From

Hedgerows to Windsor

A Pride and Prejudice Variation

Eselle Teays

Eselle Teays Publisher

Princess Amelia of the United Kingdom (1783-1810)

A grey-scale rendition of the Portrait by William Beechey

Source: Adapted from Wikipedia, Public Domain

About the Author

Eselle Teays has been an Austenphile for too many years to count. She discovered Pride and Prejudice variations and fanfiction several years ago and has read and enjoyed hundreds of them. One day, she realized that there was this one angle that had not been explored. Like the researcher that she is, she jumped on it right away. The result, "Pride Under Good Regulation," was published in 2020. She thought she would never have the inspiration to write another, but she was wrong, The second novel, "Such Novel Notions," is another of her attempts to write about something that has been hitherto scarcely explored in this very much loved, well canvassed genre.

The third novel is her answer to challenges from some reviewers. One said, "Write about the Bennets being poor." A few said, "There's no angst!"

The result is "From the Hedgerows to Windsor," which has both and much more.

After having written three novels, the author acknowledges she enjoys the research behind her novels as much as writing them.

KDP **ISBN:** 9798398484724

Independently Printed

Keywords:

1. Regency Romance.   2. British Royalty   3. Adventure

4. Mad King George III   5. Bluestocking   6. Clean and Wholesome

7. End of the Longbourn Entail

Cover design by Eselle Teays. The image is licensed from Adobe Stock Images.

Printed in the United States of America

Acknowledgments and References

All characters and some excerpts from Pride and Prejudice belong to Jane Austen. All verifiable historical characters, buildings and events, and characters and events from literary works of the period appearing in this story are borrowed purely as vehicles in a work of fiction, which does not claim any degree of historical accuracy.

I wish to thank the readers at fanfiction.net, where this story was posted. Most of all, I wish to thank Elaine C. for expertly proofreading and editing the story before publication.

The primary references used for this story are:

1) The Diary and Letters of Madame D'Arblay, 1892-Public Domain
2) A Humble Companion by Laurie Graham, Quercus Editions Ltd, London, 2013

Various episodes on the "Real Royal" channels and "History Tea Time with Lindsay Holiday" among many others on YouTube, and the Wikipedia writeups of some of the historical persons and places mentioned in this story are also acknowledged for providing background material.

Contents

Prologue

1993

"To His Royal Highness The Prince Regent, This Work Is, By His Royal Highness's Permission, Most Respectfully Dedicated, By His Royal Highness's Dutiful And Obedient Humble Servant, The Author."

Underneath the dedication was a line written by the Royal Librarian during the Regency, Mr. Stanier Clarke: 'A Scribbler: The Honorable Miss Elizabeth Bennet'

The historian, Dr. Jenny Carter, a member of the volunteer group to salvage as many of the damaged articles as possible at Windsor Castle after the electrical fire six months earlier, looked intently at the title page of a completely charred volume on her worktable. Being also an Austen scholar, she was intrigued because the title, though nearly entirely blackened by soot, could be distinguished to read 'First Impress...'

Could it be 'First Impressions?' Have I discovered the hitherto lost draft of 'Pride and Prejudice?' That would be awesome! Wait! This one was written by an 'Elizabeth Bennet,' a titled lady, no less. Is this work related to Miss Austen's timeless classic in any way? Authors of that period borrowed names and even plotlines from their contemporaries. Miss Austen was no exception. Did Miss Austen use Elizabeth Bennet's name for the heroine in 'Pride and Prejudice?'

What is the story behind this novel, which was distinguished enough that the Prince Regent, later George IV, requested a dedication to himself? Was the author from the peerage, or did she earn the title?

So many questions!

Dr. Carter reported her findings to the supervisor of her group, a gentleman who preferred 'Wuthering Heights' to all other novels by women authors of the nineteenth century. He took one look at the severely damaged page and said dismissively, "There are too many worthwhile objects in far better shape to rescue. We are running out of time. This one is obscure and ruined beyond hope. Let's move on!"

The basket labeled 'Ash Heap of History' was directly in front of her. At the last minute, she stretched her hand further to the bin marked 'To Be Sorted Later.' What the supervisor said was true: there was simply too much to do, and she had to prioritize. However, somebody else might have the time and energy later to investigate such a rare find. She could not stop wondering.

Who was The Honorable Miss Elizabeth Bennet? Did this novel, likely called 'First Impressions' as well, have anything at all to do with the incomparable 'Pride and Prejudice?'

Note: The quote above was what Jane Austen wrote when she dedicated 'Emma' to the Prince Regent in 1816. It is borrowed here for the dedication of The Honorable Miss Elizabeth Bennet's work.

Chapter 1

July 1812

Pemberley, Derbyshire

Before Elizabeth Bennet set off on a pleasure trip to the Peak District in Derbyshire as a guest of her uncle and aunt, Mr. and Mrs. Gardiner of Gracechurch Street, Jane, her elder sister and confidante, expressed concern that Elizabeth might run into Mr. Darcy, whose offer of marriage Lizzy had refused.

"Derbyshire is very large, Jane. I could enter the county with impunity," boldly quipped Lizzy. Inside, however, she was indeed a little worried about the encounter, unlikely as it might be.

Elizabeth had not simply refused the gentleman's proposal; she had delivered her rejection in a fiery tirade, enumerating his character flaws and dastardly actions. Seeing the gentleman under any circumstances, let alone on his home grounds, would be intolerably awkward.

The morning after that regrettable event, she encountered the gentleman on her walk, and he handed her a long letter of explanation. Since then, her feelings toward Mr. Darcy had undergone so material a change that she questioned herself regularly whether she had been so hot-headed and unjust as to be unladylike. Yet she had accused Mr. Darcy of being ungentlemanly.

Mr. Darcy's letter left no doubt in her mind that her charges against the master of Pemberley were based solely on the deceit of that scoundrel, Mr. Wickham, and her own misinterpretation of Mr. Darcy's intent. After months of introspection, she had traced her intense dislike of Mr. Darcy to their first meeting at the Meryton assembly. She had laughed when telling others how she overheard Mr. Darcy call her not handsome enough to tempt him for a dance. Now she admitted that making light of the insult was but a disguise for her deeply hurt feelings. She had fallen quite hard for the newcomer from Derbyshire, not only because of his noble mien and handsome figure, which spoke of honor and good breeding, but also a strong, though inexplicable, feeling of connection. She was shocked, profoundly disappointed, and humiliated when he behaved as a brute and demeaned her in public.

The only saving grace was the certainty she would never see him again.

Then Mrs. Gardiner wished to add a visit to Pemberley on their way to Lambton, her birthplace.

That was an entirely different proposition from merely being in the same county. She was petrified by the possibility of encountering the gentleman in his own home, acting as a common tourist with vulgar curiosity, poking around his ancestral home and personal sanctuary.

She thus told her aunt she had no interest in touring yet another grand estate. However, after learning from the innkeeper that the Darcy family was away, an enormous sense of excitement came out of nowhere, startling her. She told Mrs. Gardiner about her change of mind, and her aunt insisted on knowing why her usually steady and sensible niece was suddenly whimsical.

"Aunt, you remember Miss Bingley, the haughty lady who came to return a long-overdue call to Jane? It occurs to me I cannot reconcile your account of Pemberley, given your refined taste, with Miss Bingley's rapturous declarations about the beauty of the place, given how gaudy and pretentious she is. I am curious, that is all."

Elizabeth was indeed curious to see the property, but it was to see what she had lost by not agreeing to be its mistress.

12

℘℘

Pemberley was enthralling. She had never seen a place for which nature had done more, or where natural beauty had been so little counteracted by an awkward taste. Inside Pemberley house, from the soaring ceiling of the grand hall topped with skylights letting in streaming natural light, to the elegant rooms decorated with exquisite yet functional furniture, everything was sparkling, warm and appealing. Even the housekeeper of Pemberley, Mrs. Reynolds, was cordial and welcoming toward the ordinary visitors from London. Elizabeth's preconceptions of grand houses—magnificent but cold, and their head-servants—stoic but obsequious, began to crumble.

During the house tour, Elizabeth had to remind herself she was far better off as a tourist of the grand estate than as its mistress. The all-revealing letter had not exonerated the master of Pemberley of being haughty and condescending. He would surely forbid her, as his wife, to have any contact with her family, especially those from trade.

No, my family would be lost to me forever. Pemberley would become nothing but a gilded cage, albeit a breathtakingly beautiful one.

Meanwhile, Mrs. Reynolds showed the visiting party into a somewhat austere-looking room where many paintings and portraits were on display. Mrs. Reynolds explained, "This was my late master's favorite room. He has been gone these five years. The young master keeps the room exactly as his late father had it."

While showing the miniatures of the Darcys, Mrs. Reynolds found out that the young lady in the party was an acquaintance of the master. The old retainer became downright affable and extolled the virtues of her master in the most glowing terms: best brother, landlord, master. She had known him since he was four years old and never had a cross word from him— such a sweet temper! "There is not one of his tenants or servants but will give him a good name. I have heard some people call him proud, but I am sure I never saw anything of it. To my fancy, it is only because he does not rattle away like other young men."

Am I such a simpleton that I have willfully ignored his laudable personality traits during our acquaintance?

She wished to hear more.

Her uncle came to her aid unknowingly and asked Mrs. Reynolds, "Will Mr. Darcy be home soon? If I were in his position, I would never want to leave."

Mrs. Reynolds' countenance dimmed, and she said with notable melancholy, "The master came home unexpectedly after Easter. We were all very surprised but extraordinarily pleased, as he rarely takes up residence here until around this time of the year."

She paused and spoke softly, as if to herself, "He seemed different from his pleasant, solicitous self."

The housekeeper ordinarily would not talk about her master to strangers. However, unlike all the other young ladies who came to Pemberley and insinuated a non-existent intimacy with her master, the young lady of the party claimed only a casual acquaintance. She had an inkling that *this* young lady might be a genuine friend and could not help but confide more of her master's life to this special visitor.

"Perhaps he had some premonition about what was to happen. Just two weeks ago, he received an express and had to leave for the Continent." Mrs. Reynolds sighed deeply. "This war on the Continent... it is a bad business!"

Elizabeth gasped audibly when she heard this. All eyes turned to her, but she forgot to be embarrassed. She needed to know what had happened.

She asked somewhat anxiously, "Mr. Darcy went to the battlefield on the Continent? Was it because Colonel Fitzwilliam..." She stopped abruptly. It was not her place to ask such a personal question.

"Ma'am, since you are friends with both the master and the Colonel, I feel I would not overstep by telling you that the master has gone to the Continent to... escort the Colonel home since no one in the Colonel's own family could go to him at present. My master and the Colonel are like brothers. It was out of the question for him to sit in comfort at home, knowing his cousin could be in danger in those forsaken foreign lands. By now, the master is probably on-board ship to Portugal. I hear it is a long and hazardous voyage. Since the day he left, I have been worried about him. I and the rest of the staff pray every day for his safe travels."

Elizabeth reached out to squeeze the loyal servant's hand and said reassuringly, "Mr. Darcy is very capable. The Colonel will be in excellent hands. I shall join you in praying for their safe journey home. How is Miss Darcy dealing with these difficulties?"

"Ma'am, do you know Miss Darcy as well?" asked Mrs. Reynolds with even more gladness.

"I have not had the pleasure of meeting Miss Darcy in person. I have heard her mentioned frequently by her friends, the Bingleys, and her aunt, Lady Catherine de Bourgh."

"Ma'am, you are far more than just a mere acquaintance of the master then, being in the master's intimate circles. Mr. Bingley is among the few whom he invites to Pemberley. In fact, the Bingley party was supposed to have arrived two days ago if not for this unforeseen journey that has taken the master away... oh, please excuse me for going on. You were asking about Miss Darcy. She is coping as best she can. She is with Lord and Lady Fitzwilliam while the master is away. It is a pity you have not met her. She is the handsomest young lady that ever has been seen."

The housekeeper showed the miniature of her young mistress to the visitors and renewed her lavish praise, this time about her young mistress.

"With all her accomplishments, she is extremely modest, unlike other young ladies you might know..." Mrs. Reynolds gave a meaningful look toward Elizabeth, and Elizabeth knew immediately the housekeeper meant Miss Bingley.

The party from London enjoyed an especially hospitable visit from the Pemberley staff. Everyone—from the housekeeper to the under-gardener—wanted to show friends of Mr. Darcy how proud they were of serving a wonderful master, the best in all England. Mrs. Reynolds even offered tea to the travelers, who declined with regrets because they were expected to arrive in Lambton before dinner.

Elizabeth's last vestige of discontent against Mr. Darcy gradually, if reluctantly, faded away. When confronted with the genuine fondness and respect his dependents held toward him, even in his absence, she had to concede a truly vain and disdainful person would never be so beloved by his entire staff and tenants. The only conclusion left was that she had thoroughly misunderstood and misjudged the master of Pemberley.

This realization caused her attitude toward Pemberley to shift. The longer she had walked around Pemberley, with its magnificent house and grounds, the more she yearned to call it home... her home. This was an unexpected, and unwelcome, feeling. From deep in her heart emerged a sense of regret because Pemberley would never be her home.

She had felt the regret most keenly when standing outside of the stable block. Suddenly, she heard behind her the rustling sound of a hound and accompanying footsteps.

Could it be... no, it could not... but what if it is...

She turned around quickly, half convinced the gentleman she both longed and dreaded to meet was coming around the hedge. Alas, the person rounding the corner was but a groom walking a pointer back to the kennel. She berated herself for being ridiculous, but she could not help being inordinately disappointed. She realized then that she had hoped for a chance encounter with Mr. Darcy since discovering she would visit Pemberley. This imagined accidental meeting would have allowed her to apologize for her uncalled-for cruelty during his proposal, and for her gross misunderstanding of his character. Perhaps from there...

She shook her head somewhat violently to halt her train of thought. The master of Pemberley had left for a long and arduous journey. She had to acknowledge she would never see Mr. Darcy again.

As her carriage was leaving Pemberley. Elizabeth Bennet could not help turning around to take a last look at the grand stone house sitting majestically on a rise. An irrepressible feeling of belonging surged from the depths of her heart.

And of this place, I might have been mistress!

She sighed involuntarily when she turned to face the road again. The carriage was approaching the bridge spanning the stream in front of the house. Her eyes, of their own accord, were drawn to the river.

As they say, it is all water under the bridge.

℘℘

Early the next morning, Elizabeth went out alone for a walk. The quaint town of Lambton seemed larger and more prosperous than Meryton. It also gave an air of being more genteel. After all, Derbyshire was full of grand estates. Pemberley was but one among them. Elizabeth felt a sense of kinship with a town she had not known prior to this trip, simply because of its proximity to Pemberley.

By the time she got back to the inn, it was after breakfast. Her aunt and uncle had left a note telling her they had gone out to visit the village church and its graveyard, and they urged their niece to join them. However, she also saw the post on the table. Choosing between the ghosts of people from her aunt's past and news from home, there was no competition, especially when the last letter from Jane was from a week before.

Elizabeth took the bread roll saved for her breakfast and made herself comfortable in the window seat to read her letters.

She wished she had gone out to walk with her aunt and uncle so that the world as she had known since birth would last just a little longer. The contents of the two letters from Jane had obliterated that world.

Her youngest sister, Lydia, had eloped with that scoundrel Wickham! They left Brighton together and were believed to be in London rather than Gretna Green, because Mr. Wickham had let it be known that he had no intention of marrying Lydia at all. The disgrace this scandal had brought to the Bennet family was unfathomable. Her parents were in great distress, as were the sisters, especially Kitty, who was privy to Lydia's plan to elope but concealed it from her parents until it was too late. What was most troubling to Jane was that her father, though appearing very ill, insisted on going to London with the regiment commander, Colonel Forster, to find his wayward daughter.

17

Such was the situation as it stood at the end of Jane's second letter. The only thing Jane wished was for the prompt return of her favorite sister, who always knew what to do, no matter how dire the situation.

Overcome by grief and shock, Elizabeth dropped both letters onto her lap. Her own future, and those of her remaining sisters, were now in tatters. Mr. Darcy and Pemberley no longer mattered because they could not exist in her new reality.

Jane's confidence in her was obviously misplaced. What could she do? She could not go to London to help in the search, as she did not know the city well at all.

However, Uncle Gardiner does...

"Where is my uncle?" cried Elizabeth aloud, while hastily putting on her outer garment to go find her uncle and aunt. Just then, the door opened and in walked Mr. and Mrs. Gardiner, quite relaxed after a pleasant stroll around Mrs. Gardiner's old haunts.

Elizabeth, hitherto dry-eyed, burst into tears now that her relations were here to share her burden. Once the Gardiners had read the letters, and Elizabeth had explained what an unsavory character Mr. Wickham was, the Gardiner party directly quit the inn and was on the road to Longbourn.

Chapter 2

It had now been five days since Elizabeth and Mrs. Gardiner arrived at Longbourn. Mr. Gardiner had gone back to London immediately after dropping off his wife and niece.

Things were just as Jane had described on their arrival—Mary sermonized, Kitty sulked, and Mrs. Bennet stayed in her chambers, not coming downstairs even once. She received her sister Gardiner while abed and wailed incessantly that Lydia should come home.

"If it had been Lizzy, who ran away to marry, I could understand. She has always been headstrong, wild even. She never pays me any heed. But Lydia? My amiable, lively darling girl! I always knew she would attract a fine gentleman and beat her sisters to the altar. But why an elopement? Why? They should come home to Longbourn! I would buy her the best trousseau anyone in these parts has seen. And their wedding? It would be the talk of Meryton for years to come! Oh, my poor nerves! My poor, poor shattered nerves!"

Mrs. Gardiner's calm presence proved a comfort to her sister by marriage. The assurance that Mr. Gardiner would surely find Lydia and Mr. Wickham calmed Mrs. Bennet, whose self-pity was the reason for her desolation.

Just as the excitement caused by the return of Elizabeth and Mrs. Gardiner died down, an express from Mr. Gardiner came, heralding the return of the master of Longbourn the following day. The household was in an uproar once again. So much depended on the outcome of Mr. Bennet's search! The only inmates of the manor house who could keep their composure were the young Gardiner cousins.

At the appointed time, all in the Bennet household, including Mr. and Mrs. Hill, long-time butler and housekeeper of Longbourn, stood outside the front door, awaiting their returning master.

The carriage finally arrived. Mr. Gardiner descended but did not approach the waiting family members. Instead, he turned back toward the carriage door while the coachman entered the carriage from the other side, evidently to help Mr. Bennet step down.

What the Bennet ladies saw next shocked them speechless. Mr. Bennet was carried out of the carriage instead of climbing out on his own. Mrs. Bennet shrieked and rushed toward her husband.

"Mr. Bennet! What is the meaning of this? Are you... are you...?" asked the mistress urgently and breathlessly. Then she stopped, understood what she saw, and wailed, "Oh, you have no compassion for my nerves!"

"I am still breathing, Mrs. Bennet. No need to sing my elegy yet," said Mr. Bennet with amusement, even though his jesting cost him noticeable exertion.

By then, his daughters had come up to their parents, calming one while comforting the other.

Jane said to her mother, "Mamma, why don't I take you to your rooms to rest? Worrying about Lydia has been difficult for you. Hill will bring you some tea to calm your nerves."

"Oh, I want to know this instant what has happened to my dearest Lydia! But you are right, Jane, I need to be composed to hear the news. It does not bode well, judging from your father's condition. Oh, what will happen to us all?" Mrs. Bennet's hysterics went on, as she leaned heavily on Jane and Mrs. Hill to go back to the house.

Meanwhile, Mr. Gardiner asked Elizabeth to ready her father's bookroom as Mr. Bennet wished to rest there instead of in the parlor. Elizabeth complied but looked back worriedly at her father, who could not walk at all.

Mr. Gardiner settled Mr. Bennet on the bookroom sofa. Elizabeth hovered close by, adjusting the cushions and wringing her hands. Mr. Bennet smiled weakly at his favorite daughter but was too exhausted to say anything. He gestured with his hand to send his family away, allowing only his man, Hill, to care for him.

"Uncle Gardiner, what has happened? Is papa alright?" asked Elizabeth, as scared as she was nervous.

"Lizzy, let us go to the parlor. The rest of the family needs to hear this as well," replied Mr. Gardiner calmly but with a deep frown, portending the grim news he was to deliver.

Once in the parlor where the Bennet sisters and Mrs. Gardiner had gathered, Mr. Gardiner sat down heavily by his wife and was handed a cup of tea.

"Thank you, dearest. You know better than anyone that a bit of tea and scone could fortify me enough to face even a dragon!"

He meant to lower the anxiety in the room a little by jesting, but he was unsuccessful. There was not a single smile among the faces anxiously staring at him. He heaved a weary sigh and began his account.

"Your father arrived at my house about a week ago. I am very glad he thought of staying at Gracechurch Street instead of an inn. He already looked tired and worn by the time I arrived, but would not heed my advice to hand over the search to me. He told me he went out each day looking into places where derelicts would frequent based on what he knew about the city thirty years ago, when he was still at Oxford. More than once did he get into dangerous situations..."

There was a collective gasp when the ladies heard this. Mr. Gardiner realized his mistake and hurriedly reassured his wife and nieces that all was well as far as Mr. Bennet's personal safety was concerned.

"However... Let me be brief and direct. You are all old enough to understand the severity of the situation without knowing every detail. Your father has a weak heart..."

Another collective gasp emanated from the ladies, but Mr. Gardiner did not stop this time. He continued, "He has known about this for at least two years. Yesterday, when I came back from the office, I found him in the parlor, clutching his chest and breathing harshly. I immediately summoned a doctor. The doctor said the attack your father experienced was rather severe, and he must not get too agitated about anything or else..." Mr. Gardiner stopped and looked at his nieces. Every one of them was crying at this point.

Elizabeth said between sobs, "I have noticed papa rubbing his chest with his fist quite often in the past year. He did that especially vigorously when he told me he wanted Lydia to go to Brighton to learn her lesson and grow up. I guess he preferred some tranquility at home with his health condition."

Her uncle replied, "Lizzy, you are always observant. That was likely the reason he allowed Lydia to go away under the care of Mrs. Forster, who is not much older than Lydia.

"After the doctor's diagnosis, he wanted to come home to Longbourn, as his search was rather haphazard and fruitless. He has not recovered from the attack, and the journey back to Hertfordshire was difficult for him. I should be able to count on you girls to keep the house quiet for your father, and that means keeping your mother away from him as much as possible."

The sisters looked at one another and nodded meekly. Jane, being the oldest, thanked her uncle on behalf of her sisters.

"Uncle Gardiner, we are grateful for your care of papa. We shall try our best to ease papa's worries and keep mamma calm. As for mamma, knowing something of Lydia's whereabouts would go a long way toward lowering her anxiety. Is there nothing we could tell her?"

Mr. Gardiner looked defeated. He said, "London is an immense city. Among the million people living there, how do we go about finding two people unless they want to be found? Fortunately, I know a large network of people, and I will let them know—discreetly, of course—what, or rather, whom, I am seeking. I met Mr. Wickham here over Christmas and saw a miniature of him at Pemberley just a week ago. I can describe his appearance. I believe this is a better strategy than going aimlessly into the maze of alleys and nooks. Your aunt and cousins will return home with me tomorrow so that you will not have a crowd of guests here while you focus on getting your papa and mamma well."

Mr. Gardiner dismissed the sisters, but he asked Elizabeth to stay behind; something about their recent trip.

Once the Gardiners were alone with Elizabeth, Mr. Gardiner sighed again and said solemnly to Elizabeth, "Lizzy, you are the most capable among your sisters. Your courage always rises to meet every challenge. You are also your father's favorite. He treats you as the son he never had."

Elizabeth started on hearing herself called her father's son, but she remained silent. Mrs. Gardiner reached over to squeeze her hand.

Her uncle did not seem to notice the startled look on her face and continued. "I need you to be very brave for not just yourself, but also for your sisters. There was something I left out because I did not want to distress your sisters further. I did not want word of your father's true condition to reach your mother. With you, I can be frank."

Elizabeth sat up straighter to brace herself for the bad news she had 'earned' the privilege of hearing. The grim prospect did not surprise her, as she saw how her father struggled to speak or stand on his own. She wished she had not been so honored as to be chosen to bear the news alone.

"Your father's attack was far more serious than I said. Fortuitously, two doors down from my house lives Dr. Donaldson, a retired naval doctor. If not for his timely intervention, your father might have died—his breathing was so shallow I was not sure he was living."

Elizabeth burst out crying when she heard this. Mr. Gardiner said comfortingly, "Now you understand why I could not say this in front of your sisters."

Elizabeth wiped her tears, nodded, and urged her uncle to continue.

"Dr. Donaldson administered many powerful pushes on your father's chest until he breathed again. To me, it seemed an eternity before he awakened. Dr. Donaldson said he saved your father with a technique he learned while in the navy to revive drowned sailors. This approach is not commonly practiced among physicians."

Elizabeth scarcely breathed until this narration ended. She asked worriedly, "Is papa well now? Is it likely that such a traumatic attack will not have consequence? We must thank Dr. Donaldson for averting such a devastating crisis."

Mr. Gardiner replied, "Your father's left side seems to be paralyzed to a degree. That is why he has so much trouble speaking and standing. According to Dr. Donaldson, the situation will probably worsen until... Lizzy, I shall not make light of the situation. You should be prepared for the worst. In the meantime, keep your father very comfortable. I shall teach Hill the way to compress your father's chest should he have another attack. Dr. Donaldson has taught me the technique. It is simple enough and may yet prolong your father's life.

"As for your mother, try to keep her as much in the dark as possible. However, your mother is not dimwitted, even though she may appear frivolous and uncaring. I think she has sensed for a while that your papa's health has been deteriorating, which triggered her many nervous complaints regarding the entail and the prospect of being thrown out to the hedgerows when your papa dies."

Elizabeth, crying profusely, exclaimed, "Poor papa! This is too much! I must let Jane know about this pending calamity. She and I together may bear this weight of losing our dear papa! I alone will be crushed!"

Mr. Gardiner put his hand gently on Elizabeth's shoulder but said firmly, "Lizzy, that was why I told you this news alone, because you are the strongest in disposition and the most courageous among your sisters. You are like the captain of a ship in a stormy sea. Your sisters and your mother are like the distressed seamen who would wreck the ship without your direction. You will bear it, and you will think of a way to explain it to your sisters. You could choose Jane to be the first to hear this sad news, if you wish. I have faith in you. You will overcome this."

"Uncle Gardiner, you have always been so kind to us, and I promise to draw strength from your faith in me. Would to heaven that your faith is not misplaced! But first tell me this: is there truly no hope for papa?"

"Lizzy, there is always a chance for miracles, and we will all pray for your father to be whole. However, there are five of you, all females and none married, not to mention Lydia's foolishness. This is not the time to rely on a very faint, very remote chance your father will come through this ordeal unscathed."

Elizabeth became somber after hearing the "none married" part. She was to blame, as she had turned down two marriage proposals within the last year. Her family's current untenable difficulty was all because of her, and so she had to take the responsibility to save her family.

"Uncle Gardiner, forgive me for my hysteria. I am calmer now, and I will do whatever it takes to keep our family in good stead. However, with Lydia's scandal and Papa's...." Elizabeth simply could not mention her father's inevitable sad end.

Mr. Gardiner held her hand and said reassuringly, "Dear Lizzy, you have endured too much in one day. Your father will be incapacitated, but the doctor said there should still be at least a few weeks, perhaps longer, if your father does not have another shock. I shall be back in London tomorrow and continue the search. Who knows, perhaps I shall find Lydia soon and make her marry. Your father would get the boost that might prolong his life, if not cure him completely; your mother would be so happy about having one daughter married she might become sensible again."

Elizabeth smiled wanly at her uncle. Deep in her heart, she was certain this happy-sounding scenario would not come to pass, for she alone knew the depravity of Mr. Wickham. Without a large monetary enticement, he would never marry Lydia. This was her fault again. She could have exposed his treachery to her own family, but she did not. So poor Lydia became the sacrificial lamb because of her 'sensible' elder sister's folly.

25

How I wish it all to be different!

Chapter 3

The next day, the Gardiner family left Longbourn. Mr. Gardiner looked significantly at Elizabeth before stepping into his carriage. Elizabeth felt a pang in her chest. She must now act as the son her father never had... whether she liked it or not.

The previous evening, Jane had come to her before bed. She looked exhausted after having spent the entire day calming and comforting her mother, hardly leaving her mother's chambers. Mrs. Bennet kept feeling faint and asking for her smelling salts every time she thought about Mr. Bennet's ghostly appearance.

"Oh Lizzy, my heart broke for mamma. She could not stop asking me, 'Jane, what will become of us?' I have no answer. Do you think papa's health is precarious?" asked Jane in a tired and strained voice.

By now, Elizabeth could hardly remember the serene elder sister she had had before she went away on her pleasure trip. The last thing she wished to do was to tell her kind and beneficent sister, now looking harassed and haggard, about the cruel fate awaiting them all.

She put on a brave smile, held Jane's hand, and said in a soothing voice that surprised even herself, "Papa is exhausted. He was unfamiliar with London and could not manage the demand on his body and mind. Now that Uncle has taken over the search, papa can rest. Uncle Gardiner and his extensive network of friends and associates will find Lydia and make her marry. All will be well. You will see."

"Lizzy, without you, I feel completely helpless to do anything for the family. I am so very grateful you came home when I asked," said Jane with her usual beatific smile, now tainted with weariness.

"Jane, dearest, you can always count on me. I will not rest until all my sisters are well-settled, including Lydia. As for you, I will be the doting aunt to your children, teaching them all to play the pianoforte very ill!"

"Lizzy, be serious. You are the one with two proposals from two esteemed gentlemen in the past nine months alone. You may yet be the first to marry, but then who will take care of Longbourn now that papa is indisposed?"

Elizabeth was glad Jane's mind was now on a somewhat less dismal topic— her papa being ill rather than dead.

She decided to add some levity, even though it hurt to jest about this subject. "Do remember I refused both offers. I promise, however, if I am lucky enough to meet another Mr. Collins, I will instantly accept his proposal of marriage... if he asks!"

"Mr. Darcy has not married. Perhaps he might propose again. You seem to think better of him after having read his letter."

"Oh Jane..." Elizabeth choked up before she could answer her sister.

Jane was alarmed. She anxiously asked, "Lizzy, what is the matter? Did something happen while you were in Derbyshire?"

"Dearest, forgive me for being emotional. The anxiety of the past week has caught up with me. No, nothing of import happened while I was in Derbyshire. I, in fact, visited Mr. Darcy's estate, Pemberley..."

Jane eagerly interjected, 'Oh, did you see Mr. Darcy there?"

"No, he was on his way to the Continent to take care of his cousin, the Colonel. I told you about the Colonel, did I not, when I came back from Kent? Mr. Darcy had to go bring him home. He must have been gravely injured."

Jane looked puzzled, but she expressed her well-wishes for the Colonel's speedy recovery before asking, "You are sad because the Colonel is hurt, or because you missed seeing Mr. Darcy at his home?"

Elizabeth put on a brave smile and went back to jesting. "Neither. I am not sad about gentlemen so wholly unconnected to me, even though I wish them 'Godspeed' on their journey back to England."

She paused and continued carefully. "It is quite impossible for a gentleman, once refused, to offer to the same lady again, especially one from a disgraced family of ill fortune and connections. Pemberley is a very grand, yet also exquisite estate, a rare combination. Mr. Darcy deserves a lady of impeccable lineage and a large dowry to be mistress of his noble home."

"I see," responded Jane thoughtfully. "We have enough trouble at home as it is. Let us not look too far afield—nor too distant in the future—for what might yet happen. We must have faith that once papa is restored to health, everything will return to how it has always been. Uncle Gardiner will find Lydia and Mr. Wickham and make them marry."

"Yes, Jane," answered Elizabeth, with a forced cheerfulness. "You always see through the dark clouds to the silver lining. We should have faith and hope that all will end well."

After this, the sisters said their goodnights, and Jane, though exhausted, went back to her mother.

Elizabeth's mind was in turmoil. The momentary peace and optimism induced by her sister's ever-sunny outlook evaporated as soon as they separated for bed.

She had never felt more alone, her only companion the darkness of night—engulfing her, pressing in from all sides until it penetrated her to the core.

When had she become *the* strong Bennet son taking the helm of the sinking Bennet ship? No! She was nothing but the impertinent Miss Elizabeth Bennet of Longbourn... but for how much longer?

She could not suppress the sob rising from the depths of her heart.

ଚ୨ଚ୨

Mr. Bennet, who now lay on a narrow bed in his bookroom, insisted he should not be disturbed, while the household lived in dread and despair against the terrifying gloom of so much uncertainty.

On the third day since his arrival home, he asked to see his two eldest daughters, but he would not admit his wife until his heart had grown stronger. Mrs. Bennet, who had been monopolizing Jane's company since the day her husband returned, wailed pitifully at this slight, and was altogether hysterical. Jane could not leave her mother in this state. She told Lizzy to proceed with the interview without her.

When Lizzy entered the darkened bookroom, she was taken aback by how the former joyful chaos of her father's cluttered room had become dim and cheerless.

Lizzy took a few quick steps to approach Mr. Bennet, who was reclining on a pile of pillows, facing away from the window. She said softly, "Papa! I am heartened to see you awake, and you wanted to see me. How are you feeling?"

Mr. Bennet looked at his favorite daughter and croaked out her name in a weak voice, raspy from several days of disuse.

"Lizzy."

"Oh, papa!" Elizabeth did not want to cry, but she could not help herself. She rushed over to the bedside and buried her face in their joined hands.

"Now, now, darling girl. You must be strong, not only for yourself but also for your mother and your sisters," whispered Mr. Bennet soothingly, which made Elizabeth cry even harder.

After a few moments, Elizabeth, not made for melancholy, lifted her head and smiled bravely at her father, saying, "Forgive me, papa. I will be strong for you. I will be the son you never had."

"Lizzy, just as you are, you are already the child all parents wish for. I have no cause to repine when I have you, for however much longer." Elizabeth tried to protest, and Mr. Bennet pressed her hand to stop her. "In fact," he continued, "I am very glad you are not a son."

"Hear me out, Lizzy." Mr. Bennet stopped another one of Elizabeth's interruptions.

"The Bennet males have had weak hearts for several generations. I watched my brother James die in front of me, clutching his chest while we were running in the fields. He was twelve years old, and I was ten. I remember being very sad to have lost my playmate. I comforted myself by saying that he would have left home for school by the end of summer, anyway.

"Twelve years later, my father also died of a weak heart. He was bedridden for six months. On his deathbed, he admonished me to avoid agitation if I wished to escape this curse on the Bennet men. Bennet women do not seem to be affected. Mr. Collins's grandmother, your great aunt, lived to be over seventy. Over the years, I believed I had perfected a philosophical composure that not even your mother's nervous disposition could disrupt. I never once experienced any discomfort in the chest until now. But then I had not figured Lydia into my calculated peace..."

"Oh, my dear papa!" interjected Elizabeth quietly, taking care not to appear too agitated herself. "You will recover from this temporary setback yet. You shall see. With plenty of rest, good food and..." Elizabeth frowned at the closed windows and drawn curtains. She continued, "... fresh air, you will be back to your favorite books in no time!"

Mr. Bennet smiled weakly and indulgently at his daughter. "What I would not give to finish reading the Canterbury Tales I just acquired! It is a first edition, you understand. That reminds me: the books with my book plates belong to me and then to you girls when I am gone. The entail does not cover such personal properties. If the price of this book was any sign of how first-edition books have risen in value through the years, I have—responsibly, if inadvertently—left you and your sisters a sufficiently rich legacy, enough to save you from going into service. Promise me, Lizzy, that neither you nor your remaining sisters will seek employment, even as a lady's companion. I cannot allow myself to be the cause of ending hundreds of years of Bennet gentility."

Mr. Bennet lifted his other hand wearily to rub his chest after this proclamation. Elizabeth instinctively tightened her grip on her father's limp left hand and urged, "Papa, I will do as you bid. Please do not worry. You have been talking for a long time. Rest now. I will come in later to read for you from the Canterbury Tales. I often think those stories are better for listening to than reading."

"Thank you, Lizzy. You are a good girl. I am indeed getting fatigued."

Elizabeth kissed her father on the forehead and left to find Jane.

୨୧

Elizabeth knocked softly on the door to her mother's chambers. Jane opened it a crack, and seeing that it was Lizzy, whispered, "How was papa?"

"Jane, who is it? If it is that ingrate Lizzy, let her come in. I want to speak to her," hollered Mrs. Bennet from a chaise in her room. She might be unwell, but her voice remained clear and far-reaching.

Lizzy and Jane exchanged glances, and Jane stepped aside to let Lizzy through the door.

"Mamma, how are you feeling?" Elizabeth asked tentatively. When her mother was in her nervous state, she should not expect any pleasant exchange.

"How am I feeling? What do you think? You alone could have saved us from the hedgerows, and you hid behind your father to defy me. Are you happy now? He will not be here much longer to protect you. I know all about his weak heart. It is not something a man could conceal from his wife. That was why I was so eager to secure a roof over our heads sooner rather than later. Now it is too late! That hateful Mrs. Collins will turn us all out before your father is even cold in the ground! It is all because of your disobedience!" Mrs. Bennet's voice rose higher and higher during this tirade.

Elizabeth was glad her father had the foresight to stay downstairs. She calmly rebutted her mother, "Mamma, papa said he had never had any problems with his heart until now. He may pull through this difficulty yet. Let us give him some peace and quiet to restore his strength. You know how

32

the London air does not agree with him. Back here in the country, he will recover in no time."

"Oh, Lizzy, you know nothing. Everyone around these parts knows that, for generations, the Bennet men have died young of heart troubles. How is your father going to escape this curse? He has lived longer than the rest of them as it is. No, he will die soon. Mark my words! And what will become of us?" Mrs. Bennet was inconsolable.

Elizabeth tried to comfort her mother. "Mamma, all will be well..."

"Coming from the most selfish of daughters! This is rich! I cannot endure your presence any longer. Jane, where are my smelling salts?" Mrs. Bennet waved her handkerchief wildly in front of her own face.

Jane handed the salts to her mother while talking soothingly to her. She turned to Elizabeth to signal with her eyes to leave her mother's room. Elizabeth nodded and fled.

She leaned against the wall of the hallway outside her mother's room, breathing deeply. She did not cry. Over the years, she had become inured to her mother's rather frequent verbal criticisms. However, her mother was right on many levels: her father might not be around for much longer to shield her against such harsh rebukes, and her mother was not being paranoid about losing their home to the entail. Tears seeped into her eyes at these thoughts. She might as well go back to her father's room to spend as much time with him as possible.

Mr. Bennet was lying very still when she went back to his bookroom. She panicked, thinking her father might have died while she was away. She walked gingerly to the bed and heaved a sigh of relief when she saw his chest moving gently up and down.

Her mind was still roiling from the confrontation with her mother. She thought she would start organizing her father's books, but it felt too much like a betrayal, as if she were anticipating her dear papa's death. The only thing that could give her peace was physical activity. She looked over at her father, making sure he was not exhibiting any distress, and left to take a walk to Oakham Mount.

She worked up quite a sweat on that sweltering summer day, walking briskly toward the summit of Oakham Mount. Once there, she surveyed the rolling green fields of Hertfordshire, which were as dear to her as the family hearth in the Longbourn parlor. This was her first solitary moment for introspection since receiving the terrible news in Lambton.

"Lydia! How could you?" Elizabeth screamed exasperatedly into the winds, letting out her pent-up anger and frustration against her youngest sister.

It was simply not fair that the four of them—three of them and by-and-large, Kitty—always minding their decorum in public, should suffer disgrace because of the scandalous behavior of one sister, who should have been regarded as too young and too unruly to be out in society.

Her mind then hopped over to the recurring supposition which, though absurd, would not leave her alone: had she seen Mr. Darcy at Pemberley, perhaps they could have started anew. Images of the divine beauty of Pemberley came to mind unbidden. What woman would not want to be mistress of such a place, especially when the handsome master had proven so honorable and had loved her so ardently? If she had accepted his proposal—no, this would not have been possible since she found him repugnant when he proposed. Perhaps... if she had met Mr. Darcy at his own home a few weeks earlier, and they had come to an understanding, she was certain he would have taken the entire burden off her slim shoulders. Their troubles would all be over, and her father's health would not have been so perilously endangered.

Her calm ruminations turned more and more agitated as she thought how the present difficulties would not have occurred if she had accepted Mr. Darcy. She knew she was being ridiculous, as there was no possibility of a future with Mr. Darcy after the exceedingly cruel words they exchanged in the Hunsford parsonage.

However, people in despair are not expected to be rational, she reasoned with herself.

To calm her increasingly tumultuous thoughts, she started down the path toward Longbourn. Walking was the only elixir to calm her troubled mind.

Chapter 4

When Elizabeth arrived back at the house, it was almost dinnertime. On the way to her room, she heard weeping coming from Kitty's chamber. She knocked and opened the door without waiting for permission.

When Kitty saw who was entering her room, her keening became bawling. Lizzy rushed over to her younger sister and asked anxiously, "What is the matter, Kitty? Has something happened to papa or mamma while I was out?"

Kitty glanced at Lizzy with a frown and immediately turned to look out of the window. She petulantly complained, "Do you even care? You roam about without a care in the world. Did you know when I went to town with Maria just now, the townspeople, even the milliner's clerks, turned their backs on me? Maria distanced herself when she saw people shun me. The talk in town is that Papa failed to talk Lydia out of living in sin, and he was so upset he had an apoplexy, which was true enough, except he did not even find her. They also said it would not be long before Mr. Collins throws us out of Longbourn, for papa will surely not survive this shame."

Elizabeth embraced Kitty and soothingly said to her sister, "Kitty, I know it is very hard right now, but it will be better, I am sure. Papa will recover, and Lydia will return to us."

Kitty shook off Elizabeth's embrace and said testily, "How can you say that? You know better than anyone that none of what you just said will turn out as you predict. Although papa sees none but you, even I know he is dying. Oh, Lizzy! You should have married Mr. Collins. At least then we would not have to worry about losing our home!"

Elizabeth started at this unjust accusation. Lydia was the only one to blame for their impending calamity. Kitty herself was far more culpable in endangering the family's future by having concealed Lydia's intention to elope.

Elizabeth felt exhausted. She did not deign to defend herself against such a diatribe from her sister, who had never been notable for independent thinking. She suspected Kitty had been listening to her mother.

Not one made for bitterness, she abruptly stood up and left Kitty's room. To find some solace, she went to her father's bookroom. Even though her father lying weak and helpless on the bed was a heartbreaking sight, the room itself had become a sanctuary for her.

She sat in the chair, where, in happier times, she played backgammon or chess with her papa and stared at her father's chest rising and falling for a few moments. Such small indications that he was yet alive comforted her immensely after the nearly nonstop bombardment of unjust accusations. She decided it was as good a time as any to start the inventory of her father's books. It no longer felt like a betrayal because the practical side of her felt that, regardless of the outcome of her father's current health crisis, it would be a sensible undertaking to secure the future of the family.

She settled down to look through the ledger for the book collection. Even though he was lackadaisical in his general attitude, he had kept a meticulous record of his book purchases since his Oxford days, and most of the books were in the master's chambers.

Elizabeth set down the ledger and sighed. It would be difficult to enter the rooms adjacent to her mother's when her mother was still so angry at her. She understood on a rational level her mother was grasping at straws because she was so distraught, but Elizabeth felt the sting keenly.

She continued working on tallying the amount spent on the volumes, as well as on categorizing them. Hill came in with her father's dinner of broth and bread. Elizabeth left the bookroom, knowing instinctively that Mr. Bennet, master of Longbourn, would be embarrassed to have his daughter watch him being spoon-fed.

Elizabeth went back to her bedroom and requested a tray be sent up. Jane came in, looking harassed. After ascertaining that her usually robust sister was not ill, she returned to her mother, who could not bear to be alone for more than a few moments.

Elizabeth looked out of the window at the walled garden. This lovely sight, for once, could not lift her spirits. In the quiet of her own room, alone and feeling disconnected from even her closest sister, she finally conceded, reluctantly, that Kitty was right. It would have been unconscionable for her to have accepted Mr. Collins's proposal. But Mr. Darcy's...

Stop! Stop deceiving yourself once and for all.

Heeding the reprimand of her inner voice, she turned her thoughts to actions she could take.

She was not one to shirk her duties, but what could she do under the circumstances? She could not join in the search for Lydia and that blackguard Wickham, nor could she find a lucrative job as she had no employable skills other than some small fluency in long-dead languages.

As a young, poor gentlewoman, her only path to prosperity was to marry a rich husband, a nigh impossible feat for one like her—no beauty, no connections, no enviable dowry. Yet, against all odds, this otherwise unattainable prize could have been hers to claim had she simply said yes to Mr. Darcy's proposal.

She was exasperated by this recurring intrusion into her thoughts, which sounded more and more like regret.

Why doesn't this ridiculous supposition simply go away? What's done is done—no need crying over spilled milk!

And yet, the thought kept returning. She brought vividly to mind the scene when Mr. Darcy walked around a hedge outside the stable block at Pemberley and came face to face with her. The stunned expression on his handsome face was so vivid it could not have been just in her imagination. And yet, this chance encounter never happened... it was just a groom, and he did not look at her at all. But what if it had been Mr. Darcy?

"I have become deranged!" Elizabeth muttered. She decided to go back to her task of organizing her father's books.

As Mary would quote from the Bible, 'and through idleness of the hands the house droppeth through.' For once, she would have quoted appropriately. Those books will indeed mean the difference between a farm hut with a leaky roof or a respectable cottage. They deserve my laboring diligently on them.

She had almost reclaimed her steady, cheerful self when she lost it again: clearly emanating from the dining room were her mother's loud lamentations of the disaster soon to befall them. She sobered immediately and hastened to her father's bookroom.

Elizabeth sat down at her workspace, a small roundish table by the window. Its placement far from her father's bed meant the least amount of disturbance to the invalid. She glanced over at the immobile form on the bed and sighed.

She did not understand what came over her; instead of picking up where she left off in the ledger, she pulled a sheet of paper from under it and began to write.

The owner of Pemberley, still in his traveling clothes and preceded by his favorite hound, made his way past the hedge outside the stable yard. He stopped dead in his tracks when he saw who was standing in front of him. Why was she here? Was she purposely throwing herself in his way again? (No, that would have been what I thought of myself, not what he would have thought of me.) Their eyes met, and the cheeks of both were overspread with the deepest blush...

By the time Elizabeth stopped writing, it was almost midnight, and she had finished the fictional account of their reacquaintance at Pemberley. Elizabeth (she called herself L, for Lizzy, in the writing) had been introduced to Miss Darcy (called G), a young lady who was not proud but only extremely shy. The Bingley family was there, and Miss Bingley (called C) was none too happy to see the target of her affection, Mr. Darcy (called

F, for Fitzwilliam—yes, he was Fitzwilliam to her) paying court to that country nobody L. Mr. Bingley, called Mr. C in her account, appeared to savor the memory of the Netherfield ball the previous November. She stopped when F came to the inn and found L distressed because of LL (LL stood for Loathsome Lydia—*what a bother that so many people involved had the same initials!)* had eloped with WW (WW stood for Wicked Wickham. How fitting!). F quitted the inn soon after, ~~and L knew in her heart that he had gone to look for the wayward couple.~~ *(L could not have known that; it was just L's delusional wish.)*

Even though in this fanciful creation Mr. Darcy had not yet rescued Lydia, Elizabeth felt a heavy burden had flown off her shoulders. She left the writing on the table, checked her father one more time, and went back to the room she shared with Jane.

Jane was already in bed. She had been spending every night in her mother's chamber since her father came home. Their mother was doing better if she allowed Jane to come to her own room to rest.

Elizabeth quickly undressed and got underneath the light summer counterpane. For the first time in almost two weeks, she felt a glimmer of hope, even though this hope was built on an illusion—Mr. Darcy was forever out of her life and could not possibly be her knight in shining armor. She fell instantly into a deep sleep.

Whenever working on the book collection became tedious, or her mother's verbal abuse was more scurrilous than usual, or her father had a bad day, she turned to writing her story.

℘℘

Since returning from London with his heart ailment two months before, Mr. Bennet's condition had been gradually sliding. Elizabeth watched her father closely and caught him weeping sometimes. Her reading of the Canterbury Tales or other volumes cheered him somewhat, but his mood plunged noticeably when the next letter from London came.

Sensing the end was near, he sent for Mr. Gardiner to remove the book collection to London to avoid any potential contention from Mr. Collins about ownership, even though the documentation for his purchases, all dated and in good order, could stand up to any scrutiny. The more than five thousand volumes had cost three thousand pounds in total to purchase. Mr. Bennet estimated that a good portion of the collection might have risen in price by three to ten times.

The week before he died, he finally admitted his wife of twenty-three years into his study. Mr. Bennet told Mrs. Bennet about the book collection, and how Lizzy and her Uncle Gardiner would make certain that the sale of the collection would help put a roof over their heads once he was gone. On hearing this, Mrs. Bennet started crying hysterically, unable to speak. Mr. Bennet had no choice but to have his man take her back to her room.

He then asked each daughter to come in individually. Every one of them wept so miserably he found he could not say much to them. He apologized briefly to each one for failing them and bid them to bind together, navigating life as a group, and he enjoined them not to seek employment.

Lizzy was the last daughter he sent for. He was very weak by then, but he rallied when Lizzy came to his bedside. They had had many opportunities to speak in the last few weeks, but he had something important to discuss.

Mr. Bennet held his daughter's hand weakly and said, "Lizzy, I can let go of life because my heart is at peace. You have made it possible."

"Papa, please do not let go. You should yet fight to stay with us!" Elizabeth's eyes were shining brightly as she urged her father not to give up.

"Let us not argue over whether I shall live or soon die. My mind is willing, but my heart does not follow. My only regret is that Lydia remains lost. If she came home tomorrow, safe and sound, perhaps my broken heart and spirit could revive. As it is, I now entrust the wellbeing of the family to you. You are sensible. You will do your best. If you see Lydia again, tell her I have forgiven her. She is just a little girl. I cannot fault her for being silly. If she cannot be found, always remember—and remind your sisters—that you have a fifth sister. Forgive her in your heart if you are able."

"Papa..."

Mr. Bennet was exhausted, but he needed to continue. He whispered softly, "I must ask for your forgiveness..."

Elizabeth was startled to hear this and felt compelled to contradict her father, but Mr. Bennet did not allow her the opportunity. "I noticed the large stack of paper on the table by the window and asked Hill to bring me a few sheets. I had thought they pertained to my books, but I found out quickly it was a story you are writing. Hill has been reading the pages to me since.

"Lizzy, you are a talented writer. Do not waste this God-given gift you are so fortunate to possess. Forgive me for reading your story without permission. I could tell from the first half it is at least partially autobiographical. Those are the best sort of stories. I truly enjoyed it, even more than the Canterbury Tales. Your vivacious wit, so precious to me, shines brightly through. It also assures me you are far from succumbing to all the adversities thrust upon you. I especially enjoyed the heroine's fiery refusal of the offer of marriage from that conceited man–*the last man I could be prevailed on to marry*! It is more than very well done. It is sublime! It made me smile. Tell me truthfully, Lizzy, did you refuse Mr. Darcy's proposal as you have described in your writing?"

"Oh, papa!" Elizabeth wept softly. After a few moments, she nodded. She would not lie to her father, even though the truth might make him hate her. If only she had agreed to marry Mr. Darcy!

"My headstrong, passionate Lizzy! His letter... did he truly write that letter and give it to you?" On seeing the slight nod from his daughter, he smiled again.

"If I could do anything from beyond the grave, I would help bring you two back together. You two are made for each other. Your story is far from over."

"Papa, writing the story has helped me to... vent my anguish. Various scenarios of how things could have been different if I had accepted Mr. Darcy's proposal kept churning in my head—it was too much for my sanity. Having written it out on paper has calmed these thoughts, making them less confusing somehow. Papa, can you forgive me for turning down his proposal and putting you in such a difficult position?"

"Lizzy, there is nothing to forgive. Lydia has done wrong and needs forgiveness, not you. You must follow your heart. Judging from your story, I am optimistic your hearts will lead you and your young man back together. It is a comfort to me that such a prospect is in your future."

"My dear papa!" exclaimed Elizabeth softly. If it had been three months earlier, she would have contradicted her father with her sharp tongue, as her father afforded her the privilege of speaking to him frankly and as an equal.

Mr. Darcy? In my future as my husband? No, that can never be! How shall I even see him again?

She could not allow herself to take away his fond hope when he was on his deathbed; she swallowed her rebuttal and just smiled.

"Go now, sweetheart. I am truly fatigued. Take care of yourself first, before you take care of your mother and sisters. Remember, use the proceeds of the book sale to keep your sisters together and from needing to seek employment."

Elizabeth promised solemnly and kissed her father's forehead. After gathering up the pages of her story, she turned to look at her beloved father one last time before leaving his bookroom, which was now far more spacious as most of the books were gone.

Two days later, shortly after another letter from Mr. Gardiner bearing the disheartening but expected news that there continued to be no trace of Lydia, Mr. Bennet breathed his last.

His passing was particularly devastating to Elizabeth. Only she and her dead father knew what she had lost, and how desperately she wished she had not lost it—the salvation of her family from a destitution brought about by her father's death and Lydia's foolishness. She was determined to finish her story with the ending her father wished for as a tribute to her father.

Chapter 5

A s the Bennet family grieved the death of its patriarch, Mr. Darcy finally arrived in the Iberian Peninsula.

He had spent over a month on the voyage to Portugal alternating between too calm seas and gale-force winds. He said a silent prayer of thanks when the ship, the HMS Gallant, finally docked. There had been a few days during which the roaring winds and stormy seas so battered the ship that he was not sure he would ever see Pemberley again.

The journey overland to the last known location of his cousin, Colonel Fitzwilliam, was less traumatic. It had been almost two months since the Battle of Salamanca. Signs of battlefield devastation were everywhere he looked: burned villages, trampled and charred fields, and most of all, gaunt faces of villagers who stared at him with empty eyes. England and Portugal were allies, but the relationship with Spain was ambiguous. So even though the route from Portugal to Salamanca in Spain ran through territories friendly to the allies, in the eyes of those whose lives had been destroyed, the line between friends and enemies might be indiscernible.

In the past, he had always avoided any discussion of war and carnage. His own father, like his father before him, had hammered into Darcy's head since childhood that the Darcys must renounce any direct connections to the seat of power. The first Darcy, known as d'Arcy in those days, was a brilliant baron of William the Norman. The d'Arcys became immensely wealthy and were a force in military might in the first few hundred years of the country's history. Then came the Wars of the Roses. Lord Darcy and his adult sons took the wrong side at the wrong time. As a result, they lost their titles, their properties, and their heads.

When the Tudors took power, the only surviving descendant of the once-great family, Joan Darcy, regained an appreciable amount of Darcy properties claimed by the Crown with the help of the queen, Elizabeth of York, her friend from childhood. Miss Darcy married an untitled gentleman, who changed his name to Darcy to inherit her riches. She also vowed that the Darcys, from then on, would remain gentleman farmers and nothing more.

Over three hundred years later, the idea of shunning the pursuit of power for power's sake had become a family tradition, but not sacrosanct. For Mr. Fitzwilliam Darcy, he simply had no time for fame and glory outside of managing Pemberley.

On the way to his cousin's last known location—a small village near the battlegrounds—Mr. Darcy could not help chuckling at the irony of the situation: he, the pacifist by tradition, was rushing to a battlefield to rescue his cousin, the warrior, who eagerly hurtled toward war to advance his career. Darcy had thought the only way he would have anything to do with the war was if Bonaparte dared to invade English soil. Then and only then would he pick up arms, without a second thought, to defend his country, his home, and his dependents.

He stopped his musings at the thought of his 'dependents.'

If I had married, would I have been willing to abandon my new bride so readily as I did my dependents—my sister and my people at Pemberley? After all, Cousin Milton could not leave his wife so soon after she had given birth to his heir—what idle thoughts! I did not marry her—and that's that!

This was the first time since the start of his journey that Elizabeth Bennet came to mind. Curiously, the thought of her brought him only a small prick, unlike the turmoil that had plagued his whole being since returning from Kent. For three months, he was morose and temperamental to those around him, but inside of him, he felt profoundly humiliated: to be called ungentlemanly, to have judged so wrongly about Elizabeth's feelings toward him, to be named the last man she could be prevailed on to marry...

Added to the humiliation was self-doubt. Many nights when tossing and turning in bed, he looked into the darkness and her bright eyes flashing with righteous passion as she spewed those bitter accusations seemed almost real. His tumultuous mind compulsively examined his own behavior toward others. His staff and tenants seemed as admiring of his person as ever. Did they truly appreciate his ways of handling their affairs, or did they dole out adulation merely to please their master? He had been unsure of his place when he took over the management of Pemberley five years previously, but his success in increasing the prosperity of the estate and its people had given him confidence. Had this confidence turned into conceit, of which Elizabeth had accused him?

Elizabeth! Numerous high society ladies with enviable fortunes had thrown themselves at him at every turn, some even resorting to arts and allurements. Yet he succeeded in repelling them all. The only time he succumbed to temptation, he was brutally, unceremoniously, and unjustly rejected! He could not have concealed his distaste for her connections—disguise of every sort was his abhorrence! He would not bend his principles for anyone, even the one he ardently loved! Perhaps the rejection of his offer of marriage was a godsend. It had saved him from a lifetime of unpleasant interactions with her vulgar family and relations.

He could have ordered her to cut all connections with her family! But could he? He had often thought about the potential consequence for his sister, Georgiana, if the secret of her failed elopement had leaked. He could not count on even his closest family not to shun her. Lady Catherine, for example, certainly would. He, however, would never desert his sister. Even the notion of this was detestable to him. So how could he expect Elizabeth to forsake her family because of her new husband's disdain for her family and connections, which was far, far less harmful than a potentially serious scandal?

Elizabeth told me to my face that she would never marry me. Why do I keep torturing myself with such thoughts?

Yet, for the next several weeks, torture himself, he did. If not for the express from his uncle, Lord Fitzwilliam, telling of his cousin Richard's dire situation, everyone at Pemberley would have thought the master had been in an unceasingly dark mood since he came back from Kent after Easter.

Without wasting an extra moment, Mr. Darcy wrote his uncle volunteering to venture to the Continent to nurse his cousin back to health and to escort him home. In typical Darcy fashion, he jumped into action immediately. Within three days, he put his affairs at Pemberley in order, persuaded one of his own physicians to accompany him and his men, and arranged for passage to Salamanca. A week after that, he set sail for Porto, Portugal, the closest port on the Peninsula not occupied by the enemy.

℘℘

When their carriage arrived at the village where the field hospital was supposed to be, the exhausted travelers found the English army had moved to their next engagement location. They left behind only the severely injured who were languishing in village huts to await death. With only the limited Spanish he crammed into his head during the long voyage, he could not understand much of the villagers' explanations about the English soldiers stranded there. They all looked at him sadly and shook their heads as if to tell him that whoever he was looking for was not long for this earth.

Mr. Darcy prayed he had not been too late.

After visiting a few dilapidated huts where seriously injured British soldiers were moaning in deplorable conditions, Mr. Darcy felt a visit to the local nobility might bring him the information he sought.

He was not disappointed. In fact, he found his cousin residing comfortably in a chateau with several other wounded officers.

"Darcy!" A strange voice reached him before he could positively identify the person pronouncing his name. The face he saw was gaunt, hidden by an eye-patch and an emerging beard; the voice, soft and raspy, was so unlike the rather loud, sonorous one his cousin was wont to use to catch his attention.

Mr. Darcy rushed toward his cousin, overjoyed to the point of choking up. His cousin was alive! He had not realized how worried and tense he had been about his cousin's fate.

"Richard!" He crouched down to the low sofa on which the Colonel was reclining. "Are you well?"

He felt foolish asking a clearly inane question. His cousin was alive, but beyond that, the usual exuberance was uncharacteristically subdued, even on seeing his cousin so far from home.

"Today, I woke up with an inkling that I might live. Now that you are here, my odds of staying alive have increased tenfold! Oh, wait! Are those tears in your eyes? Perhaps I am mistaken! I have already died and gone to heaven. My manly cousin is shedding tears for my departed soul!"

Mr. Darcy was so relieved the jovial side of his cousin was pushing again to the fore that he rebuffed, if mildly, the embarrassing rub from the Colonel.

"Don't jest, Richard. I came as soon as I learned about your injuries. In the village, they have no hope for the soldiers left there. I could not but agree with them from the few I saw while going from house-to-house looking for you." Darcy saw his cousin's face darken at this grim news and sought to inject some levity. "But then I remembered you always find a way to get the best accommodations regardless of circumstances, and that led me to this rather grand chateau."

"I wish I could claim credit for scoring this almost luxurious place to rest my broken body. From what Fergo—Ferguson, my brigade's surgeon—told me, I was insensible until two weeks ago. I have no recollection of coming to Spain, let alone almost getting killed in battle. He addressed me as colonel when I came to, and I did not answer him because I thought I was Major Fitzwilliam. Hell's bloody bells and damnation!" The Colonel cursed despondently.

Darcy was taken aback by the hopelessness in the Colonel's voice. The worst appeared not yet over for his cousin. He asked anxiously, "What happened in battle? How did you get hurt? What did the surgeon say? Have you written to your father since you woke up?"

Realizing he might have vented his frustrations too freely, the Colonel put on a somewhat more cheerful mien lest he burden his too conscientious cousin unnecessarily.

"Easy, man! I was serious when I told you I would live. There is no concern there. Not only did Fergo assure me so, I have also been feeling stronger every day. If you had come a week ago, I would not have been able to utter two words to you. Now, if you could find some good port, I could talk through the night. Brilliant, eh?"

Mr. Darcy finally looked relieved but still wore a small frown. He again asked, "How did you get injured?"

"According to Fergo, and he heard it from my batman, Hughes, who was right alongside me when it happened, my horse was shot out from under me. We were charging, and I was thrown off my horse, and my head hit a sharp rock. Since that moment, I remained unconscious until two weeks ago. A Frenchie tried to finish me off with his bayonet, but before he could thrust the blade all the way in, Hughes shot him. The damage to my chest, unfortunately, had been done. They carried me here, and I was feverish for weeks. Right before I woke up, my fever broke, and here I am, entirely certain the worst is behind me."

The Colonel saw Mr. Darcy look quizzically at his covered left eye. He continued, "I did not lose my sight in this eye. However, if I take the patch off, I shall see two of you, and one of you will be tilted. It is very strange. I don't mind the eye-patch at all. I look quite dashing with it, do I not?"

Darcy smiled and responded in the same light-hearted mood, "Aye, that you do. Along with your beard, you would make quite the credible pirate to bring home French frigates in case the army will not take you back."

Darcy noticed the Colonel's face become gloomy once again. He realized his cousin's perpetually sunny disposition off the battlefield might now be a thing of the past. He asked gently, "Is there a possibility you will leave the army? You know your parents would be overjoyed if you did."

"The choice is no longer mine to make, I reckon. I have not told you the part about my memory loss and my vertigo."

Again, Mr. Darcy's eyes opened wide, but he said nothing.

The Colonel continued, "My head injuries were more severe than they first appeared. Fergo said the vertigo should get better, but it might recur. Imagine charging the Frenchies on my horse without knowing for certain I could keep my seat in the next instant! There is also the problem of my not remembering things that I just heard yesterday. I cannot tell how far back the memory loss goes since no one here knew anything about me until you got here. Does your father still live? My last memory of him was when he was ill with something or other."

"Father passed on five years ago. I suspect he died of a broken heart. He was never the same after mother died. We can now say for certain you remember things that happened some five, six years ago."

"Perhaps. I cannot say I remember everything from that time. Fergo said the memory might come back as well. I wonder how he knows these things. He is not God.

"I cannot lead a squadron—oh, I am a colonel now, a regiment then—when I constantly forget my orders! What a lamentable time to be giving up my army career! I understand when I fell in battle, I had taken over the command of the entire brigade from my commanding general. You remember General le Merchant? He was a great man. What a shame he died by a single shot that pierced his spine! The saber he perfected apparently obliterated the French battalions one after another. We were on the brink of a grand victory! My life goals, at least the ones from five years ago, were to be the youngest general in the army, and to send Bonaparte packing. I was so close to achieving them, but now they are forever out of reach. The tragedy of it is that all of this might as well not have happened."

"Richard, you are one of the youngest full colonels in the army, and you got there entirely on your own merit. That ought to count for something," Mr. Darcy reasoned.

"Well, a consolation prize, then? Does the master of Pemberley with vast holdings have an opening for a full colonel with a confused mind?" asked the Colonel wistfully.

If not for the small twinkle in the Colonel's uncovered eye, Mr. Darcy would have been concerned his ever-optimistic cousin had lost heart about his own future.

So he answered with a smile, "Hmm... I am but a pauper compared to your padre. Uncle owns half of Yorkshire and has connections to the Crown. Perhaps he can recommend you to be an equerry for a monarch with an even more confused mind?"

The Colonel could not help laughing. "Oh, has good old George relapsed? Your suggested job for me might even be better than the one I have been mulling about—a guard for Prinny. He has so many lackeys around him he would not miss the forgetful one. Do not tell me Prinny has reformed while I fell into oblivion!"

"Unfortunately for the country, His Royal Highness is worse than before. He has grown to such a bulk he needs all those hangers-on to hold him up in case he falls while inebriated," answered Mr. Darcy. He paused, sighed and continued, "Having seen you and all those dying men in the village suffering so terribly for the sake of country, I find Prinny's wastrel ways even more repugnant than ever."

"You Darcys have felt disgusted by the monarchy for ages, if I remember correctly. I am comforted that not everything has changed in the last five years. Tell me about my older brother. His wife was heavy with child, from what I remember. Has he been busy procreating, pushing me further down the line of inheritance?"

"Milton has indeed been hard at work. Your sister-in-law just birthed the heir, and the babe has three elder sisters. He could not come to nurse you back to health because he was needed at home..."

The cousins talked for a long time about the changes to family and friends that were all new to the Colonel. From this conversation, they pieced together what memories had been lost and what remained.

Over the next month, the Colonel's health improved steadily. The vertigo had mended itself for the time being, but the confused eyesight and the spotty memory remained.

The Colonel planned to submit a request for leave to his commanding officer, General Lord Wellington, who was leading the siege of Burgos in the north. Afterwards, they would travel as far south as Gibraltar. This would be a belated grand tour for Mr. Darcy, who had to forgo the trip on account of his father's illness. Both cousins welcomed a break from the weariness and care that the previous six months had brought on.

Chapter 6

J ust three weeks after Mr. Bennet's funeral, the Bennet ladies left Longbourn for good.

Not even a week after the funeral, talk about the Bennets' disgrace, which had subsided as a show of respect for the gravely ill Mr. Bennet, flared up again on rumors that Miss Lydia had met with the most unspeakable fate for a woman, and, in doing so, had thoroughly ruined her sisters' prospects. Several tradesmen, including the draper's apprentice and the butcher, came to the house to offer for any of the Miss Bennets, but 'preferably' either of the eldest two sisters.

"My nerves! My nerves! My girls' father is not even cold in the ground, and you dare come to the manor house to insult us all with your indecent offers! We are gentry, and my girls' father left them a handsome legacy. They will marry rich, deserving gentlemen. And what are you? Hill! Hill! Shove these scoundrels out the door!"

Mrs. Bennet's fuming anger roused her out of the crippling self-pity she had imposed on herself since the day Lydia ran off. She made no more fuss about her fear of being thrown into the hedgerows. Her nerves also suddenly became steady and unobtrusive. Instead, she was energetic in putting her possessions in order, sorting out those things that were outside of the purview of the entail—the china and the furniture she bought through the years.

As soon as she had gathered all that belonged to her, she moved the family to a modest cottage her brother Edward Gardiner had leased on her behalf. It was located at the edge of a sizable market town just outside the south side of London. She took no leave of anyone other than her own sister, Mrs. Philips.

"Mary, what is that Bible verse about shaking off the dust?"

"Mamma, do you mean the act of defiance against the people who treated the apostles badly? There are similar verses containing these words found in various books of the Bible: three of the four Gospels, the Acts of the Apostles..."

"Oh, never mind. In our new life, you will not have so much time studying useless things."

Mrs. Bennet then turned in the general direction of Meryton and spat out her discontent with righteous indignation, "I am shaking your dust off my feet, you cruel, vile vipers!"

Then she turned toward Longbourn, intending to say the same thing. However, the sad faces of the long-time Longbourn staff standing outside the front door, many weeping openly, made her stop and stare.

She turned around abruptly, sobbing uncontrollably, and cried, "Woe! Woe is me!"

If not for Jane and Elizabeth supporting her on each side, she would have fainted dead away.

Mrs. Bennet, her four daughters and their maid-of-all-trades, Sally, all crowded into a hired carriage for the twenty-six-mile journey to their new home.

Three days later, Longbourn received its new master and mistress: Mr. and Mrs. Collins. Mr. Collins, as expected, raised a ruckus about the missing books, china, silver and pieces of furniture from the manor house. He had, during his previous visits to Longbourn, surreptitiously inventoried quite thoroughly the contents of the manor. He appealed for justice to Lady

Catherine de Bourgh, his former patroness, instead of his father-in-law, Sir William Lucas, the magistrate of the region.

Mr. Bennet had anticipated trouble from his heir presumptive. He asked his brother Philips to show Sir William all relevant documents pertaining to the entail and receipts for the Bennets' personal property. Even though Sir William wanted to gain as much as possible for his daughter, Mrs. Collins, he was a just man. As a last benevolent gesture toward his old friend, to whom fate had dealt such a cruel and undeserved hand, he tried to convince Mr. Collins to give up pursuing a futile legal dispute against the Bennet ladies.

He would not have succeeded if not for Charlotte's argument that, as a respectable landowner with a handsome income of two thousand pounds a year at his disposal, he could afford to show a little charity, as befitting a gentleman of his new station, toward a widow and her daughters with no male protection. Besides, she, as the newly-installed mistress, would like the opportunity to purchase new things to show off to their neighbors their wealth. Mr. Collins, not entirely sure what a gentleman in his position should do, acquiesced.

Lady Catherine, always mindful of the distinction of rank, let a suitable amount of time lapse before she attended to her former dependent's request. She finally arrived at Longbourn in December to supervise the transition of Mr. Collins into the gentry class.

She was seriously displeased that the Collinses dared to move forward without waiting for her. By then, Mr. Collins had grown used to, and been vastly enjoying, the superior position of master of a prominent estate in the neighborhood. He no longer saw the need to ingratiate himself to his erstwhile patroness. Furthermore, Mrs. Collins had announced she was increasing. He was certain he would soon have an heir to end the entail, and he would then be the progenitor of the Collins line of landed gentlemen at Longbourn for generations to come.

Mr. Collins, out of habit, started worrying that he might have offended the noble lady, who was stomping out of his door. However, just then, his bailiff came in to deliver the tenants' quarter rents. Once he started counting the coins, he completely forgot why he had asked Lady Catherine to interfere with his affairs.

℘℘

Despite Mrs. Bennet's ingrained and intense fear of the hedgerows, she adjusted well to life in a modest cottage with a sound roof. After all, she was not manor-born. The cruel shunning from people she had known all her life finally shook her enough to comprehend the severity of Lydia's scandal. For the sake of the rest of her daughters, she could exercise enough discretion to keep the secret in their new environs. The ache in her heart caused by the disappearance of her favorite daughter, however, would never lessen.

The cottage was a former bailiff's house on an estate called Wayleigh, and it was just five miles from the Gardiners on Gracechurch Street. The comings and goings at such a busy place so close to London made the Bennets almost invisible.

They attracted some initial attention, of course. After all, a family with an exceptional beauty like Jane and three other handsome sisters could not go unnoticed for long. However, once the novelty had worn off, the family in deep mourning was left mostly alone.

The rent of fifty pounds a year was a stretch of the Bennets' financial resources. However, Mr. Gardiner had already received some estimates on the value of Mr. Bennet's book collection—it could command as much as eight thousand pounds. He therefore took the risk and leased a cottage that would appease his sister. It was far away enough from Meryton that Lydia's scandal, if it ever spread to Wayleigh, would not affect the reputation of the Bennet women too grievously.

As soon as the family had settled in, Mr. Gardiner urged Elizabeth to come to London and help him organize the book collection for auction. There were over five thousand volumes, which took up a considerable part of Mr. Gardiner's warehouse. Since a new shipment of goods would arrive in a month, he urgently needed to clear the space to receive his goods.

Elizabeth was loath to leave her family in their new home so soon after such life-changing events. The night before she was to leave for London, she and her sister Jane spoke while preparing for bed.

"Jane, truly, will you be alright dealing with mamma, Mary, and Kitty all by yourself?" Elizabeth asked anxiously.

"Lizzy. You should not worry. Mamma seems content. I think she takes immense comfort among familiar things she took from Longbourn. I am truly relieved her nerves have not been bothering her much, if at all, since we have moved here."
Lizzy interjected, "Mary is still smarting from mamma's not allowing her to bring the pianoforte here."

Jane answered thoughtfully, "She will have to learn to sacrifice. She is coming around, I think. Seeing the tight space in the parlor has made her realize mamma was right.

"Kitty, however, seems anchorless. You have seen how she looks out of the window for hours doing nothing. Without Lydia, she does not know what to do next. I am worried about her."

Elizabeth said apologetically, "Jane, forgive me for not giving you the help you need to keep the family together. I have been dealing with the tradespeople in the village to set up accounts and such..."

"Oh, Lizzy. Please do not apologize. Without you, the family would have sat around waiting for Uncle Gardiner to help with these things. No, the book collection should take priority over everything. I have seen you busy writing at that round table from papa's bookroom...." Jane could not help choking up when her father was mentioned. Lizzy squeezed her hand as she herself also started weeping.

Jane exclaimed softly, "Oh, I wonder when mentioning papa will not make us cry!" She sniffled before continuing. "Cataloguing five thousand books must have been a Herculean task. You will save the family yet. I do not think I could help even if I tried. I did not attend to papa's lessons on Greek and Latin as you did. And now you have to bear the entire burden by yourself!"

Elizabeth was a little shamefaced. She was spending more time on writing her story than on the book catalogue when she was scribbling away at the small table now placed by the window of the dining room. The stack of paper on the table was more likely a part of her manuscript than the itemized list of the book collection. Her story was a secret she had shared only with her father.

Just that afternoon, she had accomplished the seemingly impossible twist—a happy ending—in her fictitious fate:

After rescuing Lydia, forcing Wickham to marry her by discharging his debts and purchasing a commission for him in the regulars—these burdens totaling almost ten thousand pounds!–Mr. Darcy came back with Mr. Bingley to Netherfield. Mr. Bingley immediately resumed his attentions to Jane as if he had not abandoned her for eight months. Although Elizabeth felt this was rather contrived, she could not think of anything better. With Mr. Bingley in attendance at Longbourn every day, inevitably, Mr. Darcy, who accompanied him on every occasion, would offer for her again. Of course, this time, like the rational being she was, she accepted with pleasure and gratitude! Her papa was not happy at first but was persuaded by her vehement defense of the gentleman's character and honor. The most important thing to Elizabeth was that her papa remained healthy, his sarcastic wits intact.

She leaned back in the small cane chair and let out a sigh of satisfaction. She could not help smiling at how the story ended—no lost Lydia, no death of her papa, no leaving Longbourn, and last but not least, she married the man she loved and became the mistress of Pemberley.

She had long ago admitted to herself that she could have loved Mr. Darcy, had she known about the perfidy of Mr. Wickham. She had forgiven his part in separating Mr. Bingley and Jane. She herself had done the same with Charlotte, trying to dissuade Charlotte from accepting Mr. Collins's proposal the day after the bumbling parson, now master of Longbourn, had proposed to her. Charlotte disregarded her wrongheaded advice and had done very well for herself. Her husband adored her, and she could be carrying the heir who would break the entail for the Collinses. Mr. Bingley could have been like Charlotte and ignored Mr. Darcy's equally wrongheaded suggestion, but he did not. Only Mr. Bingley was the true villain for deserting Jane...

"Lizzy!" Jane almost shouted at Elizabeth to gain her attention. Elizabeth started and looked at Jane quizzically.

"What?"

"You were far away, Lizzy. You stared into the room just like Kitty staring out of the window, and then you smiled, followed by a deep frown. That was when I tried to get you out of your reverie."

"Oh! Forgive me, Jane. These days my thoughts are everywhere. When you mentioned learning Latin and Greek, I remembered the evil eye you gave me when I begged papa to teach us Latin. That must have been the first and only time you thought ill of someone and showed it on your face!" Elizabeth prevaricated.

Elizabeth's explanation of her absentmindedness did not really convince Jane, but the memory of her little sister, who was then only five, clambering onto her papa's lap and demanding to learn Latin, diverted her.

To distract Jane further, Elizabeth continued on Latin and said, "Oh, speaking of Latin, why don't we call our cottage 'Vita Nova?' It means 'new life.' We cannot keep calling it the bailiff's cottage. There has not been a bailiff here for quite a few years, I understand."

"Mamma will not like it, and I am uncertain I do either," said Jane with a frown.

"How about 'Wayleighs End?' This cottage is at the edge of the Wayleigh Estate. Uncle Gardiner said the previous owner had sold off the farmland long ago. The new owner, a trade associate of Uncle's, purchased the house for his mother to live away from London, and the bailiff's cottage came with it," suggested Elizabeth, who was very glad her tactic had led Jane away from the carefully guarded topic of her story.

"How about a simple 'Rambler Cottage?' There is a mass of these roses outside the kitchen. 'Wayleighs End' sounds too grand. It is more appropriate for the manor house than its former bailiff's cottage. Besides, with such a grand name, mamma would insist on getting her own carriage once she has access to the proceeds of the book auction," advised Jane sagely.

"'Rambler Cottage' it is! You have always been the voice of reason, Jane, and you know your roses even when they are not in bloom."

The two sisters shook hands on the agreement regarding the name. Elizabeth continued, "And you know mamma better than anyone else. You must try your best to dissuade her from any such grandiose purchase. Uncle Gardiner said the entire proceeds from the book auction would go into the funds, yielding three to four hundred pounds a year on top of mamma's two hundred. With five women in the cottage, and none of us in service, that income should be adequate for plain living. Maintaining a carriage with horses and a coachman, however, is a luxury we cannot afford. They cost at least two hundred pounds a year, even if we just rent them and not purchase them outright. Besides, the proceeds will be for our dowries as well. I shall probably not marry, but the three of you will still be in need of dowries."

"Lizzy, I have said it many times, and I shall say it once more: you will end up being the first among us to marry. As for mamma, I promise I shall try. She has been more yielding since the funeral. I think she will listen to reason. Let us go to bed. I shall get up to see you off early tomorrow morning," said Jane while yawning in a rather unladylike manner.

"Good night, dearest. I thank God every day that we are sisters," said Elizabeth, feelingly. She did not feel ready to be separated from her family, especially her favorite sister, for the next two months or however long it might take to sell the books.

"Good night, Lizzy." Jane fell asleep almost instantly, while Elizabeth tossed and turned, thinking about the books, which would soon belong to someone else. She would lose a significant link to her dear papa. What a blessing it was to still have the dear dodecagonal table (her father had taught her that word—the tabletop was a twelve-sided polygon even though

59

everyone in the family, including her father, called it the round table,) which her father bought while a student at Oxford. She felt comforted she had given the story the ending her father desired. Her father's fond wish would always live in her story, and that had to be enough.

Chapter 7

Elizabeth had been in London for a week. She finally completed the catalogue of the volumes, hundreds of which were first-editions or rare. Her father had an interest in just about everything ever published, including Anglo-Saxon history, and even books and manuscripts from foreign countries.

One morning, while her Uncle Gardiner was away from the office, Mr. Gardiner's warehouse clerk came in to announce that a lady and her business associate had requested to view the books.

Elizabeth was curious. Her uncle had not told her to expect anyone regarding her father's collection.

An elegantly dressed lady in lavender was examining the volumes with deep concentration when Elizabeth entered the front part of the warehouse. The lady was quite young—perhaps ten years older than herself, had a full and pleasing figure, and a handsome face with a self-assured air.

The man accompanying the lady seemed surprised to see her instead of her uncle and hurried over to inquire impatiently, "Ma'am, I am here to speak with Mr. Gardiner. Could you please announce to him that Mrs. Trumbull and Mr. Peters are here to view the Bennet collection?"

"Oh, my uncle has been called away on urgent business. I am Miss Elizabeth Bennet. This was my late father's..." Elizabeth still choked up when mentioning her father.

On hearing the suppressed sob emanating from the young woman, the lady came up to Elizabeth and gently said, "Miss Bennet, forgive me for intruding. Please accept my condolences for your loss. Was it recent?"

"Yes, madam, in early September," answered Elizabeth more calmly, now that she had a moment to contain her emotions.

"I see. Please allow me to introduce myself. I am Mrs. Lillian Trumbull."

Mrs. Trumbull scrutinized Elizabeth for a moment to discern any sign the young woman in front of her recognized her name.

At her husband's death the previous year, followed by the death of his seven-year-old son and heir six months later, she became one of the richest heiresses in all England. Rumor was she had inherited half a million pounds from her husband, who had been a Member of Parliament and the most successful timber merchant in the land. The money was from trade, but Mrs. Trumbull, nee Morgan, was descended from a long line of distinguished Anglo-Welsh gentry. Her father was a baronet.

Her formal reentry into society had stirred much excitement now that her mourning period was officially over. Mrs. Trumbull, anticipating eyes would be on her wherever she went, resorted to wearing half-mourning dresses to fend off unwanted attention.

Seeing no reaction from Elizabeth, Mrs. Trumbull relaxed and continued, "I heard this is an unusually extensive collection rich in the classics, including one of the two known first-editions of 'Hamlet.' I wish to learn more about it. If it is as outstanding as it is reputed to be, then I wish to purchase the entire collection before it goes to auction. Miss Bennet, you are a gentlewoman, and so I shall not trouble you further with any more talk of business dealings, especially during your period of mourning."

Elizabeth could never hold her tongue when she saw any inconsistency in an argument. She retorted, "Madam, you yourself are a gentlewoman still in mourning, and yet you intend to negotiate with my uncle on acquiring the book collection." She paused abruptly as her mother's admonishments for her being too sharp entered her mind unbidden. She apologized meekly, "Please excuse my impertinence."

Mrs. Trumbull eyed Elizabeth with interest. She was indeed not at all offended. Instead, she answered gently, "Miss Bennet, I commend you for speaking frankly. You are right, of course, about my intending to conduct the negotiation personally. Society is slower to censure a widow for trespassing outside of proper decorum than a young unmarried lady. I usually have Mr. Peters with me for propriety's sake. Miss Bennet, allow me to introduce Mr. Peters, my steward and solicitor."

Elizabeth curtsied, and Mr. Peters bowed.

Mrs. Trumbull continued, "Miss Bennet, am I correct to assume that you are more informed about the collection than Mr. Gardiner?"

Elizabeth nodded slightly. She did not want to assume false modesty when Mrs. Trumbull asked such a direct question.

"I understand your grief over your father's passing is still fresh and painful to you, and you may not be ready to talk about these books, which must have been very dear to him."

Elizabeth quickly said, "I thank you for your kind consideration, madam, but I am well now. It *is* a conundrum. I love talking about my father, but I cannot help weeping when speaking of him. If you could ignore my tears, it would be my pleasure to answer your questions to the best of my ability. I grew up with many of these books and can take some pride in my knowledge about them."

Mrs. Trumbull again looked at Elizabeth with fascination. "Indeed!"

The two ladies enjoyed a lively exchange about various aspects of the collection.

Mrs. Trumbull picked up a book. She remarked, "'Il newtonianismo per le dame'—'Newtonianism for the ladies.' Was your father enlightened about educating girls? Did he encourage you and your sisters to pursue interest in the natural sciences? Miss Bennet, I am pretending not to have just mentioned your late father again."

Elizabeth answered with a genuine smile, "My father left the pursuit of knowledge entirely to his daughters' own initiative. Those who cared to learn never lacked masters. I was the most inquisitive of his five daughters from the start. One day—I was twelve years old—I spotted my father studying Newton's 'Principia.' I had some rudimentary Latin at that age, but I did not recognize the limit of my meager knowledge and implored my father to teach Newtonian physics to me. In all honesty, the diagrams and the strange symbols in the treatise were fascinating to me, not the theory of the workings of the natural world. To pacify me, and I am certain playing a practical joke on his troublesome daughter was part of his intent, he purchased the 'il newtonianismo per le dame' for me, knowing full well I did not know a word of Italian. Being very stubborn, I muddled through the book, learning hardly anything about color and light, but picked up enough Italian to understand the lyrics of the arias I learned to sing a few years later."

Mrs. Trumbull laughed heartily over this anecdote. Her countenance was open and pleasant when she laughed, making her look younger.

"Thank you for putting me at ease talking about my father's love for his books," Elizabeth told Mrs. Trumbull feelingly. She was beginning to like this lady, who seemed very kind and quick-witted.

Mrs. Trumbull said in response, "I have not laughed for a long time. I also must thank you for telling me such diverting anecdotes of your life. Hmm, the Italian you learned was about color and light. You favor happy Italian arias then? But aren't most of them about lost love and heartbreaks?"

Both ladies laughed merrily some more. As if on cue, Mr. Gardiner entered the room and immediately approached Mrs. Trumbull. He apologetically greeted her, "Mrs. Trumbull, I beg your forgiveness for not being here to receive you this afternoon. Henderson, my clerk, alerted me to your interest in the Bennet collection. Allow me to re-introduce myself. I am Edward Gardiner. I met you and Mr. Trumbull at one of your soirees many years ago. You may not remember me—it was quite a crush, as I recall. Please accept my condolences on Mr. Trumbull's passing. He was a great man."

Mrs. Trumbull nodded to acknowledge the kind compliments but said nothing in response.

Mr. Gardiner looked from one lady to the other and said, "I see that you have met my niece, Miss Elizabeth Bennet. She is the only person who could answer questions on this collection."

Before Elizabeth could say something to moderate her uncle's high praise, Mrs. Trumbull interjected, "Indeed, you are right, Mr. Gardiner. Miss Bennet has explained the merits of this collection admirably. She also reminded me that as a gentlewoman, I should leave the business end of my interest in acquiring this collection to the men."

Elizabeth again wanted to rebut, as she had not said any such thing. However, on seeing the mischievous but good-natured glint in Mrs. Trumbull's eyes, she acquiesced.

"If you allow me a few minutes with Mr. Peters, I shall inform him of my wishes regarding the book collection, and then I shall continue the very edifying tour through these fascinating books under Miss Bennet's tutelage."

Mrs. Trumbull excused herself and went over to Mr. Peters. They conversed for a few minutes with Mr. Peters glancing over at Elizabeth a few times.

Mr. Peters then followed Mr. Gardiner to an inner office to discuss business.

Meanwhile, the two ladies talked further, not only about the books but also about themselves.

Elizabeth learned that Mrs. Trumbull had studied Latin, Greek, French and Italian as a child from her clergyman uncle. After marriage, she bore seven children in quick succession; and being the wife of an ambitious industrialist and Member of Parliament, she had not had the time for her own scholastic pursuits. Now that she was free of the many obligations imposed on her by her previous status, she wanted to build back the library of her childhood, which was lost because of her father's bankruptcy.

Elizabeth told Mrs. Trumbull about having four sisters and the circumstances that led to the sale of the book collection.

Mrs. Trumbull was thoughtful for a few moments. She asked, "Will you and your sisters be seeking employment then?"

Ever perceptive, Elizabeth sensed that Mrs. Trumbull was about to offer employment to her. She was momentarily lost for words. Mrs. Trumbull was likely to purchase the book collection, and she might risk offending a potential savior of the Bennet family by not accommodating the older lady's wishes.

To her surprise, Mrs. Trumbull did not wait for an answer but disclosed something quite personal. "My father lost more than he had in speculative investments and put his family in a dire financial situation, possibly worse than your family's current one. By the time my future husband came to purchase the woods of my father's estate, I had a fair idea that he would be buying the last of what my father owned. He had already lost my dowry years before that. When Mr. Trumbull asked me for my hand in marriage, I saw him as the way out of poverty and a life in service. I accepted his offer instantly. My father, however, had some exaggerated perception of his own importance as a gentleman with a hereditary title. My family has a rather illustrious history in my part of the country, and my father was a baronet. He refused to give his consent to the marriage of his only child, the last of his noble lineage, to a despicable 'cit,' as he so spitefully called Mr. Trumbull. I eloped, and sadly, my father had an apoplexy and died when the news reached him."

"My husband, Brent Trumbull, was the only son of a prosperous timber tradesman. He had been sent to Eton and then Oxford. When he inherited, instead of fulfilling his father's wish of purchasing an estate and becoming a gentleman, he expanded the business to include ship- and canal-building. He saw in me an opportunity to place himself in a social circle even beyond what his own father had aspired to. I was fortunate. My husband was a good man, and we had a felicitous marriage."

Elizabeth did not know what to say to this frank telling of a stranger's intimate family history, and so she remained silent. After a brief moment, Mrs. Trumbull appeared to have woken from a trance. She looked at Elizabeth with an embarrassed smile and said wryly, "Miss Bennet, you must think me daft to be telling you all this. If you knew me better, you would know that being frank is in my nature. During my year in mourning, I did not see many people or have any deep conversations. And then my only son died of scarlet fever six months after my husband's death. Forgive me for telling you what you care nothing about."

Mrs. Trumbull signaled to Elizabeth, who was about to interrupt, to let her finish. "Miss Bennet, what I intended to say to you before I digressed to this long exposition of my personal history was that I understand the dilemma faced by gentlewomen impoverished by circumstances not of their own making. I explained how I escaped the impending financial ruin created by my reckless father. I do not know whether marriage is a viable solution for you and your sisters. Unfortunately, for young women without means, the options for a secure future are scarce."

Elizabeth was tempted to tell Mrs. Trumbull that the death of her own father was also due to the shock of Lydia's elopement, but Lydia's scandal was far worse than Mrs. Trumbull's. After all, no one knew whether Lydia had married. As for Elizabeth marrying for security, that ship—with Mr. Darcy in it—had long sailed.

She focused on the issue at hand instead. "Mrs. Trumbull, I am grateful for your taking me into your confidence and for your advice. Please be assured what I just heard will go no further, and also accept my condolences for your loss.

"I have an unusual predicament that my father stipulated adamantly before his death that his daughters would not go into service and charged me with upholding his dying wish. The Bennet family is of old lineage as well, but there have been no titles in our branch of the family. Nonetheless, pa... my father felt a deep remorse for leaving his daughters in a state of need. He felt the sale of his books should be able to preserve our status as gentlewomen. I suspect he also worried about what ill fate could befall us, for my elder sister is an exquisite beauty."

"I see. Miss Bennet, I have given instructions to Mr. Peters to offer Mr. Gardiner fair value for the collection. I hope the sum will be enough to maintain six ladies in genteel living. Have you found a new place to live?"

"Thank you, madam. I also hope all will come to a satisfactory conclusion. As for my family, my Uncle Gardiner found us a cottage on the edge of a village close to Clapham, which is about five miles from here. They are settling in tolerably well," answered Elizabeth. She had to bite her lip to stop spilling the truth that there were only five of them left in the family.

"Ah, Clapham is but three miles from Brixton Park, my country house."

Mrs. Trumbull left Elizabeth's side and walked away for a few moments. When she turned around, she looked at Elizabeth and said intently, "Miss Bennet, we have only met today. This may seem abrupt to you. I, however, have been contemplating for months what I shall offer to you, or rather, someone I would hire to fill the position I think you are well-qualified for, and hope you will accept."

Elizabeth was indeed surprised after telling Mrs. Trumbull in no uncertain terms she was not available for employment. She looked at Mrs. Trumbull quizzically.

Mrs. Trumbull smiled and said pleasantly, "Please be assured there is nothing sinister about my scheme. My husband, and by association, I as well, were active in the circle of Tory politics. For instance, General Wellesley attended at least one gathering at my house every time he was in town. He has been, of course, very seldom in town these past few years. I greatly enjoy the intellectually stimulating discussions with these brilliant minds and intend to continue these meetings when I formally come out of mourning in the coming season. However, without my late husband's presence, the atmosphere of the meetings may become awkward. My widowed aunt has agreed to be my companion, of sorts. She is quite erudite—the uncle who gave me my education was her husband, but her health is becoming more and more delicate, and she dozes off every few minutes, hardly adequate to be a chaperone. I have been searching for another lady to help me host these soirees, but a lady with the qualifications I am looking for has not appeared until today. You are perhaps a little younger than what I had in mind, but your education, though self-taught, is impressive. You claim your sister is an exquisite beauty. Could she possibly be more beautiful than you? Your eyes flashing with passion, as they did a few moments ago, would turn most gentlemen into puddles. Your intelligence, liveliness, your fine countenance and figure, and last but not least, your Italian arias, will divert the attention of the gentlemen away from me."

Elizabeth started on hearing this.

What could she mean? And she said she did not mean anything sinister!

Mrs. Trumbull looked amused and smiled widely at the younger lady's astonished expression.

"Be not alarmed, Miss Bennet. The gentlemen who gather at my house are of the honorable and clever sort. Their collective sarcastic wit can easily vanquish the occasional rake or dandy and chase him out of the house within three minutes. Besides, there are usually some matrons of exalted standing in attendance. No one would dare misbehave."

"Then, madam, why the awkwardness?"

"Let me be completely frank with you, and perhaps a bit indelicate. I have the feeling you expect more than vague answers. Rumors are rampant all over London that I am worth half a million pounds or more. An eligible lady worth that much has always been the target of attentions from even honorable gentlemen. In years past, these gentlemen viewed me as the wife of their esteemed friend. Nothing untoward happened. Now... I do not know what they think, or how they will act."

Elizabeth stood dazed. The great wealth of the lady stunned her and made her slow to respond to the question placed before her. She had been certain the riches of others, as in the cases of Mr. Darcy and Lady Catherine, hardly impressed her, but why was Mrs. Trumbull's wealth different?

Is it because of the change in my status? Before, I was a gentlewoman from Longbourn. Now, I am a nobody... it would have been different if I had married Mr. Darcy... Stop being ridiculous!

Mrs. Trumbull paused. Mistaking Elizabeth's stupefied look for wariness, she explained further, "In the past, my interactions with a few of these gentlemen could have been construed as flirtations. My frank and open manner may give the impression I am free and easy with my favors, but I have never been. My husband kept me... say, I have no wish for any marital affection in the foreseeable future. Perhaps you might comprehend better now from whence discomfiture may spring. I shall make clear to everyone you are a friend in reduced circumstances. They will leave you alone. Those who do not will probably have honorable intentions."

Oh. Mr. Darcy thought my frank exchanges with him were flirtations as well!

What was she thinking? Didn't she long ago give up all hope of being Mrs. Darcy? She chastised herself for holding onto a fancy. Finally, her wits caught up with her while Mrs. Trumbull looked on with amusement again, which made Elizabeth feel challenged.

Whomever Elizabeth had become, her courage did not stay suppressed for long in the face of intimidation.

"Madam, if my mother were to hear what you just said, she would offer all her daughters for your service!"

While laughing at her own joke with Mrs. Trumbull, Elizabeth could regain her composure. The two weighty reasons she could not accept Mrs. Trumbull's offer of employment came to mind: her father's charge on his deathbed, and, equally important, Lydia's scandal, which she would feel obligated to disclose to a prospective employer.

Elizabeth became sober and spoke with unease, "I am still newly in deep mourning. My mind cannot presently fathom any such prospects." It was shame she felt because she was about to repay the lady who had been generous and open with falsehood.

"Of course, Miss Bennet. I apologize if my comments sounded importunate. I only meant to assure you that your presence at my soirees would benefit me without hurting you in any manner. There will certainly be no lascivious employer lurking in a dark hallway to take advantage of you."

"Mrs. Trumbull," said Elizabeth after a quick moment of contemplation, "I am honored and gratified you deem me suitable to assist you in reentering society. Meeting the learned and worldly guests at your gatherings would be something a country girl like me could only dream of. Unfortunately, I must honor my father's last wish that none of his daughters go into service, and so, I regret that I must decline."

Mrs. Trumbull was astonished by the refusal.

"Miss Bennet, was the reason behind your father's wish that his daughters should not lose their status as gentlewomen?"

Elizabeth nodded, once again marveling at the lady's insight and the straightforward way Mrs. Trumbull expressed herself.

"In that case, isn't it fortunate there is a simple solution to your late father's objection? I need a lady to help me navigate my way around the ton. Whether the lady is a friend, or a paid companion disguised as a friend, does not signify. Mr. Peters will add two hundred pounds to the book sale transaction. All I ask is you commit to be my assistant for two years, unless you marry before the two years are up."

Elizabeth was beginning to admire this rich lady's forceful character. However, her somewhat officious attempt to arrange affairs to her own liking without regard to the wishes of the person involved reminded her of another strong-willed lady: Lady Catherine de Bourgh. Inevitably, her ladyship's nephew, with his own high-handed way of interfering with other people's lives, came to mind.

Why is it everything reminds me of him?

Without giving herself too much time to ponder on the persistent presence of that confoundingly confusing gentleman in her thoughts, she answered Mrs. Trumbull firmly, "Madam, your solution to circumvent my father's last wish is indeed clever. Would you give me until tomorrow to think things over and discuss with my uncle? I am of age as of last month, but I am not prepared to make a decision which may dishonor the memory of my father without my uncle's approval."

"Of course," answered Mrs. Trumbull. "Let me make one point clear before I leave this topic. I am a bluestocking, as you may have surmised, and I feel it is a pity learned ladies are no longer in vogue. One can find ladies who have enough education to be governesses to my daughters, but finding one

71

with the classical education of a gentleman, independence of thought, and the willingness to assist me has been impossible."

She paused to look Elizabeth in the eye. "I have made the offer based on long, careful contemplation and not an impulse. After talking things over with your uncle, if you have any preferences of your own, please do not be afraid to discuss them with me and see whether we may come to a mutually beneficial arrangement. From what I have seen so far, you are not afraid to be open with me."

Elizabeth's opinion of Mrs. Trumbull turned for the better again. This lady was not inconsiderate after all. The opportunity to be introduced to the level of society filled with important people who controlled the fate of the country—and perhaps even the world—was indeed exhilarating. Before Lydia's scandal, she would have jumped at the offer in a heartbeat. However, the family's shame was an enormous gallows staring down at her. There was no going around it.

For all she knew, she and all her sisters had been forever banned from polite, let alone elevated, society.

Chapter 8

Mr. Gardiner was all smiles when he came out of the office where he and Mr. Peters had been haggling over pricing.

As soon as the visitors had left, Mr. Gardiner said exuberantly to Elizabeth, "Lizzy, Mrs. Trumbull has purchased the entire collection for nine thousand pounds! That is at least a thousand pounds more than the auctioneers' estimates, and because this was a direct sale with no middlemen involved, I have also saved on the commission. You girls will have much more than I had thought for your future!"

"Oh, Uncle Gardiner, this is good news indeed! Why do you think she paid so much more than what the auction houses predicted?"

"Items like rare books do not have an actual intrinsic value. It depends on what the purchaser thinks the books are worth to them. Auction

houses have more experience with doing an evaluation like this, but

even they told me the proceeds could come in much higher or lower than the six-to-eight-thousand-pound range. As soon as we had entered my office, Mr. Peters asked me outright what return I expected from the auction. I took a risk and told him what I believed it would gross. That was when he offered nine thousand pounds if I canceled the auction. I could hardly maintain the stoical face I have perfected for negotiations. He then drew up all the papers for me to sign and handed me a bank draft for the entire amount! The rumor of Mrs. Trumbull having sold her late husband's businesses for half a million pounds must be close to the mark; and even with that much wealth, she would not have spent such a large sum unless there was something in the collection she desperately wanted."

"Perhaps I could ask her myself..." said Elizabeth thoughtfully. She paused, realizing that, in her own mind, she had already accepted Mrs. Trumbull's offer to be her companion.

Before he could ask questions, she explained, "Uncle Gardiner, Mrs. Trumbull offered to me the position of companion. I told her I had to discuss with you because papa..."

After taking a deep breath, Elizabeth recounted her conversation with the rich heiress.

Mr. Gardiner looked at Elizabeth in awe and exclaimed, "Lizzy, this is an extraordinary opportunity! The Trumbulls' gatherings were renowned in the city for attracting distinguished artists and the best minds in Tory politics. The late Prime Minister, Mr. Spencer Perceval, General Wellesley, and the famous painter, Mr. Thomas Lawrence, were regulars.

"If Mrs. Trumbull thinks you are the ideal person to help her manage her soirees, then you will have made your father proud! I am certain he would have encouraged you to accept. If you must honor your father's last wish to the letter, you could refuse the monetary compensation. The extra one thousand pounds she paid for the book collection is a more than fair compensation for your assistance to her."

The incredible privilege of entering elevated circles finally sank in. However, she remembered the reason for her reservation.

"What about Lydia? Mrs. Trumbull could not possibly be willing to have her name tarnished by associating with me."

"Lizzy, you are not important enough to cause any harm to Mrs. Trumbull's reputation. Besides, you are not obligated to tell her anything about Lydia. For all we know, Lydia could have gone on a holiday without telling her family. If she left Brighton with a man, no one witnessed that event. There might also have been a chaperone. We must not think the worst of her until we know more.

"Even if such a scandal was proven, you need not tell anyone about it. In a small village like Meryton, what happened to Lydia was noteworthy and caused people to gossip because they have nothing better to do. Here in London, people are too busy to notice an ordinary little girl running away from home. I am not being cold-hearted or facetious. It is the truth. Even the Prince Regent's scandalous antics do not always cause a sensation. Did you not just tell me Mrs. Trumbull herself had eloped? I cannot say I heard anything about it because it did not happen in London, and the Trumbulls were not as prominent as they are now. I wager even among your own acquaintances, there are secrets that could erupt into scandals if they became known."

Mr. Gardiner's comments made Elizabeth think of Miss Darcy. It became instantly clear that her uncle was right. She also saw for the first time that Lydia's shame was Lydia's alone, and should not hang over her sisters like a gallows. She solemnly vowed she would look for her wayward sister the rest of her life, and she would forgive Lydia's actions, but she would not allow this to taint herself or her other sisters.

"Uncle Gardiner, if you think my family can do without the extra hundred pounds yearly, I think I should honor papa's wish by not taking compensation. I am indeed very excited about meeting the great minds of our time at Mrs. Trumbull's home, and I am humbled she thinks me worthy of this position. Could you send a note to Mrs. Trumbull informing her of the terms for my acceptance of her kind offer?"

"Of course, Lizzy! I am happy for you. This is a once-in-a-lifetime opportunity for you to see the world without having to travel."

"Uncle, what about my mourning?"

"Why don't we suggest to Mrs. Trumbull you begin your tenure with her when you enter half-mourning in a month? Meanwhile, Mr. Peters said his employer is staying at her country house with her three daughters. Brixton Park is just three miles from your cottage. Whether you are in London or her country house, you will not be far from family."

'Tis a good plan, Uncle Gardiner. I shall do as you wish."

ᏇᏇ

Meanwhile, in Salamanca, Colonel Fitzwilliam had gained enough strength. The cousins were preparing to travel for the Colonel to submit his request for leave to his commanding office, General Lord Wellington.

However, just as they were ready to set out, the General unexpectedly came to them.

The siege of Burgos had turned out badly. General Wellington ordered the army to retreat to Portugal via Salamanca. Fighting against a French army 80,000 strong with his own 65,000 was decidedly to his disadvantage. He refused to waste any English lives unnecessarily.

The pursuing French caught up with the British at Salamanca.

Colonel Fitzwilliam and Mr. Darcy went up to high grounds to watch the incredible sight of two enormous armies facing off in the same open fields where Colonel Fitzwilliam had been so grievously injured three months earlier. While the Colonel could not recall any military confrontation of this scale, Mr. Darcy was astounded how many men were willing, at the sound of the bugle call, to charge the opposing army and kill as many of their opponents as they were able. It was a sobering scene.

Fortunately, the French army chose not to attack, and General Wellington did not waste any time ordering the evacuation of Salamanca.

The cousins loaded the few remaining recovering soldiers into their small caravan and moved with the army to Portugal, where General Wellington intended to winter.

The allies' retreat to Portugal was arduous and fraught with danger. Mr. Darcy's group narrowly escaped capture by the pursuing French calvary. General Paget, General Wellesley's second-in-command, was a family friend of the Fitzwilliams and the Darcys. He rode over to their small contingent and urged them to make haste, as the French were coming fast. The next day, they discovered General Paget had been taken prisoner, along with many in his command.

Mr. Darcy, instead of feeling repulsed by the fighting or frightened by their narrow escape, experienced a kind of exhilaration he had never known. He felt useful and connected to what he believed to be an important moment in history. Back in England, viewing Bonaparte from afar, he had felt admiration for the military ruler, who had conquered a large part of Europe seemingly without effort and implemented a sensible code of law where there had been none. Having now seen the utter destruction of life and property in places where battles raged, he changed his mind about his erstwhile hero—Bonaparte was nothing but just another self-aggrandizing usurper with no regard for humanity.

Mr. Darcy felt energized that he was contributing to the eventual downfall of this ruthless tyrant.

Once the army had reached safety inside Portugal, Mr. Darcy helped his cousin with the logistics of the army's encampment. He offered everything in his possession to the troops—his physician, his men from Pemberley, his carriages and horses, and his money, which he loaned to the army until official funds arrived via the long and winding parliamentary process. He even went into the surgery ward to assist his physician in caring for the wounded.

When life at camp had calmed down sufficiently, Colonel Fitzwilliam asked to see the Commander-in-Chief about resigning his commission. He had had some doubts about yielding to Darcy's advice to give up his army career for good. However, since the retreat from Salamanca, he had to admit he could no longer physically shoulder the demand of a high-ranking military officer. Without Darcy's help, he would have been lost and unable to fulfill his assignment of matériel procurement.

"Colonel, let me commend you for your valor and outstanding tactics in the battle of Salamanca. Your leadership of the brigade after Le Marchant's fall was brilliant!" General Wellington was always generous in giving credit where credit was due.

"Sir, thank you. It is a pity I do not remember any of my own actions during that battle. I lost five years' worth of memory when I fell from my horse."

"Shame! I have lost le Marchant, Beresford and Paget already. You would have been a strong candidate to fill le Merchant's position. This war is far from over."

"It has been an honor to serve directly under you, sir, but I am afraid my military days are over. I have come here to submit my resignation from the army."

"Resignation? I read reports that you have been laudable in speedily settling the troops and the animals for encampment. If we had had this kind of competence during the retreat, it would not have turned into such a disaster.

"I understand you could not wield your saber in battle any time soon, but the army needs your organizational ability. I will recommend you to be head of battlefield logistics and make sure your contribution to the victory at Salamanca will count substantially toward your next promotion."

Colonel Fitzwilliam was proud that the General, who never doled out undeserved praises, wanted him to continue serving in his command despite his disabilities. He did not want to deceive the General, however.

"Sir, my cousin, Mr. Fitzwilliam Darcy of Pemberley, Derbyshire, has been assisting me. Without his help, both physical and financial, matters here would not have gone so smoothly."

"Is that right? You lured Darcy the Pacifist to the battlefield, and he even involved himself in the business of fighting! Is he here? I need properly to meet the scion of the most peace-loving family in the entire Kingdom."

"Darcy is outside, sir." The Colonel was worried about the sarcastic tone in the General's speech. There was, however, nothing he could do to mitigate the impending clash between two outsized personalities: the most illustrious general in the land, accustomed to being revered, and his intensely proud cousin, who would stand up to any challenge to the honor of the Darcy name. His cousin had accompanied him because they thought the interview with the General would be brief, and they could then go on their way to secure conveyance for a pleasure trip through Portugal. How he now regretted this decision!

Instead of asking the Colonel to send for his cousin, General Lord Wellington walked out of the room himself to meet Darcy.

"Ah, Mr. Darcy of Pemberley!" called the General in his booming voice.

Mr. Darcy was watching with interest the hustle and bustle inside headquarters and did not expect to be called upon by the head of the army like an errand boy. He had met the General briefly for the first time soon after they arrived in the border town inside Portugal. However, things were chaotic then, and the General was in a melancholic mood because of the enormous losses during their retreat. In addition to a large number of casualties, thousands of troops remained unaccounted for. Many who made it back to camp were in poor physical condition because they had marched four full days through cold, pouring rain without food. For the first time in his life, Darcy experienced true hunger and intense cold. He was very worried about his cousin's well-being. Fortunately, the Colonel, though newly recovered from severe injuries, had built up his physical resilience through years of harsh military marches.

"Sir!" Mr. Darcy answered, lifting his arm as if in a salute but dropping it self-consciously. The only salutes he had ever executed were when he had played in boyhood war games.

Colonel Fitzwilliam relaxed when he saw the General walking up to Darcy and shaking his cousin's hand cordially. Even though the General was not large of stature, he had a larger-than-life presence.

"Mr. Darcy, I beg your pardon for not thanking you promptly on account of all you have done for the troops since we have arrived. They have high praise for the swiftly supplied food and provisions for both men and horses. I must commend you on your excellent organizational skills. Now that your cousin Colonel Fitzwilliam proclaims himself out of commission, could I persuade you to take his place serving in His Majesty's army? I understand your distaste for battles, but we need all the good men we can get to aid us in vanquishing Bonaparte!"

Mr. Darcy was unprepared for this sudden—without preamble—offer of a position. He worried about declining the offer, as he had heard the reputation of General Wellesley's fondness for having his way, always. Then he noticed the crinkled corners of the General's laughing eyes and hoped to disarm the ferocious warrior with some levity.

"Sir, my paltry attempt at easing the suffering of our brave troops is unworthy of your generous praise. As for your allusion to the Darcys' aversion toward fighting in wars, that has not been the case for the last two generations. We simply have not had enough males in the family. We have had to make do with farming our lands as profitably as possible to pay into the government coffers to fund the war efforts. I have learned to be content basking in the glory brought home to England by warriors like your Lordship. I wonder how your Lordship's own eldest brother, Lord Mornington, endures watching the entire nation pinning their hopes on you, sir, to save us from the deranged ambitions of Bonaparte."

General Wellesley looked at Mr. Darcy with narrowed eyes, but Darcy stood his ground. Then the general burst out laughing.

"Darcy of Pemberley, I usually detest flattery, but I find no fault in yours! Well played!"

He then turned to the Colonel and said, "Fitzwilliam! Fortune favors us younger sons! And speak nothing of the balls we soldiers are privileged to enjoy between battles!"

The Colonel breathed a sigh of relief and just smiled and nodded in agreement.

"Incidentally, Colonel, your request for resignation is denied. I received a dispatch from Whitehall this morning—you have been reassigned to equerry duty for His Majesty beginning in March next year. You have also been given leave until you report for duty at Windsor. If you wish to squabble about this assignment, take it to Whitehall yourself. I am no longer your commanding officer. Dismissed!"

The General walked away, still chuckling.

The Colonel turned to his cousin, looked at him suspiciously, and asked, "Did you have a hand in this?"

Mr. Darcy put up both hands and shook his head. "Not at all, on my honor! I simply reported your physical condition to your father after I found you. However, before I left for this journey, I heard your parents discussing positions suitable for keeping you safe in England."

"I wager you suggested posting me as an equerry during the discussions!"

Mr. Darcy again put up his hands to deny he had anything to do with the new assignment, but the Colonel put up his own hands to cover both eyes. He exclaimed, "I wish I were completely blind! I cannot bear having to wipe the royal arse!"

"Don't flatter yourself. You will be His Majesty's equerry, not his Groom of the Stool."

"Thank God for small mercies!"

The cousins left the camp three days later, foregoing the ball that was to be held in a week.

Ladies arrived from London, including the Duchess of Richmond and Lady Caroline Lamb. They would follow the army and did not waste any time organizing balls and dinners to make the warriors' lives gay and festive until the next battle.

In the middle of January, the cousins departed for England with cases of excellent port and art by notable Spanish and Portuguese painters. The Colonel's health had improved significantly. The new injuries incurred during the arduous retreat from Salamanca had healed completely. Although his memory of the previous five years and normal vision in his left eye had not returned, the vertigo and headaches had become scarce. He could also again maintain his balance while riding. He greatly exerted himself in this last endeavor because his cousin constantly teased him that His Majesty, known for his kind heart before he turned mad, would surely promote the horse-averse equerry to be a Gentleman of the Bedchamber.

Chapter 9

Whilе Mr. Darcy and the Colonel were enjoying a leisurely trip along the picturesque coastline of Portugal, Elizabeth was having an adventure of her own, a literary one.

Elizabeth had been Mrs. Trumbull's companion for a few weeks when they started addressing each other by their Christian names. Each knew the other as sensible, frank, and without malice.

Since the season had not yet begun, Elizabeth resided with the Trumbulls in the country, and helped her patroness to integrate Mr. Bennet's books into the existing collection.

One day, Mrs. Trumbull came into the library, waving a sheet of paper. She looked at Elizabeth in awe and exclaimed, "Elizabeth, genius like yours should come out of hiding to shine. I feel very honored to have made your acquaintance."

Elizabeth was at first baffled by this sudden high praise from her friend. Once she had recognized the page in Mrs. Trumbull's hand was not the list of Welsh histories she had handed to her patroness earlier, but a page of *the* letter, she was horrified. She had copied the letter from Mr. Darcy so she could read the letter as many times a day as she pleased without fear of soiling the pages of the original, which she carefully hid in her trunk. Somehow, a page of the copied letter had gotten mixed in with the lists of books.

How could I have been so careless?

Before she came out of her stupor, Mrs. Trumbull continued with her effusive praise. "Your writing is mesmerizing: passionate, heartfelt, and so unexpectedly real for a fictional gentleman! I have suspected that you are writing something substantial at the round table you carry around, but I never would have guessed it to be a manuscript of such superior quality. What must I do to convince you to let me read the rest of your story?"

Elizabeth was mortified that her most precious and private possession was so cruelly exposed but felt strangely relieved Mrs. Trumbull did not realize its import. She said a silent prayer, thanking heaven for her foresight of leaving out the names of the people in the copied letter.

She played along and asked, "But Lillian, you have read only one page! How could you be so sure whatever I have written is good?"

"I fancy myself a connoisseur of brilliance. The most celebrated talents in the arts, be they painters, playwrights, poets and writers of note, or even preeminent craftsmen in their trades, have gathered in my drawing room. Some are household names, while others will be recognized in due course because of their undeniable talents. You will meet Mr. William Blake, not yet well known but no less an exquisite poet. You belong in this group. The world would be a better place to see such human emotions so aptly described. You should publish it. Have you finished the story?"

Elizabeth did not know what to say. She had not written the page in question; Mr. Darcy had. Perhaps if she met Mr. Darcy again, she would encourage him to write novels!

This idea seemed so ludicrous to her she could not help laughing out loud.

Mrs. Trumbull raised an eyebrow and looked at Elizabeth bemusedly. Elizabeth hurriedly apologized for appearing disrespectful of Mrs. Trumbull and the company she kept.

"Forgive me, Lillian, for laughing inappropriately. You know I dearly love to laugh at follies and..." Elizabeth paused and felt her explanation was going in the entirely opposite direction when Mrs. Trumbull's face now showed a distinct frown.

"Oh, I was not making myself clear. You must make room in your kind heart to forgive such blundering. What I meant to say is I simply could not see myself among such illustrious company. I would feel like an imposter, and that would be laughable—little me walking among giants!"

Mrs. Trumbull's face relaxed and smiled a fond smile. She said, "Your modesty does you credit. You must have read Lord Byron?"

Elizabeth nodded enthusiastically. Was it possible to find someone who had not read 'Childe Harold's Pilgrimage?' It had been published earlier in the year, and Lord Byron became a celebrity overnight.

"Lord Byron is a genius... the Shakespeare of our generation. He is rumored to be publishing another epic poem early next year. I met him two years ago at one of our gatherings. He is very young, not much older than you, very beautiful to gaze upon, and so brilliant that everyone, himself included, knows he is destined for greatness. Elizabeth, I believe your talents are of that magnitude, and yet you are humble. You owe it to the world to share your extraordinary gift with the common people."

Elizabeth was blushing furiously now. To be compared to Lord Byron? Impossible! She stuttered out, "Lillian, I do not know what to say. I think you should read more of what I have written before you give me accolades I simply cannot accept."

As soon as she inadvertently issued this invitation, she regretted it. However, Mrs. Trumbull had to know that what *she* herself had written could be completely worthless. She admitted she too loved reading Mr. Darcy's letter, and had read it hundreds of times, but she thought it was the contents of the letter, and how they made her reflect on her life and character that had her reading it over and over, not the style of the writing, or the turn of phrase, and definitely not how it might affect other readers.

She quickly continued, "I wrote a story while caring for my father after he had taken ill..." She again had to stop to collect herself. It had been over three months since his death, but mentioning him without becoming teary remained difficult.

She took a deep breath and resumed her account. "Seeing him lying on his bed day in, day out, and gradually understanding the end was inevitable, I wove together experiences from many places and people to write a story with a happy ending. My father read the story and... and was amused... and comforted, which was all that mattered to me. I wrote only about provincial things. Many characters in the story are based on real people. I even recorded what these people said, word for word. I cannot publish the story because it would be a betrayal."

"Elizabeth, you have just made me more eager to read your creation. Novels have had such a poor reputation because they are, in fact, mostly frivolous and unrealistic. Take Mrs. Radcliffe's novels as an example. They have their own worth, of course, but serious people may feel they are only for whiling away the time. Mme. d'Arblay—you probably know her as Mrs. Fanny Burney—is among the few exceptions. A work of fiction based on real people and real lives infused with your power of description and genuine passion will be a welcome breakthrough for this much-maligned genre of writing. To tell you the truth, I had attempted to write a work of fiction based on my life, of which you have had a glimpse. Would you not call it quite eventful, and I am only two-and-thirty?"

Elizabeth nodded in agreement.

"What I had written felt leaden to me. It was to be expected. I felt as if I had to squeeze my brain simply to put words on paper. If I managed to deaden the drama of my life into a boring chronicle of events, I might as well just write what I do best, and so I have switched to writing a history of Wales. If you agree to edit my manuscript when it is finished, I am certain your suggested changes would enliven my writing—you are a superb writer."

"Lillian, you have struck me dumb. I do not know what to say."

Mrs. Trumbull smiled widely and said, "I must congratulate myself for having achieved the impossible! No impertinent comeback from the quick-witted, saucy Miss Elizabeth Bennet!"

Elizabeth smiled as well. She had found a sympathetic friend in Mrs. Trumbull. She rejoined, "Indeed you should. It has never happened before!"

The ladies turned serious again when Elizabeth resumed her thoughts, "I had no intention to share my story with anyone except my father—in fact, he found my story by accident as well. Your generous comments based on such a small sample of my story have made me extremely curious. I do not have names for my characters right now. They are Mr. A, Miss B, Mrs. C and so on. Let me come up with some names for the characters, and then I shall give you a few more pages to evaluate. I fully expect you to retract your high praise after you have read more of the story, and then I shall not fool myself with any ambition of being a creditable novel writer. Instead, I shall focus on helping you improve your treatise on Wales if you find my editing useful."

Mrs. Trumbull feigned a look of exasperation, showing her displeasure at Elizabeth's unwarranted self-deprecation. She then smiled to show that her goodwill had not been lost and said, "I am seldom wrong. Now could you please hurry with inserting names in your story? I am impatient for it."

Before walking away, Elizabeth asked, "Lillian, how did you guess I was writing a story?"

Mrs. Trumbull cordially replied, "You have been scribbling constantly at your round table. The expressions on your face were a sight to see—sad, angry, sarcastic, longing—one succeeding another as if you were experiencing the events causing these emotions. I thought you could have been writing a play. The page I just read surprised me in that it is a work of fiction, and an outstanding one."

Elizabeth smiled weakly before turning to walk away with inner turmoil. On the one hand, she was worried about revealing so much of her life to a relative stranger; on the other hand, she was intrigued by the possibility she could be a good writer, asserting again what her papa had told her.

Three days later, Elizabeth handed over about twenty pages of the story, covering her heroine's visit to Mr. Keynes's estate, Detosny Park in Cheshire, their accidental meeting outside the manor's stable block, the very material change in Mr. Keynes's manners—from haughtiness to solicitousness, even tenderness toward Isabella—until when Isabella received a letter from her family about the elopement of the youngest Delancey, Marianne.

Mrs. Trumbull adored the sizzling passion between the two 'undeclared lovers,' and especially appreciated Elizabeth's techniques describing this passion through their interactions with others.

"Elizabeth, are you trying to kill me with this suspense? What happens next? The pending scandal would derail this seemingly made-in-heaven romance. My heart is melting—and I am no impressionable young thing! I thought you were brilliant with the page I had read before. This chapter only affirms it. No wonder your father was so pleased, him being such an eminent scholar."

After the usual brief moment she required at the mention of her father, Elizabeth said haltingly, "Lillian, I do not know what to say to your generous praise..."

Mrs. Trumbull interjected, "If you must say something, just say thank you. You deserve my heart-felt adulation of your talent, and the world will, too."

Elizabeth swallowed slowly to give herself time to formulate an answer. She said, "Lillian, thank you. I am overwhelmed. I do not mind sharing the story with you, but I am not ready to share it with the world."

As straightforward as ever, Mrs. Trumbull asked, "Is there a reason to avoid the world?"

Elizabeth had to think fast without exposing her true concern—Mr. Darcy would be scandalized that his most private conversations and actions were so cruelly exposed, and he would be justifiably offended by her delusional wish of being united to him.

"Novel writing is not a reputable calling, and especially for a woman. Most authors publish their novels anonymously. I also am afraid the actual people whose lives I have detailed would sue me for libel."

"I see. You worry about your reputation, which is a legitimate concern. Does it have anything to do with your youngest sister's situation?"

Elizabeth's eyes grew round in shock. How did her friend find out about Lydia? *This is calamitous!*

She decided there was nothing else to do but to own up to the scandal and leave the Trumbull household. The burden of concealment had weighed heavily on her even before coming to live with the Trumbull family.

"Lillian... Mrs. Trumbull, forgive me for keeping the truth from you all these months. Let me assure you the reputations I wish to protect are chiefly those people whose life experiences I have stol... incorporated into my story without permission. As for my youngest sister, Lydia, we do not know what has happened to her. She just disappeared. My father's death was in part due to his blaming himself for his inability to locate her. My mother, to this day, has not reconciled herself to the loss of her favorite daughter. The rest of us, my mother's four remaining daughters, are trying to cope with our family being broken, our family home taken away from us, and our new status as gentlewomen in poverty."

Elizabeth wanted to weep but remained dry-eyed. She had been sad for so long that this last strike was simply a small increment to what she had already endured. She detested living in fear of her sister's shame being discovered, and so, with the truth out in the open, she felt relief.

Before she could continue, Mrs. Trumbull interrupted, "Elizabeth, I knew of your sister's disappearance before you came to live here in Brixton Park. Mr. Peters, of his own initiative, sent a man to your home village, Meryton, to investigate your background once I had offered to have you for my companion."

On seeing Elizabeth's knitted brows, Mrs. Trumbull said reassuringly to her young friend, "Mr. Peters was my late husband's most trusted steward and has been with this family since Mr. Trumbull was a boy. I allow him to manage my affairs with great autonomy. Please do not blame him for his inquisitiveness."

Elizabeth's countenance relaxed, and Mrs. Trumbull continued, "He told me about the Bennet family's disgrace due to Miss Lydia's misdeeds, and the cause of your father's death was attributed to her elopement. I shall never blame you for something you could not have controlled. Mr. Peters said Miss Lydia's seducer was a scoundrel of the first order, almost twice her age, a swindler, and a cheater, leaving many debts behind when he left."

"I could have prevented it. I had known of the debauchery of... of that man, but I decided not to tell anyone except my dearest sister, Jane, thinking he would leave the area in just a few short weeks. Lydia had no money, no connections, nothing that could have tempted him to..."

Elizabeth finally broke down and cried. Mrs. Trumbull rubbed Elizabeth's upper back to show her support. "Elizabeth, an unprincipled, dishonorable man does not require a good reason to commit an indecency or even a crime. If Miss Lydia was not married to him, and they lived as if they were, it would be dire for your family indeed, but only for a time. People who look down on you will not do it forever. Besides, you have left your village. You remember I myself eloped. My husband and I moved to London from Wales after our marriage. I never knew whether my elopement created any gossip in the area where I had lived. Frankly, I did not care."

"I promised my father on his deathbed that I would never forget Lydia. Until my last breath, I will never give up looking for her. My uncle is still searching, but how does one find a young girl in a city with one million people?"

"You will find a way. You are resourceful. If there is anything you think I can do to help, just say the word."

"Lillian, if I publish the story, will it earn some money? If it does, I will have more resources for my uncle's search."

"I looked briefly into the business of publishing a novel when I thought I could write one. A well-written, well-publicized novel might earn a large amount of money. Mrs. Burney's third novel, 'Camilla,' earned her over two thousand pounds."

"Oh, so much!" Elizabeth exclaimed. She had never dreamed novels could be that lucrative. She had, of course, read all of Mrs. Burney's novels, and 'Camilla' was not even her favorite. 'Evelina' was.

"Did 'Evelina' make even more money? I like 'Evelina' the best out of her three novels," inquired Elizabeth.

"So do I. But 'Camilla' made such a large profit because Mrs. Burney was very well known then, and she had an extensive circle of influential friends supporting her. The novel was sold by subscription." Elizabeth nodded as she had bought a subscription herself—the first book she had ever purchased independently of her father's purchases.

"If you decide to publish your story, which has the potential to be superior to 'Evelina,' I shall do my utmost to help spread the word on it being a superb work of art. Who knows, you may earn enough to fund a large search for your sister."

"Lillian, I feel I am at a crossroads. If I can materially change the outcome of the search for Lydia, I shall do it. Having this entirely unexpected avenue to earn the needed resources to help find my sister gives me... a large measure of hope. It has been over three months without even a clue to her whereabouts. On the other hand, I still feel it is morally wrong for me to tell a story about real people's lives without their permission. Some details are rather intimate..."

Mrs. Trumbull arched an eyebrow on hearing this. Elizabeth, though an innocent, understood her friend's direction of thinking immediately and hurriedly added, "Oh, I meant very private details... such as a marriage proposal. I have taken the liberty to describe, almost exactly a proposal from a cousin to a lady, without the cousin's approval."

"And you have the approval of the lady in question?" Mrs. Trumbull smiled knowingly.

Elizabeth could not deny her friend's insinuation was correct, and so she gave as non-committal an answer as she could, "Eh... yes."

"Elizabeth, we could be here talking in circles for the next three months without coming to a decision. What do you need to do to think more objectively on this conundrum?"

Elizabeth pondered for a moment and said firmly, "Only the first part of my story was borrowed from my personal experience and observations. The second half is purely fictional. I may alter the first part without damaging its integrity. My dear sister Jane always puts sense in me when I feel befuddled. If you do not need me for a few days, I would be grateful for that time to spend with my family."

"You are not my employee. Please spend as much time as you would like and take the carriage. This close to London, the three miles of country lanes between here and your home may not be as safe as they ought. Please convey my greetings to your lovely sisters and to Mrs. Bennet. You did not go home last week because of Hester's illness. She and I both thank you for your tender care. I believe Hester prefers you to her own nurse and governess."

"I am used to taking care of my sisters. Hester is like another sister to me and..." Elizabeth was about to say Miss Trumbull had taken away some of the emptiness left behind by Lydia but stopped herself in time. She did not wish to appear overly sentimental.

Elizabeth took her leave and went to her room to collect the large stack of paper containing her story to bring home with her. Jane had never seen the manuscript, but she had looked curiously at her sister's scribbling away at the small round table. Elizabeth was apprehensive about Jane's reaction to her having put down on paper the events that led to her elder sister's heartbreak over Mr. Bingley's abandonment, but a chance of restoring Lydia to her family was at stake.

Jane's unbiased opinion would decide the fate of Elizabeth's story.

Chapter 10

When Elizabeth arrived at Rambler Cottage, all was quiet. She could just make out her mother sitting by the window, gazing out but not seeing her.

When the Bennet ladies first began cottage life, Mrs. Bennet, though none too pleased with the limited aspects of her new home, energetically directed her daughters and their maid of all work to set up the household. She then waited impatiently to access the proceeds from the book sale. However, her most impertinent daughter, Lizzy, and the most unjust brother in the world, Edward Gardiner, informed her that the money had been invested in the funds, and only the interest would be dispersed quarterly to supplement her pin money and household expenses. Mrs. Bennet was outraged that, as head of the family, she had to kowtow to her younger brother and her least favorite daughter.

The neighborhood of her new home was also not what she had expected. Virtually all the people she had met were exceptionally devout—they were all like Mary! She found out later that Clapham, the closest market town to the cottage, was home to a large sect of the religious and anti-slavery community. To her, it was incomprehensible why people would concern themselves with topics so wholly irrelevant to her, when her most pressing concern was to marry off her daughters despite their reduced circumstances, scandal or no.

Over the weeks which were void of any news of Lydia's homecoming, Mrs. Bennet became increasingly lethargic and lifeless. When Lizzy walked through the door that day, she only briefly turned her head to glance at her second daughter. She was more miffed than usual because, for the first time, Jane, her most compliant daughter, had acted impertinently toward her— and because of Mary!

Unlike the rest of the family, Mary's spirits were raised by the religious community surrounding them. She had struck up a reciprocal friendship with the lady of the manor, Mrs. Lytle, whose son had leased the cottage to Mr. Gardiner's family. As a condition of the low rent, Mr. Lytle had requested the Bennet ladies look in on his elderly mother. During her initial visit, Mary found a kindred spirit in the old lady in their shared desire to study scripture. Since coming out of full mourning, Mary had been accompanying Mrs. Lytle to worship at the Clapham Common church.

Mrs. Bennet had had a glimpse of the young man when he came to visit his mother and felt a handsome young man with such a large fortune must be in want of a wife of Jane's beauty. She worried that Mary, being so plain, would spoil things for everyone.

"Jane, you must visit the manor house to get to know the old lady. Her son is obviously devoted to her, buying her such a fine house in the country. To be mistress of Wayleigh is nothing to sneer at!"

"Mamma, we are in mourning. I do not want to appear too forward," explained Jane gently. Being the eldest, she ought to put herself forward to secure the wellbeing of the family, but that was easier said than done.

"Mourning has not stopped Mary. You should not be too bound by tradition about this. I am sure your father would have approved."

Jane was just like Elizabeth: every time her papa was mentioned, tears came into her eyes. She forced back the tears and said patiently, "Mamma, Mary has found a genuine friend in Mrs. Lytle. Don't you think Mary has become more mature? She is much more willing to listen to others' opinions instead of merely reciting passages from Fordyce's Sermons to explain everything."

"She was willful, and it is true she is less so now. I love all my daughters, but when it comes to finding husbands, I am far more adept than any of you. Mary is simply not attractive enough for a prosperous, worldly man like Mr. Lytle. He will desire a beautiful wife like you, Jane, to be on his arm when out in society—to be a credit to him. Mary is more suited for one of those religious young men she is meeting at that church she attends with old Mrs. Lytle. Your Uncle Gardiner said Mr. Lytle may someday become the youngest director of the East India Company. Those directors are richer than many lords!"

Jane had never been cross with anyone, let alone her mother. However, after Lydia's scandal, she was painfully aware of the situation in which her wanton youngest sister had placed them. How could her mother say any gentleman would want to be seen with someone like her, a woman from a disgraced family?

"Mamma, it looks like rain. I must collect the wash from the lines before it is drenched. I shall speak with you later," Jane said hurriedly. She wanted to be away from her mother before she did the unthinkable: shaking her mother until her mother understood things were different now. If any of the sisters could secure a decent match, the whole family should rejoice rather than to undermine one another.

"Ask Sally to do it. You should not get your hands calloused," cried Mrs. Bennet.

"Mamma, Sally is busy in the kitchen. I shall be just a moment." Jane hardly finished her sentence before hastily leaving the parlor.

Mrs. Bennet muttered to herself, "Even Jane has become recalcitrant. No one listens to me anymore. My poor nerves!" She did not bother to ask for her salts. There was no one to fetch them for her.

That was how Elizabeth found her.

"Mamma, how do you fare?" Elizabeth asked solicitously.

"Why do you ask? You know very well that until Lydia comes home, I shall be unhappy. The rest of you are simply here to vex me!" Mrs. Bennet huffed.

94

Elizabeth was no longer upset hearing cruel and unjust accusations from her mother. Since writing her story, she had become a keener observer of human emotion. Before, she had taken note of people's superficial behaviors and prided herself on being discerning. The debacle of completely misreading Mr. Darcy's and Mr. Wickham's true characters had humbled her. Now she knew to search deeper when confronted with any seemingly irrational behaviors.

She believed her mother, having lost more and being more set in her ways, would need more time to adjust to their new circumstances. She should learn to be more tolerant of these occasional tantrums.

"Mamma, where is everybody?" Lizzy asked, completely ignoring her mother's rude putdown.

"Mary is visiting Mrs. Lytle. Kitty is hiding away somewhere with her cursed drawing book, I reckon. Jane is in the back garden taking care of the laundry," Mrs. Bennet answered woodenly, still gazing out of the window.

"I shall go help Jane then."

On the way out of the house, Elizabeth added, "Oh, Mrs. Trumbull sent with me a leg of lamb, some apples, tea, and sugar as well. We shall have a feast for dinner!"

This news cheered Mrs. Bennet. She missed designing menus without the constraint of a tight budget. Even having a good cup of tea, which, like so many other essential things in life, had become a luxury out of reach.

Seeing her mother was appeased, Lizzy went to the back garden to look for her sister.

"Jane!"

"Lizzy! I was not expecting you today!" Jane left the last piece of washing on the line and stretched out her arms to her dearest sister.

"That should make me all the more welcomed!" exclaimed Lizzy while stepping into Jane's open arms. Jane was, in fact, very glad to see Lizzy, who had shouldered so much of the burden of caring for their family.

The sisters brought in the clean clothes, sat on their shared bed, and started folding.

Lizzy hesitated to state the purpose of her visit because she had never told Jane about the story she had written.

"Out with it, Lizzy. You cannot hide things from me," chided Jane.

"Dear Jane, you know me better than I know myself! I have come home today mainly to solicit your opinion."

"That sounds ominous!"

"It is momentous!" Lizzy took a deep breath and continued, "Jane, I have written a story, a work of fiction, but it contains many things I took from what actually occurred, including what happened to you... and Mr. Bingley."

Jane looked shocked, but she quickly returned to her serene self.

"Lizzy, is that what you were scribbling on sheets of paper all the time? I wondered why you did not use a notebook. How did you keep the sheets in order?" Jane asked good-naturedly.

"Oh, at the beginning, I was just jotting down disjointed thoughts. Before long, I connected all the pieces, rewrote many sections, and somehow, I completed a coherent story even before I went off to stay with Mrs. Trumbull. A few days ago, Mrs. Trumbull accidentally discovered and read a few pages. She urged me to publish it. I told her I must discuss it with you because the first half of the story is virtually an autobiography involving actual conversations among us, our former friends, and neighbors. The rest stems from my fancy. There should be no issue there... except that I have given you and Mr. Bingley a happy ending. Jane, tell me what to do! Mrs. Trumbull believes the book could earn a substantial amount of money, enough to make a difference in our search for Lydia."

Jane assumed a faraway look on her countenance deliberating. Presently she replied, "I believe I have not done or said anything of which I am ashamed. I will not have any objection to your including my conversations with others. As for making me and Mr. Bingley... it is all fictional, anyway. I cannot disapprove of anything that is only in your imagination. I know you felt deeply about Mr. Bingley's abrupt departure. I have long accepted that if Mr. Bingley did not return to Netherfield Park, he must have had unimpeachable reasons."

"Jane..." Elizabeth almost blurted out it had been the interference of his friend, Mr. Darcy, and sister, Miss Bingley, but stopped herself. There was no use digging up these old grievances. She had already shifted the blame entirely to the party who deserved it, Mr. Bingley himself. If he had truly loved Jane and been so easily swayed by others, then he was not a man good enough for Jane. Even after everything, Elizabeth had not given up hope for steadfast love.

"Ah, Lizzy, I love a good novel. I am confident yours will be brilliant. You told us entertaining stories of your own creation when we were younger."

"Dearest, now that I have admitted to having written a novel based on our lives, I am nervous about sharing it, even with you. Please give me your honest opinion. I do not want to publish something that critics and readers will hate."

The manuscript was over an inch thick. While Jane was reading from the beginning, Elizabeth finished inserting the names of the characters in places of their ersatz representations. By dinner time, Jane had read about a quarter of the pages. She was up to the part about her stay at Netherfield Park while she was ill.

Dinner was scrumptious by the standard of the Bennets' new economy. Mrs. Bennet ingeniously put some apples in the lamb stew, giving it an unusually pleasant, tangy favor. After dinner, everyone enjoyed a cup of very fine tea.

Jane excused herself to go up to her room and continue reading the manuscript. Elizabeth remained with her sisters to do some mending. The room was cozy, reminding Elizabeth of happier times in the bright and cheerful Longbourn parlor, where all the sisters were engaged in some needlework, and her mother walked about checking their progress.

Kitty came to sit next to Lizzy on the sofa and showed her a sketch of herself with head bowed and a smile on her face while working on mending a pillowcase. The likeness was adequate, but it was the peace and serenity on Lizzy's face conveyed by the drawing that made Elizabeth gasp in wonder.

"Kitty, what a fine sketch! I like the way you make me look like Jane, so tranquil and beatific!"

"You appeared calm and relaxed, but your brain was working. You seemed to be entertaining agreeable thoughts in your head while sewing," explained Kitty. "Look, this is you, not Jane. Jane would not have had a busily working mind while sewing!"

"You are absolutely correct, Kitty. The likeness is definitely mine. I was simply surprised I was capable of such serenity... and..." It struck Lizzy then that Kitty was truly gifted. Her sketches had depth. She would benefit greatly from the instruction of masters—but they were no longer the Miss Bennets of Longbourn.

"Kitty, you are so talented! Why did you not ask papa... for lessons from a drawing master?" asked Elizabeth, while suppressing the tears that threatened to appear. She was at last getting better about the weeping.

Kitty looked very pleased with her sister's praise. She exclaimed, "You think I am good at drawing? Truly?"

Lizzy said with a big smile, "Of course! Mrs. Trumbull has a collection of sketches, even one by Leonardo da Vinci! I cannot say where you stand among famous artists, but this sketch you made is very me, more than just a likeness. I am proud of you! Tell me, why did you hide this talent of yours?"

"It is that... Lydia said my drawings were stupid, and she would throw them away if she saw me waste my time on them again. I hid my drawing supplies because of her threat. Then I was sad for a long time. I blamed myself for causing papa's illness and death..."

Both sisters suppressed their emerging sobs.

"... because I concealed Lydia's scheme to elope until it was too late. One day, I saw my drawing pencils and paper while looking for a shawl. I started sketching. I sat at my window looking out to the lane and drew the people walking by. Sketching soothes me. The day stops being interminably long, and the night is not so sleepless. Mary said she could now sleep better as well without me tossing and turning till dawn."

"Oh, Kitty! No question you did wrong..." Hearing this, Kitty burst out crying.

Mrs. Bennet had gone off to bed, but Mary was sitting at the table doing needlework, quite an unusual occurrence in her mother's absence. She had ignored the sisters' conversation until she heard her own name mentioned. Instead of calling out some quotes from the Fordyce's Sermons from across the room, she came over and rubbed Kitty's back. She then said firmly but not harshly, "Whatever you did wrong, you have paid for it with your penitence. I have forgiven you, and I am sure Lizzy has as well."

Elizabeth was astonished by Mary's compassionate and sisterly attitude toward Kitty, whom her pious sister used to despise or ignore.

"Yes, Kitty. Listen to Mary. I have forgiven you as well. I don't think Jane has ever been angry with you. Now, now..." Elizabeth cooed while gently squeezing Kitty's shoulder.

"What... what about papa?" Kitty hiccupped.

"Kitty, papa is in a better place now. He has no pain, no sickness, and no sadness. He is living in one of the many rooms that our Lord had prepared for him. When we pass to the next world, we shall see him there," Mary comforted Kitty by paraphrasing some Bible verses.

"How do you know that, Mary?" Kitty questioned, unconvinced.

"Well, in the Gospel of John, chapter fourteen, verse two, it clearly states that."

Kitty calmed down substantially. She nodded at Mary and said meekly, "I envy you, Mary. You know the Bible so well that you can call up reassuring verses instantly. I feel better now. Thank you."

She then turned to Elizabeth and said, "Thank you, Lizzy, for your forgiveness and your encouragement for my sketching."

Elizabeth squeezed Kitty's hand and said, "Kitty, I am sorry I sounded so harsh, but I was about to say the same thing Mary said. Would you like to see Mrs. Trumbull's art collection? I could ask her, and I am quite certain she would not mind."

Kitty clasped her hands to her mouth in surprise and delight. She looked at Elizabeth as if her elder sister were an angel from heaven heralding the best news ever.

"Oh, Lizzy! That would be wonderful! Thank you! Do you think Mrs. Trumbull will let me go soon?"

"I shall ask her when I go back in a few days. If she agrees, which I am quite certain she will, then I shall send the carriage for you."

Elizabeth then turned to Mary. "Would you like to come as well, Mary? Perhaps all my sisters can come together. Miss Trumbull will assist me as hostess."

Kitty cried, "Oh, Mary, come! We have been sad for so long that this outing will be jolly!" She then rose with a smile almost splitting her face and exclaimed, "I shall certainly have sweet dreams tonight. Good night, my dearest sisters!" Kitty made a dramatic curtsy and left to go upstairs.

Both the remaining sisters watched Kitty dance up the stairs and were glad a semblance of their happy times at Longbourn was finally rising from the embers.

"Does Mrs. Trumbull have a good instrument?" asked Mary with some curiosity, still wearing a smile from Kitty's antics.

"The best! Mrs. Trumbull does not display, but she loves music. She always stays with Miss Trumbull during the girl's music lessons. The music master, Mr. Rocco, is Italian. He plays beautifully—with such feeling—even though he is quite young. I sometimes stay outside the door to listen to him play as well."

"Oh, I should like to come then, if I could see the instrument. Mrs. Lytle has an ancient, out-of-tune pianoforte, but she does not notice because she is quite deaf. She cannot hear unless one speaks directly into her ear. If I miss anything from our life at Longbourn, it is to have an instrument to play whenever I want. There is room in the dining room for a spinet."

"I see..." Lizzy left off what she was going to say and smiled brightly at her sister. "Life at the cottage is not so bad after all. In time, we shall have our little wishes fulfilled, to be sure."

Elizabeth then noticed Mary was sewing a piece of unraveled lace. She was curious on two fronts: Mary did not wear lace, and the lace looked familiar to her.

Oh, it is from my old dress!

"Mary, why are you mending that piece of lace? It was from my dress, wasn't it? I thought I asked Jane to give the dress to Sally. Are you mending it for Sally because she is too busy?"

Mary started at this inquiry, and her cheeks burned like fire. She stuttered, "I... I... I am sorry I did not ask your permission to take this lace, but Jane said you would not object. Since you did not come home last week, I completely forgot about asking you. I... I... decided... that I could use it in my half-mourning dress. If you mean to give this to Sally, I shall finish mending it and give it to her." At the end of this confession, Mary had bent her head low to hide her tears.

"Oh, Mary, of course, you can take for yourself any clothing I have left behind. I had not thought of giving you my old dresses because you are taller than I, and you never liked the colors or any lace adornments I wore."

"Oh, thank you, Lizzy. I... have made the decision to start wearing dresses that a young woman my age wears instead of insisting on plain dresses. At Longbourn, I read 'Fordyce's Sermons to Young Women' and other religious tracts but did not realize that I misinterpreted the meaning of modesty. I have been having Bible studies with Mrs. Lytle and Mrs. Hines, her companion. Now I understand that dressing modestly does not mean dressing like a nun. Some lace and brighter colors are acceptable. Mrs. Lytle said the Fordyce's Sermons were published when she was a girl almost fifty years ago. I should not read the Sermons too literally, or I would not fit in society today.

"The two ladies took me to their church at Clapham Common last Sunday. I noticed ladies, many of them known for their piety, were dressed very fine—like mamma and you when we were at Longbourn. That led to my decision to give up dressing with excessive austerity. Since I have no lace of my own, I thought I would start with pieces from your old dresses. I admit to depriving Sally of what is rightfully hers, but I shall compensate her once I have saved up some pin money."

Elizabeth inspected her formerly severe-looking sister. She immediately noticed Mary's brown hair was no longer pulled back tautly as before, and she could see the natural curls framing Mary's face. Her spectacles were also on the side table instead of being on her face. In their former life, Mary never took off her glasses from the time she left her room each morning.

Elizabeth reached out to pat Mary's shoulder. "Mary, your new looks become you. Mrs. Lytle is an invaluable influence in leading you to the true meaning of biblical truths. I must meet her someday to find my enlightenment."

She returned to dresses and said, "Mrs. Trumbull insists I take an allowance for clothing and other personal needs because I have refused a salary. Because of the company she keeps, I need to dress more fashionably, even when in half-mourning. In fact, she had recently given me a small mountain of dresses from her own half-mourning to alter for myself. I shall bring those home next time I come. You will have some very fine dresses to alter to your liking."

"I am just beginning to alter my... way. It seems strange, but being so far away from our old lives makes it easier for me to change. I would have been embarrassed to suddenly start wearing different clothes. It is only outward appearance. I should not have minded so much."

"Dearest, we are only human. When you came over to comfort Kitty, I was speechless with shock! I had expected you to spew—forgive my indelicacy—random quotes from your favorite reading material, unrelated to Kitty's state of distress. Now you are trying to moderate your behavior and appearance. I am certain you will be successful!"

Mary smiled at Lizzy's mild rebuke at her erstwhile habit of using ubiquitous quotes from Fordyce's Sermons for all occasions.

Seeing that Mary had not been offended, Lizzy continued, "I used to pride myself on my ability to discern others' characters. Lately I realize that I have been wrong more often than right. But bad habits die hard. I will attempt one more time to explain your change in behavior. I venture to say you and Kitty were the two 'neglected' daughters in the family. Mamma fawned over Jane and Lydia, and papa... doted on me. To gain some attention from your negligent parents, you wanted to be contrary: if mamma valued beauty and vivaciousness, you would be stern and severe in appearance and decorum. Kitty, being younger, was not so resourceful, and decided to follow Lydia, hoping for some left-over attention. Oh, did you see how she coughed to attract notice? She usually coughed only when papa and mamma were present, and lately, not at all."

Mary lowered her head, thought for a long moment, and said, "I do not know why you said your ability to read people's characters was faulty. I think you hit the nail on the head in my case, and likely in Kitty's as well."

Mary tried to suppress a yawn and continued. "I have really enjoyed this conversation with you. In my recollection, this is the first time we have talked like this. You have given me a lot to think about. However, thinking should not require candlelight. I have been tasked with monitoring candle usage since you left. Uncle Gardiner's rule is that the candles, once used up, will not be replenished until the new quarter begins. So we had better snuff out the candles and go to bed!"

"Oh, heavens—of course! I have been spoiled by the riches of Mrs. Trumbull's household in only a few weeks. Let us walk upstairs together, sister. I need to check in on Jane, to be sure."

"Is Jane alright? I assumed she had something to take care of. She manages the household accounts."

"I think so. I am not aware of anything out of the ordinary about Jane. Almost nothing can ruffle her. You know that."

As the sisters approached the landing of the first floor, they could see light leaking from the bottom of the door of Jane's and Lizzy's room.

Mary, wearing her former solemn look and speaking in the stern voice she had been wont to use when scolding, "Need I tell you, that men of the best sense have been usually averse to the thought of marrying a female who burns candles without restraint?"

Elizabeth's eyes went round, and an expression of utter astonishment showed on her face.

"Could this be from Fordyce's Sermons? It has the sound of it, but..."

Mary burst out laughing and had difficulty speaking clearly. "Not all of it. It should have been 'that men of the best sense have been usually averse to the thought of marrying a witty female.' Lizzy, this quote is meant for you. Take care!"

Lizzy retorted without missing a beat, "Who is the witty female now? Mary, you take care!"

Both sisters laughed until tears of hysteria rolled down their cheeks.

Chapter 11

When Lizzy entered the bedroom, Jane was in bed with a heavy shawl around her shoulders, reading Lizzy's manuscript. The fire had burned low in the fireplace, while a candle burned brightly by the bed. She looked quizzically at Lizzy, who was hurrying to get undressed for bed, and said, "I am certain I heard Mary laughing with you. How could that be? I have not heard her laugh since she was thirteen!"

"Jane, it was the wonder of wonders. Not only did Mary laugh, but she also told a joke, at the expense of Reverend Fordyce, herself, and me. I laughed so hard my sides hurt! I will tell you all, but I need to get into bed first. It is cold for November!"

After Elizabeth described Mary's unexpectedly light-hearted and clever quip, Jane smiled widely and exclaimed, "That was indeed remarkable!"

Elizabeth went on to tell Jane about the other dramatic changes she had noticed in Mary. She ended her retelling with this, "It seems Mary has found a new path for her life lit by the wisdom of Mrs. Lytle and the study of the Bible. And Kitty has also discovered life after being Lydia's slave is full of promise stemming from her appreciable talent in drawing."

Jane looked thoughtful. Lizzy knew that look. It did not occur often, but when Jane looked contemplative, she had come to some significant revelation.

"Lizzy, I have read your story up till Miss Wilkins's letter, oh, Miss Bingley's. I could recognize the parts that I lived through, but not the parts where I was absent in real life, such as some parts of the Lucas Lodge party..." Jane tried to find the place where these events occurred.

"The Johns's Lodge," Lizzy prompted before Jane was successful in finding the page.

"Ah, yes, and also most of my stay at Netherfield Park when I was ill. From now on, I shall just use the names of the people we know instead of what you call them in the story."

Jane paused to collect her thoughts and continued, "If I were to read this story without knowing you to be the authoress, I would marvel at the coincidences in my life. I would just assume life in such a confined and unvarying society as ours would be pretty much the same, no matter where the village is located. I am not very imaginative and would never have thought my sister could have written such a story."

"Jane, I tried to change things around a little because I always meant it to be fiction. I did not want it to be a precise replica of my life, because the second part of the story sprang entirely from my head. If you see only shadows of our lives in it, I am relieved. The point I am most concerned about is whether you feel unjustly exposed in the section where I describe your... relationship with Mr. Bingley."

"I am reading this part right now. If you worried that I would be embarrassed, you would be right..."

Lizzy seized Jane's arm and cried, "Oh, Jane, forgive me! I will burn the manuscript! I knew I should not have been so reckless to include such private matters as a near courtship in something that all parties involved could potentially see."

"Lizzy, I am not embarrassed about your including my unfortunate encounter with Mr. Bingley..."

"Why then?" Lizzy interjected.

Jane hesitated, but continued determinedly, "Reading how you describe the events last autumn, I cannot help but notice what a colorless dullard I was."

Elizabeth was ready to jump in and defend her most serene and beautiful sister, who was lovely in every way, but Jane placed her finger on Lizzy's lips to stop Lizzy from interrupting again.

"Calm down, Lizzy. Would you let me speak my piece before I lose my nerve?"

Lizzy nodded, and so Jane continued, "You did not describe any conversations between me and Mr. Bingley, as you probably did not hear any of them. However, I also cannot remember anything of note about them, either. Mr. Bingley sat with me and talked to me numerous times. But what did we talk about? Do I know anything about Mr. Bingley beyond the superficial facts such as where he was from, his closest family, and the most important piece of information as far as mamma is concerned, his annual income? I can honestly say I know nothing else. Then why did I fancy myself in love with him? Why have I been feeling melancholy since the Christmas after the Bingley party left Netherfield, almost two years ago?

"I do not like the image of myself in the story, which, to my chagrin, is very accurately presented. You just told me that both Mary and Kitty have found new outlets for their God-given talents, which they were previously forced to conceal, whereas I have done nothing but mourned the loss of our status as gentlewomen living on our own estate."

"Dearest, do not be so harsh on yourself. You are beautiful, compassionate, a peacemaker, and extremely competent in running the household when mamma seemed incapacitated. You will make a brilliant match and have many children. I am determined to be the most doting spinster aunt to your children and teach the lot of them to play the pianoforte very ill!"

"Ah, I have the talent to be an excellent housekeeper!" Jane exclaimed with forced cheerfulness.

"Oh, Jane, forgive me for even suggesting you have no gifts other than managing a modest home..." Lizzy saw Jane wince when the tactless sister put her foot in her own mouth for a second time in the same evening. "I am making the matter worse..."

"No, do not blame yourself for speaking your mind without artifice. That is the same manner you tell the story. Your exchange with Mr. Darcy in the parlor of Netherfield is quite diverting: *your defect is to hate everybody*! I would never have the courage to say something like that to a gentleman. Did you truly say that?"

"Eh... yes, or something very like it. I wanted to change those words but have not come up with anything."

"You should not change anything in the story, at least up to the part I have read so far."

"Jane! You are forgiving, and do not mind my telling people your private affairs, but what about... Miss Bingley, or Mr. Bingley?"

"I think if I could not remember anything Mr. Bingley said, it is likely he probably has no recollection of anything about me either. As for Miss Bingley, she is entitled to think whatever she wants, being so wholly unconnected to us."

Lizzy looked at Jane with a new admiration. "Jane, you said I had courage, but yours is ten times more. I should call you brave... and wise! I never desired her good opinion. Why should I start now?"

Elizabeth then looked troubled and wrung her hands under the counterpane. She said worriedly, "The same cannot be said about Mr. Darcy. What I expose of him is of far greater concern—a rejected proposal! And my abusive assessments of his person and character! He would be furious to see all those unflattering things on paper for the world to see!"

"I have not yet reached that part of the story. So far, you have revealed nothing said in confidence. You were never alone when you conversed. As for your saying not so favorable things to him on paper, if he ever reads them, perhaps they will have the same effect on him as your portrayal has on me."

Elizabeth got on top of the counterpane, kneeled, and prostrated herself on the bed, facing Jane. She exclaimed dramatically, "My dearest Jane, I cast my face down before you in adoration! You are truly the great sage of our time, and I am not in jest!"

Jane laughed and said, "Get back under the blankets, or you will catch your death of cold! Stop being ridiculous! I am merely giving you my honest opinion. There is nothing profound about it."

"You have given me so much to think about. I had expected you would not outwardly disapprove, as that is against your nature. However, your honest opinion is not only objective but sensible in a way I would never have considered myself. I cannot wait to hear your impression of the entire story when you have finished; at this rate, perhaps by tomorrow night?"

"It is indeed possible because I might stay up till dawn reading it. I am eager to see how you determined our fates. You said papa... approved of it?"

Elizabeth nodded, feeling a warm camaraderie with her sister, who also missed her father deeply.

"Then this story has the best recommendation from the most trustworthy person..." Jane wiped her eyes and continued, "I miss papa, but I hope this weepiness will stop soon."

"Dearest, it has become better for me. I do not cry every time he is mentioned anymore. I will not forget papa, and I will do what he bade me even if it kills me, but just like you, I do not want to have to suppress a sob every time someone says his name."

Jane smiled and said, "As I was saying, I cannot wait to get to the end of the story, but I think the journey to the end will be equally gripping. Lizzy, you are a truly talented storyteller. Nay, you are more than that. The story weaves through such common everyday occurrences, and yet you draw your reader in. I know I may be biased because my life is in the story, but I believe that a common indifferent reader will feel like she lives among us, too."

"Oh, Jane, I have already prostrated myself once, and I cannot blush any more than I have with your acclamation. If you wish to stay up, please do. I hope Mary will not get up in the middle of the night to make you snuff out the candle."

Jane smiled and said, "Good night, dearest. I shall not be much longer."

℘℘

The next morning was Sunday. Mary walked up the drive to accompany Mrs. Lytle and Mrs. Hines to go to the Sunday service at the Clapham Common church. The rest of the Bennet ladies went to the chapel in the village. Mrs. Bennet, however, resolved to take her daughters to the Clapham church starting the following week to show off her handsome daughters, especially Jane, to the prosperous congregation there.

The ladies usually enjoyed a small repast after church and would then be engaged in various activities in the parlor. This day, Mary came in with a large party: Mrs. Lytle and her companion, and two unknown gentlemen, one of whom Mrs. Bennet recognized to be the elusive Mr. Lytle.

Mrs. Bennet's countenance immediately brightened as soon as the gentlemen entered. Both gentlemen appeared to be in their mid-thirties. Both were quite handsome and amiable.

Mrs. Lytle made the introductions. The tall, sun-tanned gentleman was indeed Mr. Jeremy Lytle, and the other, less remarkable gentleman, was the Vicar of Trinity Church, Mr. Samuels.

"Mrs. Bennet, Miss Bennet, Miss Elizabeth, Miss Catherine and Miss Mary, I am honored to make your acquaintance and beg your forgiveness for disturbing your Sabbath. However, since I accompany a clergyman, I can only hope you may find it less offensive."

"Mr. Lytle and Mr. Samuels, we are indeed honored to have you pay us a visit. We have been leading a retired life here at Wayleigh because of our mourning state. The girls, however, have been in half-mourning for the past two weeks, and may indeed begin to enter society again, only small gatherings in close circles, of course. Since you are our landlord, and Mr. Samuels is a man of the cloth, we certainly do not have any objection." Mrs.

Bennet noticed that Mr. Lytle was throwing a few glances over at Jane, who was seated with her mother and Mary on the sofa by the window.

The irrepressible instinct to find husbands for her daughters immediately raised its indecorous head.

"Mrs. Lytle, Mrs. Hines, gentlemen, since I am still in deep mourning, I shall ask my eldest, Jane, to be hostess. You probably much prefer a beautiful girl such as Jane to serve you tea than an old lady like me, don't you?" Everyone winced when they heard this, and Jane wanted to find a hole to crawl into. But Mrs. Bennet did not see any of this and continued, "In a few more weeks, I shall visit Mrs. Lytle at the manor house, and I hope to see you there as well. Mr. Lytle, please take my seat here by Jane. Mary, would you go bring in another chair for yourself as there is not enough room for all three of you? Good day, ladies and gentlemen."

Mrs. Bennet curtsied and left the parlor with a half-hidden smile on her face. She could spot a smitten gentleman from a mile away, and she was certain that Mr. Lytle had already fallen in love with her Jane. Who would not be? Jane was not so beautiful for nothing!

She did not go far. She went into the dining room, where every word uttered in the parlor could be heard quite clearly. However, she did not reckon Mr. Lytle would come in after her to retrieve two chairs for himself and Mr. Samuels. Mrs. Bennet was slightly mortified her scheme had been so easily discovered, but curtsied and left the dining room.

Elizabeth was ashamed of her mother's blatant attempt at matchmaking in the first meeting between the gentlemen and her sisters, but Jane and Mary were rendered frozen in their seats. As usual, Elizabeth's courage rose when the situation demanded it. She thanked the gentleman for bringing chairs and left to order tea. She was glad the tea from Mrs. Trumbull was available for their esteemed guests.

When she arrived back in the parlor, Mr. Lytle was seated between Jane and his mother, and Mr. Samuels had placed his chair between Mary and Kitty. She was trying to decide which group to join; Jane seemed to have regained her composure, but Mary appeared to be exceedingly shy, and her cheeks bloomed pink becomingly.

Interesting! Is Mary sweet on Mr. Samuels? I hope he is not married! Elizabeth was musing to herself and was startled when she heard Mrs. Hines hail her, "Miss Elizabeth, come join us."

Mr. Lytle was so deep in conversation with Jane that Mrs. Hines had to speak directly into Mrs. Lytle's ear to ask the mother to touch her son's elbow before he smiled apologetically to Jane and stood up to move Elizabeth's chair closer to his mother's.

Mrs. Hines said pleasantly to Elizabeth, "Miss Elizabeth, Mrs. Lytle–she is my cousin, you know, and I look forward to having you and your sisters visit us at the manor house. Mrs. Lytle has been out of mourning for the old Mr. Lytle for a few months, but she prefers to wear her black clothing because she sees no reason to have new dresses made. She is frugal, that one, even though her son is high up in the East India Company."

Elizabeth glanced over to Mrs. Lytle to make certain the elder lady did not mind her cousin speaking of her when she herself was present. Mrs. Hines took the young lady's meaning and said, "Oh, do not worry, Miss Elizabeth. Mrs. Lytle cannot hear very well unless the room is completely quiet. With all these conversations going on around her, she could hear only if you speak directly into her ear. She does not mind my telling you all this.

"We moved here only two months before you. Mrs. Lytle had heard about the Clapham sect and, being so devout herself, she asked Mr. Lytle to move her out of the city. She also likes to breathe the clean air in the country. Her late husband owned a clock-making business. I wonder whether all those clocks chiming at all hours of the day affected her hearing." Mrs. Hines nodded sagely.

So far, she had not given Elizabeth any opportunity to speak. Elizabeth, never one to let others direct their interactions, interjected when Mrs. Hines appeared to be taking a breath. She would prefer to talk to Mrs. Lytle, who seemed very interesting based on Mary's description of the lady being wise and truly intelligent. However, there was no polite way to lean over and speak into the old lady's ear.

"Does Mr. Lytle often come to visit his mother and you?"

Mrs. Hines smiled knowingly, looked at Elizabeth meaningfully, then looked over at Jane, and said, "Ah, young ladies are always setting their caps at Mr. Lytle..." Elizabeth wanted to object to this cloaked accusation, but Mrs. Hines continued before she could utter the first sound of protest.

"Mr. Lytle is married. He ran off to India when he was not yet of age and married a native woman there. All I know about her is her name, Arati. Even my cousin does not talk much about her. When the elder Mr. Lytle passed away suddenly about a year and a half ago, her son came back alone to help with settling his father's legacy, which, I understand, is quite substantial. He is to go back to India in a fortnight now that my cousin is well-settled in the country."

Elizabeth said absentmindedly, "I see." She remained inattentive while Mrs. Hines, who really did not care much whether her audience was responsive, talked on.

Soon after that, Mr. Lytle took his leave on behalf of his party. He again apologized for intruding upon the Bennets' restful Sunday afternoon because he was to go back to the city in a few hours and would not return for some time. He did not wish to appear even more uncivil to have waited over three months to introduce himself to the Bennets.

As soon as the front door closed behind the visitors, Mrs. Bennet descended the stairs and was eagerly asking about the rich gentleman.

"What bad luck it was I had to leave the dining room! So, Jane, have you made Mr. Lytle your new conquest? I know he must capitulate to your beauty!"

Jane was extremely embarrassed and momentarily tongue-tied. The uncouth manner her mother displayed every time a single gentleman with a large fortune came into their midst was, somehow, more scathing than ever before.

Elizabeth did not know whether Mr. Lytle disclosed to Jane the fact that he was married, and she definitely did not wish to further embarrass her older sister if Jane favored the gentleman.

Finally Mary chimed in, "Mamma, Mr. Lytle is married. He is also leaving for India in a fortnight. He left his wife there when he came back to England nine months ago."

"What? He is married? What a scoundrel! Why is he here to seduce our beautiful Jane?" fumed Mrs. Bennet.

Jane broke her silence and said calmly, "Mamma, Mr. Lytle came to meet his tenants before he leaves for India. When Uncle Gardiner took the lease on this cottage, one condition of the lease is that we look in on Mrs. Lytle regularly. He was here to meet the ladies who will keep his mother company and not to seduce anyone."

"But he sat next to you and talked to you the whole time he was here!" exclaimed Mrs. Bennet.

"How do you know that, mamma?" asked Elizabeth, truly intrigued, since she had just seen her mother come down the stairs.

"Of course, I know. There are large cracks in the plaster next to the beams all over the ceilings. I could see through the plaster from above stairs. I could hear hardly anything, but I could see," answered Mrs. Bennet shortly. She never cared much for Lizzy's inquisitive nature.

Mrs. Bennet then turned her attention to Mary and Kitty. She said, "Mary and Kitty, you two were talking to Mr. Samuels, the clergyman. No doubt he is also married."

Mary blurted out, "No, mamma, he is not."

"Oh, good girl, Mary. He seemed very attentive to you. I hope he has a living that allows him to marry. You have not studied the scriptures so diligently for nothing."

"Mamma, Kitty and I spoke with Mr. Samuels in equal measure. We were discussing the Bible verses that bring comfort when one feels one is drowning in grief..."

"Oh, Mary, you must change the way you talk—one did this, one thinks that. It sounds so... unseemly," scolded Mrs. Bennet.

To her surprise, Lizzy agreed with her mother on this point. Mary had very often spoken in that manner, but, to Mary's credit, she seldom used that turn of phrase anymore.

"Well, perhaps Kitty will have a better chance with Mr. Samuels."

Mrs. Bennet turned to Kitty, looked over her fourth daughter from head to toe and said matter-of-factly, "Kitty, you are not as lively as Lydia..." At her mention of Lydia, Mrs. Bennet's countenance suddenly became anguished, and she cried out, "Oh Lydia, where are you? Why do you treat me so? If only you were here, and we would not be in this predicament! A house full of girls with no settled home or prospects!" Mrs. Bennet left her daughters abruptly and went back upstairs.

The four sisters looked at one another grimly. Although they knew their mother had not become more sensible under the new circumstances, witnessing her unreasonable behavior was not any easier, even with this knowledge.

As usual, Jane, the peacemaker, left the room to try to soothe their agitated mother.

Elizabeth noticed Mary's countenance when her mother commented Mr. Samuels might prefer Kitty. Mary abruptly stood up and rushed out of the parlor, followed closely by Kitty. Elizabeth was left standing in the middle of the room, alone. She sighed and slowly retreated to the bedroom she shared with Jane to await her closest sister, who might once again spend most of a day trying to pacify her mother.

Chapter 12

When Lizzy entered the bedroom, to her surprise, Jane was reading the manuscript as if nothing had happened. From the look of it, she was well past the middle of the story.

"I thought you were with mamma."

Jane looked at Lizzy with her usual serene expression. "I was going to go to her, but then I changed my mind. I do not know what to say to her. From the description of mamma in your story, I have realized that mamma is a little like Lydia. Coddling would only make her tantrums worse, and I was always the one to do the coddling."

Elizabeth was astonished to hear that. Her eyes went round, and her mouth gaped open.

"Oh, Jane. I certainly hope mamma's nervous attacks are really temper tantrums in disguise and not a health condition. Now that you have pointed it out, I must commend you for being uncannily perceptive. I used to be on the receiving end of these tantrums. Now that I do not live at home, I had hoped they would come less and less regularly."

"They have. What happened just now was the first in a few weeks. I do not mean that mamma's calmer demeanor was because of your absence. Perhaps she is shifting her wrath to someone else. I hope she has not decided on Mary. Poor Mary, how does she fare? That was a cruel and unjust put-down."

Elizabeth got another jolt at hearing Jane's critical assessment of their mother.

"I have not been to see Mary after she left the parlor. Kitty went with her, and so I came to my room, and you were already here! You are making good time reading through the manuscript. You may finish it by tomorrow."

"Or sooner... if I stop correcting your mistakes along the way. I did not alter anything. I just put to right some obvious spelling errors and such. I am surprised there are as many as this. You are usually a careful writer in your correspondence."

"Oh, thank you! I have found that writing a manuscript of one hundred thousand words is another matter altogether from writing letters. This is already the second draft of the story, and I thought I had taken out all the mistakes. I read somewhere that an author cannot edit her own writing because she sees what she intends to write and not what is on the paper. You have proven that right."

Elizabeth paused and asked apprehensively, "Where are you in the story exactly, and what do you think of it so far?"

"You are at Pemberley, and you just met Mr. Darcy again outside the stable block. Lizzy, tell me, do you think that if you had actually seen Mr. Darcy during your trip to Derbyshire, everything would have been different? And Mr. Darcy would have saved Lydia?"

"It was this scene–my seeing Mr. Darcy at Pemberley–that started the story. The scene was so vivid I had a hard time convincing myself it did not happen. I know that as a story, this encounter at Pemberley seemed too coincidental, and I often criticized other novels for having too many implausible encounters for their heroes and heroines, but I felt compelled to include it.

"As for Lydia–oh, I mean Marianne in the story, being saved because of my... Isabella's seeing Mr. Keynes at his Cheshire estate, you will soon find out. I think, deep down, I wish so much for Lydia's rescue that I have written an entire story to justify my irrational longing."

117

"It comes out loud and clear from your pages that you wanted to see Mr. Darcy again for yourself, and not just for the rescue of Lydia. Your impression, or rather, your prejudice against him, has changed materially since his proposal in Kent, which is... amazingly enthralling. The passion exuding from each of you is so palpable and mesmerizing. It makes the reader realize how well-matched you are. Besides, it really is not a completely implausible meeting at Pemberley. If not for the unexpected call to duty that compelled Mr. Darcy to leave for the Continent, all that happens in the story could have happened in real life."

"Your analysis is insightful. I cannot wait till you have finished reading the manuscript. I am very pleased reading about yourself in my story seems to make you stand up to mamma more."

"Your story cannot claim all the credit for my having grown a backbone. When you saw me in the back garden the other day, I had just defied mamma and insisted on going away from her to take care of our dry linens. It was a small thing, but my heart was pounding. You remember how you always say your courage rises at all attempts to intimidate you? I understood the meaning of the word 'courage' for the first time. Even just now, when I turned away from mamma's door, my heart was thumping so hard I almost went into her room to ask her for smelling salts!"

"Do you regret your newfound defiance? I do not wish you to gain courage while losing your nerve!"

"It may sound contradictory, but I feel the burden on me lessening. Just now, when mamma went on and on about Mr. Lytle favoring me, I could calmly correct her. Mr. Lytle did not mention his marital status during the conversation, and I never considered him a potential match. If we were still at Longbourn, I would have thought him very amiable because he singled me out to converse, and therefore I should be expecting a proposal! Remember, that was the reaction I had after Mr. Bingley asked me to dance twice at the assembly."

"Jane, asking a young lady to dance twice at a first meeting is a very different matter from conversing with your tenant during a short visit. I do not think you were wrong to assume that Mr. Bingley was going to court you. He was.

He paid no attention to other young ladies in your presence. Mr. Lytle was also focused on you and you alone in the parlor. Are you sure that he does not favor you? Ah, no, I forgot he is already married. In that case, he had better not favor you!"

"We were merely talking on a topic of mutual interest. He asked me about naming the cottage 'Rambler,' and I told him I was partial to roses. He then told me he also specialized in plants, but the ones that made good spices. He is in charge of transplanting nutmeg, mace, and cloves from the Spice Islands to the other parts of the Empire in case the Dutch, who ruled there until recently, snatched the islands back. It was fascinating, really, but not conducive to romantic feelings."

"Ah, you have no trouble recalling the contents of your conversations with Mr. Lytle, unlike the ones you had with Mr. Bingley."

"I believe I shall remember this conversation for a long time. I love my herb garden and am constantly looking for new herbs to include in my collection. I wish I could grow those exotic spices here, but Mr. Lytle said the climate here was unsuitable. Now that we are no longer at Longbourn, and we do not have mamma's constant harping on finding husbands, I feel the world has opened up for me. Lizzy, would it not be wonderful if we could take a voyage to the Spice Islands? They are very far away, even beyond India."

"What do you mean by not being constantly reminded of finding husbands? Mamma did just that not twenty minutes ago."

"I mean mamma can talk about finding husbands all day long, but if we could not find husbands when we were daughters of the master of Longbourn, what is the likelihood we shall find them now that we are penniless cottage-dwellers? I almost sound bitter, but I am not. It is a relief to me to no longer need to make marrying a rich young man my priority in life."

"Jane, we have talked our entire lives about marrying for love. I do not believe you have truly given up on that hope. Here at Wayleigh, Brixton, and Clapham, our world seems so much bigger than our corner of Hertfordshire with four-and-twenty genteel families. In time, you will meet many more fascinating people like Mr. Lytle, some of whom may even be single, eligible men!"

"That may be true. In the meantime, however, I would like to get to the end of your absorbing tale."

"Oh, I know when I am not needed. I shall go see how Mary fares. By the time I come back, I expect you to be ready to give me your unbiased opinion on this story!"

Jane smiled and said, "Unless you are to spend the day and night in Mary's room, it is unlikely I shall finish the story before you come back. Now go!" Jane playfully waved Lizzy away.

℘℘

Mary could not stop the tears that threatened to emerge as she ran up to the bedroom she shared with Kitty.

Kitty came in directly after her and said earnestly, "Mary, please do not be upset with me. You should not take mamma's words seriously. Mr. Samuels talked chiefly with you, and he only glanced at me from time to time to make sure I was engaged in the conversation. I am not at all interested in marrying Mr. Samuels. He probably thinks I am just a silly girl as papa did."

"Do not worry, Kitty. I am not upset with you, and you have become much more sensible since Lydia left."

Kitty was never one to take care of another. She was relieved she had not been blamed and left the room to go back downstairs to continue her sketching.

When Lizzy came into the room, Mary's tears had dried. Lizzy sat down facing Mary and squeezed Mary's hand, but she remained silent. She had caused much anguish for her sisters since she came home two days ago, and she had learned it was often wise to avoid saying the first thing that came to her mind.

After a few minutes, Mary squeezed Lizzy's hand and started speaking. She spoke, not curtly, as she was wont to do, but dejectedly.

"Lizzy, I do not even know why mamma upset me. She said nothing I had not expected her to say, but this time, for the first time, I felt the injustice of it."

"Dearest, I need not remind you since you have lived with mamma for nineteen years: what mamma says usually means nothing."

Mary responded only with a slight nod.

Lizzy ventured into making a guess of Mary's distress. She continued, "Could it be you are upset because you do like Mr. Samuels? You dress yourself with more care and study the scriptures as they were written instead of through some outdated sermons. Do you think these could be because of Mr. Samuels?"

Mary thought for a while and answered, "I do not know. After you refused Mr. Collins's proposal of marriage, I had hoped he would offer for me because he was a clergyman, and I always imagined myself marrying a man of the cloth. When he chose Charlotte, I was very disappointed. Since meeting with Mrs. Lytle to study scriptures, I have striven to banish such worldly thoughts of treating every unmarried clergyman as a potential husband. However, two weeks ago, when I accompanied Mrs. Lytle to the Clapham church and discovered Mr. Samuels is not married, my heart leaped! Now you have associated my wanting to dress according to the norm as a sign that I have set my cap at Mr. Samuels. I am truly disgusted with myself."

"Do not blame yourself too much, Mary. It is natural for a young lady to think about marriage, especially in the Bennet family. Mamma has instilled in all her daughters that a single man with a large enough fortune must be in want of a wife, and she seizes every opportunity to push her daughters forward when such a young man appears. We all entered society when we were only fifteen. Even though you hid behind your austere appearance for the past four years, you could not help being affected by this thinking. Jane and I just spoke on precisely the same topic. She said she is moving herself away from mamma's machinations. We are now freer to pursue our lives in the directions we wish because we are no longer the desirable marriage targets of Longbourn."

"Lizzy, I have never viewed things this way, and it is a lot to think about. I have one question: why is it that you seem immune to the desire of marrying eligible young men?"

"I am stuck on the notion of marrying only for the deepest love. Mayhap I am rebellious in nature. You remember I am the one who has been going against mamma's wishes since I was a young girl. There you have it. You are not like me, and you are not looking directly at the fate of being a spinster aunt to all my nieces and nephews!"

"Lizzy, don't jest! So far, you have been the only one among us sisters who has received a marriage proposal. Lydia does not count because she eloped. Lizzy, I feel better now. It is wonderful to have a sister to confide in. I shall certainly miss you when you return to Mrs. Trumbull."

"Mrs. Trumbull's homes are not far from Rambler. You should send notes as often as you like. Mrs. Trumbull does not mind franking any post coming to her house. I shall also try to come home regularly. In the meantime, if you need a sister's shoulder to cry on or just to talk, you should go to Jane."

"But Jane is always so serene and predictable, like a warm blanket, but I sometimes need to be challenged in my thinking, as you just did. You are irreplaceable, Lizzy."

"I truly am pleased you think my ideas are intellectually stimulating. But Mary, try Jane. She is different now. She is far more discerning than I am, but she used to bury her keen perception of people and events to avoid any possibility of unpleasant situations. Her talent to understand acutely the world around her is unique. We are now impoverished young women without much protection except for Uncle Gardiner, who has plenty of worries and cares of his own. We must band together, consult one another, help one another, and we shall be stronger than we ever were!"

"I like the sound of your charge very much! Hmm... what if you and I band together and go to the kitchen to help Sally prepare dinner? She must be so hassled from morning till night by the five of us. She is a young woman in the family as well!"

"What an excellent idea, Mary! Let us go!"

At dinner, Mrs. Bennet was uncharacteristically silent. It was also evident she had been crying. The sisters were discomfited that their usually spirited mother seemed so out of sorts.

At the end of dinner, after Sally had removed the dishes, Mrs. Bennet sighed deeply and glanced over at Mary. She then bent her head and said, downheartedly, "Mary, I ask your forgiveness for being cruel this afternoon. I should not have said what I did, especially when you have begun to discard your drab habits of dress. Don't think I have not noticed. Without your spectacles, you look almost pleasant."

Mary's cheeks became flaming red, and she could do nothing but lower her head to hide the shame she felt at her mother's tactless insult.

Mrs. Bennet, entirely insensitive to Mary's embarrassment on her account, paused to look at each daughter by turns and sighed again before continuing, "You girls are daughters of a landed gentleman and were the Miss Bennets of Longbourn. I could not get any of you a husband. Now, your prospects are so much less favorable that I need to maximize the chance of getting at least one of you settled advantageously, or else we shall remain in this mean cottage for the rest of our lives. If I appear cruel, that is because desperate times call for desperate measures, you understand."

The rebuttal against Mrs. Bennet's statement came from the least expected source. Kitty, who had never in the past gainsaid her mother, said quizzically, "Mamma, Rambler is quite tolerable. It is far better than the hedgerows you had warned us about for years before papa's death. The rooms are pleasant, and the cottage is so well situated that I am never bored if I just look out of the windows."

Mrs. Bennet looked at Kitty with distaste. She said irritably, "Kitty, you know nothing. Without my dear clever Lydia, you have become inane. You have never been the mistress of an estate, or among the important matrons

123

of a neighborhood. You will never know how I feel. Lydia, if she were here, would understand me instantly. This cottage is nothing!"

She then swept her gaze around the table again and sighed heavily once more. "None of you will likely become the mistress of an estate. I had wished for better futures for you."

She turned to Jane and gave her a pointed look. She said, "Jane, perhaps you still have a chance if you listen to me and put yourself forward more..."

Jane, once again, felt the need to repeat the tactic of absenting herself.

"Oh, mamma, I just remembered to work on something Lizzy brought back from Mrs. Trumbull for me to look over. I had better go now." Jane got up and left the room.

"I do not understand how you do it, Lizzy. You have been home for two days, and you have already managed to turn my most obedient daughter against me. I blame it on your father. Not only did he die without leaving adequate support for his family, but he also spoiled you to be more than impertinent. You are downright disrespectful," scolded Mrs. Bennet while looking at Lizzy severely.

Through the years, Elizabeth had grown a very thick skin against her mother's unjust verbal attacks. However, such unkind words about her dearest papa were beyond what she could bear.

"Mamma, papa's investment in his book collection yielded over three times the return. The interest from the book sale should provide adequate support for his widow and unmarried daughters if we economize to suit our current circumstances. As for being spoiled, at least I did not elope with a scoundrel and plunge the family into such a scandal that all her sisters, and mother, are now disgraced."

"Oh! My nerves! My nerves! You ingrate! If you had accepted Mr. Collins, we would still be at Longbourn. It is all your fault!" Mrs. Bennet's agitation and speech were worse than Elizabeth had ever heard.

"Mamma, do you truly think that had I married Mr. Collins, and he had inherited Longbourn, he would have allowed you to stay at Longbourn with Lydia's shame?"

"If you had married Mr. Collins, your father would still be alive!" screeched the mother.

"Why? Lydia would still have gone to Brighton and run away from there. And I, I would not have been there to take care of papa in his last days. For that alone, I thank heavens I refused Mr. Collins. Poor papa! I think I have stayed too long at Rambler. I shall go back to Brixton Park tomorrow. Good night, mamma."

Mrs. Bennet stared at the retreating figure of Elizabeth with fire shooting out of her eyes. She turned back to look at her two daughters remaining at the table. Both Mary and Kitty had their heads bent low and were trembling.

"You have seen how your sister insulted your poor mother. 'Going back to Brixton Park!' This humble cottage, her mother, and her sisters are not good enough for that high and mighty Lizzy! Oh, Mr. Bennet, why did you have to die? You left me at the mercy of your ungrateful wretches of daughters!"

"Mamma, why don't I take you back to your room? You are over-wrought," asked Mary meekly.

"Over-wrought! Over-wrought! That is all you have to say! I am not over-wrought. I am suffering! Don't you think I know Lydia has caused our problems, and we must suffer the consequences of her actions? But what can I do? I have tried my hardest to raise all of you the best I can. What do you want from me? What is it you want..."

In the middle of her tirade, Mrs. Bennet fainted dead away.

Chapter 13

Kitty screamed while Mary ran to try to catch her mother. Both Jane and Elizabeth rushed downstairs when they heard the commotion. All four daughters supported their mother and carried her to her bedroom.

Jane waved the smelling salts in front of her mother's face for a few minutes. Mrs. Bennets came to gradually, looking confused. Seeing all her daughters hovering over her, she asked groggily, "What happened? What is going on? Why are you all here? Oh, has Lydia come home? Let me see her!"

Jane soothingly said, "Mamma, you fainted. No, Lydia has not come home, but Uncle Gardiner has been working very hard on finding her. No doubt she will be home soon."

"I feel exhausted. I shall go to bed now. Would one of you call Sally please? I shall see you tomorrow," said Mrs. Bennet softly. The sisters looked at one another. Jane nodded, and the three younger sisters filed out of their mother's chamber.

"Mamma, would you like me to help you undress for bed? You look extremely fatigued," asked Jane solicitously.

"Jane, you are not a maid. Go ask Sally to help me. My nervous attack has passed, and I am feeling much better now."

Jane did not move. Mrs. Bennet, on seeing her favorite daughter refusing to leave her as she had earlier, continued with a downcast countenance, "I am worried about Lydia. Until she comes home, I shall be desolate. I was unjust, first to Mary and then to Lizzy. I knew when it happened. I just could not help myself. When you become a mother, you will know how I feel.

"I might have spoiled Lydia, but she was my last-born. I put all my hopes on her being the heir. When she turned out to be another girl, and I could not even have another child, I just treated her like the heir I could never have. It sounds absurd even to me, but that is how it was. And now, she is out there in the world all by herself. I am not a simpleton. If she had eloped and wed, she would have come back to Longbourn, prideful she was the first among her sisters to marry. And yet, she has not come back, and your Uncle Gardiner cannot locate her. Something has happened to her, and if I let myself imagine what has befallen her, I doubt I could live."

Mrs. Bennet rose on her elbow to look around her room, and Jane hastened to help support her mother to recline on the pillows. The matriarch continued, "I really do not mind this cottage. It is far more comfortable than I had imagined we would have. But there is not much to do here, and I have too much time to think about Lydia. Tell Lizzy I am sorry, and she does not need to leave on my account. Now go get Sally, please."

Jane squeezed her mother's hand and nodded. Sally was already at the door, as Mary had gone for her when first their mother asked.

In their own room, Jane and Elizabeth both sat, looking glum. Soon, Mary and Kitty knocked on the door and were allowed entry.

The sisters all sat on the bed, listening morosely as Jane recounted what their mother had just explained. No one said a word when Jane finished.

Finally, Elizabeth broke the silence and said, "I should apologize to mamma tomorrow and stay here for another two days as planned. We sometimes forget that, while the four of us appear to have found new directions for our lives, it is much more difficult for mamma. As the former mistress of Longbourn, she has given up far more than any of us. But what she said about Lydia's fate is extremely disconcerting. I have been thinking that locating Lydia is the most important mission in my life, but I have thought little about whether she has suffered. In fact, I have felt that, because she caused us so much grief, she deserves whatever befell her. I agree with mamma that Lydia must have gone through tremendous hardship we cannot even fathom."

"It was all my fault..." Kitty started crying. Before she turned hysterical, all three sisters surrounded and embraced her, telling her she was too young to know the full consequence of such reckless actions.

After Kitty calmed down, Mary said thoughtfully, "Perhaps I should encourage mamma to join me and Mrs. Lytle in our study of the scriptures. It has enlightened me to a degree I never expected. Perhaps mamma would benefit from knowing the scriptures better as well."

Both Elizabeth and Jane looked at Mary skeptically. They exchanged looks, and Jane said gently, "Mary, you are insightful to suggest mamma needs to find extra activities to occupy her time so she would be too busy to think often about Lydia's fate. However, we must proceed cautiously. Mamma was accustomed to being active–visiting, supervising Longbourn's staff, and teaching us those accomplishments she considered important. Perhaps all of us, except Lizzy, will engage mamma in our daily lives together. I shall invite mamma to choose plants for the garden..." Jane looked over to Kitty and smiled, "while Kitty may show mamma her sketching, and you, Mary, may read to mamma. And all of us, mamma included, will go visit Mrs. Lytle more frequently. The important thing is we do not leave mamma alone for long."

"Wonderful idea, Jane!" exclaimed Elizabeth. "Perhaps I could ask Mrs. Trumbull for permission to have you all visit regularly. She often tells me I am her guest, not an employee. I think she may be receptive to these suggestions."

Bit by bit, the gloom that enshrouded the sisters lifted. They looked forward to the day when their mother returned to her former cheerful self, but perhaps without the brashness stemmed from her false sense of superiority among the neighbors.

After their younger sisters had left the room, Jane sighed and said, "I shall have to stay up to finish your story. I am very close to the end."

"Take your time, Jane. Unless you vehemently object, I shall go ahead with the publication of the story with the goal of earning money. I do not think anybody's hurt feelings are more important than maximizing our chance at finding Lydia. Now that mamma has reminded us that Lydia could be suffering terribly out there somewhere, we must find her!"

"I completely agree with you on making finding Lydia our most important priority. I do not think your story will hurt anybody's feelings..."

Elizabeth wanted to interrupt, but Jane stopped her by taking her hand.

"Let me finish... please," Jane gently implored. Lizzy nodded reluctantly.

"In your story, Mr. Darcy, once having his character flaws clearly pointed out by you, underwent some serious self-contemplation, resulting in his becoming a much more attractive character. I did not think Mr. Darcy was particularly handsome. His fearsome scowl more than scared me—it was forbidding. I confess I hardly looked at him at all. After your transformation of him, I think he will go down in literary history as one of the most beloved gentlemen by ladies!"

Elizabeth smiled indulgently and shook her head, "Oh, Jane, you should write a story yourself! Such imagination!"

"No, Lizzy. It is not my fancy exactly. I told you how seeing myself described on your pages has made me reconsider how I should live my life. So, if Mr. Darcy reads your story, he may react the same way. Is there any possibility your paths will cross in the future? I am very curious to find out whether he will become the person at the end of your story."

"You spoke of fancy—that was precisely the reason for me to write it out on paper. I blame myself for papa's... health collapse. Without thinking up this impossible scenario of Mr. Darcy coming to our rescue, and by so doing, exonerating me for my sin of refusing his proposal of marriage, I think I would have gone mad. And now I perfectly comprehend mamma's outburst today. She had no outlet for her worries, guilt, and frustration, and so she lashed out at all of us.

129

"I think Mr. Darcy hates me, as he should, for my cruelty and my stupidity in misreading his character. I dreamed up that precise scenario where Lydia was rescued, because Mr. Darcy had the best chance of doing so as he grew up with that scoundrel Wickham. Alas, this all only happened in my head."

"But it makes sense Mr. Darcy might know how to look for Mr. Wickham. Now that we have decided to make it our first goal in life to look for Lydia, should we not try to find out from Mr. Darcy whether he might have any idea where Mr. Wickham could be? If we found him, he would likely know where Lydia was, if she were not with him."

Elizabeth stared at a spot on the wall opposite her, as she was deep in thought. She finally said, "You are wise and astute as usual. I have been so convinced the second half of my story is purely fictitious that it never occurred to me the real Mr. Darcy could know something about finding Wicked Wickham–Henry Wolfe in the manuscript. I shall send a note to Uncle Gardiner to see whether he could find out the whereabouts of Mr. Darcy. Do not forget, Jane, we must be discreet in our inquiries about Lydia. Mr. Darcy already thinks little of our family. His knowing of Lydia's scandal will either make him hate me or congratulate himself on his narrow escape from the Bennet family millstone around his neck for the rest of his life. He may likely do both. On the other hand, if he hates me a little more than what he already does because of my novel, it does not signify."

"Is it likely you might see him again now that you move in Mrs. Trumbull's circles?"

"I do not know. The chances of my seeing him again have certainly increased because of Mrs. Trumbull. However, she is not completely in society yet, and she is active in Tory politics, whereas the Darcy-Fitzwilliam clan is in the opposition because of Lord Fitzwilliam's prominent leadership position in the Whig party."

Elizabeth yawned and said, "It has certainly been an emotional day. I am going to bed."

"I think I shall as well. My mind feels very unsettled. 'Tis a new sensation for me. I am only about thirty pages from the end. I should be able to finish the story in the morning."

The next two days went by calmly, but the underlying tension was palpable. Everyone in the Bennet household tiptoed around one another to maintain the truce. Various apologies were offered and accepted. Mrs. Bennet, after her violent outburst, appeared subdued. She seemed otherwise physically robust after the fainting spell, which was a relief for her daughters, who could not handle the loss of the only parent left to them.

Before Elizabeth departed for Brixton Park, Jane handed over the manuscript with corrections added for all the misspelled words and grammatical errors she had found. She also gave her blessing for the publication of the story.

"Lizzy, I am very proud of you. Your story goes deep into my heart. I am sure that it will resonate with other readers as well."

"Let us first wait and see whether there will be other readers. I expect some of Mrs. Trumbull's important friends will subscribe but then cast the book aside. I care only that it will aid us in discovering Lydia. Who knows? Perhaps Lydia will read it and come back to us."

"I think it is possible. Lydia would like this story."

"That is the highest praise indeed! No dungeon and no damsel in distress and Lydia would like it? She will most likely hate it. However, if she comes back only to tell me to my face how the story is a waste of time, I will thank God for it."

At the appointed time, Mrs. Trumbull's carriage arrived at Rambler Cottage. The sisters went out to see Lizzy off. Right before Elizabeth stepped onto the carriage, her mother broke through the crowd of sisters and gave Elizabeth a fierce embrace. And wordlessly, just as quickly as she came, Mrs. Bennet retreated to the house. The sisters stood dumbfounded momentarily, but then broke into wide, teary grins.

"All will be well," said Lizzy through her tears and stepped up to the carriage. Her sisters waved until the carriage rounded the bend down the lane.

Chapter 14

"May I come in?" Elizabeth asked when the door to the music room was opened by the Italian music teacher.

Mr. Rocco nodded and said, "My business is finished here." He slipped out of the room without another word.

Mrs. Trumbull was sitting on the sofa with her youngest daughter, Cecily. She greeted Elizabeth cheerfully, "Ah, Elizabeth, there you are. Do you think Cecily is ready for music lessons? Perhaps you could start teaching her some simple children's songs."

"Oh, I should think Mr. Rocco is much better at it than I could ever hope to be." Elizabeth smiled and walked over to the three-year-old girl sitting by her mother.

"Hello, Cecily. Are you ready to play the pianoforte? You are a lucky girl to have Mr. Rocco as your teacher. He plays beautifully," cooed Elizabeth. She rarely saw the little girl, who stayed mostly in the nursery.

"I am going to start both Helena and Cecily on music lessons since they are only one year apart. Now that we are through with mourning, I would like very much to go back to normal life as soon as possible."

"Oh, Mr. Rocco will be very busy."

"Yes, he will be. With three young budding pianists needing lessons every day, you will see a lot more of him. He stays at the gate lodge when we are in the country."

"I see. It is considerate of you, Lillian." Elizabeth thought her patroness had to be the world's best employer—perhaps in competition with Mr. Darcy for that coveted position.

"I do what makes sense. Have you decided on the publication of your story? Will I have to wait much longer to read your masterpiece?"

Elizabeth smilingly replied, "It will be published if you deem it worth the effort and the expense, but I just realized that I do not know the cost of printing. Is it possible to see how many subscriptions the story attracts before I decide on how many copies to print? If the cost is not prohibitive, my Uncle Gardiner may allow me to borrow from the book-sale money to pay for the printing."

"You have learned something about business, I see," Mrs. Trumbull looked at Elizabeth with a self-satisfied smile.

"The expedient way is for me to pay for the printing, and then you pay me back when you have collected the subscription fees. After all, I instigated turning you into a published authoress. Mr. Peters will arrange for the publication. I have heard rumors Lord Byron's poem is at the final stage of editing, which could mean it may be another two weeks or two years before he is completely satisfied and allows its publication. Regardless, we should try to get your story out as soon as possible. Once his poem is available to the public, it will be all but impossible to take any attention away from all the hubbub surrounding his person and his work."

"Lillian, I am so very grateful for your generous support and sound advice. I was going to ask my Uncle Gardiner, but he is already so busy with the additional care of the Bennet women. Mr. Peters is very capable. I am certain none will do better than he."

"Mr. Peters was my late husband's most trusted manager. Now that I have sold all the businesses, Mr. Peters would be more than happy to have an interesting project or two to amuse him. I must thank you for providing one because I live in fear he will retire out of boredom!"

Elizabeth could not believe how easily the business of publication was proceeding. The power of wealth astounded her anew.

If I had married... Stop! No more of this capricious thinking!

Four weeks later, right before three hundred copies of her novel were ready to go to press, Mrs. Trumbull and Elizabeth went to see Mr. Charles Burney to view Mr. Burney's book collection, which numbered over thirteen thousand volumes. Mme. d'Arblay, his sister, was staying with him until she went back to France to unite with her husband.

Elizabeth was, of course, awe-struck. Standing before her was her idol. She simply adored the older novelist's first novel, 'Evelina.'

What she did not expect was that Mme. d'Arblay appeared to be quite awe-struck as well.

"Forgive me, Miss Bennet, for staring at you so indecorously. When I first laid eyes on you, I thought I was dreaming. You look so much like Princess Amelia. The same color hair, the same shape of the face, very similar physical build, and especially the self-assured air about you all reminded me of our dear departed princess. On a closer look, the resemblance is not so pronounced, especially when compared to the princess in the last few years of her life, when her health was very poor.

"You may not know I was the Queen's Keeper of the Robes for six years, and all the princesses, and Her Majesty in particular, condescended to treat me as a friend. Princess Amelia was the youngest, and only a little girl then. However, since I left Her Majesty's service, I have returned regularly to visit the Royal household. I am proud to claim Princess Amelia as a friend. I saw her not long before her tragic death two years ago. You cannot imagine how devastating it was for Their Majesties, especially the King, to lose their favorite daughter. Her Royal Highness was only seven-and-twenty at her death."

"I remember reading about the princess's passing in the newspaper. The entire nation mourned with Their Majesties. I understand they are doting parents." Elizabeth paused and thought of her own family's desolation in losing Lydia, not to death, but to the unknown.

She then tried to direct the conversation back to more light-hearted topics.

"Madam, will you give me some hope a new novel is in the offing? I adore all your novels."

The renowned authoress smiled indulgently at Elizabeth and admitted, "I am planning something, but all I have at present is a vague notion of a plot. If you are waiting to read something new, perhaps Mrs. Trumbull's will satisfy your wishes sooner. Many are eagerly anticipating that happy event. You are the bosom friend of Mrs. Trumbull. Do you know when it will be published? I hope it will be before I return to France."

"Mrs. Trumbull's? It is by A Scribbler! How have people even heard about the novel? It will not be ready for a few more weeks," exclaimed Elizabeth, and, sensing she may have said too much, blushed deeply.

"Ah, I have been wondering what made Mrs. Trumbull change her mind about putting her creative energy into the novel format. Perhaps she did not?"

Madame d'Arblay looked at Elizabeth pointedly and observed, "You see, Miss Bennet, I have known Mrs. Trumbull since she and her husband began their soirees years ago. She is, without a doubt, one of the finest traditional bluestockings. I am very glad we have someone like her to keep the blue flames burning. Interestingly, not many of us blues have ventured into novel writing, myself among the few exceptions, but I am also by far one of the least learned. Even then, I concealed the fact I had written a novel until it was discovered by my father.

"Where was I? Oh, I have digressed. Mrs. Trumbull once asked me to read a few pages of a draft about her life in fiction form. I gave her my honest opinions. Soon after that, she told me she had given up on the novel genre altogether. Her style was quite distinctive—concise and scholarly. I should be able to tell whether she has, as everyone assumes, written the novel. I have already purchased a subscription."

Madame d'Arblay continued to scrutinize Elizabeth, and with a twinkle in her eye, quipped, "If, as I suspect, she is not the authoress, I have an excellent idea who may be."

Elizabeth was shocked when she heard Mme. d'Arblay's insinuation. She could not refute the older lady's keen perception but did not know how to respond. Instead, she remained tongue-tied and looked like a thief caught in the act.

"Miss Bennet, when people found out I was the authoress of 'Evelina,' nothing really happened. I cannot account for my fear of being discovered to have written a novel. However, I shall not say a word to anyone else. I am eagerly awaiting this work of fiction so many have been talking about."

Mr. Burney and Mrs. Trumbull came over and joined the two authoresses, one renowned and the other anonymous. Mrs. Trumbull directed the conversation to the situation on the Continent, where General d'Arblay remained to serve the exiled French emperor.

On the way back to the Trumbull residence on St. James Square, Elizabeth looked troubled, and soon could not contain her anxiety anymore. She blurted out, "Lillian, I should call off the publication. Madame d'Arblay figured out I am the authoress without having read a word of my story. I shan't bear it!"

Mrs. Trumbull was half surprised and half amused to hear this almost childish cry from one so sensible; she counseled, "Elizabeth, you talked to the only person who had the misfortune of having read my disastrous attempt at novel-writing. There is nothing you need to fear about Madame d'Arblay. Her discretion is legendary. It is well known the Queen and the royal princesses favor her because she has never leaked a word about her years serving at Court."

Elizabeth calmed down substantially, and her short-lived decision to not publish was reversed when Mrs. Trumbull disclosed, "Did Madame d'Arblay tell you that the proceeds from the sale of 'Camilla' allowed her to build a cottage for her family? General d'Arblay was an impoverished émigré from France during the Terror. He, like many of his fellow countrymen, escaped with only the clothes on his back. Her family would have been homeless if not for the large number of subscriptions garnered by the novel, which Madame d'Arblay wrote specifically to provide a home for her family."

Well, if the celebrated Madame d'Arblay could write novels for the financial means to build a cottage, then it is not wrong for me to do so to find Lydia. If Mr. Darcy does not like the way I tell the world about his private business, I hope he will someday understand I meant no disrespect.

Somehow, Elizabeth felt no relief after again rationalizing her decision to publish.

In early 1813, the novel, 'First Impressions,' by A Scribbler debuted. The three ladies sponsoring the subscriptions were Mrs. Trumbull, Lady Nottingham, and Mrs. Mulvaney, all well-known bluestockings. Because of their reputations, no one mistook the novel for a gothic thriller aimed for the younger set.

That Mrs. Trumbull herself was the authoress was not a mere rumor, it was well accepted as the truth. Many gentlemen bought subscriptions, hoping to have suitable conversation topics when they attended the wealthy heiress's soirees. The first printing of three hundred copies, quite an ambitious number for a new author, sold out in one month. At a guinea per copy, the author earned over two hundred pounds after printing costs.

During the twice-per-week at home receptions, which were quite a crush, Mrs. Trumbull seated Elizabeth away from herself to spread out the crowd. It worked to a certain extent. The younger (and some not so young), unmarried gentlemen could not be persuaded to leave the heiress alone, but their mothers, sisters and the older gentlemen found Mrs. Trumbull's pretty friend an engaging, amusing sort of diversion.

Elizabeth could not help eavesdropping on the conversations occurring in her patroness's group. The gentlemen piled accolade upon accolade on the superiority of the writing, the humor, and the depth of the writer's

138

understanding of human nature. Elizabeth's own group also talked a fair amount about her novel, trying to entice Elizabeth into confirming Mrs. Trumbull was indeed the authoress. In addition, ladies, both young and old, gushed about Mr. Keynes, saying he was the most delectable gentleman who had ever appeared in literature—more appealing even than Romeo. The rest of literature's heroes should not be mentioned in the same breath as Mr. Keynes.

Elizabeth did not know what to make of this onslaught of praise. Were her guests trying to use her as the messenger to convey their flattery to Mrs. Trumbull? Or were they in earnest?

Even with so much attention focused on the authorship of the novel, conversation moved to the important events of the day: the war on the Continent, Bonaparte's retreat from Russia and potential ramifications for England, likely election winner for presidency of the Royal Society, the state of the King's health, and many other equally fascinating topics.

Elizabeth never expected to be so exhilarated to be among the erudite, intellectually sophisticated people of the world. She found she enjoyed their company very much.

Meanwhile, the letters from Rambler Cottage were also encouraging. Her mother had settled into a more amiable state. Mrs. Bennet seemed to have accepted she could not change Lydia's fate by being anxious. Helping Mary to get her wardrobe renewed had become her new mission in life. She had also stopped grumbling about her daughters doing housework. They would likely need domestic skills in their futures if they were lucky enough to marry.

Jane's letters told of a somewhat puzzling occurrence. The winter was dreary, but unaccountably, Mr. Lytle came to visit every week, even though he was supposed to be back in India! Jane assumed he had put off his journey till the weather had turned more favorable for the voyage. His visits added interest to their otherwise uneventful life.

Chapter 15

It was mid-February 1813 when Mr. Darcy finally found himself back in England.

Over the previous months, he had relived much of his recent life for his cousin so that when they arrived in England; the Colonel would not feel disconnected from his family or those events which occurred during his forgotten years. However, in the retelling, he merely narrated events but said nothing about matters of the heart. The oppression he had felt between the previous Easter and his departure for Portugal, which had made his life so burdensome, had thankfully disappeared. This alone made him feel like a new person.

During their return journey, at a time of a calm sea, Darcy and the Colonel leaned on the rail at the bow to look past the endless rippling ocean toward England, the Colonel asked absent-mindedly, "Do I have to worry about running into a jilted lover or two once we are on dry ground?"

Darcy chuckled and answered, "You would more likely run into the countless lovers who jilted you."

The Colonel's uncovered eye grew round, and his eyebrow rose to his hairline. He feigned a disappointed frown, "Jilted or jilting, it is all the same. A regular Casanova! Well, some things are better forgotten. Why was I jilted? Was it the same old story of my rich, handsome cousin snatching my catch?"

Mr. Darcy chuckled again.

"I cannot tell. It was you who claimed being jilted every time a woman turned her attention away from you. I never thought you were serious. You were far more focused on your army career than settling down with a wife."

"Ah, that is undoubtedly the truth. What sensible lady would pick a poor soldier over a rich bloke like you? Speaking of wives, why don't you have one? You had better not prevaricate as mother would tell all when I see her. I am certain, over the past five years, she has not ceased matchmaking for either of us."

Darcy knew then his cousin had no inkling about his proposal to Elizabeth Bennet at Rosings. As every disguise was his abhorrence, he was glad he could tell the truth.

"No one wanted me," Darcy said with an ease that surprised him. He remembered, at one point, his heart felt as if it were punched—as nonsensical as it sounded—every time he thought of his rejected proposal.

"How could that be? You are the best catch of our time! Filthy rich..." He paused and stared at his cousin with his one good eye. "And quite manly— I noticed you did not look at all shabby next to Wellington. You are also honorable, almost unheard of for someone in your position. Your wife would never have to worry about your stepping out with actresses and courtesans or gambling your daughters' dowries away. So, what did you do to scare women away? That fearsome scowl alone could not possibly have been enough to fend off the determined ladies of the ton!"

Mr. Darcy really wanted to change the subject. He feigned deep contemplation for a long moment, and then said, "Since you are unwilling to give up your inquisition, I have no choice but to confess there was one lady..."

The Colonel perked up instantly and cried, "Aha! I knew it!"

Mr. Darcy put on a serious look and asked innocently, "Do you remember Bingley's younger sister..."

Before Darcy could even mention the name of the lady, the Colonel yelled, "Stop! Stop! You want me to believe the harpy with a peaked face and the most disgusting, obsequious manners is the possessor of your heart? Not a chance! I often thought you paid too high a price to be friends with Bingley when his manacle of a sister would latch onto you every chance she got."

"Bingley has become a good friend in the last five years. I have done him wrong."

"What? What did you do to that puppy?"

Darcy looked at his cousin for another long moment. Convinced the Colonel had no memory of what happened at Rosings the previous Easter, he felt there was no harm in mentioning his foolhardy attempt to separate Bingley from Miss Jane Bennet.

"Oh, was she the fortune-hunter you had told me about?"

"When and where did I tell you about a fortune-hunter pursuing Bingley?" Although glad to see the Colonel might have regained some of his memories, Mr. Darcy was alarmed that the wrong ones might have resurfaced.

"You must have told me two or three instances of Bingley falling in love with this or that unworthy lady in just the first year of your acquaintance with him. That hapless young man simply could not help entangling himself with unsuitable young women of every sort. You were always trying to extricate him from one ruinous courtship after another."

"Oh, I had forgotten about that."

"Now, who is the one with the bumped head?"

This exchange finally distracted the Colonel from his relentless probe into Darcy's lack of marriage prospects. Darcy made a note to himself to never interfere in others' private affairs again.

$\wp\wp$

The season was slowly rolling along, and Mr. Darcy felt compelled to be in town to help his sister, Georgiana, to prepare for her debut the following year. He longed to be back at Pemberley, but he would wait till April, just before the planting season.

To him, even after their seven-month separation, Georgiana was the same shy, diffident girl, but she had grown noticeably taller.

She is taller than Elizabeth now.

Darcy started at this thought. This was the first time her name had come unbidden to his mind since he landed in Portugal.

At least she no longer causes the anguish that nearly killed me. I am certain if we meet again, it would be as common and indifferent acquaintance.

Darcy's mind was at ease with this realization. The devastation of having his heart trampled was not an experience he cared to repeat.

He detested wallowing in idle thoughts. It was high time he got back into society after a week at home. The first place to visit would be his club.

He rode over to Rockingham House on Grosvenor Square to invite his cousin along.

It was an unseasonably sunny and warm late-winter day. The cousins took their time wending through the elegant streets of Mayfair towards St. James Street, where the gentlemen's clubs were located. They were so deep in their own banter they did not notice a young lady, who was out walking in the garden at St. James Square. On seeing the men, she scampered away to hide behind the newly erected statue of William III, to the astonishment of her companion, the young Miss Trumbull.

"Miss Bennet, why are you standing behind the statue? Are you afraid of those two men?" asked Miss Trumbull with curiosity. The girl, though only ten years old, was exceptionally observant. Elizabeth's astonished stare at the two gentlemen on horseback did not escape the girl's notice.

"Forgive me, Hester dear, for acting so abruptly. I am not avoiding anybody. Seeing the soldier on horseback prompted me to inspect the statue of William III. I never noticed the king dressed as a soldier before since I have not been living in London for long, and the weather has been gray and cold.

This is the first time I have been able to really enjoy the square." Elizabeth hated to lie to her young friend, who had become dear to her.

Hester Trumbull lost her father and only brother within a short span of six months. Her two remaining sisters were still in the nursery. She felt drawn to Miss Bennet, who was interesting and had far more ideas on how to amuse her than the governess.

"Let us go to the park. The weather may not hold for too much longer," Elizabeth suggested.

Miss Trumbull happily agreed and forgot about the riders.

To the young girl, Elizabeth appeared calm and cheerful, but inside, she trembled with panic. The fear of discovery by Mr. Darcy had always been overarching.

Yet, she had known, deep in her heart, the day of seeing Mr. Darcy again would be inevitable, but she never expected it would be so soon. After all, her uncle had informed her the previous week Mr. Darcy had not yet returned from the Continent, and no one knew when he would be back in town.

Whether or not Mr. Darcy would read her novel was immaterial. She was simply not ready for any face-to-face encounter with the gentleman.

Chapter 16

When the two cousins entered Brooks's, men gathered there spontaneously erupted into "Hurrah." Mr. Darcy stepped back to let the returned war hero bask in the well-deserved adoration of their friends.

Mr. Darcy had not previously cared for many of those who swarmed around them. He thought them frivolous or worse, only coming to the club to gamble and gossip.

While standing next to the window watching the men show their appreciation for his cousin's heroism, someone of that not so savory ilk came up and greeted him, "Darcy!"

"Westerham," Mr. Darcy replied curtly.

Viscount Westerham, a notorious gambler who had trouble holding onto his family fortune, paid no attention to Mr. Darcy's rather haughty demeanor, and asked with genuine curiosity, "You were away a long time. Are you back now to pursue the Trumbull fortune like every unmarried man here?"

"I went to the Continent to escort Fitzwilliam back. He is being hailed as a conquering hero over there. As for the Trumbull fortune, I know nothing about it, and I have no interest in finding out."

As if he had not heard the indifference and aloofness in Darcy's answer, Westerham pressed on, "You were here when Brent Trumbull died more than a year ago, weren't you? His heir also died right after Easter last year. Mrs. Trumbull is worth more than half a million pounds—all liquid assets! Some even say a million, if you could believe it. She sold all her late husband's businesses. The money is from trade, of course, but cash is cash. No one cares about its lineage, and Mrs. Trumbull herself was born of the finest Welsh blood. She was a Morgan."

Mr. Darcy knew of Mr. Trumbull's passing but was unaware of the loss of his heir. He was again reminded of that period when he was desolate, confining himself at Pemberley and shutting out the world.

Seeing Darcy's stoic demeanor did not change with this momentous news, the viscount asked directly, "I cannot believe you are not planning to join the fray! I remember the puppy looks you gave Mrs. Trumbull when you first came into society. You certainly had a thing for her then."

Mr. Darcy looked severely at Westerham and said sternly, "I was nothing but a callow youth then. Mrs. Trumbull was already married with one or two children. I admired her and her husband's intellect. I did not have a 'thing' for her."

"Ah, you have forgotten that you were not so dour then as you are now. I swear you would have..."

Before Westerham went on with his lurid allusion, another of Darcy's friends came up to greet him, "Darcy!" Seeing who was conversing with Darcy, the newcomer nodded perfunctorily in the viscount's direction without even a verbal greeting.

"Bentinck! Oh, pardon me, Lieutenant Colonel Lord John Bentinck! Congratulations on your well-earned promotion! I heard much about your exploits in Salamanca," greeted Darcy cordially.

The Bentincks and the Darcys had been neighbors in Derbyshire for centuries. Lord John Bentinck was the third son of the Duke of Bridgestone. He joined the army when he was seventeen and rose to be a major on his own merit. During the siege of Burgos, he was sent back to England as a courier of top-secret dispatches. He received his promotion based on his brilliant performance at Salamanca. When he returned to the Continent, he was to be put on General Wellesley's staff.

"Thank you, Darcy. I came across Fitzwilliam in surgery after the battle and was worried about him. I am very glad to see him looking well."

The newly minted lieutenant-colonel glanced over in admiration at his comrade-in-arms before turning back and smiling at Mr. Darcy. "I did not come over to talk more about the war. I shall be back there soon enough— next month, in fact. I meant to tell you I met Miss Darcy for the first time in seven years, and could not recognize her..."

Mr. Darcy frowned when he heard that. His sister was not out. How did Bentinck meet her?

"Darcy, put that frown away! It is I, Bentinck. You would not think I would do anything with a young girl not yet out—and immediately before I go away to war? I was visiting Milton at Milton Hall, and he showed me his little boy, his heir. Miss Darcy was in the nursery. That was all. Do not cut my head off because I had a glimpse of your precious sister!"

Mr. Darcy apologized immediately. "Forgive me, Ben. Georgiana is all I have had for so many years that I tend to be over-protective..."

Westerham, who had hung on every word even though he was not included in the conversation, chimed in. "When will Miss Darcy be out?"

Mr. Darcy looked at the rake with another stern expression and said icily, "She will not be out until she has learned how to keep fortune-hunters at bay."

He then turned back to Bentinck and said, "Look, the crowd around Fitzwilliam has thinned out. Let us go join him." They both walked away with another perfunctory nod toward Westerham.

After the cousins left the club, Mr. Darcy asked the Colonel, "What do you think of Bentinck as a match for Georgiana?"

"Darcy, Georgiana is still a girl. As her co-guardian, I *will not* allow her to be matched with anyone until she is at least two to three years older. From what I have seen of her since I came home, she is not yet ready for society, and definitely not ready for marriage. She seems afraid of her own shadow. You know I say all this as her loving cousin and guardian and not with any intent to insult her. I am surprised you would think about marriage for her when you are not yet wed. If you hurry to get yourself hitched soon, your future wife will be a perfect guide for Georgiana to venture into society."

Mr. Darcy realized that, while telling his cousin what had occurred in the previous five years, he had omitted to tell him about Georgiana's near elopement with Wickham. If he had not shown up at Ramsgate just two days before the planned elopement, his sister would have been lost to a life of misery, and it would have been entirely his fault. Perhaps, unknowingly, he had tried to forget this particularly painful incident as well.

"Richard, I neglected to tell you what happened to Georgiana eighteen months ago at Ramsgate..."

After Mr. Darcy's heart-wrenching account of that episode in the Darcy siblings' lives, the Colonel thundered, "Georgiana agreed to elope with Wickham? No doubt he knew of her fortune of thirty thousand pounds. Remind me why I let the scoundrel live? I would have found him and wrung his neck!"

"You were on the Continent. You came home for leave only once in two years, and that was last spring," replied Mr. Darcy.

"You said you found the blackguard in Hertfordshire. Why did I not do anything?"

"We both agreed that as long as he did not come close to our family again, there was not much we could have done. After I left Hertfordshire, I discovered he was maligning my name in that neighborhood, but he did not leak a word about Ramsgate. That was all I cared about, and I let it be."

"Ah, he is in the militia. Now that I am back, I shall keep a keen eye on his whereabouts. It should not be difficult unless he has quit already. I cannot imagine him being content with the pay of a militia lieutenant given his expensive tastes. Exhausting four thousand pounds of inheritance in less than four years! How did a son of a steward manage that?"

"You had been away since Wickham and I were still at Eton. I could see even then that he was envious of the lifestyle of boys from wealthy families. At Pemberley, he knew his place. But at Eton, he became a lackey for the rich boys who bullied him on one hand and let him have some scraps of their wastefulness on the other. And that was his way of living through Cambridge as well—as a hanger-on of the wastrels. Once he received his inheritance, he knew all the depraved ways to spend it. Three of the four thousand pounds came from me as cash compensation for his giving up the claim to the Kympton preferment. I doubt very much any of the inheritance went—as he claimed it would—into studying law."

The Colonel paused and asked thoughtfully, "Is Georgiana's withdrawal into herself the consequence of that regrettable event? Is that why you want to match her to Bentinck as soon as possible to avoid another rake's foul scheme once she is out?"

"It is certainly on my mind. Bentinck is an honorable man. I trust him. His family and ours have been neighbors for so long he would not dare do anything dastardly to hurt my sister and your ward. Rakes, like Westerham, were asking about her.

"I truly do not believe I have what is required to see to the happiness of my sister as she grows into a mature young lady. Since being back, I have seen her only when she emerges from her room during mealtimes. She and I have not exchanged more than a dozen words each day."

"I shall come by your house tomorrow to judge for myself how she fares. I saw little of her as you hurried her back to your house before I could get away from my mother's hovering."

"What was Aunt's hovering about? You are almost entirely healed except for your vision and memory loss, which she can do nothing about."

"At the beginning, she wanted to make certain I was not at death's door. Once she was sure I would live, she started nagging at me about settling down with a wife and children. Milton has given her four grandchildren in the last six years, and he has shown no signs of slowing down. Why is she so eager for more?" asked the Colonel exasperatedly and rhetorically.

"Has Aunt identified young ladies for your choosing? It will not be long before she pushes a similar list on me. After all, the season will be in full swing in a few more weeks."

"She kept hinting at, nay, more like advocating for, the widowed Mrs. Trumbull. For reasons known only to my dear madre, Mrs. Trumbull's fortune from trade has no stench. From what she has heard, the widowed heiress is worth almost a million pounds."

"I wonder which number is closer to the truth. At the club, the rumors were she was worth more than half a million pounds."

"The unfortunate lady has a target painted on her back then. I am but a poor soldier with rich parents and have no qualms about mooching off my old man. The incentive to pursue an enormous fortune for fortune's sake is not as strong for me as for others. I would be content with just fifty thousand pounds. Why, that would be a handy sum to gain from one's bride!

"The last time I heard about her was that she had already given birth to five children in seven years, a feat even Milton's wife cannot match, unless my dear sister is increasing again. If Mrs. Trumbull were to become Mrs. Fitzwilliam, I wonder whether she would lock the door to her room at all times! I need a willing wife to appreciate my prowess and appetite for love. She is also a Tory. What will father say?"

"You seem to have had the time to look at this potential match from many angles. Remember, though, the Tories are ascending, and General Wellesley is a leading Tory. You happily served under him till only recently. Perhaps Uncle William would be pleased to have you claim the most coveted Tory prize for the Whigs."

"Why do you not go after her? She is a few years older than you, but nothing that signifies. She has also proven herself fertile, and might agree to give you a child or two. By the way, did you not have a tendre for her when you first entered society in your first year at Cambridge?"

"No, I did not, and I do not plan to pursue her for marriage. I have no need for her fortune. I confess a marriage of convenience no longer disgusts me as it used to, but I am certainly not ready to consider such a fate for myself."

150

"Does that mean that you will succumb to Aunt Catherine's machinations and marry Cousin Anne? That would be the most convenient of all marriages of convenience," said the Colonel with a smirk.

Mr. Darcy did not think such a question merited a response.

"Anne is quite an heiress, but probably too sickly for you, and definitely for me. She has not turned into a robust beauty in the last five years, has she?"

Mr. Darcy rolled his eyes but did not answer. He regretted telling his cousin about his current view on marriage before he had thought it through himself. The gross disappointment in his first foray into love, and his subsequent experience with the transient nature of life, happiness, war, and peace, made him re-evaluate the purpose of his life's pursuits. Of late, he felt perhaps marriage was for procreation more than anything else.

"Just as well. Let the greedy men fight tooth and nail for Mrs. Trumbull then. She must be the richest heiress to grace the ton, ever. Meanwhile, if I do my equerry duty well, His Majesty might promote me to general; then I would have a fat pension and could take the most delectable damsel for my wife without regard to her fortune."

"If you were to get a promotion from His Majesty, it could as likely be to his Groom of the Stool."

The Colonel rolled his good eye and sighed. "Not *that* again!"

Mr. Darcy was glad the discussion on *his* marriage was over, for now.

Chapter 17

On his way back to Darcy House, Mr. Darcy contemplated his relationship with his sister. The culpability of their lack of conversation since he returned from the Peninsula was partially his. He had been so busy catching up with the estate business that he allowed his sister to lock herself in her room. In fact, he had not lately even heard Georgiana's practicing on the pianoforte.

Mr. Darcy decided to seek his sister out and went straight to her rooms.

After a few quick knocks on the door, he heard his sister call out, "Come in."

She has not closed herself away after all. It is all my fault, Mr. Darcy chastised himself.

When he opened the door, his sister was sitting in the window seat, reading. The smile that must have been from some amusing passages fell off her face instantly when she saw whom she had admitted.

"Brother! I did not know it was you!" cried Georgiana while trying to hide the book she was reading in the folds of her dress.

"Georgiana, I apologize for neglecting you since coming back from the Continent. Would you show me what you are reading? I have never seen you so absorbed in a book before. Let me guess. Mrs. Radcliff has a new novel out?"

"Oh no, Brother, this is not by Mrs. Radcliff. I know you do not approve of Mrs. Radcliff's novels, even though you never forbid me to read them. I would not openly defy you..."

Mr. Darcy interjected, "Sweetling, you are all grown up. You can, and should, choose your own reading material without my input. I do hope, though, you will still allow me to make recommendations for books I think you will enjoy. However, this time, you could recommend a book to me, especially since you seem to adore it. Until you saw your somber brother enter, you had a wide, lovely smile on you."

Mr. Darcy regretted this jest as soon as the words came out of his mouth because his timid sister was not used to teasing.

Instead of immediately withdrawing into her shell, to his surprise, his sister proudly showed him the book and excitedly said, "Brother, I would love to! I am certain you have not read it because it was published when you were still away. This copy belongs to Aunt Charlotte. She has not yet finished it. All her friends have read it, and they talk of it incessantly—but those are Aunt's words. She wanted me to read it and tell her what I think of the story from a younger person's point of view so she could bring up something new when they next discuss the novel."

Mr. Darcy took the book from his sister, careful not to lose her place in the book. He truly treasured this talkative version of his sister, something not seen since the Ramsgate debacle.

Perhaps she has finally got over it, thought Mr. Darcy with renewed hope for the happiness of his sister.

"Please look over the book as much as you like. I have read it once already. I am just re-reading sections I particularly enjoy."

Mr. Darcy was now quite intrigued. Georgiana was a reluctant reader. She usually would much rather play on her pianoforte.

"'First Impressions' by A Scribbler," Mr. Darcy read the title and the author aloud softly. "Hmm..."

He opened to the page where his sister was reading with such glee. He might as well start there.

"'Implacable resentment is a shade in a character. But you have chosen your fault well. I really cannot laugh at it. You are safe from me."

"There is in every disposition a tendency to some particular evil—a natural defect, which not even the best education can overcome."

"And your defect is to hate everybody."

"And yours," he replied with a smile, "is willfully to misunderstand them."'

Georgiana was watching to see whether her brother would find the passage as diverting as she. Instead, he stood abruptly, his face drained of blood. Not only was his hand holding the book shaking, but his body also swayed slightly, as if he would fall.

"Brother! Are you well? You have turned ghostly pale. Did I do wrong to read the book? I shall return it to Aunt directly!"

Mr. Darcy steadied himself and apologized to his sister. "Forgive me, sweetling. I stood up too fast, and that was all. I am well now."

Seeing the worried look on Georgiana's face, he reassured her, "Georgiana, I am indeed well. I might have imbibed more than what was good for me. At the club, there were many rounds of cheering toasts for your cousin's heroic return."

Georgiana appeared to be satisfied with this explanation, as her only experience with drinks was from an occasional glass of sweet sherry.

Mr. Darcy detested disguise, but this time, it was necessary. He had been shocked out of his wits when he read the exchange he had with Elizabeth in the early days of their acquaintance. He carefully, tentatively, asked his sister, "Does anyone know the identity of 'A Scribbler?"

"Aunt says the general assumption is that Mrs. Lillian Trumbull is the authoress because she promotes the subscription most ardently. She is also well known for her intellect. Aunt said she might have written the novel to pass time during her mourning period. I am uncertain what a subscription is. I do so want to buy one, but I do not know how."

Mr. Darcy was silent for a long moment. He finally smiled at his sister and said, "Selling books by subscription is just another way to sell books. The author, or authoress in this case, simply did not want to go through a commercial publisher. She has the means to cover the expenses of printing the books, and she is also influential in wide circles to ensure her book will get into the hands of her readers. There is no mystery about it."

"Oh, may I buy a subscription then? I so want to have a copy of my own since I promised Aunt I would keep this copy for only a week."

"Of course, sweetling. I have read hardly anything of the book, but I trust your judgement. I shall ask Mr. Nolan to acquire a copy for you."

"May I have the subscription in my name?" asked Georgiana hopefully. "Aunt said the Prince Regent's name was on the subscription list—Aunt's good friend, Lady Nottingham, is one of the sponsoring ladies. She has told Aunt tidbits about this book. Lady Nottingham said the book has sold six hundred copies since January and was one of the best-selling novels of our time."

"Yes, sweetling. You will have your own subscription, and I am glad that you have found something you enjoy so immensely. Your own copy will arrive shortly if you will excuse me to speak with Mr. Nolan."

Georgiana thanked her brother profusely, and before he was out of her room, she called him back and said, "Brother, I truly think you would like the story as well."

Mr. Darcy turned and smiled at his sister. "Any book that makes you so animated and enthusiastic must be good. I look forward to reading it."

A footman all but jumped aside when he saw his master barreling down the hall in an agitated manner.

"Nolan!" Mr. Darcy barged into his secretary's office. "Could you order two subscriptions for a novel called 'First Impressions' by 'A Scribbler' for Miss

Darcy? Lady Nottingham is a sponsor. Please hand the books to me directly, preferably this afternoon."

"Of course, Mr. Darcy. I shall get on the errand myself. I know my counterpart at Lady Nottingham's house well, and I shall be back here in an hour."

Mr. Darcy smiled, a little embarrassed, and said, "Thank you, Nolan. Please excuse my abrupt manner."

Mr. Nolan replied, "There is no need to apologize, sir. Through the years, you have not once asked me to do something frivolous, and I shall not disappoint Miss Darcy."

As they exited his office, his master said once again, "Thank you, Nolan. I can always depend on you."

Mr. Nolan had only seen his master so agitated on two previous occasions: the first was when he came back from Rosings the previous year and needed to return to Pemberley in all haste; and the second was when he was in London making preparations for his trip to the Peninsula to rescue his injured cousin. Mr. Nolan had heard about this new novel from his contacts in other great houses. If Miss Darcy wanted it desperately, it would be his pleasure to procure it for her, although he had a strong suspicion Mr. Darcy was equally eager to see the book.

Even though it had not taken Mr. Nolan above half an hour to complete his errand, his master had almost worn a hole in the Persian rug in his study.

Mr. Darcy's furrowed brows smoothed instantly when he held the books in his hands. Mr. Nolan swallowed the chuckle that was on the verge of breaking through. He wondered why everyone thought his master inscrutable and stoic. To him, his master wore his heart on his sleeve.

"Thank you, Nolan. That will be all. Could you hold all business matters for the next couple of days? You should, of course, let me know of any genuine emergencies."

As soon as Mr. Nolan left the room, Mr. Darcy tore into the book.

While waiting in his study, his overly active mind imagined all kinds of scenarios for how this impending disaster would play out. The most worrisome were the contents of his letter to *her*, specifically the part about Georgiana. It was all his fault. How could he have risked his dearest sister's future by exposing her past to someone not yet connected to him? He had made a fatal mistake, and now *she* had betrayed him for profit! Perhaps he could pay a large sum to stop her from printing more copies. However, that would cause too much attention and perhaps even unforeseen damage. What to do? What to do...

He skimmed the pages hurriedly until he found the proposal—he nearly cried out in agony when the proposal was there, as he predicted. There was now no doubt in his mind who had written this book.

He placed his finger underneath every word as he read, as if his life depended on it. When he saw those fateful words: 'God bless you' and the signature 'Egerton Keynes,' he let out the breath he did not know he was holding.

She had not exposed Georgiana!

In the story, the girl Ariana Grey was Keynes's distant cousin and ward. She was an orphaned heiress left in Keynes's care. The girl was eighteen years old and on a pleasure trip to Bath. She met Henry Wolfe, who pursued her assiduously. After she accidentally observed an assignation between her companion, Mrs. Evans, and Mr. Wolfe, she distanced herself from the wicked man. But when Wolfe did not cease his pursuit of her, she wrote her guardian and asked him to come retrieve her, as she no longer trusted her companion. Her life was imperiled when the villains attempted to kidnap her to Gretna Green, but the timely arrival of Mr. Keynes thwarted the foul scheme. Mr. Keynes made sure the villains were suitably punished, and the near scandal was hushed up.

Once his greatest fear proved unfounded, Mr. Darcy went back to the beginning of the book to skim through the pages, reading a few lines here and there to get an idea of the plot line of the story.

Just before dinner, he reached the last page. He had very little doubt the first half of the story until the letter was about him and Elizabeth, but the second half was quite unknown to him. There were two points that stood out. First, the heroine, Isabella Delancey, married the hero, Mr. Keynes, for love. Her poor first impressions of him began to fade when she visited his estate in Cheshire, and then underwent a material change when he rescued her silly youngest sister, who eloped with that scoundrel, Henry Wolfe. Having found them in London, he forced them to marry, thus saving the Delanceys' reputation.

Anger and despair took the place of the initial fear. Mr. Darcy was devastated that Elizabeth should have treated his feelings as a commodity to be publicly exhibited for monetary gain. He had never loved any woman but her, and now his deepest feelings were on display like the animals in a menagerie.

He was still extremely upset when he heard the dinner gong. As agitated as he was, shutting himself in his room would surely drive him mad. He needed his sister's presence more than ever to distract him from the upheaval within him.

The siblings had never been lively conversationalists. Despite exerting himself, Mr. Darcy could not break the dark mood he was in. Miss Darcy, still fearful the novel she was reading somehow offended her brother, was equally silent.

Finally, Mr. Darcy could not stand the strained atmosphere any longer and blurted out, "Georgiana, did you find the novel disturbing?"

Georgiana almost jumped off her seat when her brooding brother suddenly spoke to her.

"Brother, what do you mean? I... I... I found the story engaging. There are villains in the story, but Mr. Keynes finds them out and defeats them. Should I find any of this objectionable?" Georgiana added timidly.

"No, no, little sister. I am glad that you enjoy this work of fiction. With the little I have read, I could see characters resembling people I know in real life."

"Aunt said the same thing. She said Lady Paddington in the story reminds her of Aunt Catherine and Lady Northam. She also said this was a sign of a great novel—the characters popped out of the pages like real people we recognized. She also said..."

Georgiana stopped suddenly, looking abashed.

Her brother urged her to continue. He said, "Georgiana, you can say anything to me. I am interested."

"She said Mr. Keynes reminded her of you in some respects, and some other gentlemen whose names I did not know or recall. But then she said you were the steadiest and most honorable young gentleman she knew, and you would never be so impetuous as to propose to a lady in such a rude manner."

Mr. Darcy forced a smile on his face and asked with a feigned lightheartedness, "Do you agree with Aunt on this?"

"Oh, I have never connected you with any character in novels I have read. You are always kind, and so good to me."

"You do not think Lady Paddington resembles Aunt Catherine?"

"Uh... no. Aunt Catherine scares everybody, and I try to avoid her attention as much as I can. But Lady Paddington is not nearly as scary, or at least she does not intimidate Miss Isabella Delancey. I wish I could have Miss Delancey's courage."

Mr. Darcy touched his sister's wrist for reassurance. "You are full young, sweetling. By the time you get to Miss Be... Delancey's age, you will be as poised and self-assured as this character in the novel."

Miss Darcy looked at her brother with gratitude in her eyes. She clasped her hands in front of her and said, "I truly hope so!"

After dinner, Mr. Darcy presented a copy of "First Impressions" to his sister, who gave her brother a most brilliant smile. This reinforced her esteem for her kind and most amiable brother, who was not at all like the haughty but enigmatic Mr. Keynes in the novel. She volunteered to play a piece on the pianoforte before the siblings parted ways for the night.

Mr. Darcy removed to his study to continue reading the novel, which had created such turmoil in him. He reminded himself that his wartime experience on the Continent had changed him. Women, love, heartbreaks were simply follies. He had witnessed momentous events in the annals of history: two enormous armies facing each other, ready to decimate their opponent at the order of their commanders-in-chief.

After this self-introspection, he was finally calm enough to open the book to the first page and begin reading.

'*It is a truth universally acknowledged...*'

When the maid came into the study to tamp down the fire for the night, the master asked her to bring in more wood instead, as he intended to stay up for a few more hours.

Chapter 18

By the time his cousin the Colonel showed up to speak with Miss Darcy, Mr. Darcy had finished reading the book and formed a plan of action.

His identity in the novel, though well disguised for most people, might not evade discovery by his closest friends, such as the Colonel and Mr. Bingley. He felt fortunate Richard had lost his recent memories. Bingley, though intelligent, had trouble remembering faces and conversations. Miss Bingley was sharp enough to recognize some conversations, but she would never believe he would have fallen for a 'country chit,' as she called Elizabeth. So it was reasonable to assume he would be safe from being associated with the novel.

What he needed to find out, first, was how Mrs. Trumbull came to be recognized as the authoress; second, whether George Wickham had almost become his brother-in-law...

Mr. Darcy stopped abruptly and muttered, "What nonsense! Thank heavens she refused me."

Just then, the Colonel bounded into his study. An idea came to Mr. Darcy: his cousin was an intelligence officer, and he would be eminently and conveniently—since he remembered none of the Bennets—qualified to help with coordinating the investigations.

"Richard," Mr. Darcy said solemnly.

"Darcy! What is the matter? You look as if you had not slept last night. It is already four o'clock in the afternoon!" cried Colonel Fitzwilliam in his usual frank and unceremonious manner.

"I have come across some information about Wickham and would like to consult with you about that. For now, however, let us call Georgiana and have tea. She was quite excited about your visit."

"Where is my little 'Sweet Pea?' Why is she not here to welcome her favorite cousin?"

"Please do not call her 'Sweet Pea.' You remember her as a twelve-year-old. She is now seventeen."

"She did not object when I called her that at Rockingham House. However, if her glum brother does not like it, she will be Miss Georgie."

"Just Georgiana. She has no nickname."

"Alright, alright. Order tea and let me see my sweet Georgiana!"

Georgiana came in a few minutes later. The incident at Ramsgate made her uneasy about seeing her guardian again.

Within ten minutes, her jovial cousin made her lose most of her nervousness. She could never be described as lively, but she was at ease, and her cousin decided to tease her a little.

"Georgiana, would you allow me to call you Georgie? Your brother said you had no nickname." The Colonel glanced over at Darcy, who seemed surprised by this overt disregard of his request.

The Colonel smiled mischievously and said, "You need not allow anyone else the privilege. I always called you by a nickname. Do you remember?"

Georgiana looked over at her brother. He shrugged.

The young lady smiled broadly and answered, "I would love to answer to 'Georgie' from you, just like Izzy and her sisters. They all have nicknames."

Mr. Darcy's heart skipped a beat before he realized his sister had said 'Izzy' for Isabella Delancey in the novel, and not 'Lizzy' for Elizabeth Bennet. If

162

he had any doubt before about getting to the bottom of the mysteries surrounding the confounding book, it all disappeared with that irrational reaction; he refused to live in fear of being discovered as the real-life Egerton Keynes.

On seeing the look of bewilderment on her cousin's face, Georgiana smiled again, a rare thing for her to do twice within a minute, and explained, "Oh, I am sorry, cousin. I have been reading a novel in the last few days, and the main characters, four sisters and their female cousin, all have nicknames. I was thinking I would like to have one as well—but not the one you gave me when I was young."

"You do not prefer 'Sweet Pea,' Georgie?"

The cousins all laughed. The Colonel felt relieved Georgiana appeared to be not as gloomy as they had perceived.

After a musical interlude by Georgiana after dinner, Mr. Darcy and the Colonel retired to the study to enjoy some port and cigars.

"Richard," said Mr. Darcy solemnly, "I might have a lead on the whereabouts of Wickham."

The Colonel responded with a feigned solemnity of his own, "Why should we worry about the scoundrel now? Did you not tell me if he did not come close to our family, we would do nothing?"

Mr. Darcy stood up and paced back and forth for a minute. He said carefully, as if weighing every word, "This time he appears to be trifling with a gentleman's daughter. The family—I met them in Hertfordshire—needs help."

"I see. How am I supposed to assist this family I know nothing of?" asked the Colonel with obvious curiosity. He had not expected to talk about anyone but Georgiana. Darcy seemed to think somebody else was more important than his precious sister.

Mr. Darcy detected skepticism in the Colonel's response. He needed to explain the matter in such a way so as not to expose his true intention, which was to find out why Elizabeth made him the hero who saved her sister.

"First, Wickham was in the militia. He might have deserted his regiment to elope with this young lady. You, as ranking officer, may arrest him on the spot. Second, the family of the unfortunate young woman believed they had gone to London and no further. If Wickham is in London, it is my business to know he will not come near Georgiana."

"How long ago did the elopement occur? Is it possible they might have left London? I have heard enough about elopements for one day. There is one just as you described in a novel Mother said was all the rage in town."

"When did you start reading novels?" Mr. Darcy asked sharply. He could not believe his ears! His cousin might have found his source for the information on Wickham. He should have proceeded with the investigation on his own without involving anybody else.

"Don't look at me as if I were a three-headed monster! God help me if I ever read such things! Mother was nagging me about pursuing Mrs. Trumbull again, and she believes it would help my case if I could converse about the novel she has written. A good conversation starter, so to speak. I do not know why I remember rubbish like that and forget what I did to earn a medal. Father said I would get one soon."

"You deserve the highest honor the country bestows upon you. Congratulations! What did Uncle William think about your going after Mrs. Trumbull's money from trade?"

"Padre said he was quite certain the sales proceeds from her late husband's business interests were close to a million pounds, in addition to the two estates in Wales she inherited from her father. They would not be worth much, but they are on either side of the Dolancothi gold mines, and there is a chance there is gold under those grounds. He rather likes the idea of my owning gold mines, which is far more glamorous than owning coal mines. I think it is all rubbish, as gold, if there is any, would have been discovered long ago. The Morgan family has owned those estates for hundreds of years. You are aware Father and Devonshire have an ongoing rivalry about who is richer. So, he thinks it would be excellent sport for him and his younger son together to beat his rival indubitably."

"I see. What about you? You seemed against the whole idea yesterday."

"To be honest, I do not think I have any chance with such a grand heiress. Besides her wealth, she is also renowned for her bluestocking attributes. What does some impossibly rich lady with brains want from a rough-shod cavalry officer who reads only military manuals with only one eye? My pride will not allow me to fight a losing battle against hordes of eager men who could act out whole tragedies and comedies at the drop of the lady's handkerchief."

Darcy was perturbed by this unusually pessimistic attitude from his proud cousin. Perhaps their hoped-for success in tracking down Wickham would rejuvenate the down-trodden warrior's spirits.

"I see your reason to focus on finding your fifty-thousand-pound ladylove instead of wasting time running after what all the men of the ton are pursuing. Your reading of the military manuals has not been in vain. Tell me what you think of my strategy to find Wickham."

The Colonel signaled Darcy to continue.

"My plan is to visit Mrs. Younge's boarding house tomorrow." On seeing the Colonel's frown, Darcy explained, "Mrs. Younge was Georgiana's companion. She colluded with Wickham to plan the elopement. I suspect she and Wickham had been co-conspirators from the start. Poor Georgiana never had a chance. After I discovered their foul scheme, I dismissed her without reference. I put some men on watching her and found she owns a boarding house on Edward Street, not exactly a fashionable neighborhood. We may have to bribe her, but I shall not rest until she tells all."

"You are hell-bent on flushing out Wickham. This family in Hertfordshire must be important to you." Colonel Fitzwilliam looked at his cousin with curiosity, but his cousin remained inscrutable.

"Not forthcoming with your reasons? If we are going to pay Mrs. Younge a visit tomorrow, count me in. Mother said Mrs. Trumbull would be at home tomorrow, her first since coming out of mourning, and she strongly hinted I go pay my respects."

165

"Tomorrow it will be, then. Care for some billiards?"

Colonel Fitzwilliam stayed till past midnight, winning a few games to the astonishment of his cousin. The Colonel said he no longer needed to close one eye to take aim, and the realization that playing billiards was one thing he could do as well as before energized him.

The next day during calling hours, Mr. Darcy and the Colonel knocked on Mrs. Younge's door.

When the door was opened, Mr. Darcy received the shock of his life—the one answering the door was none other than...

"Miss Lydia Bennet!" Mr. Darcy could not help exclaiming. Then he noticed she was heavy with child.

Lydia was shocked as well, and she stood motionless for a long moment. Then she tried to close the door.

"Wait, Miss Bennet. This is my cousin, Colonel Fitzwilliam. We are here to see Mrs. Younge. Is she at home?" asked Mr. Darcy solicitously.

"Mrs. Wickham has been dead these two months. You are too late. If your business is finished here, please excuse me. I have work to do," answered Lydia matter-of-factly. The frivolous young girl of yore was nowhere to be seen.

"Miss Bennet, may I have a few moments of your time? We need to know where Wickham is. Could you help us?"

On hearing Wickham's name, the girl burst out crying. Mr. Darcy took her arm to let her lean on him for comfort. The Colonel closed the door, the trio walked into the front parlor, and Mr. Darcy helped Lydia sit down.

"Miss Bennet, would you allow me to ask your maid to bring you some tea? You are distressed," asked Mr. Darcy gently. Regardless of what he previously thought of Lydia, the girl in front of him, too young to become a mother, evoked nothing but pity from him.

Lydia was now downright bawling. Mr. Darcy gave her his handkerchief. After a few moments, she calmed down. Between loud sobs, she told of her woes.

"Wickham got both his wife and me with child and disappeared. I have not seen him for five months, since he found out I was increasing. He dropped me here with Mrs. Wickham, told her I would work for her while she was increasing, and he left without another word. Mrs. Wickham was further along with her babe than I was, and she was always tired. She dismissed her maid and turned me into her maid!

"It did not take her long to notice I was pregnant as well. She became kinder to me and asked me how I got into the family way. She said both she and I were victims of Wickham's debauchery. She forced him to marry her when she found out she was carrying his child. She held some debts of his that she would cancel if he agreed. All she wanted was to give her babe a name and did not care whether he would be a good husband. He finally agreed.

"I was having a wonderful time in Brighton with Colonel Forster's regiment, surrounded by so many dashing redcoats. George... Wickham came back from London a married man, but he told no one, and he showed no sign of being married. He flirted outrageously with me. Before that, he never paid me much attention. I fancied myself in love. One day he asked me to leave with him for Gretna Green because I was not of age to marry. Naturally I agreed. In fact, I jumped for joy. I later found out he needed a naïve girl to help him get out of Brighton. He was dallying with the camp foreman's daughter, and the father had been watching his every move. An officer, who had a tendre for me, warned me about Wickham when he heard that nasty blackguard brag about using me and my pin money to escape to London. I thought he was just jealous of Wickham for having my love and not him. I did not listen. How I regret that! I was a stupid girl. I wish I were as discerning as Lizzy!"

Mr. Darcy winced noticeably on hearing Elizabeth's name again. Fortunately, the Colonel was focusing his attention on Lydia and her tale.

"George... rented a room in an inn not too far from here. The place was in worse shape than this. I was having an adventure and did not notice. Soon after we arrived, Wickham said Gretna Green was far away, and he could not wait any longer to... hmm, I was unwilling because I was a gentleman's daughter, and I had my morals. He said it was not unusual for an engaged couple to anticipate their vows. As soon as I heard the word 'engaged,' I softened. It was always my ambition to be the first to marry among my mamma's five daughters. I thought if I did as Wickham wished, he would surely marry me sooner. So we stayed in the inn week after week, but Wickham was not always there. Mrs. Wickham told me Wickham came to her during that time to search for the deed to her house. Even though he was the legal owner of the house after the marriage, Mrs. Wickham hid the deed from him. The house was her inheritance from her first husband, and that was all she had left to make a living. She said Wickham forever ruined her prospects for any respectable employment. She regretted her involvement in a scheme nearly ruining a young daughter of a gentleman, but she did not tell me any more about it.

"One day, when she was feeling particularly poorly, Wickham came and ransacked her bedroom with her lying weak and helpless right there on her bed. He heaved up the mattress with her on it and snatched the deed hidden under there. He told Mrs. Wickham he was not selling the house, just mortgaging it. As long as she let out rooms to boarders, the rents would cover the mortgage payments, and she would not notice any difference. He promised to pay back the note on the mortgage as soon as his luck at the gaming table turned.

"Mrs. Wickham knew the house was lost and did not argue. It was a few days after that he brought me here. Mrs. Wickham was a good teacher, and she taught me some lady accomplishments when we had free time. She told me to marry Wickham if she died, but I do not want to marry him. I know my life is ruined. I may die like Mrs. Wickham. If I live, I solemnly vow that I *will* be a better person."

Mr. Darcy could not help admiring the young girl's pluck. Having been so abused by Wickham, she had learned from her mistakes and kept her spirits high.

"Does your family know you are here?" asked Darcy gently.

"No!" Lydia shouted. By now, her tears had dried up. She had not felt so good for a long time. Telling someone, anyone, especially one Wickham hated, relieved her of a tremendous burden. She had learned from Mrs. Wickham that whatever Wickham said was bad must be good, and according to Wickham, Mr. Darcy was a thoroughly evil villain.

"I cannot go home in this state. Papa probably is not even aware I have been missing from home. He cares only about his books and Lizzy. Mamma... oh mamma, she would be heart-broken to see me like this. She would be ashamed of me, and I cannot bear it!"

"What of your family in London? Have you thought to contact them?" Mr. Darcy simply could not understand how a young girl could think she would survive in a vast city such as London without support. He had, of course, heard of young girls "disappearing" after a disgrace, but such disappearances were usually arranged by the fallen women's families.

"Both my Uncle and Aunt Gardiner would just preach to me about how I should have learned from my elder sisters to become a genteel young lady. I can see now they would be right to do so, but it is too late. Worse, they would immediately tell my mother about my sorry state, and my poor mamma..." Lydia started crying again and wiped her eyes furiously with Darcy's handkerchief.

Mr. Darcy spoke soothingly to Lydia as if she were his own sister. "Miss Bennet, the Colonel and I will leave you for a few minutes. When we come back, we shall offer you suggestions to help you through this difficult time. You are about to give birth. We shall think of a way for you to do so safely."

Lydia did not expect this kindness from one who seemed so disdainful in Meryton. She was deathly afraid of giving birth, having heard Mrs. Wickham's incessant blood-curdling screams and then the silence that followed when the poor lady died, her child never born.

She lowered her gaze and nodded gratefully.

When they stepped out of the house, Colonel Fitzwilliam raised his one eyebrow and said, "I am all ears. What is the connection between you and the miserable little girl inside? I want the truth."

Mr. Darcy sighed. Seeing Lydia Bennet here, another victim of Wickham's treachery, threw him off-kilter. He felt frustrated that the woman he had convinced himself was forgotten kept coming back from so many angles. He did not know how much to tell his cousin.

"Miss Lydia Bennet is the youngest of five daughters of Mr. and Mrs. Bennet of Longbourn, Hertfordshire. When I was staying with Bingley at his leased estate, Longbourn was his closest neighbor. Bingley and I had a number of encounters with the Bennet family. Miss Lydia Bennet, from my estimation then, was spoiled by her too indulgent mother. Her two eldest sisters, however, are everything genteel and decorous..." Mr. Darcy paused, mindful he might accidentally digress to territories he was not ready to reveal.

He continued, "Wickham appeared on the scene as a member of the militia encamping just outside the closest market town, Meryton. When I was in residence there, he and I avoided each other. I did not have any inkling he favored any of the local women. Later, I found out through a chance encounter with one of Miss Lydia's sisters that Wickham maligned me once I was out of the area, and he had gained the neighborhood's trust. You know what a silver tongue Wickham has."

Mr. Darcy paused, gathering his thoughts on how to continue without telling any untruths. "From this same source, I learned Wickham might be in town playing his usual mischief. As we have found out today, his dastardly acts have found two victims, both ladies of gentle birth. I will not allow him to go on jeopardizing innocent women's lives. It makes me shudder to think of him coming near Georgiana again."

"And Miss Lizzy Bennet?"

Mr. Darcy was completely blindsided by this probing question.

"Don't look so surprised, Darcy," chided the Colonel. "I saw how you were taken aback when Georgiana mentioned the name Izzy while talking about the novel she was reading. I thought that was noteworthy but could not fathom how a character in a novel could have caused such powerful emotion from your usually stoic self. Just now, when Miss Lydia mentioned her sister

Lizzy, I saw the same kind of shock from you, though not as strong. I surmise Miss Lizzy Bennet is also the reason you care so deeply about helping Miss Lydia. So do not prevaricate, as disguise of every sort is your abhorrence. I can better help you if I know how much assisting Miss Lydia means to you."

To gain himself time to come up with an acceptable narrative of his relationship with Miss Lydia's sister, Mr. Darcy resorted to levity. "I was under the impression you could see with only one eye. How have you seen so much, which may or may not have been there?"

"I may have lost proper sight in one eye, but none of my wit. I was a stellar intelligence officer of His Majesty's army, and a chest full of medals to prove it. Now own up!"

Mr. Darcy walked a few steps away but turned back quickly. He sighed deeply and said, "I do not deny Miss Elizabeth Bennet... captured my fascination for a while, but nothing came of it. After my time on the Continent, I thought I had gotten over that infatuation; but somehow her name has kept coming up since our return a few days ago. I will tell you the whole sorry tale, but this is not the time. Miss Lydia is waiting for an answer. Do you have any suggestions?"

"What did you do with the girls around Pemberley who fell in the family way because of Wickham?"

"I am aware of two such instances around Pemberley before I became master. Father found a young man among the tenants to marry the first victim and compensated the young man for taking on a child that was not his own. In the second case, the girl did not want the babe, and Father helped to find a family who would be glad to take on a child and compensated them for their trouble.

I lost sight of Wickham after he had claimed his inheritance. I thought I had finally rid the cancer of the family when I found him once again wreaking havoc in Ramsgate. No doubt he has preyed on many more naïve young women besides Miss Lydia and Mrs, Younge through the years."

"The world will be populated by Wickham's bastards! His one legitimate child, ironically and sadly, did not live! Why could you not do the same with Miss Lydia?"

"Miss Lydia is a gentleman's daughter..."

The Colonel interjected, "And her sisters' reputations need to be safeguarded?"

Mr. Darcy did not deny this. He nodded.

"Well then, we shall marry Miss Lydia to a dying gentleman!"

Mr. Darcy raised his eyebrows, seeing where his cousin's thoughts led.

"There are, unfortunately, many worthy young officers dying of one cause or another. Some of them came from genteel but impoverished families. If you shell out a couple thousand quid, it should be possible to find a man who would marry Miss Lydia. We will have to act quickly since Miss Lydia looked as if the babe would pop out soon."

"An excellent plan. If Miss Lydia agrees, I will act on it immediately."

When they returned to the small parlor where Lydia sat embroidering, the Colonel laid out the plan to her.

Mr. Darcy added, "Once you are married, your babe will be your husband's legitimate child. You can return to your family as a widow when your husband dies."

"Please find me a husband from the navy instead. I have sworn off redcoats—I mean no disrespect toward you, personally, Colonel," said Lydia quite matter-of-factly.

The Colonel answered, "As you wish. Do you know when you will give birth?"

"Mrs. Baker—she was the midwife who took care of Mrs. Wickham—said the babe would come in early March by the look of me," Lydia answered shyly.

"We have no time to lose. Darcy!"

The gentlemen took their leave, telling her to be ready for her wedding. Mr. Darcy left her some banknotes to buy wedding clothes. Lydia was very pleased with this gift because she had been wearing Mrs. Wickham's dresses. On second thoughts, she would buy new dresses once the babe had come. To her newly acquired practical mind, it made no sense to spend money on a fine dress that would fit her for only a week or two.

Chapter 19

After leaving Lydia, the cousins went their separate ways to enact the plan to salvage the Bennets' reputation.

The Colonel went to the military hospital. His memory of the place from five years before was that it was crammed and understaffed. Now, the place was pure chaos.

It did not take him long, however, to find a suitable candidate for Miss Lydia. Midshipman Daniel Cieran had been badly burned on a frigate that caught fire while up on dry dock at Deptford Naval Yard a few miles down the Thames. More than half of his body was covered in burns and scabs, but his face and head were largely spared except for a bare patch at the back of his otherwise full head of red hair. He had been brought in two days earlier. There were signs of infection already, which did not bode well for the handsome young officer from Ireland.

His conditions for marrying Miss Bennet were simple: if he lived, the Colonel would help him gain a promotion to lieutenant. He had already passed the lieutenant's examination, but promotion slots went to candidates with connections. If he died, his body should be given a proper sea burial befitting an officer of the Royal Navy; and his bride's dowry of one thousand pounds and any annuities due him after his death should be sent to his mother, a widow with five young children at home.

When the Colonel went back to Darcy House to report his progress, Mr. Ford, the butler, informed him Mr. Darcy was away visiting a Mr. Gardiner on Gracechurch Street.

The Colonel made himself at home in the master's study. He heard Georgie practicing on the pianoforte, but he also saw "First Impressions" on his cousin's desk. He had never opened a novel before. This novel, however, appeared to hold some important clues to the uncommonly impassioned behavior of his stoic cousin.

The novel opened naturally in the middle, as if the previous reader had read and reread the passages there.

'*I have struggled long and hard, but my feelings will not be repressed. You must allow me to tell you how ardently I admire and love you...*'

The Colonel was so engrossed in reading he did not hear his cousin entering the study.

"Richard! What are you reading?" exclaimed Mr. Darcy, more agitated than the Colonel had ever seen.

"Ah, Mr. Keynes! Colonel Harlan Egerton, at your service!" greeted the Colonel with a flourish.

"You know! I have been in dread of someone realizing the story was based on me. You have, despite not remembering any of it!" said Mr. Darcy, looking pale and distraught while pacing and turning his head from side to side as if he were trying to find a place to hide.

"Calm down, Ke... Darcy! I only recognized you because I am privy to your being associated with this novel somehow. This Miss Elizabeth Bennet, if she is the author of this novel, is an exceptionally talented writer. I cannot abide novels. But this, this is brilliant!"

Mr. Darcy looked up to heaven and wanted to cry. He also felt the novel was mesmerizing—the sentiments were genuine and deep, the reflections of contemporary social mores were spot-on, and the vivaciousness of Isabella Delancey made him fall in love with Elizabeth Bennet all over again. The trouble was, the characterization was so true to life he felt he had been put on display for the entire world to see.

"Miss Delancey appears to favor Colonel Egerton. Did Miss Bennet favor me in real life?"

Mr. Darcy's countenance turned glum. It was possible Elizabeth favored the Colonel. However, he did not wish to admit that to himself.

He said, "I do not know. I was, in a fair way, blind when it came to her feelings. I thought she was flirting with me, expecting my address when she actually loathed me!"

"Ah, if she had fifty thousand pounds, I might attempt to woo her. As it is, she is safe from me. I had been wondering why I set my price at fifty thousand. I did not think five years ago I had such expensive aspirations. But she ended up marrying you, or rather, the fictional you. She must have had a change of heart."

"This is just a novel. It is not unusual for a writer to use actual life experiences in their stories. However, I do not believe I feel the same about her today as I did last Easter, and I am just concerned whether anyone associated with these events could tell I was this arrogant prig in the story."

"Arrogant prig? Hmm... Knowing Keynes is you, I could see you in him. However, you are not the only arrogant prig out and about. Among the arrogant prigs of the ton, you are at least a good one—rich, honorable, dutiful, and kind toward all in your care. I would not worry too much about it."

"But could others, say, Aunt Catherine, or Mrs. Collins—the parson's wife—see me in Keynes?"

"When was the last time Aunt Catherine cared about anybody but herself? She is too wrapped up in her own self-importance to observe others. I do not recall a Mrs. Collins. My feeling is the only person who might have some inkling is the elder sister, the confidante. The reason you could so easily pick yourself out was because you were the only other participant in the interactions between the two lovebirds."

Mr. Darcy rolled his eyes at hearing this moniker. He was serious when saying that his ardent feelings for Elizabeth Bennet were in the past.

Just then, the dinner gong sounded. The cousins separated to get dressed for dinner. The Colonel had his own room at Darcy House and sometimes stayed there instead of going back to the barracks or his father's house.

It was a pleasant dinner. After Ramsgate, Georgiana felt awkward when alone with her own brother. With their cousin in their midst, she was at ease. Mr. Darcy was jealous initially, but he had reconciled himself to it. It was a blessing there was at least one person from whom his sister did not shrink away.

After Georgiana's pleasing performance on the pianoforte, she excused herself for the evening, at which point, the two male cousins removed to the study to discuss the progress of their plan.

The Colonel began by telling Mr. Darcy about Miss Lydia's future husband.

"At the risk of sounding callous, I must ask, what if Midshipman Cieran survives? By the way, is he Catholic?"

"No, he is not a papist. It may be easier to find a parson than a priest to perform the wedding ceremony when the bride and groom have so blatantly anticipated their vows. If he lives, Miss Lydia will not repine marrying such a fine naval officer. He risked his own life pushing his half-comatose commander up the stairs away from the gunpowder kegs stored below them, which were about to explode."

"I see. I have obtained the approval of Miss Lydia's legal guardian, Mr. Gardiner. I went to meet him at his warehouse earlier today. He was absolutely delighted with our help to restore the Bennets' reputation. What did you promise as Miss Lydia's dowry?"

"I promised Cieran a thousand pounds."

"I told Mr. Gardiner I would bear the whole financial burden of ensuring Miss Lydia's marriage. He protested, of course, but to no avail. It is my fault alone that Wickham wreaks havoc wherever he goes, but this is his last time.

"I have also asked Nolan to apply for a common license as soon as Miss Lydia has agreed to this arrangement. He should be able to get it in a day or two, and then Miss Lydia and Midshipman Cieran may wed. I hope both of them will hold out until the necessary moment."

"You have done all you can to help her. If the babe appeared tomorrow, it would not be your fault."

The Colonel continued, "I have moved Cieran to Dr. Stowe's premises. If Miss Lydia would like to meet her future husband before the wedding, she should not risk her health going to the hospital. It is a disgrace our injured warriors must endure such filth while trying to recover, even on their home turf. My accommodations in Spain were far better by comparison. You, of course, will not mind the extra expense."

Mr. Darcy nodded and added, "If Wickham were around, and Miss Lydia insisted on marrying him, I assure you Wickham would demand no less than ten thousand pounds before he would wed her."

"You got off cheap then. If we have finished our business for the evening, I shall stay here for the night, and remain perhaps until I report for duty at Windsor to avoid mother's machinations. Will that suit you?"

"Of course! You are welcome to stay here as much as you like. You make Georgiana happy."

"I am developing such superb skill at picking husbands for girls! My mother would be envious. When it is Georgiana's turn, I shall be an expert. Goodnight, Darcy. May I borrow this novel? I only had time to skim parts of it. I would like to read it in some detail and see whether it will further jog my memory."

Mr. Darcy waved his hand in resignation and bade his cousin goodnight.

After the Colonel's departure for his chambers, Mr. Darcy refilled his glass of port, and sat by the fire, thinking over the meeting with Mr. Gardiner earlier that day.

℘℘

It had taken a matter of minutes for Mr. Nolan to find the business address of Gardiner Imports in Cheapside, and Mr. Darcy immediately went to see him without an appointment.

When Mr. Darcy called at his office, Mr. Gardiner had just received Lizzy's note that morning informing him that Mr. Darcy had arrived in town. The gentleman's visit had saved him the trouble of coming up with a plan to approach the haughty landowner from Derbyshire about that blackguard Wickham without betraying any association with Lydia.

Before he could determine the purpose of Mr. Darcy's visit, however, he needed to be cautious.

"Good afternoon, Mr. Darcy, I am Edward Gardiner, proprietor of Gardiner Imports. It is my honor to receive you at my place of business. How may I be of assistance?" asked Mr. Gardiner.

Contrary to Mr. Darcy's expectations, the brother of Mrs. Bennet appeared to be urbane and have genteel manners. He silently chastised himself for disdaining the man solely because of his social status. The way Mr. Keynes behaved in the story came to mind unbidden.

He took extra care to greet the businessman courteously. "Mr. Gardiner, I have some urgent business... about your family to discuss with you. Specifically, it is about your niece, Miss Lydia Bennet. May I have a few moments of your time?"

If there had ever been a time when one could knock Mr. Gardiner over with a feather, this would have been it. He stood there, staring and speechless. As a savvy tradesman, he had never believed he could have been so taken by surprise.

He closed the door of his office and invited Mr. Darcy to sit down while he poured a spot of brandy for himself and his guest.

"Mr. Darcy, allow me to offer you some liquid courage. You may not need it, but I do." He drained his glass in one go.

Mr. Darcy took a sip. It was exceptionally good French brandy. He complimented his host accordingly.

"Excellent cognac, Mr. Gardiner. Thank you."

"Being in trade has its perks, sir. I am pleased my humble offering is agreeable to you."

Mr. Gardiner paused, eyed his visitor a moment, and said, "From your demeanor, Mr. Darcy, I would venture you have information about my niece Lydia her family does not know. Please hold nothing back. I am eager to know all."

Mr. Darcy was impressed by the fellow's straightforward, yet civil, manner, which betrayed no sign Lydia was in trouble.

"Mr. Gardiner, I will be forthright. I have found your niece, Miss Lydia Bennet, at a boarding house previously owned by a former employee of mine. This woman had passed away in childbirth as Mrs. Wickham..."

Mr. Gardiner started at hearing Wickham's name but did not interrupt, even though he became more and more amazed as Mr. Darcy finished his account.

Mr. Gardiner let out the breath he was holding and said, "Lydia has always been intractable. From what you said, she has finally learned her lesson, but at what cost? At least she is safe. Words alone cannot express my gratitude, and the gratitude of her family for your generous help in locating her and finding a solution to save not only her reputation but also her sisters'. My other nieces do not deserve the sullying of their names because of a foolish act of a most foolish girl.

"I am Lydia's legal guardian, as her own father died of a broken heart five months ago."

It was Mr. Darcy's turn to be shocked by the news.

"I have no wish to speak ill of the dead, but my brother-in-law, always an indolent parent, learned his fault too late. He had a weak heart, which could not stand the strain of the loss of his youngest to the worst fate that could befall a young woman. Lydia, even now, is but sixteen years old.

"I, as Lydia's guardian, shall do my utmost to bring her back to the fold of the family. Her mother—you met her, I understand—has been a shadow of

180

her former self. She is very drastically changed—far calmer, and she devotes a great deal of time learning to fit into their local society, accompanying Mary to religious meetings with their devout neighbors. They are staying at a cottage near Clapham, you see."

Mr. Darcy knew of Clapham as an enclave of evangelicals and non-conformists. The great crusader for slave trade abolition, Mr. Wilberforce, was a resident.

He could not resist inquiring, "And the rest of her daughters?"

Mr. Gardiner was surprised by this inquiry. Why would Mr. Darcy ask about his other nieces, whom—according to Lizzy—this rich, prideful gentleman had disdained?

He answered dutifully, "Her sisters are doing well under the circumstances. They are with their mother except one, who is in London staying with a friend. In fact, this news about Lydia having been found and her reputation restored would help her eldest sister greatly. She is being courted by a worthy gentleman. It has been our worry he may give up his suit if he finds out about Lydia."

Mr. Darcy was again startled. In two days, he was to meet Bingley at the club. He was planning to tell Bingley his role in separating him from Miss Bennet. Even though he had sworn off interfering with his friends' love lives, he should at least warn Bingley his former angel might no longer be available should Bingley consider resuming his interest in courting Miss Bennet.

"Miss Bennet is serious about marrying this young man, then?" asked Darcy hesitantly.

On seeing the puzzled look on Mr. Gardiner, he hurried to explain, "Forgive me, Mr. Gardiner, for asking such an intrusive question. There is, in fact, a reason for my being so forward. I shall soon meet with my friend, Mr. Charles Bingley. He might wish to renew his acquaintance with Miss Bennet, whom he admired very much."

181

"You may as well tell your friend he need not bother to call on Jane. He raised expectations while he was in Hertfordshire, monopolizing Jane's dance cards, and showed every sign he favored my beautiful niece. Then he left suddenly, and his sister made it clear her brother would not be back because she was expecting a union between her brother and... oh, your own sister, Mr. Darcy."

Mr. Darcy wanted to deny this ridiculous claim, but Mr. Gardiner was not finished.

"Jane was here in London last winter and spring and called on Miss Bingley. Miss Bingley did not return the call until three weeks later, and she did it with obvious coldness. Jane was heartbroken. And then her dear papa died. She had been melancholy until only recently. She is finally smiling again even though she is worried about the exposure of Lydia's shame. She is certain Mr. Lytle—the young man courting her—will not blame her for her sister's folly, but Mrs. Lytle, the mother, a pious woman with strict morals, may not be so sanguine."

Mr. Darcy felt he ought to defend his friend. He said in a measured tone, "Bingley's decision to leave Hertfordshire was not entirely his own. He adopted advice which he believed to be true, but was mistaken." He stopped, feeling exceedingly ashamed of his part in breaking up his friend and Miss Bennet.

"Sir, I understand Mr. Bingley is still quite young. Let that be his excuse for such ungentlemanly behavior. Jane is far better off with Mr. Lytle. He is an entirely self-made man—he sailed to India as a very young man and built a stellar career with the East India Company. He came back to England to take charge of a very prosperous clock-making business left as a legacy from his father, a genuinely estimable gentleman. The business had several royal warrants. Whether he is to continue the family business or to become one of the youngest directors of the Company, his brilliant future is assured. The cottage where the girls and my sister are staying is on the grounds of the country house he purchased for his mother. He has been visiting his mother rather often these days."

"I see," muttered Mr. Darcy. He continued thoughtfully, "I shall not mention Miss Bennet when I see Bingley then. I must clarify, however, there is no understanding of any kind between Mr. Bingley and my sister. She is now almost seventeen, but she is not yet out. I will ask Bingley to tell his sisters to desist in such despicable gossip-mongering."

Reverting to his initial stoic attitude, he said, "Bingley will take care of his own personal affairs. Let us return to the urgent business at hand regarding Miss Lydia. Since her current plight was entirely caused by that reprobate, George Wickham, who was my late father's godson, I would like to take the responsibility to restore Miss Lydia's reputation, both financially and logistically."

It was Mr. Gardiner's turn to attempt a protest, but Mr. Darcy was not finished.

"Mr. Gardiner, Miss Lydia Bennet is only the most recent of a long string of victims of Wickham's debauchery. I deeply regret that I, who have known of his depraved conduct since we were at school, did nothing to stop him. My father and I simply cleaned up after him because all the victims I knew of were associated with my estate, and they requested the scandals to be hushed up. This time, it is different. He has hurt an innocent young gentlewoman and her family without a care. I must do all I can to compensate Miss Lydia for such an immense loss. My cousin, a colonel in the army, is, as we speak, scouting for an honorable officer—gravely injured and likely to die—to marry Miss Lydia, so she would be a respectable widow with a child. I believe sympathy for her misfortune will go a long way toward restoring her respectability."

Mr. Darcy turned solicitous again. "Mr. Gardiner, I do not want to appear insensitive and arrogant. You have a growing family, whereas I am master of a substantial estate with only my sister and myself to see to. It would please me immeasurably to be of use to the Bennet family, if nothing else, as a token of my respect for the late Mr. Bennet, whom I esteemed for his intellectual acumen."

"What is your plan to stop Wickham from harming more young woman?"

"Wickham is a gambler in addition to being a womanizer. He has accumulated substantial debts at the gaming table and from tradesmen. I have purchased a fair portion of these debts as a threat to keep him away from my family. I will now call in the debts. The Bow Street Runners in my employ will look for him to bring him to justice. Miss Lydia Bennet told me she had no wish to marry that scoundrel even though he is a free man after the death of both his wife and child two months ago."

"Heaven forbid! He impregnated two women at the same time!"

"Yes. I am certain Wickham is immoral—a thoroughly wicked man."

Mr. Gardiner thought for a moment and said, "Sir, I still believe you have taken on too much for yourself. I do not blame you for Wickham's crimes. However, I know about your estate, Pemberley, as my wife hails from Lambton, the village where your family has been the primary patron for hundreds of years. I cannot deny you are far more able to afford the financial burden of Lydia's hasty marriage. I shall do as you wish, but the entire Bennet and Gardiner families are in your debt. It is unlikely, but it is my greatest wish that someday I would be of use to you in some small way, just to repay a minute amount of the immense generosity you have shown the widow and her defenseless daughters."

Elizabeth's luminous eyes looking up at him with gratitude immediately came to Mr. Darcy's mind's eye. He shook his head slightly to chase away such an absurd thought, but it reminded him to tell Mr. Gardiner he wished the whole transaction to be kept strictly confidential since Wickham was well known to be associated with the Darcy family. In fact, the scoundrel often used the association for ill-gotten gains.

"You have my word, Mr. Darcy. However, it is virtually impossible for me to keep any secret from my clever wife. I shall not volunteer any information, but if she asks, I will have no choice but to tell her the truth. She, thankfully, is very discreet. I can guarantee what we have discussed today will go no further than my wife. Since the whole affair should be concluded within the next few days, I will not need to keep the secret about Lydia for long."

184

"What will you tell your nieces... and Mrs. Bennet?"

"I shall say the many investigators I have hired finally turned up solid leads to Lydia, who has already married. You may not know, but my second niece, Elizabeth, turned out to have some literary genius. She authored a novel that garnered not only critical acclaim but also quite a financial windfall. She has turned the entire proceeds over to me and charged me to spend all of it to search for Lydia. She has taken seriously, almost too much so, the responsibility of restoring her sister, if not her reputation, at least her person. Her attitude is partially my fault, as I called her the son her father never had, and she felt it keenly. She refused to keep any of the profits for herself, saying she published the story solely to raise funds to find Lydia. I finally persuaded her to purchase things for her sisters, a spinet pianoforte for one sister and drawing lessons for another.

"Oh, you must excuse me for forgetting you may remember my niece as one of your neighbors while residing in Hertfordshire. I have certainly heard about you through her, although her description of you bears scarcely any resemblance to you in person. I will correct her first impressions of you when the occasion arises.

"It is unlikely a busy gentleman like yourself would have time for novels, let alone talking about them to others. I am certain I can trust you not to disclose her authorship of the novel to others on the off chance that the novel is mentioned in your circles. Even the Prince Regent is rumored to like it. Being her uncle, I am inordinately proud of her achievement, but finding time to sit down to enjoy such an impressively thick tome has been impossible. Now that Lydia's affairs are near the end, I shall make time for it."

Mr. Darcy assured Mr. Gardiner of his secrecy concerning Miss Elizabeth Bennet's authorship, asked about Mrs. Gardiner as his neighbor in Derbyshire, and the two gentlemen parted on excellent terms.

By the fire in his study, Mr. Darcy could not help lifting the corner of his mouth. It was an amazing irony that Elizabeth's publishing her novel located her sister, but in a way she would never have foreseen. This realization somehow rendered his former animosity toward Elizabeth's exposing him in her book much less stinging.

Chapter 20

The next morning, the Colonel, Mr. Gardiner, and Mr. Darcy visited Miss Lydia Bennet at the boarding house. Lydia shrank from the sight of her uncle.

Mr. Gardiner, however, rushed up to Lydia and embraced her. Lydia leaned on her uncle's shoulder and cried copious tears.

"Lydia, my dear girl, do you not know what kind of heartache you have caused your family?"

Even though this came out gently, it was clearly a rebuke. Lydia cried almost hysterically after hearing it.

"Calm now, Lydia! You should not get too worked up in your present condition. It is important your marriage to Mr. Cieran takes place as soon as possible. The reputation of your whole family is at stake."

The old Lydia would have sneered that her uncle cared only about her sisters. However, the new Lydia understood the consequence of her own folly and quietly, though still somewhat reluctantly, conceded her uncle's point.

The entire party boarded the Darcy coach and was at Dr. Stowe's surgery in half an hour. Lydia was excited about meeting the man they had chosen for her: she would be the first to marry among her sisters, after all.

Just before she entered the house, she blurted out petulantly, "But... Mr. Cieran has not proposed!"

The three gentlemen looked at one another, shamefaced. Every young lady wanted to be proposed to—Mr. Darcy could not help thinking, *except for mine*—even when the young lady in question was a fallen one.

"Of course, my dear Lydia, Mr. Cieran will propose as soon as you two meet," said Mr. Gardiner reassuringly.

Mr. Cieran had had a restless night caused by a raging fever. He was lucid, however, when his betrothed entered his private chamber.

Fever had heightened the color of his cheeks, making him look youthful and his eyes exceptionally bright. Lydia showed her approval by clasping her hands in front of her to hide her round belly.

The Colonel did the introductions, and then Mr. Gardiner whispered in the midshipman's ear. After that, the three gentlemen left the room.

"My fair cailin, will you marry me?" asked the naval officer with a faint Irish lilt.

Lydia clasped her hands even more tightly together, and exclaimed, "Yes! Yes! My dear Mr. Cieran. But my name is Lydia, not Colleen. I do not mind. Even if you call me the silliest girl in all England like my papa, I will still marry you! I promise you I am no longer silly, and I will be the most faithful wife to you for as long as we both shall live!"

Mr. Cieran was charmed by Lydia's vivacious artlessness. He had agreed to marry a fallen woman for monetary advantages, but he rather liked this pretty, sprightly girl. The fever, however, was making him very uncomfortable, and his smile looked like a grimace.

Lydia took in his flushed face and said solicitously, "You are unwell. Let me wipe your forehead with cool water. Mrs. Wickham taught me how to do it when she was ill, and I made her feel better. I am your betrothed. My uncle will not mind."

She took a rag, rinsed it in cold water, and gently wiped the young man's face while softly singing a song she had learned from an Irish boarder:

"In a little town they call Belfast..."

The young man could not remember such tender care from a woman, not even his mother, who had to divide her attention among her eight children. The song 'Black velvet band' meant a great deal to him because singing that song had ameliorated his homesickness when he first went to sea at age twelve after his father, who lost his small landholding to consecutive poor harvests, died of a sudden illness, which plunged his large family into poverty.

Lulled by the sweet voice singing slightly out of tune, and the cool comfort of the soft rag on his head, he fell asleep. Lydia, however, remained diligent in her nursing duties.

The three gentlemen looked on at this touching scene with mixed feelings. Both Mr. Darcy and Mr. Gardiner were gladdened that Lydia seemed to have matured, but their attachment had the potential to be very short-lived. Either or both of the young couple could die very soon.

Just then, Dr. Stowe joined the gentlemen. He peered into the room and said, "Cieran is finally getting some rest. It will do him an immense amount of good. The young lady's care is just what he needs."

Mr. Gardiner asked, "Dr. Stowe, what is the prognosis for Cieran? How much longer will he live?"

The doctor sighed deeply and said, "It is in God's hands. He was not that badly burned. He had soaked himself quite thoroughly while dousing the powder kegs with water before rescuing his captain. However, the open sores on his burns appear to have become infected at the hospital. Now, he must fight the infection, and we can only hope for the best."

"What a waste of a good life! It should not be his time to shuffle off this mortal coil!" exclaimed Mr. Gardiner.

Mr. Darcy was impressed Mr. Gardiner could quote from Hamlet with ease, and the Colonel vaguely remembered the quote being from somewhere.

The doctor, however, felt more deeply about these words, as he saw too many of his patients die.

"Aptly quoted, Mr. Gardiner! Are you a lover of the Bard as well?" the doctor inquired.

"I enjoy his works very much, especially his plays, and of those, Hamlet in particular. My brother-in-law, the late Mr. Bennet, owned a first-edition Hamlet. It was one of no more than a handful in existence. Reading that copy, the one where Shakespeare's words first appeared to the public, got me thinking: why was dying described as 'shuffling off the mortal coil?' I have been pondering this lately, and so it came to me as fitting just now."

"Do you still have that first-edition copy, sir? I would love to see it," inquired the doctor.

"No, not for the past four months. A lady came and bought the entire collection at an extraordinarily good price. My second niece, who is now helping the lady curate her ever-growing book collection, told me the lady bought the entire collection mainly for the copy of Hamlet, which held special meaning for her when she was a girl. Apparently, her father had been forced to sell his collection, and she wanted it back because she could afford to. It has certainly benefited my fatherless nieces. Bennet's estate was entailed from the female line, and six defenseless women were left without a home at his death. Everything will be better now that Lydia... will soon be married," Mr. Gardiner checked himself before he accidentally exposed the family's shame.

Mr. Darcy, outwardly nonchalant, was in fact listening intently. He now had the full narrative of how the novel came to be.

The Colonel, always tactically focused, signaled to his cousin to leave. Mr. Darcy, however, ignored the signal because he wished to know more. The doctor obliged and continued with his inquiry. "That is indeed fortunate for your late brother's family. Is your second niece a bibliophile?"

"Yes, indeed. She volunteered to catalogue the book collection and regularly accompanies her friend to evaluate collections of interest. She went to see Mr. Charles Burney's collection, and through some fortuitous encounters, my niece is now expecting an offer of the most fantastic honor. Forgive me..."

By now, the Colonel felt it was past time to enact the next step in their plan. He discreetly pulled on his cousin's sleeve to guide him toward the door.

Mr. Darcy reluctantly followed his cousin. His heart clenched when he heard Elizabeth was to receive an offer. *What kind of offer could it be? Most fantastic honor? For a woman, especially one with Elizabeth's fine qualities, now thrust into contact with distinguished men, it is natural she would be snatched up. But she is still penniless, more so now than before. Who among the young bucks in Parliament could afford to ignore her lack of fortune and offer for her...*

"Darcy!"

Mr. Darcy jumped this time and looked embarrassed. The Colonel scolded, "Did you hear even one word of what I just said? You looked as if you were pondering a matter of life and death. What was it: to be or not to be?"

Mr. Darcy replied stoically, "You quoting 'Hamlet'? Lady Catherine would ask, 'What has this world become?' You know I have been eying Mr. Burney's collection. He has over 13,000 volumes, many very rare, and you dragged me from that titillating conversation." Mr. Darcy hated to prevaricate, but there was no untruth in his words.

"I know no such thing. By the way, if a tradesman could quote the Bard, why can't I? I, however, would not dare, in a thousand years, to question the Bard's choice of words. Mr. Gardiner is no ordinary tradesman!"

"So, Richard, what is the urgency?" asked Mr. Darcy, resignedly.

"Cieran may not last much longer. A common license will require him to be carried to Gardiner's church to be married, and the carriage ride could finish him off. A special license is more likely to make our plan successful. Now that I have drawn myself into this harebrained scheme, I do not want it to fail!"

"But the rules for obtaining a special license are against Cieran and Miss Lydia Bennet. It is unlikely they will get one."

"Cousin Darcy, Master of Pemberley! Rules are not made for the privileged with impeccable connections. Our dear Uncle Dundas is a close friend of his

Grace the Archbishop. You are Uncle's favorite nephew. He will not refuse to speak to his Grace on your behalf, especially if you invite him to hunt at Pemberley whenever he pleases."

"He already has that invitation, but I see what you mean. I could say Cieran is a war hero, and his dying wish is to marry his betrothed. Being a former naval captain himself, he has a soft spot for the Royal Navy. You should come too, as you are a *bona fide* war hero, and you have your war injuries to prove it."

"And my medals too. Let's take our leave of these gentlemen and be on our way. If we catch Uncle before he leaves for the club, we may have the license in hand by tomorrow."

When they joined the others again, there was a third gentleman, a naval officer, among them. He turned out to be Commander Wilkes, whom Midshipman Cieran had saved from certain death. Cieran had not only saved him but also the ship. The captain had gone to the Admiralty to petition for Cieran's promotion and now came to pin the lieutenant insignia on Cieran's uniform.

Mr. Darcy and the Colonel did not stay to see the ceremony. The Colonel was pleased that one of Cieran's conditions to marry Lydia Bennet was fulfilled without his lifting a finger.

By evening, Mr. Darcy and the Colonel had accomplished their mission. The Archbishop did not ask a single question before signing the special license Lord Dundas handed him.

The two cousins had a celebratory toast after dinner. The Colonel was quite exuberant because he relished triumph, but Mr. Darcy seemed pensive. When questioned, he claimed to be wondering about the vast privilege he enjoyed just by being master of Pemberley. The Colonel, not prone to introspection, left his moody cousin be.

Mr. Darcy was still mulling over what Mr. Gardiner meant when he said Elizabeth would soon receive an incredible honor. He wished he had stayed just a few minutes longer to find out what that honor would be. Not knowing put him in a foul mood. His head said whatever offer she was to receive should not be his concern, but his traitorous heart ached when he thought someone else would succeed where he had failed so miserably. He made up his mind to return to Pemberley the following week when the Colonel began his equerry duties at Windsor.

The next morning at eleven o'clock, a small group gathered in Lieutenant Cieran's room for his marriage to Miss Lydia Bennet.

Mr. Gardiner walked the bride to the Lieutenant's bed, where his commander would stand up with him; the parson from Mr. Gardiner's parish officiated. Miss Stowe, the doctor's spinster sister, stood up with the bride, and it was done.

Both bride and groom were appropriately radiant—Lieutenant Cieran because of fever, and the new Mrs. Cieran because of that particular bloom pregnant women often possess.

After the wedding, Lydia stayed in the sickroom with her new husband. The doctor was impressed by the young woman's diligence in taking care of her severely injured husband, but saddened that the groom's condition continued to worsen.

Three days later, Lydia gave birth to a healthy baby boy, named Daniel Aidan Cieran for his legal father, but he would be called Aidan. Lieutenant Cieran was happy his legacy would continue in his son, even though the fiercely crying babe was not his blood. Commander Wilkes promised to stand as godfather and see to the proper upbringing of the child. There was hope that perhaps this good news would give him further will to fight the fever. Unfortunately, the sepsis causing the fever won, and a week after his son was born, he breathed his last, with both his wife and son crying.

Lydia was inconsolable. She had somehow convinced herself Lieutenant Cieran was the love of her life and true father to her child. Mr. Gardiner felt compelled to take her and his new grandnephew back to his home on Gracechurch Street instead of sending them back to the boarding house, which had been his original intention until he had had sufficient time to coach Lydia on the story she must tell of her discovery.

Mrs. Gardiner was shocked when her husband told her his searchers had found Lydia and her newborn son. Her husband had died in the service of His Majesty as a lieutenant in the Royal Navy, and she preferred to return to her own family instead of going to her late husband's family in Ireland.

Mrs. Gardiner had many questions for her niece. However, seeing Lydia was genuinely distressed about her husband's recent death, Mrs. Gardiner decided to discover the truth from her husband later. For now, she was both relieved and happy her two favorite nieces' future was safe with the return of their lost sister as a widow with a legitimate child.

Chapter 21

Mr. Darcy had another night of fitful sleep, thinking about Elizabeth marrying another. He was in poor humor when he entered the breakfast parlor. His cousin was already at the table, enjoying a hearty meal, but he had no appetite.

He noticed the Colonel wearing a large smirk and eyeing him with mischief.

The evening before, the Colonel had received an urgent summons from his mother. He dutifully went and was 'requested' by his mother to be her escort to the first evening soiree at the Trumbull residence. Having heard so much about the rich widow, the Colonel accompanied her without complaint.

"Good morning, Darcy! I met your Miss Elizabeth Bennet last evening at Mrs. Trumbull's soiree!"

Mr. Darcy visibly started when he heard his cousin's proclamation. She had tortured him through the night, and tortured him still, but he would resist her relentless hold on him. He forced down his emotions and said nonchalantly, "Yes? How did it go? Did she tell you she had met you before?"

The Colonel was intently watching Darcy's reaction to this piece of intelligence, and he did not miss the initial shock. He decided to play with his stoic cousin a little.

"I could not get within three feet of her. So many distinguished men from government crowded around the vivacious Miss Bennet that one would have mistaken her to be the heiress! I also sensed she was avoiding me."

Mr. Darcy's remained stoic, but his strained voice betrayed his inner turmoil when he said, "Indeed."

That was the entire response for the Colonel to decipher, and decipher he did. He sometimes felt that he knew Darcy's heart and mind better than his own.

"You know well enough you cannot hide from me. I can tell she is still very important to you. Out with it! Perhaps I could help before I disappear into the nadir of Windsor Castle."

"You cannot help, Richard. Only time will help. Elizabeth Bennet is the only woman I have ever... who has ever turned my head—the same head that says I am over her. I will forget her. Too much water has passed under the bridge and, as cliché as it sounds, it describes how I feel."

"As stubborn as ever! You should know I cornered her in the hall, so to speak, when she was sneaking away after spotting me making my way toward her. I, of course, did not allow it. She is a well-mannered young lady. She asked about my battlefield injuries and my trip back from the Continent. Apparently, she visited Pemberley, and Reynolds told her about your going to Spain to rescue me."

"I should talk to Mrs. Reynolds about discretion."

"Darcy! Don't be an ass! Reynolds is the height of discretion and loyalty. Please do not embarrass and humiliate the dear old lady. Miss Bennet was mindful to tell me Reynolds mistook her as an intimate friend of the Darcy family and volunteered the information."

"And of course, Miss Bennet failed to correct the wrong impression she conveyed."

"What has come over you, Darcy? You proposed to Miss Bennet. If she had accepted you, Reynolds could have been speaking with the mistress of Pemberley!"

"Ah, there lies the catch. She did not accept the proposal. In fact, she said I would be the last man she could be prevailed on to marry. She should never have gone to Pemberley."

"Still bitter about the rejection, I see. I agree she was excessively harsh. I shall not bother you further about the woman who so vexes you. She, on the other hand, was gracious and asked about you."

"What did you say?"

"Why do you want to know?"

"She knows far more about me than I do her. It is only fair I know what you told her."

"The logic is not so clear to me: you did not want her to know about you, and now you want to know about her because she knows about you. My headache returns just thinking about this tangled mess of your feelings. Have mercy! I am but a poor soldier!"

The Colonel watched his cousin closely during this exchange and understood for the first time how much Miss Elizabeth Bennet meant to the outwardly stoic but inwardly passionate master of Pemberley.

"I told Miss Bennet you and I experienced some harrowing events during the retreat to Portugal."

"What was her reaction?"

"She seemed thoughtful for a long moment, and then expressed her warm regards for our successful return to England."

Mr. Darcy stared ahead, but his face was solemn.

"You do not want to know anything else about the gathering? Miss Bennet's numerous admirers? The heiress herself?"

Mr. Darcy winced ever so slightly when he heard the second question. He replied woodenly, "Miss Elizabeth Bennet is an accomplished and beautiful woman, inside and out. I am heartened to find out I did not waste my affection on a nonentity. I wish her felicity in matrimony with a worthy gentleman. She will choose well. As for Mrs. Trumbull, she is unknown to me. What she does with her life is none of my business. When will you begin your equerry duty?" Darcy changed the topic suddenly.

The Colonel saw exactly what was going on—his cousin was finished with Miss Bennet. He, however, would not give up so easily. He had to put in one last word.

"Darcy, beginning tomorrow, I need to be at Whitehall to be drilled for Court etiquette. Today is the last day you will see my bonny face for a long while. Eventually I will be assigned a two-week on, two-week off schedule to tend to every need of our dear monarch. Before I leave tomorrow morning, I must get this into your thick skull: you are not over Miss Bennet, no matter how you convince yourself. I suggest you go over to the Trumbull residence and confront your own demons. It is possible when coming face-to-face again with Miss Bennet, you may decide nothing of your former... love remains, and you will know it was an experience in your past and move on with your life without her. Otherwise, knowing you, you would always wonder, and turn into a bitter, sour man before your old age."

The Colonel half expected Darcy to just ignore his advice and remain glum. However, his cousin's face relaxed to show a pensive but no longer sullen expression. Further, he rejoined with a hint of lightheartedness, "You have indeed become a matchmaker par excellence. More than just making the introductions, you also give advice to imbeciles lost in the matters of the heart. Let us talk in my study."

Once inside the completely private sanctuary, he continued in a detached voice, "I convinced myself I should have gotten over her rejection. After what I saw on the Continent, my humiliation at the hand of a country maiden seems insignificant. However, the mere mention of Elizabeth receiving a highly coveted offer has made me lose sleep for the past few nights. I must concede that the feelings and ardent love I could not then repress, which led to my impulsive proposal, have not at all diminished. I almost drove myself insane trying to figure out who might have won her hand. And then you confirmed for me what I have been dreading—Elizabeth was surrounded by admirers. I apologize for being so short with you just now, Richard. I am a novice in the land of love, and it shows."

The Colonel was heartened to hear such a fervent confession from his very private cousin. He jumped up and said, "There is no time like the present. Carpe diem! Let's go to the Trumbull residence this minute to snatch back your love."

Mr. Darcy laughed out loud at the enthusiasm of the Colonel.

"You remember the Bard quotes and Latin phrases from your schooling but forget common civility. It is not yet polite calling hours, and the ladies are also probably not available for callers if they had a late gathering last night. Moreover, I am not convinced it is up to me to reclaim 'my love' after what she said—in no uncertain terms—she would never marry me. If Elizabeth has found someone she favors, I was serious about wishing her joy in matrimony. What you said about 'facing my own demons' is more to the point. I need to know once and for all that—regardless of how I feel—I must submit to the lady's choice."

It finally dawned on the Colonel that Darcy's continuous denial of his deep feelings toward Miss Bennet was a desperate measure to protect his still-broken heart. Knowing full well that his stubborn cousin would not be receptive to this new understanding, he said instead, "You may be right, but then you may be wrong. However, I feel a certain premonition that this matter needs to be settled as soon as possible. I often have feelings like this before major battles."

"Tell me about the heiress. If I am going to call on her, perhaps I should know what, or whom, to expect."

"If there was a crowd around Miss Bennet, there was a mob around Mrs. Trumbull. Those men were shameless, pushing one another to jostle for the best position. From what I could overhear, they were all complimenting her on her novel, even though she has never admitted to being the authoress. No one could have known those obsequious fools were, in fact, august gentlemen, among whom were up-and-coming stars of Parliament. Other than that, Mrs. Trumbull appeared to be quite delectable—ah, was that too indelicate? She is more handsome than I remember. Her only fault is she is too clever for the likes of me. If you decide to give up Miss Bennet, Mrs. Trumbull may be an adequate substitute. They both possess an air of...

playful impertinence, and Mrs. Trumbull possesses an immense fortune besides."

"I do not understand the concept of substitution in love. If I pursued Mrs. Trumbull, it would be for her alone. However, her fortune precludes any potential interest from me. Any lady that wealthy must prefer to have her own way all the time."

"You are no beggar, and you also like to have your own way all the time—and usually get it. But I see your point. Too many people wanting their own way usually leads to war. Ask Boney."

Mr. Ford, the butler, knocked on the door. The carriage to take the master to his club was waiting.

"I almost forgot. I am meeting Bingley today at the club. What are your plans?" asked Mr. Darcy.

"I shall spend some time with my other cousin. She should be in the breakfast parlor by now. Then I shall put my affairs in order before going off to serve the King."

The two cousins went to the breakfast parlor together. Miss Darcy was indeed at the table with the all too familiar novel open next to her eggs and kippers.

Mr. Darcy chatted with his sister for a few minutes before leaving to see Mr. Bingley. He did not know what to expect. His friend's letters had been even more indecipherable than before—or could it be he had less patience now for Bingley's frivolous goings-on?

Chapter 22

Mr. Bingley greeted Darcy enthusiastically, which reminded Mr. Darcy why Bingley had been such a constant companion for the last five years: his friend's cheerfulness always brought a smile to his face.

"Darcy! So good to see you back in England!"

"Bingley, you look well. I must apologize again for abruptly canceling your visit to Pemberley last summer."

"Ah, yes, that. We were disappointed, of course. A visit to Pemberley is always a treat, especially in the summer. Caroline was inconsolable about having to ride past Pemberley without entering, but I understood and sympathized with the urgency of your journey. Having only arrived in town two days ago, I have not yet congratulated the Colonel on his miraculous recovery. Fellows here filled me in on his hero's welcome. I salute you for rescuing the Colonel and bringing him safely home!"

"Thank you, Bingley. It was a chilling sight—the battlefield, an endless sea of men, standing ready to kill one another; it truly was a life-changing experience. The arduous retreat to Portugal gave me a taste of what our soldiers must go through because of that mad man Bonaparte. But how has life been treating you in my absence?"

"Caroline has been complaining bitterly that, without you here, life has been too dull for her liking. She misses the house parties, hunts, balls and such. To her, my other friends are simply not good enough. We spent the summer in the north, traveled to Weymouth, and then to Bath. We had to return to Scarborough because my aunt fell ill and passed away. I had to put her affairs in order, thus the delay in coming back to town. Caroline complained incessantly we would miss the beginning of the season. She was especially incensed with me after she heard you had returned, and she was convinced you were attending balls and parties without us." Bingley laughed a little, embarrassed by his sister's antics.

"My condolences on your aunt's passing," said Mr. Darcy, which Mr. Bingley acknowledged with a nod. Mr. Darcy continued, "I have been extremely busy due to my long absence. In fact, I shall go back to Pemberley after my annual visit to my aunt, Lady Catherine. I am afraid I shall not be socializing for the foreseeable future."

"Oh, Caroline will surely be disappointed. We shall have to fend for ourselves."

Mr. Darcy did not respond. Somehow, it sounded absurd to him that their entire conversation had so far centered on what Miss Bingley wanted.

Has it always been this way?

Hearing no response, Mr. Bingley lowered his voice and said almost conspiratorially, "Caroline has been urging me to pursue Mrs. Trumbull. She said Mrs. Trumbull was from a distinguished Anglo-Welsh family, and that should overcome her connection to trade through her late husband. I have no desire to follow her dictate this once. From what I know, Mrs. Trumbull is a brunette, and she is at least eight years older than I. What do you think?"

Mr. Darcy raised one corner of his mouth and asked, "You are not giving up your blonde infatuation for a million pounds?"

Mr. Bingley's eyes bulged on hearing the sum and exclaimed, "So much? Fellows here said half a million." He pondered for a moment and replied, "What is half a million pounds more than what one already cannot spend?

My inclination is 'no.' I must love my wife. I have never loved a brunette, and so it would be a significant risk for me to pursue a brunette."

Mr. Darcy looked at Mr. Bingley intently for a long moment, making his friend squirm. No one could say Mr. Bingley had no principles. Was he frivolous? Yes! Easily swayed? Yes! But if it concerned the color of his love's hair? Non-negotiable!

"What?" Mr. Bingley asked defensively. "I love blondes. I own it without disguise."

"Just as well. From what I have heard, there is no shortage of men chasing Mrs. Trumbull, or rather, her large fortune. Since both of us are disinterested in winning the lady's hand, perhaps you do not mind paying a call tomorrow? I am curious about all the fuss."

"You? Curious about things like this? Your experience on the Continent must have truly altered you. You used to stay as far away as possible from the alleged heiresses of the ton."

Mr. Darcy knew he could not hide his true intention of the visit if Mr. Bingley went with him. He said, hesitantly, "The Colonel told me he had seen Miss Elizabeth Bennet at a gathering there. She is a close friend of Mrs. Trumbull. I thought I would pay my respects when I call. I did not tell you, but last Easter, she was in Kent visiting her cousin while I was visiting my aunt, and we met a few times at my aunt's house. Lady Catherine was fond of inviting the vicar's family to Rosings."

Mr. Bingley looked lost for a moment but soon said, "The Bennet family! I have almost forgotten about them. It has been more than a year since we last saw them at the Netherfield ball. Caroline told me some terrible scandal befell the family, and they were forced to leave their home. What a pity!" Mr. Bingley shook his head in sympathy. He returned to his cheerful demeanor only a moment later. "I would be pleased to see Miss Elizabeth Bennet again."

"How did Miss Bingley hear of their scandal? Did you not say your family had been gallivanting continuously around the country, far away from

Hertfordshire, until a few days ago?" Mr. Darcy wrinkled his brows in puzzlement.

"Gallivanting! I cannot deny we sought pleasures everywhere we went. I believe Caroline has spies all over. If your retainers were not completely loyal to you, she would know your every move as well."

Mr. Bingley laughed on seeing Mr. Darcy's startled look. He said, "Darcy, for someone as clever as you, you can be quite obtuse when it comes to women."

Mr. Darcy immediately retorted, "What do you mean? A gentleman should never distrust... the sister of a close friend."

Mr. Bingley's smile grew bigger, very pleased that he was cleverer than his friend.

"Thank you for your faith in me and my ability to restrain my sister. After my father's death, my mother indulged Caroline terribly. I was away at school and knew nothing of the person my younger sister had grown into. After my mother's passing, to keep the peace, I let her have her way. You know how I detest confrontation. For important matters such as my best friend's well-being, I exert my authority and speak in the language she understands. If she does anything untoward, I will be on your side, and I will drastically reduce her pin money, which is from the interest of her dowry. My father's will allows me to exercise that right as needed. He must have seen what Caroline was becoming. The ton, the people she cares about most, will ridicule her. My father was an astute tradesman, and I learned at his knees from as far back as I can remember. He took me with him to many business meetings. Once I began school, my mother insisted I should become a gentleman and should associate myself with gentlemen's sons instead of turning into another tradesman. My father hated confrontation as I do, but he agreed with my mother on this point. So here I am, trying to be a gentleman."

Mr. Darcy was astounded by Mr. Bingley's frank confession. He asked, somewhat bewildered, "Bingley, we have been friends these past six years. Why did we never discuss this?"

"The topic never came up. You and I have a relaxed sort of friendship—remember all those Sunday afternoons when we did absolutely nothing! You never pry or argue except with Miss Elizabeth Bennet. When you were on the Continent, I had incessant complaints from Caroline about your 'desertion.'"

Mr. Darcy was again appalled by a claim of intimacy which did not exist.

Mr. Bingley clarified. "Do not be alarmed, Darcy. I am deaf to her dissatisfaction. Enough is enough, that's what I have decided. I am five-and-twenty. Caroline is younger by just one year. She should have married long ago and been off my hands, but she has this pig-headed notion you would marry her someday. Now she will have to fend for herself."

This was disturbing for Mr. Darcy. First, though, he needed to know whether Mr. Bingley truly meant what he said. He remembered clearly how at Netherfield, Bingley told Mrs. Bennet that whatever he did was done in a hurry—if he were to quit Netherfield, he would be off in five minutes. Was his friend in earnest this time, or would he change his mind in five minutes?

He asked skeptically, "Can you follow through with your resolve? Our entire conversation has centered on Miss Bingley—and we have not seen each other for more than a year!"

"I freely admit to making snap decisions. This time I am serious. She has so bothered me lately that she is on my mind constantly. You always make me see things clearly, and when you were away, everything seemed muddled."

Mr. Darcy was feeling more and more uneasy about his friend's state of mind. He had thought this trait endearing and was always willing to help one he treated as a younger brother. Now he felt his own knees had replaced those of Bingley's father.

This was a good segue into what he wanted to know. He asked, "Bingley, when you quitted Netherfield, had Miss Bingley already tried to persuade you not to return after your trip to town, or did you hear from both Miss Bingley and me at the same time?"

"That was more than a year ago. Let me remember..." Mr. Bingley placed a finger on his chin and thought for a minute. "Ah, Caroline *ordered* me to stay in London. Persuasion is not her style. Of course, I resisted. I like to maintain the peace, but it does not mean I would throw my hands up and surrender every time. Besides, the matter was of some importance to me. I loved to gaze at Miss Bennet's angelic face, framed by her silky golden hair. For a brief time, I considered offering for her because I believed my life would be tranquil having such a serene beauty by my side. I also planned to delegate the problem of Caroline to my would-be new sister. Miss Elizabeth Bennet could have vanquished Caroline's ridiculous nastiness with a few choice words."

The corner of Mr. Darcy's mouth lifted at the image of Miss Bingley cowering before Elizabeth. He returned to his serious mien, however, when his own culpability in separating Bingley and Miss Bennet needed to be addressed. He had not lied when he told Bingley he believed Miss Jane Bennet's heart had not been touched by Bingley's enthusiastic gazing. However, he now knew his perception was faulty, and Bingley's desertion had broken her heart.

"Bingley, if I had not intervened with my fool-hardy suggestion, would you have offered her marriage?"

Mr. Bingley again stopped for a moment before answering, "Possibly... to spite Caroline. I thank you for having put some sense into me. Spiting your impudent sister should not be the basis for such an important commitment as marriage. Even now, a year later, I do not feel ready to marry and settle down. My circle of friends is ever expanding. I enjoy the travels and pleasures of these engagements, despite Caroline looking down on my friends. According to her, their estates are nothing to Pemberley. No, having a wife and children would not do. They are incompatible with my life at present."

After what he witnessed on the Continent—men years younger than Bingley suffering and dying from injuries and sickness, all because they answered the call of duty to their countries—Bingley's pleasure-seeking life seemed hedonistic and aimless. He hoped and prayed his friend would not soon squander his inherited fortune, even without Miss Bingley's help.

"What? You disapprove? You are wearing a deep frown," Bingley asked with curiosity. "Don't worry. Now that you are back, I shall not be sowing my wild oats as much. My engagements have been rather innocent— hunting, fox hound racing, occasional visits to what you would consider disreputable establishments. I have not taken to gambling other than card games with friends. My father's legacy is intact, if that is what you worry about."

Mr. Darcy looked him in the eye and said solemnly, "Bingley, you are your own man. How you live your life is entirely of your own choosing. I, of course, would help in whatever way I can if you ask. I shall, however, not interfere with your life from now on."

"Why so solemn, man? At least with me, you did not always look like someone had stolen your favorite puppy. Your experience on the Continent has indeed changed you!"

"Do you think so? I have felt a shift within me. It is impossible not to have been affected by what I saw and experienced."

"To own the truth, you have always been serious. You have never sown a single wild oat that I know of. My recent change in behavior must have shocked you. Sometimes I wonder if this life of a gentleman suits me. I was an excellent student. I can apply myself, but I feel anchorless now that I have no estate to learn to manage, and no business to attend to—God forbid if Caroline heard this." Mr. Bingley sighed and took on a serious mien, quite different from his carefree self.

"I have indeed never lived an epicurean lifestyle. My early inheritance of Pemberley killed my plan of freer living on my grand tour in Portugal or even North Africa.

"I am not judging you by any means. You have not touched your father's inheritance. You are not a wastrel. As you so astutely observed, I need time to adjust my thinking back to peacetime life here in England after almost six months under threat of war.

"If you have no engagements this evening, would you come to supper at my house? My cousin, the Colonel, will leave for his new assignment at Court tomorrow. He would enjoy someone besides me for a pleasant evening. However, I must request that you come alone without your sisters."

"Thank you, Darcy. I would like to come. Caroline was extremely unhappy that I was to meet you here at the club. By the way, she had designs on your person had we stayed at Pemberley last summer, but I thwarted her plans and warned her so she understood. I have my own eyes and ears." Bingley smiled mischievously.

"I see," was all Mr. Darcy said.

Chapter 23

Mr. Darcy arrived at his town house, deep in thought about the encounter with Bingley. He concluded he should be cautious of both Bingley siblings. Bingley's guilelessness, instead of being whimsical and charming, could simply be a sign of his immaturity that could be unpredictable and cause pain to others.

Bingley, however, had become a dear friend, whose well-being he cared deeply about. With proper guidance, he believed Bingley would, in time, steer himself toward maturity.

While he was thus ruminating, he sensed a swift movement toward him. Seeing a lady was about to collide with him, he was horrified until he saw the lady was Miss Bingley. He stepped away just enough to grab Miss Bingley's elbows to steady her.

Miss Bingley gripped his forearms but could not move any closer. Mr. Darcy was never so thankful he was nimble-footed through years of fencing practice. To an onlooker, it would appear they were doing some strange sort of dance in front of his house. Peculiar? Yes. A compromise? Hardly.

Through the years, he had become an expert in avoiding compromising situations. No one, however, had been as blatant—attempting to get into his arms in broad daylight in the middle of a street.

Miss Bingley was crying hysterically and forgot the basic decorum of a lady. She practically screamed, "Mr. Darcy, how could you be so hardhearted and ungentlemanly? I need help and you refuse to give it!"

This ruckus had to stop. Mr. Darcy said sternly, "If you do not understand me, you must understand your brother."

Miss Bingley stopped immediately and released Mr. Darcy's arms, taken aback that Mr. Darcy would know of her brother's threat.

"Could you truly believe me capable of treachery? I came to visit you and Miss Darcy, but your knocker was down. When I saw you returning, I hurried to greet you, but tripped and would have fallen had you not been so quick to help me back up."

By then, a Darcy footman and the Colonel had come out to watch the commotion.

Mr. Darcy asked his footman, "Stevens, has this lady tried to gain entry into the house?"

Stevens answered, "Yes, Mr. Darcy. Several times. She even threatened to dismiss me without reference when she became mistress here." Stevens was a third-generation retainer of the Darcy family. Like all Darcy's upstairs staff, he was literate and well-spoken.

The Colonel chimed in, "I watched her walking back and forth between this door and the carriage over there for at least an hour, but I did not recognize her." He then narrowed his one eye, took a long look at Miss Bingley and exclaimed dramatically, "No wonder! Her face has become so peaked it bears little semblance to the pretty... ish young lady I had seen with Bingley years ago."

Mr. Darcy signaled Stevens to escort Miss Bingley to her carriage. He turned his back without another word, formally cutting her, and went into his house with the Colonel.

"Attempting a compromise on the street! Did she not know a lady may have an accidental fall, and the good Samaritan gentleman who helps her is not obligated to marry her?"

"I have been clear about my lack of interest in her through the years. Any clearer would have made me a brute...." Mr. Darcy stopped in mid-sentence.

Was I kinder toward Miss Bingley than Elizabeth, who certainly regarded me as rude? Was I equally rude to both ladies, but Elizabeth did not tolerate my disdainful behavior, whereas Miss Bingley would accept anything to achieve her goal of becoming mistress of Pemberley?

Mr. Darcy furrowed his brows and looked completely discombobulated.

"A brute? Yes, Darcy, I can see that. Have you just realized your manners in public could be seen as uncivil? You get away with it because you are the master of Pemberley. Those of great wealth are treated with undeserved courtesy, unlike we mere mortals. Go on!" prompted the Colonel impatiently.

Mr. Darcy ignored the Colonel's ribbing and continued, "I thought she would respect my friendship with her brother and attempt nothing untoward. Bingley told me at the club she had planned to carry out some nefarious scheme if she had stayed at Pemberley last summer. My having hurried away to extricate you thwarted her design. Something has changed. Perhaps she now feels the pressure of age. She is four-and-twenty."

"Practically on the shelf! I can see why she is desperate. Scheming to compromise you in front of your own home? What a hussy!"

"Bingley will come for supper tonight. I shall confer with him on how to prevent future incidents like this. He holds the purse-strings, and he is on my side."

Promptly at eight o'clock, Mr. Bingley arrived. He greeted the cousins jovially.

"I heard there was a lot of drama here this afternoon. My sister threw a vase at me when I told her I was coming here for supper. My coachman clued me in to the cause of her bad mood: earlier today he witnessed the two of you in a strange dance. I know you hate dancing. And in the street? I am intrigued!" Mr. Bingley ended with a chuckle.

"Bingley! That was no laughing matter. I thank you for warning me about Miss Bingley's dishonorable intentions, which prompted me to be on guard when I saw her. What can you do to stop her from trying again?"

"There is no question in my mind that she will try again. Caroline is persistent if nothing else. What exactly did you do to thwart her scheme?"

"I held her at arm's length. She could not get close enough to claim a compromise. I also told her she ought to understand your language."

"That explains why she was so angry at me. I shall meet with my solicitor tomorrow and present her with her dowry to spend as she pleases. I no longer want to supplement her outrageous spending. Darcy, thank you for providing me with a reason. She has been extremely difficult, especially with her nagging."

The Colonel, who had been watching the exchange with a smirk, interjected, "Is it a punishment when you give her the fortune to do even more mischief? What if she uses her funds to hire ruffians to kidnap Darcy and coerce him into marrying her?"

"Hmm..." Bingley rubbed his chin, trying to think of a solution. "You have a point. Caroline is devious enough that I would not rule out her trying something like that."

"Good God!" exclaimed Darcy. "She is evil incarnate if she is capable of such criminal acts. I thought you could take away her pin money altogether if she misbehaved!"

"You are right, of course, Darcy, but I have always meant it as a deterrent. Do you think I should exercise that power? It sounds awfully cruel," said Bingley meekly.

"I have made a promise to myself to never again interfere with your personal life. Business-related issues? Yes, but that is all. To protect myself from Miss Bingley, I have already cut her from my circle of acquaintances. I may have to distance myself from you as well if you cannot control your sister."

The Colonel chimed in again, "What I see, as one not involved in the situation—although Darcy's well-being is my own—you have two viable options to preserve your friendship with Darcy."

Mr. Darcy was grateful he would have his cousin's counsel more regularly now that he was back in the country for good.

Mr. Bingley's face lit up instantly. Without Darcy's help and guidance, he had been out of sorts. His sister's persistent irritation thus became almost too much to endure.

"You could marry Miss Bingley off..." Mr. Bingley immediately looked over at Mr. Darcy, who rolled his eyes.

"Not to Darcy! Are you daft?" Mr. Bingley looked appropriately chastened at this reprimand. Mr. Darcy could not help lifting the corner of his mouth momentarily. His cousin, with one eye and lingering battle injuries, could intimidate a grown man like Bingley without even meaning to.

The Colonel softened his voice to continue. "There is always a horde of men, young and not so young, who need heiresses for wives. Your connection to trade is an encumbrance, but negotiable. Your sister's disposition could be more of a hindrance. A man desperate enough, however, could be persuaded to accept both conditions. Who knows, this man may even take your sister in hand."

"But Caroline will not agree. She is of age. I cannot force her to marry where she does not wish," protested Mr. Bingley.

"That is why you need the second option," quipped Mr. Darcy. He had begun to see where his cousin's thinking was leading.

Mr. Bingley looked from one cousin to the other. He sighed and said wistfully, "I wish I had a cousin, or better yet, a brother." Again, he looked at Mr. Darcy. "You two seem to talk to each other without speaking."

The Colonel eyed Bingley suspiciously, "Give up any ludicrous thoughts! Darcy will never be your brother."

Mr. Darcy was startled to hear that. *What is Bingley about?* He had to admit to himself that, when he was walking away from the Hunsford parsonage after his disastrous, impulsive proposal to Elizabeth, it had crossed his mind that Bingley and he would become brothers if he brought Bingley and Miss Bennet together again, thus changing Elizabeth's rejection of his proposal to acceptance. Now, though, it seemed impossible. Miss Bennet had a suitor.

If the Colonel had known that particular bit of history, Bingley's allusion would not have appeared as baseless as the Colonel thought.

Bingley put up both hands and shook his head. "Of course not. Colonel, you can read minds!"

"I wager I can read your soul with both eyes. As it is, reading your mind will do. Darcy, will you tell Bingley his second option?"

Mr. Darcy thought for a moment. He said, "The second option is for you to remove a portion of Miss Bingley's pin money, say, a quarter of it, because of the infraction she committed against the rules you have set. You will finally convince her you meant what you said. Who knows? She may at last be persuaded to look more seriously at the first option because if she dares try compromising me again, you will cut her off entirely, and I will make sure society does as well."

"Bravo! Your version differs from mine only in the amount of money taken. I would remove half, at least. Make it hurt! She will come around. Bingley, this will succeed only if you do not succumb to her nagging and reinstate the portion taken away or, worse still, augment it just because she nags you further."

"Oh, no, no. I shall be firm. Thank you both for this ingenious scheme. I shall remove a third of her pin money, the average between your two suggestions."

The two cousins exchanged glances, and Mr. Darcy gave a slight nod, indicating he would give Bingley the benefit of the doubt.

Before the evening was over, it was decided that Mr. Darcy and Mr. Bingley would call on Mrs. Trumbull the next day, while the Colonel reported for equerry training.

Chapter 24

The next day, true to his word, Mr. Bingley went to his solicitor to make the needed arrangements for his sister's pin money, but he reduced the amount by just thirty pounds.

He was complaining to Mr. Darcy about how he dreaded confronting his sister when the Colonel walked in.

"Oh, good! You have not left. I will join you when you call on Mrs. Trumbull. It seems too delicious to miss: the scion of one of the richest landed families in the kingdom meeting the richest heiress of exalted Welsh blood."

"Richard! Stop this nonsense. By the way, why are you not practicing your curtsies to Their Majesties?"

"Ha! It turns out equerry duties for a mad king differ vastly from those of yore when His Majesty was sane and avuncular. My job will be to restrain him when he tries to escape his rooms, which he attempts rather frequently. As for the other Royals, my bow is good enough—or so those at Whitehall believed, and they have let me go until I move to Windsor Castle next week."

"In that case, we may as well leave now."

When the three gentlemen arrived at the Trumbull residence, they saw would-be-callers turning away. The knocker was down.

A startlingly powerful emotion bordering on despair came over Mr. Darcy. He had been extremely apprehensive about this first meeting with Elizabeth. All night long, scenario after scenario of how their reunion would happen had tumbled around his head. He decided on a simple resolution—once they had a chance to clear the air, they could continue their separate lives, and he would wish her everything good in her future.

Just then, the Trumbull carriage pulled up to the front door, and emerging from the house to step into the carriage was none other than Miss Elizabeth Bennet.

"Miss Bennet!" All three gentlemen called simultaneously.

The loudest was Colonel Fitzwilliam, but Elizabeth heard only the one voice that had been haunting her since their last meeting a year before. Blood drained from her face, and her instinctive reaction was to retreat into the house. Alas, the front door was already closed behind her.

Mr. Darcy was not much better. After having given up on seeing Elizabeth that day and feeling inexplicably melancholy, he stood there with his lips slightly parted, staring shocked and incredulous at the woman, who, he had decided, was nothing to him. It never occurred to him that his heart might not follow his head.

The Colonel watched his cousin closely and smirked, saying under his breath, "Indifferent acquaintance?"

This ironic taunt woke Mr. Darcy out of his trance. He moved toward Elizabeth, who was still standing at the door, looking undecided. However, as soon as she saw Mr. Darcy walking toward her, her courage rose, and her countenance relaxed. She curtsied, and the gentleman bowed as any ordinary acquaintances would. The only sign this was anything but ordinary was that neither paid any attention to the other two gentlemen.

Mr. Darcy, hoping to repair his poor impressions on this particular lady, asked solicitously, "Are you well? Are your family at Lo..." Mr. Darcy remembered just in time that Longbourn was no longer the lady's home and finished, "home well?"

With his obvious avoidance of saying Longbourn, Elizabeth realized Mr. Darcy knew something of the calamity that had befallen her family. She answered solemnly and hesitantly, "Yes, we are all well... Mr. Darcy, you seem to have some knowledge of what has happened to the Bennet family—my father's passing... and our removal to new lodgings."

And then, with a sudden determination to not be sad and gloomy on such a wonderful day, she stood tall, lifted her head, and said with unsuppressed elation, "But everything is so much better now than even yesterday! I received a note from my uncle this morning, asking me to return post-haste to our cottage. Sir, my youngest sister is coming home today after a long absence. She is recently widowed with a newborn babe. My compassionate friend, Mrs. Trumbull, has lent me her carriage to go home."

Before Mr. Darcy could answer, Elizabeth turned to Mr. Bingley and said apologetically, "Mr. Bingley, we have not met since the Netherfield ball..."

Mr. Bingley interjected immediately, "The 26th of November in the year '11."

Elizabeth was impressed by Mr. Bingley's distinct memory of that event, but she no longer cared what Mr. Bingley remembered and what he did not. She continued, "Yes, it has been a long time. Please send my compliments to your sisters, Mrs. Hurst and Miss Bingley, and your brother, Mr. Hurst." She looked at the Colonel and said, "Colonel Fitzwilliam, it is good to see you again."

Just then, a footman approached and handed Elizabeth a note.

She read it, blushed becomingly, and apologized. "Forgive me, gentlemen, for detaining you at the door. Please come in. Mrs. Trumbull had the knocker removed because of my having been called away suddenly; and her aunt, Mrs. Morgan, is feeling unwell. However, she would like to meet you. She has, of course, been reacquainted with the Colonel."

Mr. Darcy asked hesitantly, "Would it delay your reunion with Mrs....?" Mr. Darcy felt a jab of his cousin's elbow on his back. He looked over his shoulder at his cousin and realized he had almost given away his involvement in Mrs. Cieran's rescue, and so he hastily added, "Mrs. Bennet and your sisters?"

Elizabeth was surprised by his kind consideration, although she could not help being puzzled by the peculiar interactions between the two cousins. She smiled, eyes shining with gladness, and said, "My uncle and Lydia will not come until he has finished his day's business. I am merely impatient. It would please me greatly to assist Mrs. Trumbull in hosting you, gentlemen."

Mesmerized by luminous eyes in a joyous and enchanting face, Mr. Darcy looked fixedly at her. Elizabeth squirmed under this stare but reminded herself his steadfast gaze might not represent censure. If she dared to admit it, she detected a new softness in his eyes, resembling tenderness.

The master of Pemberley had nothing but admiration for the guilelessness and loyalty of the young woman who had devoted her life to searching for her wayward sister. At that moment, all the residual resentment he had felt about her telling the world of their most private feelings evaporated. He forgave her completely. If it had been Georgiana, he would have willingly sold his own soul to the devil to ransom his sister.

Since Mr. Darcy seemed to be distracted, Colonel Fitzwilliam stepped forward and gallantly offered his arm to Elizabeth, and the group entered the drawing room of the Trumbull townhouse.

Mrs. Trumbull, standing at the window where she had been watching the goings-on at the front door, turned and greeted the callers cordially.

"Gentlemen, well met. Colonel Fitzwilliam, welcome. Mr. Darcy, it has been a long time since I had the pleasure of your company. Elizabeth, would you do the honor of introducing me to the remaining gentleman?"

All three gentlemen were impressed by the lady's take-charge demeanor.

After the introductions, Mrs. Trumbull jokingly said, "I am glad that I could play the role of companion to Elizabeth during your visit. Please don't mind me. I shall just be across the room."

Elizabeth protested vehemently, and the gentlemen joined in, asking their hostess to join them.

The group fell naturally into two small groups: Elizabeth with Mr. Darcy and Mr. Bingley, and Mrs. Trumbull with the Colonel.

Mrs. Trumbull frequently glanced over to where Mr. Darcy was sitting and appeared to be watching him closely.

Colonel Fitzwilliam sighed, thinking his cousin had once again unintentionally snatched an eligible lady from him.

Mrs. Trumbull must have heard his sigh, for she quickly addressed the Colonel, "Sir, allow me to offer you more tea, or something stronger? I feel I have been negligent in attending to your comfort."

"Madam, forgive me for appearing morose. It has nothing to do with your excellent hospitality." The Colonel glanced at his cousin, sitting stoically and ramrod straight, listening to the conversation between Mr. Bingley and Miss Bennet. He turned toward Mrs. Trumbull and said with feigned despair, "I was lamenting that my cousin Darcy attracts attention wherever he goes, even if he appears as a lifeless vegetable."

Mrs. Trumbull could not help laughing at the Colonel's droll expression and his ridiculous but good-natured chiding of his cousin.

At her laughter, the other three occupants of the room turned to look.

"Oh, please don't mind us. The Colonel was regaling me with a diverting anecdote," said Mrs. Trumbull jauntily to the other visitors. She turned back to the Colonel and said, "Colonel, could I interest you in some paintings by Mr. John Trumbull? He is an American painter distantly related to this family. He was in London for quite a few years and is renowned for his exceedingly fine paintings of the American Revolution. My late husband commissioned a few paintings from him that have never been exhibited in public."

The Colonel understood immediately she wished to speak privately to him, and so he enthusiastically responded, "Madam, you are indeed a lady after my heart. I enjoy everything military and have seen some of Mr. Trumbull's paintings while studying the American battles. Lead on!"

Mrs. Trumbull gave the Colonel such a brilliant smile that the hardened military man's heart almost melted. For the first time, he felt perhaps he should put some effort into gaining the favor of this highly courted lady.

If she can smile like that, who cares if she also spews Latin and Greek for sport?

Mrs. Trumbull led the Colonel to the small conservatory at the back of the house. There were no battlefield paintings in sight. Colonel Fitzwilliam raised an eyebrow.

"Sir, Mr. Trumbull—the painter—is also a renowned portraitist. I sat for the painting over there when I was newly married. I hope my youthful visage is enough of a compensation for the lack of a dying general?"

"Indeed, madam. It is a far greater treat than battle scenes, no matter how expertly depicted. I..." The Colonel was going to flirt with the heiress like a regular society lady, but his instinct made him change his mind. A lady of her status would detest common flattery, even if he meant what he said. He thus switched to the task at hand. "I suspect you wished to speak in private. Let us proceed. We do not wish to fan the fire of my companions' imaginations by being away too long, do we?"

It was Mrs. Trumbull's turn to raise her eyebrows. "Do you mean to say, sir, that your upright cousin is capable of indecorous thoughts?"

"What do you think, madam? You observed him a great deal since he came into your drawing room." Mrs. Trumbull wore a sardonic smile on her face, and the Colonel could tell that she was excessively diverted by the conversation. Thinking that this particular lady, worldly and understanding of man's desires, at least her late husband's, would not fault him for stating the obvious, he quipped, "I do not know of a single man, my cousin included, who does not let thoughts of carnal pleasures intrude upon their minds."

Again Mrs. Trumbull laughed, and again, the Colonel was bewitched. She spoke through another smile, "Interesting thought, Colonel. Perhaps you and I could explore this topic at a later time." She let the sentence hang for a brief moment, stirring an upheaval of potent feelings inside the Colonel, which surprised the experienced warrior both on and off the battlefields.

221

Before the Colonel could find time to reflect on whether Mrs. Trumbull was a loose woman, or he was particularly favored, the lady continued to speak quite matter-of-factly, "I am certain you have read, or at least heard of, the new novel attributed to me. When you came to call a few days ago, I was certain you were Colonel Egerton in the story. It would follow that your cousin, Mr. Fitzwilliam Darcy, would be Mr. Egerton Keynes. However, the Mr. Darcy in my recollection was an earnest young man intent on scholarly pursuits, and not the arrogant, selfish, and meddlesome man Elizabeth depicted. In the second part of the story, Mr. Keynes begins to resemble the Mr. Darcy I used to know—a passionate and honorable man. The way he rights the wrong caused by Mr. Henry Wolfe is admirable.

"While watching Elizabeth and Mr. Darcy's interactions from the window, I became convinced that Mr. Darcy is indeed the real Mr. Keynes. The reaction of each party on seeing the other reminded me of the scene outside of the stable block of Mr. Keynes's estate. Just now in the parlor, I simply could not help wanting to solve the puzzle: which parts of Elizabeth's story are based on her actual experiences, and which parts are from her imagination? Did Mr. Darcy propose to Elizabeth in that abhorrent manner as in the story, or is it only Elizabeth's wishful thinking—the proposal, not the incivility of it? Now that I have identified the protagonists, will real life imitate the fictional one? Colonel, I consider myself a mature, level-headed, and high-minded individual, which is why I cannot understand my obsession with discovering what will happen to those two."

"Perhaps that is the effect good literature has on people? I am not a reader of anything outside of military history, but it makes sense to me. Sadly, I am not in a position to help you satisfy your curiosity since I have lost the memories of the past five years. To my knowledge, I met Miss Elizabeth Bennet for the first time at your last soiree, but she informed me we had met at my aunt's estate in Kent last Easter. As for my cousin, I shall not betray any confidence. He is an extremely private man."

"Oh, Colonel, I did not mean to seek any information about your cousin from you. Rather, I enjoy watching the mystery unfold.

"I truly admire the story, and I am inordinately proud to be the one who convinced Elizabeth to publish it. Soon, she will begin a new exciting chapter of her life, and I am very pleased I have had a hand in shaping that as well."

"Do you mean she will go down in history as a literary giant like the Bard?"

"That is indeed possible. However, I meant she will soon be leaving me and taking up a position as the co-Keeper of the Robes of the Queen."

The Colonel's eye grew round and exclaimed, "The Queen of England? Queen Charlotte?"

"Yes, she will take the position Mrs. Burney, oh, Madame d'Arblay now, used to hold. During Madame d'Arblay's recent visit to the Royal household, the authorship of the novel, which has become a favorite of the Royals, came up. Madame d'Arblay, of course, could not conceal from the Queen what she knew of the author. Her Majesty was extremely curious about Elizabeth. Madame d'Arblay believed it was because she mentioned Elizabeth's resemblance to one of the royal princesses. Soon after, Elizabeth was summoned to the Queen's House for an interview with Her Majesty. A few days later, Madame d'Arblay carried the message that the Queen wished Elizabeth to take this position."

"It must be Princess Amelia. I have met her before and, now that you mention it, I agree the resemblance is quite uncanny. The princess's recent passing has affected the King profoundly. As my equerry duty for His Majesty begins imminently, I need to know such things."

"It is good Elizabeth will have someone she knows at Court. She was reluctant to accept the position, as everyone knows being associated with the Royal household is a two-edged sword. Madame d'Arblay shared her experience when she herself served the Queen. It was far from being all mirth and laughter. Her mother and uncle, however, were jubilant about this offer and urged Elizabeth to accept, reminding her it would surely restore and even elevate their family's reputation. Madame d'Arblay weighed in with a few more benefits stemming from her own experiences. When she found a lump in her... breast, the best medical doctors here and on the

Continent were available to her to save her life. I can tell a colonel of the King's army this with impunity, can I not?"

"Of course," replied the Colonel promptly.

"Elizabeth immediately associated this advantage with her father's illness. He could have been saved by the best physicians of the land. And if her mother's nervous ailment turned into something serious, she would have the connections to get her the best treatment. She accepted the offer and will begin attending Her Majesty in another week."

Mrs. Trumbull stopped and smiled sheepishly.

"Colonel, you must think I am a gossip. Elizabeth could easily tell you all this herself, since you are friends. I cannot help it. I am proud of her. She is the sister I never had."

By now, Colonel Fitzwilliam believed himself in love. He had thought the grand heiress would be aloof and contemptuous of those she deemed less intelligent and erudite than herself. Yet, Mrs. Trumbull behaved like a caring, compassionate lady—who also was handsome, full-figured, and temptingly widowed.

Just then, Elizabeth appeared and informed her friend that the other two gentlemen wished to take their leave. Mrs. Trumbull acknowledged the summons and said, "Colonel, it has been a pleasure. We must meet again to explore the other topics we had discussed... if it suits you." She then lowered her voice and said softly, "I am at home most evenings this coming week."

The Colonel was shocked by this forward invitation, but he was skilled at hiding his emotions. He bowed smartly and quietly replied, "It suits me very well. You honor me, madam."

The trio returned to the parlor. Mr. Bingley and Mr. Darcy were both standing, ready to leave. Mr. Darcy apologized, "Madam, I regret I could not converse with you today. I hope to call again soon at one of your soirees."

Mr. Bingley enthusiastically concurred.

"Mr. Darcy, Mr. Bingley, I am grateful for your call and look forward to your valuable insights at future gatherings. Elizabeth will soon leave me, but her sister, Miss Mary Bennet, will take Elizabeth's place. I believe you are acquainted with Miss Mary as well."

Mr. Darcy could not hide his surprise. During the entire visit, he was mostly silent, letting Bingley and Elizabeth carry the conversation. He desperately wanted to ask about the offer Elizabeth had received but did not know how to broach the question without betraying his acquaintance with Mr. Gardiner. He fervently hoped she had not accepted the offer—fate could not have been that cruel.

Where is she going? Am I too late after all?

Seeing that Darcy showed an initial look of surprise before falling silent, Mr. Bingley felt obliged to interject. He turned to Mrs. Trumbull and said, "Ah, Miss Mary Bennet! Of course, I remember her. She was pious and proper, quite a different companion for you after Miss Elizabeth Bennet, madam."

He then turned to Elizabeth and asked, "Miss Bennet, you did not mention you would be leaving Mrs. Trumbull's household. Are you rejoining your family, or is there to be a felicitous event of the marital kind for which I should congratulate you?"

Mr. Bingley's almost-intrusive questions surprised Elizabeth, and not pleasantly. During their earlier conversation, he mainly talked about his sister, Miss Bingley. Even his inquiries after her family were quite perfunctory. It was obvious Jane meant little to him.

Was he always this self-centered?

No wonder her imminent departure from the house at St. James's Square did not come up.

To own the truth, her mind had been on the other gentleman, who, when she turned to look at him, seemed sullen and was frequently looking at the carpet.

Could I expect it to be otherwise? Why did he come?

Since neither Mr. Darcy nor Elizabeth was inclined to speak, the Colonel spoke up instead, "Miss Bennet will be attending Her Majesty as Her Majesty's Keeper of the Robes. She and I will begin our tenures at Court at almost the same time."

This pronouncement struck Mr. Darcy like a thunderbolt, and a profound sense of relief descended upon him. Elizabeth was not lost to him forever!

He could no longer deny he loved Elizabeth as much as he ever had. What an idiot he had been for thinking that his limited war experience could have entirely changed him. If that was the case, his cousin would have become somebody unrecognizable. Yet, he was the same fun-loving, irreverent but honorable person he had been since childhood. Bingley, on the other hand, seemed to have changed drastically in the past year, his only perilous life-changing experience being that of having ducked a vase thrown by his sister.

He could not help himself. His face relaxed, and a smile appeared on his previously stern countenance.

"Darcy is amused we would both be serving our sovereigns on our hands and knees," quipped the Colonel.

Mr. Darcy immediately rebutted, "Not at all. It is the highest honor to be trusted by Their Majesties, and I congratulate you, Miss Bennet, on being chosen for such an illustrious position. Will you have to commit to serve for a certain length of time?"

Mr. Bingley added, "I am also proud of your royal connections, Miss Bennet. Caroline will be envious."

"Thank you, gentlemen. I did nothing to attain this position. Her Majesty condescended to request my service. I shall try my best not to disappoint and shall serve at Her Majesty's pleasure."

Elizabeth did not know how long she was supposed to serve the Queen. Since Queen Charlotte was close to seventy years of age, Elizabeth would probably be in her position for the rest of Her Majesty's life. Madame d'Arblay said if she had not been deathly ill, Her Majesty probably would not have looked kindly on her resignation.

As Elizabeth spoke, she was uncertain she had made the right decision by accepting the offer. Royal connections, as Mr. Bingley pointed out, would be the envy of all who knew the Bennet family. Even their formerly contemptuous neighbors in Meryton would look at her family as extraordinarily distinguished. Jane's courtship with Mr. Lytle would go more smoothly, even though Jane had told her to decide solely based on her own inclination.

There was another important consideration. Deep down, she believed her worth in Mr. Darcy's eyes would be elevated. Why was that important to her? She asked herself this question numerous times. Judging from the gentleman's smile after hearing her news, she felt perhaps she had assumed correctly.

The three gentlemen parted ways outside the Trumbull residence. Mr. Darcy and Mr. Bingley agreed to come to the gathering Mrs. Trumbull would host the following Thursday evening, but the Colonel would have reported for duty at Windsor Castle by then.

Chapter 25

The air inside Rambler Cottage was thick with excitement and anticipation. Mrs. Bennet bustled from room to room, lamenting that the house was grossly inadequate for her darling Lydia and even more darling grandson. Her Lydia did not ruin the family after all; and was mother to a boy!

What was her husband's excuse for dying so early, leaving his widow and daughters in such a mean dwelling? It was so unfair to little Aiden, who would never know the life of a gentleman on an estate. Overflowing with pride and gladness, she exclaimed, "Mrs. Cieran! How well it sounds! And a grandson!"

The Bennet sisters were not outwardly exuberant, but all rejoiced at the homecoming of their lost and no longer disgraced sister. They genuinely sympathized with Lydia, who had already lost her husband at only sixteen. The addition of a babe, however, would lift the sadness, and they could not wait to be doting aunts. With Elizabeth's position at Court, their own positions in society would surely be elevated to a level they had never dreamed of. Except for Mary, they were ready to let bygones be bygones and forgive Lydia for the egregious behavior, which caused the death of their dear papa.

When Elizabeth arrived, the three sisters rushed up to her. They hugged, held hands, and spontaneously burst into a version of the Maypole dance.

Mrs. Bennet smiled in contentment for the first time in a long time: she and her daughters would be well despite the mountain of hardship in the past few months. In another hour, Lydia and her precious grandson would arrive, making her joy complete. Even with her tight economy, she managed to set out a fine dinner with a meat pie, a lamb stew, and a tart made with apple preserves, all Lydia's favorites.

Elizabeth and Jane stole away for a moment to talk about how Lydia's return might affect Mr. Lytle's and Jane's courtship. Jane could not help a seldom-displayed broad smile.

"Lizzy, Jeremy... Mr. Lytle... and I have reached an understanding..."

Elizabeth grabbed Jane's hands and kissed them fervently.

"Oh, Jane, I knew that you—your whole being and your soul—could not be so beautiful for nothing. I shall be proud to have Mr. Lytle as my future brother!" Elizabeth exclaimed with joy.

"We have not told our families because of Lydia's situation. He was hoping to find a propitious occasion, as he feared Mrs. Lytle might object on account of our family's disgrace. Mary had told her..."

"Oh, Mary! How could she?" Elizabeth was incredulous.

"Don't blame Mary, Lizzy. You know how impeccably honest she is. She simply does not know how to evade the truth. She and Mrs. Lytle were studying the biblical passage of the woman at the well, and the topic on disgraced women came up. Mrs. Lytle is a kind woman. She told Jeremy about a potential scandal involving Lydia, but she did not appear to judge. She felt her son should know as he was courting me. The Lytles are completely without airs, despite their wealth. Two days ago, Jeremy called here, and we walked in the garden. I told him everything about Lydia, and how you are trying every avenue to find her. He immediately offered to help. I was very touched, of course, by his kindness, and knew in my heart that he was the one for me and told him so. We were both very glad..." Jane stopped suddenly and blushed crimson.

Elizabeth smiled mischievously at her very demure sister. She could imagine there had been more than just words of heart-felt gladness. She squeezed Jane's hands and urged her sister to continue, refraining from teasing to avoid embarrassing Jane further.

"He told me there was something he had wanted to tell me but did not have the courage. Knowing that I... love him, he felt emboldened." Elizabeth squeezed her sister's hands again, showing her support for whatever was unfolding.

"Remember how we thought he had been married to an Indian woman named Arati, and it turned out his hard-of-hearing mother mistook the word 'ward' for 'wife?' And how she felt it was not her place to interfere with her grown son's life and did not ask further questions to clarify?"

"Oh, yes. We all heaved a great sigh of relief after you confronted him directly when he asked you for a courtship."

"On hearing about Lydia, he felt the obligation to tell me the truth about Arati. Arati is his natural daughter."

Elizabeth gasped. Jane signaled to let her finish the account.

"When he first arrived in India, being an Englishman, he had the privilege of living among other English colonials and high-ranking natives in a fashionable area of Calcutta, even though he only held a junior position with the East India Company. There was a young native woman staying with her aunt in the house next door. They met by chance; and they continued to meet in secret in a concealed corner of her garden. Jeremy vows he did not love her as he loves me, but he was homesick and lonely because... that is a story for another time.

"When he asked the aunt for permission to marry the woman, following the custom here in England, the elder lady not only refused to grant permission but also immediately sent her niece back to the young woman's father in a province far away from the city. Her father was a local chieftain, either a sultan or a nawab—I am confused about these titles, much to Jeremy's amusement. Eight months later, the woman's maid knocked on his door and handed him a bundle, which turned out to be a baby girl, and then she hastily left.

"Jeremy asked his friends, a missionary couple, to bring up Arati at his expense. Six months ago, this kind couple died of malaria, leaving Arati without care. Jeremy was already in England because of his father's death. He had planned to go back to India, adopt the girl and bring her up there. However, affairs here—his father's business, which was quite extensive— needed attention; the Company wanted to groom him in England to a directorship, and then he met me. He decided to stay in England for the time being and asked a married couple who were coming back to England to bring Arati with them, and he would raise her as his ward... if his future wife agrees."

"Of course you will agree. Won't you?"

"I told Jeremy I would be pleased to raise the girl with him. After all, I am very adept at helping young girls grow up—look at all my wonderful sisters! You should have seen his face—he was so relieved!"

"Jane, you are the kindest and most compassionate person I know. Mr. Lytle is a very fortunate man. Tell me the story you were delaying. Why did he fall into temptation? Are the customs of the land that young women may have marital relations with men outside of marriage?"

"No, Jeremy said the woman was from the highest level of local society, where girls are married off to secure alliances... not unlike what we have here in England. Marrying outside the rules set by the father was completely forbidden and may lead to dire consequences for the woman. That was why she was sent home by her aunt. Jeremy tried to locate her, but the state of affairs in India made it impossible. He said it would remain a deep regret that his reckless behavior had endangered the life of a young woman. He said he was young, foolish, and alone in a foreign land not of his choosing, and that must have been his excuse, feeble as it was."

"It is sad, but we must not judge him. Our own too young and stupid Lydia committed a similar infraction, and she did not even have the excuse of having been exiled to a faraway country with entirely different people and unfamiliar customs. But Mr. Lytle's life is so fascinating! Why did he go to India if it had not been his choice, and his father had such a prosperous business in London?"

"This is the part I wanted to put off. Jeremy's father was a renowned clockmaker. His patrons included the peerage and even some of the royal princes. Jeremy, as a young man, had already become an expert in this craft, good enough to service the clock collections of some of his father's most distinguished patrons. It was not uncommon for him to stay for weeks at a single estate to take care of their hundreds of clocks. During one of these stays, he fell in love with the young daughter of his patron, an earl. The young couple planned to elope to America. When he got to the dock at the appointed time, he found the earl himself waiting for him. He was forced to board the first ship that was to sail, and its destination was India. He could not return to England until the earl died three years ago, *and* his father had forgiven him, which his father finally did on his deathbed. That is another of his great regrets—to be absent when his father died."

"Poor, poor Mr. Lytle! So unlucky in love and life! But things will be dramatically better since he is marrying you. You will make him so happy and content he will have nothing to repine. Now that Lydia's scandal is no longer a factor, he does not even have to worry about his mother's disapproval..."

As if on cue, an unmistakable shriek from their long-lost sister came up the stairs, followed by the wailing of a baby. In an instant, the two sisters were transported back to their Longbourn days, when Lydia could never make an unremarkable entrance. Sensing what each was thinking, they embraced tightly and rushed to welcome home their sister and new nephew.

In the parlor, Mrs. Bennet and Kitty crowded around Lydia on the sofa. Mr. Gardiner and Mrs. Gardiner were in the chairs opposite, looking on with fond smiles. Mary stood alone in front of the fireplace, looking bemused. Jane and Elizabeth embraced their wayward sister, joining the others in joyous tears.

"Oh, look at him, precious Aiden! Lydia, you have done very well with him! He is already a handsome boy! A boy!" gushed Mrs. Bennet.

"La, my son is a treasure. He gave me no trouble when I was giving birth, unlike poor Mrs. Wi..."

A loud clearing of the throat emitted from Mr. Gardiner. Lydia looked sheepish for a second and continued her account with less bravado. "Unlike Mrs. Younge. She was the owner of the boarding house where I stayed while waiting for my Daniel to come back from sea. Poor dear! She died trying to birth her child."

Elizabeth noticed that Lydia swallowed the name of the owner of the boarding house at her uncle's warning. The new name given, Mrs. Young, sounded suspicious to her.

Could it have been Younge?

The letter from Mr. Darcy was so ingrained in her brain that any information reminding her of the letter did not escape her. Why had Lydia begun to name the proprietress Mrs. Wi..?

Could she have meant Mrs. Wickham? Lydia was supposed to have gone off with Wickham. These unusual interactions between Lydia and Uncle could provide the clues for how Lydia's initial elopement with Wickham developed into her becoming Mrs. Cieran. But how?

Uncle Gardiner had to be involved. He said the proceeds from her book sale funded the recovery of Lydia, but if she remembered correctly, the initial amount he received was not much. She would need to investigate. In the meantime, she would bide her time.

She asked, "Lydia, who was Mrs. Young? Where is the boarding house? Perhaps you should start from the beginning: tell us how you came to disappear from Brighton in July last year and return married with a babe. I am overjoyed to have you and my new nephew here with us, but we were so worried about you! And papa..." Elizabeth swallowed a sob. She could usually control her emotions concerning her father, but not this time.

Lydia grimaced before she emitted a loud keening and looked as if she might faint. Mrs. Bennet immediately scolded, "Lizzy, we are all so happy to see Lydia and Aiden. Let us leave off unpleasant things for now!" The reproof was exceptionally mild, for Elizabeth had risen high in her mother's estimation since having accepted the Queen's offer.

Mr. Gardiner interjected, "Lydia has been remorseful since hearing of her papa's death. She is young and could not have foreseen the dire consequences of her actions."

He turned to Elizabeth next and said, "Lizzy, you are always curious and need to know everything. What I wrote in the letter this morning is the whole story: Mr. Wickham used Lydia for her pin money to get to London, left her at his paramour's boarding house where Lydia met and fell in love with Mr. Cieran, an Irish Lieutenant on shore duty; they promised themselves to each other and anticipated their vows; Mr. Cieran was called back to his ship for a short voyage that turned into a long one; soon after that, Lydia found herself with child and was too ashamed to come home to her family; Mr. Cieran came back to England with severe injuries right before Lydia gave birth; they married a few days before the birth of his son, and Lieutenant Cieran could name his son before succumbing to his injuries. Lydia decided to return to her own family instead of going to Ireland to be with Lieutenant Cieran's family, whom she has not met."

Lydia issued a horrific shriek when hearing the account of her husband's death, startling the babe, who cried loudly as well. Mrs. Bennet immediately stood up with him and walked around to calm him, all the while staring with annoyance at Elizabeth. Jane took her mother's place on the sofa to comfort Lydia.

Seeing the family in turmoil, Elizabeth did not want to add to the tense atmosphere in the parlor. She meekly said, "Forgive me, Uncle." She turned to Lydia and Mrs. Bennet and apologized to them as well.

The Gardiners soon took their leave before it turned dark. While they were waiting in the small vestibule for their carriage, Elizabeth came up suddenly. She asked without preamble, "Uncle, Aunt, Lydia was not of age. How could she have been legally married?"

Mr. Gardiner knew he could not conceal the truth from his discerning niece. He said resignedly, "There was indeed more to Lydia's disappearance and recovery. I was the one who gave Lydia away at the wedding. Mr. Darcy, whom you know..."

"Mr. Darcy!" Elizabeth cried. Fortunately, Lydia and her son were still creating a fair amount of agitation in the background such that Elizabeth's astonishment escaped notice.

"I was surprised too, Lizzy, as you had told me and your aunt how disagreeable the gentleman was while he was in Hertfordshire with his friends. Yet, he was in every way a gentleman regarding the recovery of Lydia. He took everything upon himself to secure a respectable future for Lydia, and by doing so, saved all your reputations. He spared no expense. Lizzy, if you and your sisters marry well, you have Mr. Darcy to thank."

"Does that mean that Aiden is not Lieutenant Cieran's son?"

Mrs. Gardiner interjected, "Aiden is in every way Cieran's son..."

Just then, Mary descended the stairs. No one had noticed Mary leave the room. Mrs. Gardiner and Lizzy stopped talking.

The carriage was in front of the house. Mrs. Gardiner embraced Lizzy and spoke softly in her ear, "Except in blood. Keep this to yourself. I am reconciled to the deception. Try to do the same."

Mrs. Gardiner nodded to Mary, who had reached the vestibule. Mr. Gardiner opened the door, and they were gone.

Mary looked at Elizabeth quizzically and asked, "Lizzy, were you questioning Uncle and Aunt about the identity of Aiden's father?"

Elizabeth was not entirely surprised that Mary should ask this question. She composed herself and asked, "Are you questioning the identity of Aiden's father?"

Mary, straightforward as ever, answered directly without pressing for an answer to her own question. "I have my doubts. The account of Lydia's elopement and recovery seems too tidy—almost like it was made up. To tell the truth, I am a little disgusted that Lydia, who committed the sins that cost papa's life, is welcomed home with open arms and no questions. Mamma has slaughtered the fatted calf for Lydia the sinner, when she did nothing for her good daughters, especially you, who have done so much for this family. Without your money, Lydia would not have been found."

"Oh, Mary, your allusion to the parable of the prodigal son is very apt. Lydia, our wayward sister, has come home a reformed and respectable widow with a cherubic babe. We are blessed to be in the position to forgive and rejoice at her transformation, unlike the older son in the parable, whose jealousy and resentment achieve nothing other than to make himself miserable. I think we should accept the father's advice and be grateful that our reputations are safe, and our futures are now as bright as we could make them."

Mary, always receptive to a biblical interpretation, thought for a moment, and said, "I agree with you about the blessings of forgiveness, and I shall try my best to be charitable. Lydia appears to be more mature—not brash and selfish like she was. Her affection for her dead husband also seems genuine. However, I sense there is more to the eye than what Uncle explained. Someday, I hope you will let me into your confidence."

"Mary, I promise when the time comes, I shall tell you all I know, but I do not yet know everything. Let's return to celebrate and wait for the fatted lamb for dinner!"

Life returned to a joyful sort of normal after that first excitement. Mr. Lytle lost no time informing his mother of the widowed sister's homecoming, and the kind old lady was so pleased that she insisted on inviting the Bennet and Cieran families to her house for dinner.

During dinner, Mr. Lytle announced his engagement to Miss Jane Bennet. Elizabeth was very pleased she could witness this felicitous event before returning with Mary to the Trumbull residence, and from there, to the deep, dark intrigue of the Royal Court.

In the quiet of the night, Elizabeth had some time to contemplate Mr. Darcy's involvement in Lydia's rescue.

How did he find out about Lydia, and why did he do it?

236

If I were bold... and delusional, I would surmise he did it for me. But he hardly talked to me when he called at Mrs. Trumbull's. Vexing man!

Chapter 26

After calling on Mrs. Trumbull and Elizabeth, the Colonel was uncharacteristically reticent. Mr. Darcy would have teased his cousin about this unusual behavior, but he was himself deep in thought. The two cousins rode without exchanging a word.

At the door of Darcy House, the Colonel did not enter. Looking almost sheepish, he said, "I... eh... have a rendezvous with... a lady tonight. I shall see you tomorrow."

Mr. Darcy, surprised, looked at his cousin with raised eyebrows and commented, "It is only four o'clock. This lady must be very special for you to get ready so early in the day."

"You don't say," muttered the Colonel under his breath.

Mr. Darcy caught the words. "I see. *That* special then? You had better keep her out of my sight or you would blame me for stealing your fair... maiden when she inevitably leaves for greener pastures."

"There is no possibility of that!" The Colonel said with bravado.

"I am heartened to see your confidence returning full force. However, I cannot imagine an assignation of that nature happening in broad daylight. Is it not supposed to be stealthy and in complete darkness to avoid being discovered by the husband?"

The Colonel rolled his eyes heavenwards without answering.

Mr. Darcy resorted to imploring, "Please stay for at least a few minutes because I wish to consult you on a matter of some urgency."

It was the Colonel's turn to raise his eyebrows, but he followed Mr. Darcy into the house.

"Here we are in your study. Speak up!" The Colonel commanded.

Mr. Darcy paced in front of the fireplace, ignoring the impatient tone of his cousin.

Finally, he asked, "When you begin your duties for His Majesty, will you have opportunities to see Miss Bennet?"

"Ah, you want me to keep an eye on her, lest she be snatched up by a handsome and powerful courtier?"

"No! No... Perhaps. Would you take care of her? I imagine the Court is packed with the kind of cunning and backstabbing that Miss Bennet is ill-equipped to handle. What if she were to encounter another Wickham?"

The Colonel narrowed his eyes and asked bluntly, "Why—or, for whom— am I protecting Miss Bennet?"

Mr. Darcy paced some more and said with determination, "I will not deny it any longer. If Miss Bennet would have me, I want her to be my wife, mother of my children, and mistress of Pemberley."

"Humph! Why have you waited till now to offer for her? You are not wrong about Court life, although King George, mad though he is, is not known for sending courtiers to have their heads chopped off. The Monarch during his rare lucid moments and his Queen Consort are decent people, but the heir is... debauched and a wastrel. Fortunately, he is also sickly and cannot do as much harm as otherwise. His brothers, all six of them, are scarcely better, and one of them could be dangerously depraved. On the Queen's side, Her Majesty is besieged by difficulties: a mad husband and sons whose behavior is repulsive to her strict moral code—out of the seven sons, she has only one legitimate grandchild and uncountable illegitimate ones. Her daughters have turned spiteful, forced into spinsterhood, and living as recluses. Darcy, Miss Bennet is going into a perilous web of intrigue and treachery she must navigate on her own with her limited life experience."

"Is she going to be in great danger? I must go and stop this altogether."

"It is too late at this point to decline the Queen's offer, unless you want to ruin Her Majesty's reputation of not sending law-abiding subjects to the Tower. You have not answered my question: why offer now and not earlier?"

"I had not known my mind for certain. I proposed to her last year at Rosings. You were there too, but I never told you of it. To my great shock and chagrin, she rejected me most vehemently. I do not blame her, not anymore. Over the last few months, I realized how disgustingly rude and condescending I had been in my proposal.

"After my time on the Continent, I thought I *had* got over her because I no longer lived in wretched misery. Then I read her novel and became furious with her again. But the episode involving Wickham and Miss Lydia Bennet roused me into action. Now, having learned why she had published her novel, I have nothing but admiration for her. Today, seeing her face-to-face, I can tell she is not indifferent to me. I felt I could breathe again. I finally saw through my folly—my denying my love for her stemmed from my fear that she would never have me, and I would rather be the one to reject her. Now, my head is clear. I *will* ask her, repeatedly if necessary, to marry me. I understand she cannot turn down the Queen's offer at the last minute, but she may be allowed to leave after a reasonable length of time, say, six months."

"Simply from the glimpse I got at Mrs. Trumbull's door, I agree that you two have a deep connection. It was as if time stood still.

"In that case, I shall do what I can to take care of your precious Miss Bennet. I shall not see her often, for the King is locked up at Windsor Castle, while the Queen, as acting hostess for Prinny, is frequently at her House in London during the season. I can, however, ask the other equerries to leave Miss Bennet alone. They are mostly honorable gentlemen and will heed my request. One thing in her favor is that she is poor, although there could be one at Court enamored with her literary brilliance. You know, Prinny is a lover of literature."

Mr. Darcy silently paced, until he stopped abruptly and said to his cousin, "On Monday, I hope to call on her, and tell her I shall wait for her, however long it may be. If she accepts my offer, she—as my betrothed—should be able to work in the palace without unscrupulous men preying upon her, and the Queen should be prepared to lose her service sooner rather than later."

"You have too high an opinion of unscrupulous men. I agree that an engaged woman should garner fewer unwanted attentions. I wish you much luck in securing Miss Bennet's hand."

The Colonel stood and made ready to leave. "If we have finished here, I shall leave you on your own to strategize your wooing. I would be of no help to you. My roughshod way will, more likely than not, spoil your plan."

"Your way appears to work very well with Mrs. Trumbull. Have an *enjoyable* evening."

The Colonel was startled by his cousin's quip. He narrowed his eyes and said, "You should have accepted Wellington's offer for a position on his staff. With your keen observational skills, you and Wellington would have already vanquished Bonaparte while he was retreating from Russia."

"You were not at all subtle in your admiration of Mrs. Trumbull. If she adores your 'roughshod' way in return, it could be the match you have been waiting for."

"I am truly not thinking about a match with her... or her fortune. She is a widow and willing. I am a bachelor and willing. That is all. I found out this afternoon she was not a holier-than-thou, over-educated bore. To me, it was a pleasant enough surprise that I look forward to this evening."

"If you stay till after dinner, you could take from Georgiana's ample provisions for a fragrance bath to make yourself especially alluring to your estimable lady. Georgiana would be pleased to help with your pleasant diversion."

"If you leak a word about this to Georgiana, she would find your head on a platter at breakfast!"

Mr. Darcy could not help a loud guffaw. He waved the Colonel out of the house.

$\wp\wp$

It was after ten o'clock at night when the Colonel arrived at Mrs. Trumbull's.

The music teacher, Mr. Rocco, opened the door, and the Colonel managed to hide his surprise.

"Señor Ricco, is it? Is Mrs. Trumbull at home?" asked the Colonel, a little abashed. In other past encounters, there had never been another man involved. He had seen in his first visit to Mrs. Trumbull how the heiress sat close to the music teacher on the bench when he played. He thought nothing of it then.

Now, however, Colonel Fitzwilliam had to suppress a strong feeling of jealousy. The two men stood uneasily at the open door.

"Rocco. *Mr.* Rocco. Mrs. Trumbull is in the parlor. My business is finished here," said Mr. Rocco.

The butler now appeared to take his outer clothing and showed him to the parlor before closing the door. At least the pianoforte was not in this room.

Is it a good sign or a bad one?

"Good evening, Colonel," greeted the heiress pleasantly, as if the Colonel were making a polite social call during calling hours.

"Good evening, Mrs. Trumbull. Is this a convenient time for me to call?" The Colonel felt rather absurd as soon as he had asked the question. He was usually much more suave than this.

Mrs. Trumbull, who appeared all grace and elegance but was trembling inside, did not despise the Colonel for the inane inquiry. Instead, she said, "I am uncertain. I have never done this..." She used her hand to wave between herself and her guest. "I am relying on you for pointers."

The Colonel was so charmed by this innocent answer that he knelt on one knee and took her hand for a kiss. Then he said tenderly, "It would be my greatest honor to show you the way as I know it, although I am equally inexperienced when it comes to pleasing as fine a lady as yourself."

"We shall see..." She leaned down and kissed the Colonel on the lips.

There was no need for more conversation after that.

The Colonel, after an encounter like this, would usually get dressed and leave. This was not a lovers' tryst, but the satisfaction of scratching a certain itch. This time, however, he felt compelled to find out where he stood in Mrs. Trumbull's group of lovers.

Or is there a group? She admitted she was not an old hand at this sort of rendezvous. But what about Mr. Rocco? He practically lives here.

The Colonel cleared his throat while tidying up his clothes and asked, "Madam..." Once again, he felt foolish addressing the woman thus after what had just transpired. He soldiered on and said, "Mrs. Trumbull, Mr. Rocco opened the door for me when I arrived. I am curious about his.... position within your household."

"Would you rather not wonder whether you will be invited back? If you are not coming back, there would be no need for you to know more about my household."

The Colonel acknowledged the sense in Mrs. Trumbull's words. He thought for a moment and said, "I would be honored to return in the evening... late, when I am not on duty. Would you grant me this honor?"

Without acknowledging his question, Mrs. Trumbull asked, "You wonder why Mr. Rocco comes and goes as he pleases so late in the evening? He is one of those rare men who... shows no inclination toward carnal pleasures. Whatever you may think of his relationship with me or any female members of my staff, the truth is far from it. Does that satisfy your curiosity?"

"Yes, indeed. Forgive me for prying. I enjoyed our time together so much that I was curious about others who may be competing for your favors."

"I do not dole out favors, as you so tactfully described, to more than one person... at a time. Before you, I had never had intimate relations with anyone other than my late husband. To be frank, I do not have any plans to remarry, given my financial situation. I have no incentive to hand over my freedom to another man by marrying. However, I have... needs that I had not anticipated. If you are willing, it would please me to have you visit from time to time, but not too frequently."

"I see. I am honored. Would you think me unduly meddlesome if I ask why you have chosen me?"

Mrs. Trumbull said after a moment of contemplation, "Since my return to society, you and your cousin are the only two gentlemen callers who have not been fighting to get close to me. I had planned to have Miss Bennet distract the horde, but to no avail. That was when I noticed you. As for your cousin, it is clear where his heart is engaged. As I told you before, I could tell he was Mr. Keynes in Lizzy's story even before he entered my house. I wish Lizzy and Mr. Darcy the happy future she so feelingly described in the story. Before her sister's scandal was so suddenly resolved, I had encouraged Lizzy to accept the Queen's offer because I thought her position in Court would enhance the chances of her marrying Mr. Darcy. Now her court position may delay their ultimate union."

"My cousin is as constant as the craggy peaks surrounding his Derbyshire estate. A brief wait for the Queen's pleasure to release his love back to him does not signify. They have the advantage of being much younger than Her Majesty."

The Colonel paused and addressed the point about himself. "You were sick of the officious attention, and were disgusted by men who were always speaking, and looking, and thinking for your approbation alone. I roused and interested you because I was so unlike them."

"That and your military air and stance are what attracted my attention initially. I used to admire General Wellesley because of his superior, almost heroic airs, but I cannot abide his philanderer's ways. Whereas for you, I have heard nothing bad reported."

"Ah, you have thoroughly checked me out! I am glad that I passed muster."

Colonel Fitzwilliam stood up, executed a smart salute as if his paramour were an important military personage, and made his way to the door. Hearing a peal of laughter behind him, he did not turn around but knew, in his heart, he was leaving the woman he might love.

Chapter 27

At Rambler Cottage, Elizabeth was getting ready for her new post at the Queen's House, Her Majesty's official residence while in town. She was folding her many new dresses, gifts from Mrs. Trumbull, who insisted she not appear shabby in front of the other ladies at Court, when Lydia entered the room to see all of Lizzy's finery one last time.

Unlike her former self, she could admire the exquisite dresses with no outward spiteful jealousy. There was a little envy in her, but not the bitterness she used to harbor every time she did not have her way. She was serious about wearing black for a full twelve months for her dear departed Daniel. Until she was out of mourning, she sincerely wanted her sisters to have all the fun and wear pretty things.

"Ooh, look at this lace! Have you ever seen anything more lovely? And this shawl! How darling!"

While Lydia was busy admiring the dresses, Elizabeth casually asked, "Lydia, aren't there good warehouses where you were staying at Mrs. Younge's—it is 'Younge' with an 'e' at the end, is it not?"

"Oh, Mrs. Younge, and yes, there is an 'e' at the end. What a fastidious speller you are! Edward Street is neither prosperous nor fashionable. No good shops at all! Just as well—Mrs. Younge barely had enough money to buy food for the both of us. I am forever grateful for her taking me in when that blackguard just left me there."

"It never ceases to amaze me that Uncle's Gardiner's men could have found you in such an obscure place," commented Elizabeth nonchalantly.

"Uncle's men never found me. Thank heavens Mr. Darcy and the Colonel did, or else I would be rotting with my sweet babe in that decrepit boarding house and would never have met and married the love of my life."

Elizabeth could not help gasping when she heard this, even though she had already known about Mr. Darcy's involvement. She recovered quickly and pretended the noise was for discovering creases in a dress.

Lydia looked up slowly, realizing she had made a blunder. Seeing her sister had not reacted to the secret she just revealed, she was happy at first, but soon realized her clever sister could not have missed it.

"Lizzy, please do not tell Uncle Gardiner I leaked this secret by accident. He and Aunt went on and on admonishing me to seal my lips about how I was found," Lydia implored.

"Whatever do you mean? I did not hear any secret!" Lizzy fibbed.

Lydia looked at her sister with a knowing smile and said, "Thank you, Lizzy. I know I can trust you."

Elizabeth's mind whirled with this confirmation that Mr. Darcy was personally involved in saving her entire family—he did not simply send some men! She felt faint. Lydia's verification that she was with Mrs. Younge, Miss Darcy's companion, an integral part of Mr. Wickham's dastardly plan to deceive Miss Darcy, explained why Mr. Darcy readily found Lydia. But how did he know to look for her?

A moment later, Kitty ran into the room and said breathlessly, "Lizzy! Oh, Lydia! You would never guess who is downstairs in the parlor! It is that proud man, Mr. Darcy! Can you imagine? Why did he come here? How did he even know where to find us? It was so long ago we saw him in Meryton!"

Stopping for breath, she calmed and said, "Mamma asked you to come downstairs to sit with the guest. Jane has gone to prepare tea, and you know mamma cannot abide that man!"

"Mr. Darcy is a good man. Don't you slander him!" scolded Lydia. She said, "Come, Lizzy. I know you found him repugnant when he was at Netherfield. But he really is a gallant gentleman. Not warm and flattering like some scoundrels are, but decent, generous, and handsome too, I admit."

Kitty asked incredulously, "How do you know all this? You have not seen him for more than a year. I have to fetch Mary. She is taking down the wash for packing." Kitty looked longingly at the pile of fine dresses on the bed and said wistfully, "How I wish I were the one going to stay with Mrs. Trumbull!"

The two sisters watched Kitty turn to dash out of the room just as Mary entered. The four sisters ended up going down to the parlor together.

They heard the gentleman expressing his condolences on the passing of Mr. Bennet, followed immediately by his congratulations to Mrs. Bennet on the betrothal of Miss Jane Bennet to Mr. Lytle. Mrs. Bennet accepted both sentiments quietly but said nothing else; she was tongue-tied in front of this great man.

When her daughters entered, the Bennet matriarch was visibly relieved. She asked solicitously, "Mr. Darcy, do you remember my daughters? Lydia here is newly widowed. She returned home with my grandson, Aiden Cieran, a sweeter babe you will not see!"

To Mrs. Bennet, a married daughter took precedence over older, unmarried ones. Mr. Darcy bowed in greeting and expressed his condolences. Lydia, fully aware of the blunder she had just committed, curtsied but did not look at Mr. Darcy for fear he might detect her slip-up written all over her face.

"Here are Elizabeth, Mary and Kitty. Had you not come today, you would have missed both Elizabeth and Mary."

Mrs. Bennet, never missing an opportunity to boast about her second daughter's good fortune, practically crowed, "You see, sir, Elizabeth has brought great honor to our family by securing the position of Her Majesty's Keeper of the Robes. She will serve among other exalted ladies-in-waiting. It is an important position. She will see Her Majesty every day."

"Mary will stay with Mrs. Trumbull, Lizzy's benefactress. After Jane is married, there will only be Kitty, Lydia and my grandson, Aiden, here with me."

Mr. Darcy turned to Elizabeth and said, "Allow me to congratulate you again on your good fortune to be serving our monarch, if... that is what you aspire to do."

He lost his train of thought as soon as his eyes connected with those deep brown orbs, which had been invading his mind constantly over the past week.

Not willing to waste any more time before Elizabeth's imminent departure to the unreachable royal palaces, he turned to Mrs. Bennet and asked firmly, "Mrs. Bennet, would you allow me a private conference with Miss Elizabeth?"

Everyone in the room was taken aback by this request, except for Elizabeth, who had been in a stupor since Kitty announced the gentleman's visit. She stood frozen with her lips parted.

Her mother was the first to recover. The matriarch could usually scent a suitor from miles away. But Mr. Darcy's sudden appearance at her humble cottage asking for an interview with her now-favorite daughter threw her into befuddlement momentarily.

Jumbled thoughts rushed into her head: *Why on earth has he picked Lizzy? She hates him! However, if I have any say in the matter, she will, of course, accept him. He is so very rich! Rejecting Mr. Collins has turned out well then, has it not? What about Her Majesty?*

Mrs. Bennet returned to her match-making persona and suggested, "Of course, Mr. Darcy. We do not have a pleasant garden here as we did at Longbourn. A walk with Lizzy in the lane is a perfect way to enjoy this lovely spring day!"

"Mamma, it is misty and damp outside. You can barely see your own shoes if you look down!" Kitty artlessly corrected her mother.

"It is warm, and that is a far sight better than all those gloomy, cold winter days. Oh, Kitty, why don't you go with Mr. Darcy and Lizzy? Lydia is in mourning, and Jane should remain. Mr. Lytle should be here shortly."

Mary was again forgotten, but she did not mind because she still had packing to do, and she had learned to accept that her mother's inconsiderate verbal slight resulted from lacking a genteel upbringing rather than reflecting a spiteful intent. Besides, she did not wish to ruin the cordial relationship she had been enjoying with her mother since Mrs. Bennet's breakdown months ago.

Mr. Darcy and Elizabeth walked out with Kitty. They said not a word for quite a distance. Kitty could barely make them out, even though she was only a few feet behind. Being a chaperone was tedious if there was nothing to eavesdrop on or see. She wished she could go back to the cottage and draw.

What a diverting idea!

Meanwhile, the wandering couple did not realize that they had lost their chaperone. At length, Elizabeth, the more impatient of the two, hesitantly began, "Mr. Darcy, I am gratified you called on us today, else the opportunity to speak in person would be delayed for an indefinite period. Please allow me to thank you again and again from the bottom of my heart, and on behalf of my whole family, including my late father, for your generous help in restoring Lydia to her family, and saving all our reputations. On his deathbed, my father charged me to find Lydia, but I utterly failed him. I owe you a debt of gratitude I can never hope to repay."

Mr. Darcy gazed at her eager, passionate face and big, expressive brown eyes, and wanted nothing more than to take this guileless young woman into his embrace and kiss her senseless. He did not, of course. They were in a public place, even with the mist. Besides, if she was so overwhelmed by gratitude, taking her in his arms now would amount to taking advantage of her benevolent heart. It was tantamount to forcing her to accept a grand gesture of love, and that would never do. That also meant that his asking for her hand in marriage now might appear opportunistic to her.

Instead, he spoke of something else to bide his time to solve this conundrum—to ask for her hand or to wait.

"Miss Bennet, I... do not deserve such high praise from you. As for your family, much as I respect them, they owe me nothing. Could you tell me how you come to the knowledge of my involvement in delivering Miss Lydia out of her precarious situation? I did not believe Mr. Gardiner could be so little trusted."

"Oh, no, my uncle tried to keep his promise of secrecy. It was my deduction, stratagem, and Lydia's carelessness that revealed the truth. Lydia accidentally mentioned Mrs. Younge and her boarding house. I... have memorized every word in... your letter. I instantly recognized the name and suspected this Mrs. Younge to be the same as the one formerly in your employ, especially with Mr. Wickham being in the mix. After a few leading questions, which Lydia unsuspectingly answered, I found out both you and Colonel Fitzwilliam were her rescuers. I cannot say why, but I knew in my heart it was you who had everything planned, with the Colonel only assisting."

Mr. Darcy could not help smiling at the faith Elizabeth had in him. Perhaps he could ask for a courtship if an engagement was not yet appropriate. He first wanted to reassure her it was ultimately her own persistent efforts to rescue her sister that led to the fortunate outcome.

"Miss Bennet, I only followed your lead."

"My lead? How?" Elizabeth was mystified.

"When I saw how Wickham's elopement with Miss Lydia turned out, I had to find out whether the scoundrel had attempted such a despicable act in real life..."

Elizabeth, frowning deeply, interrupted the gentleman and asked, "I do not take your meaning, sir. What is real life versus... Oh! You have read my novel! And you have determined I am the authoress from the private details of your life I have so shamelessly exposed without your permission. You must hate me! Forgive me, Mr. Darcy! I am mortified!"

"Miss Bennet! Elizabeth, please be reassured I do not hate you. I was angry for a short while, but once I found out how you so tirelessly, faithfully protected your family and searched for Miss Lydia, my admiration for you welled up from the depths of my heart. I could not have suppressed it if I had tried."

He grabbed Elizabeth's hands and held them tightly. Seeing the lady did not resist, he continued, "I had thought my previous admiration for you was irrational. I had never allowed myself to acknowledge the existence of my intense feelings toward you. When I proposed to you at Rosings, I surprised myself as much as I also surprised you. When I went to the Continent, I was preoccupied with searching for my cousin and persuaded myself that the offer of marriage to you had been an impulse of the moment not grounded in affection, let alone reason. But that was just a delusion I fabricated to try to get over you because I thought you would never accept me. So once again, I have struggled in vain! My dearest Elizabeth, will you accept my hand in marriage?"

Elizabeth looked completely shocked—he was offering marriage directly after explaining why his first offer was borne of an irrational impulse.

Rationally, she was unsure if, in her tumultuous state, she should decide her fate by giving an answer to this proposal of marriage. Yet, her heart and soul leaped for joy at this second chance. She *would* not miss it!

Mr. Darcy surprised himself once again. He had thought it prudent to ask for a courtship for the time being because Elizabeth seemed so overwhelmed by gratitude. Yet the words flowed out of his mouth unbidden. They could not be retrieved. He did not regret them—far from it. He instantly realized this second offer was like the first: impulsive and from his heart. If his brain and his intellect had anything to do with it, it would have been to remind him he had better brace himself for another scathing rejection.

Elizabeth, needing assurance that what was happening was real, asked dumbly, "You wish to marry me still, after all that has happened?"

Mr. Darcy could not help another smile. This was not a humiliating scolding; not even sarcastic barbs cloaked in sweetness. He brought her hands up and kissed the gloved knuckles reverently instead of giving her a verbal answer.

Elizabeth blushed deeply. She had always known Mr. Darcy was her motivation to write her novel; it enabled her to experience fictitiously what she had lost because of her own folly and prejudice. The gentleman's romantic gesture jolted her from the agitated state she had been in since leaving the cottage. She realized she had not given the answer to his offer.

Now that her mind was calm, she looked directly into his eyes and said with determination, "Sir, Mr. Darcy, I am honored to accept the offer of your hand in marriage. I have regarded myself as your future wife since I put the first word of my story on paper."

With such an admission, Mr. Darcy felt justified pulling her into his arms for that kiss he had deemed indecorous. By then, the mist had turned into a dense fog, and from even ten feet away, they could not be seen.

After a very long moment of blissful felicity, the couple separated and smiled beatifically at each other.

"Mr. Darcy..."

"Fitzwilliam."

Elizabeth had to stop and think before she understood Mr. Darcy's request. It would take her some time to not associate her betrothed's Christian name to his cousin.

"Fitzwilliam, you were grave and silent at Mrs. Trumbull's. I had no inkling you still loved me."

"Forgive me, dearest. I had gone there to find out who had offered for you, and whether I had a chance to win back your heart. Bingley was taking up your time, and I felt ill-equipped expressing my feelings for you in his presence.

"When I found out your offer was to serve the Queen, I was both relieved and worried. How could I court you when you would go to the Queen's

House in just a few days? I suppose I am rather slow-witted when it comes to wooing."

"I thank you for this reasonable explanation. To own the truth, I erroneously assumed you would prefer the company of the hostess."

Mr. Darcy was startled to hear this, but Elizabeth reassured him it was merely a fleeting fancy.

Elizabeth asked for the entire account of how he discovered Lydia and how her youngest sister became a respectable widow with a legitimate son begat by a naval hero. By the end of his explanation, Elizabeth's eyes were glistening with thankful tears.

"Fitzwilliam, before my father died, he said if he could do anything for me from heaven, he would bring you and me together. I truly believe he is smiling at us right now.

"The main reason I consented to publishing the story was that I thought it unlikely you would read a novel, let alone one written by an unknown authoress. Yet you read it within days of arriving back in England. I must thank Mrs. Trumbull for persuading me to publish and using her influence to place copies into many homes."

"Dearest, I do read novels so I can make recommendations to my sister, but with yours, she recommended it to me. Reading most other novels has been an obligation. Reading yours provoked in me something completely new: it touched my heart, and I do not mean how it has changed my life by uniting us.

"My precious love, if you wish to continue writing novels for the world to enjoy, I shall not object. Georgiana will be delighted to preview stories you write."

"Oh, Fitzwilliam, Miss Darcy will be disappointed. I do not have any urge to write another. 'First Impressions' forced itself on me because I wanted my family's lives and mine to end differently, and... I regretted deeply my refusal of your first proposal, even before Lydia's elopement. I wished so much to see you at Pemberley that I fancied myself actually seeing you outside the stable block. This scene, so vivid to me, was the first scene I wrote for the novel."

"When I saw you coming out of Mrs. Trumbull's house, it felt like *déjà vu*. I imagine my expression then was very similar to how you described me in the novel. It is uncanny. Mr. Bennet might have had a hand in all this, after all."

Before retracing their steps to the cottage, the newly betrothed couple decided to delay publicly announcing their engagement until after Elizabeth had informed Her Majesty, whose approval must be granted before a lady-in-waiting could marry. It might only be a formality, but not soliciting approval could prove perilous. She did not want to test the Queen's temper and get sent to the Tower.

"Fitzwilliam, one advantage in delaying the announcement is your betrothed will be a lady connected to the Queen and not a penniless girl from a rented cottage. Some of your relations—in particular, Lady Catherine de Bourgh—may not vent their objections as freely as otherwise."

"Lady Catherine will object vigorously and often as long as I do not marry my cousin Anne, but it does not matter what my aunt thinks about my state of matrimony. Since you will become a Darcy, you should know that, for generations, the Darcy family has kept as far from Court as we can. The fact that I shall marry a lady-in-waiting will raise some eyebrows."

"Oh, I was not aware. Will this be a detriment to your family's reputation?"

"As long as you remain as you are, I do not care what others think, or whether you are a royal princess or a scullery maid."

Elizabeth's heart was filled to the brim with joy and love when she finally understood her betrothed's ardent love. She could not help standing on tiptoe to give Mr. Darcy's lips a quick kiss. He, however, had other ideas, and especially since they were shielded by a dense fog. Another opportunity like this might not come until they were married and at Pemberley.

They did not notice they were standing directly underneath the window where Kitty was drawing. However, the fog had become a ground fog, and

Kitty, from above, could see every detail of the passionate kiss between her sister and that proud man. Her heart started racing, and that scared her.

"Oh! Oh!" Kitty swooned.

Chapter 28

Kitty rushed downstairs to resume her delinquent chaperone duty. She was intent on not repeating her error in judgement, which led to Lydia's elopement and the death of her papa.

"Lizzy must have been coerced into this shocking behavior. Why does she not struggle to get away? She hates that proud man!" she muttered while dashing out of the house.

Everyone in the parlor followed her with their gazes, but the fog was so dense they could see nothing.

The door being thrown open prompted the entwined lovers to jump apart. By the time Kitty reached them, they were presentable, but their faces were flushed.

Kitty asked breathlessly, "Lizzy, I saw only a little of what you two were... doing just now, and I promise I will not tattle on you if you will not mention me being absent?"

Elizabeth and Mr. Darcy looked at each other, blushing crimson. Mr. Darcy cleared his throat and said, "Miss Catherine, you have my word. No one will think anything was amiss."

Elizabeth lowered her head and laughed so hard that her shoulders shook. Mr. Darcy's serious mien and Kitty's almost childlike request struck her as most comical.

Mr. Lytle was with Jane and Mary in the parlor when the trio entered. Being undoubtedly a man of the world, he took one look at the slightly disheveled appearances of Lizzy and Mr. Darcy and easily imagined the delightful activities the couple had been engaged in. He did not know Lizzy well, and Mr. Darcy even less. He would, however, suggest Miss Elizabeth and Mr. Darcy walk out together with himself and Jane to enjoy the foggy spring weather.

Jane made the introductions. Mr. Darcy stepped forward with Elizabeth on his arm. He looked around the room and was surprised to be pleased with the family he was about to gain. He smiled at Mrs. Bennet, which made his future mother-in-law's heart flutter, and said, "Mrs. Bennet, Miss Bennet, Miss Mary, Miss Catherine, Mrs. Cieran, and Mr. Lytle, I am very pleased to announce that Miss Elizabeth has honored me with her acceptance of my hand in marriage. Mrs. Bennet, Miss Elizabeth is of age, but I seek your blessing for our union, and will speak to Mr. Gardiner on the morrow, before I convey Miss Elizabeth to the Queen's House, and Miss Mary to Mrs. Trumbull's."

Mrs. Bennet, ever in awe of this tall, rich, and proud gentleman, said meekly, "Of course, Mr. Darcy. I am pleased to have you join our humble family."

Everyone in the room congratulated the couple on their pending union. Lydia, especially, was exultant. She exclaimed, "Mr. Darcy, my Aiden is so fortunate to have you as his uncle." Feeling she had slighted Mr. Lytle, she turned to the other gentleman and said, "And you too, of course, Mr. Lytle." Then she said, "Lizzy, you sly thing! I am more indebted to you than ever!"

Elizabeth was puzzled by this unexpected show of gratitude, but when Mr. Darcy squeezed her hand, she instantly realized Lydia had recognized Mr. Darcy's attachment to Elizabeth was what motivated him to come to Lydia's rescue. This idea made her heart swell.

He thought only of me!

Mrs. Bennet, grievous that her dinner menus had suffered because of her reduced income, was heartened that Mrs. Lytle had sent down a side of beef from the manor house, and Lizzy's quarterly wages advanced by the Queen would allow her to buy some fish and trimmings for a festive dinner.

She approached Elizabeth. "Lizzy, ask your Mr. Darcy what dishes he particularly enjoys. I cannot set a table like I used to at Longbourn, but you will not be ashamed of what your mamma does offer."

Dinner was indeed almost as scrumptious as those of their Longbourn days. The two future sons-in-law complimented Mrs. Bennet profusely, making the matriarch beam with pride. For the first time since his death, Mrs. Bennet thought of her deceased husband benevolently. The resentment she had held against her late husband finally dissipated.

Mrs. Lytle and Mrs. Darcy! Mrs. Cieran! Three daughters married or as good as! I shall go distracted!

While Mrs. Bennet was thus engaged in pleasant musings, the five Bennet sisters piled onto Jane's and Lizzy's bed to discuss how their lives would change in the future. Garnering the most focus was Lizzy becoming Queen Charlotte's lady-in-waiting. To the penniless sisters from a modest estate in Hertfordshire, the implication of being family to a court lady was so extraordinary it seemed like a fairy tale.

"What if the Queen forbids your marriage to Mr. Darcy?" asked Kitty. To her, what she observed outside of her window that day would scandalize both Lizzy and Mr. Darcy if they were not to marry soon.

"Mr. Darcy thought that unlikely. Madame d'Arblay had nothing but high praise for Her Majesty's character. She ended up serving the Queen far longer than she desired because she was afraid to oppose her father's wish, which was for her to serve the Queen forever. However, I have no such compunction. Worse comes to worst, we shall wait till the Queen no longer needs me," reasoned Elizabeth.

"No one wishes the Queen any ill, but that is the order of nature," interjected Mary sagely.

"What do you mean?" Kitty frowned.

Before anyone answered, she exclaimed, "Oh, you mean you will outlive the Queen!"

She then asked eagerly, "Lizzy, if you leave your position at Court before... while Her Majesty still needs a Keeper of the Robes, would you recommend me to Her Majesty? You said the Queen chose you because you look like her dead daughter, Princess Amelia. I look the most like you of all our sisters!"

Lydia interjected, "Unless the Queen allows me to have Aidan with me, I do not have any interest in taking any position that would require me to leave my son behind in order to serve her."

Elizabeth was amazed anew by the change in Lydia. It appeared her selfish and indecorous youngest sister was a thing of the past, even though she was not yet seventeen. Kitty, though a year older, was as flighty as ever. The hardships Lydia experienced at Wickham's hand had chipped away most, if not all, of her frivolous nature, anchoring her firmly on her son, whom she believed wholeheartedly to be of her beloved husband's blood. Kitty had much more growing up to do before she could be considered for a position outside of their home. For this reason, when Mrs. Trumbull had asked Elizabeth for one of her sisters to replace her, she had recommended Mary.

She would, however, oblige Kitty as much as she could. She said airily, "I doubt I would have any influence on Her Majesty's hiring, especially if she does not wish me to leave her service after only a few months, but I might arrange for your curtsies to the Queen. She asked me whether any of us had been presented, and I answered we had not because, as poor country girls, we did not have the sponsors or the means to procure the elaborate court dresses for Her Majesty's ball. She was very gracious and suggested a private presentation to save the trouble and cost of the feathers and fancy hooped dresses."

All five sisters erupted into a heated but good-humored debate on the merits of wearing the hooped dresses or not. The sadness that had engulfed the family for so long had finally lifted.

Chapter 29

In the entrance hall of Buckingham House, oblivious to the surrounding bustle, Mr. Darcy and Elizabeth stood facing each other. A page was waiting to take her to her rooms.

Neither had been prepared for their impending separation. Everything was so new and exhilarating after months of pining, especially when both had been convinced there was no hope for a future together. This separation was cruel indeed.

Taking a ring box from his waistcoat, he said, "Dearest, this ring has been in the Darcy family since the first Darcy matriarch. Knowing it is on your finger will reassure me you will come back to me no matter how long it takes."

"Oh, Fitzwilliam, 'tis a beautiful ring! I will keep it with me always. I own nothing of great material value, nor did I have any notion of sewing some handkerchiefs for you..." Elizabeth wrinkled her brows, trying to think of something to give to her betrothed for a keepsake.

"Will you allow me to keep your dodecagonal table until you return to me?"

"Of course! It is my most treasured possession. I wrote my entire story on it."

"I shall cherish it, as you do, and write all my letters to you on it. Remember, write to me through Georgiana."

With a few more lingering glances, the lovers reluctantly parted for an uncertain future.

Elizabeth started Court life with trepidation. She could not make out the Queen's attitude toward her. During her first interview with the Queen, Her Majesty had been all condescension. Now that she had joined the royal household, Her Majesty sent her wordless, sidelong glances with an inscrutable expression, which was eerie and deeply disturbing. Elizabeth worried that approaching the Queen about resigning her position for marriage would be far more difficult than anticipated.

Elizabeth, from the first day she reported for duty, became the object of fascination to the four royal princesses. At first, they stared at her and marveled at her resemblance to their dead sister, Amelia. After the curiosity had worn off, they asked endless questions about their most recent obsession—they wanted to know whether Mr. Keynes was a real person and exclaimed how they all wanted to marry him.

Because their father turned mad before he had had a chance to choose husbands for all but the Princess Royal, the princesses were unmarried. As the King's health continued to deteriorate, the Queen would not hear of any potential matches from foreign princes, and the King's own law forbade his children to marry commoners. The princesses were afraid to antagonize their mother or push their father further into insanity, even though marriage was their surest and most desired way to escape from the strict and suffocating grip of their mother.

This stalemate was relieved somewhat when their brother became Regent two years before. They begged their favorite brother to intervene with their mother. They were ready to fall in love with anybody, and rumors were rampant that some of them indeed had clandestine relationships with equerries and courtiers. It was no surprise that these love-deprived princesses readily fell in love with a fictional romantic hero.

Adding to Elizabeth's uneasy existence was her unwanted idleness. The other co-Keeper of the Robes, Frau von Waldheim, known at Court as Mrs. Waldheim, together with her assistant, handled the Queen's toilette with Teutonic efficiency. However, she still needed to be prepared and present in case the Queen had a task for her, which had not yet happened. The Queen Consort had many official duties as hostess for the Prince Regent, who had banished his wife because they hated each other.

Out of the intrigue among unhappy people came a glimmer of light. Her namesake, Princess Elizabeth, was a woman with a sunny disposition, in stark contrast to the gloomy atmosphere of the Royal residences.

Princess Elizabeth was twice Elizabeth's age, but she was active, both in mind and body. She studied nature and recorded it with her considerable artistic skills, and she loved to laugh. Her optimism made her a favorite among all who knew her.

In Miss Elizabeth Bennet, she found a kindred spirit. She often invited Miss Bennet to walk with her in the park at Buckingham House and described her garden at a rented cottage in Old Windsor Village, where she grew vegetables and raised livestock.

Elizabeth enjoyed these outings with the plain-speaking and fun-loving princess, and it helped that the Princess made excuses to the Queen for their absences.

One day, Elizabeth was pointing at a winter berry bush while wearing her ring, which she usually kept in a secret pocket sewn close to her heart in case she had to handle the Queen's dresses. She was taken aback when the Princess snatched her hand and brought it close to examine the ring.

"There are two rings very like this in my mother's collection. The rings were from our namesake, Elizabeth of York. See this red rose here? Yours is the Lancastrian Rose. One of Mamma's has white with yellow in the center, which was Yorkist. The third one is the Tudor rose. It is like yours except the center is the Yorkist's white and yellow, symbolizing the union of the two Houses. Very interesting! I often wondered whether there had been a Lancastrian rose. How did you come by it?" asked the princess with genuine curiosity.

Elizabeth was momentarily speechless. Mr. Darcy had not explained the origin of the ring to her, just that it was very old. She felt she had no choice but to admit the ring was from her betrothed, Mr. Fitzwilliam Darcy.

"Ah, the Darcy Pacifists. It all makes sense now. The first Darcy matriarch was a dear friend of Elizabeth of York. The Darcys abhor wars because they had lost all male members of their family during the Lancastrian-Yorkist conflicts. We of the House of Hanover are usually not so conversant about the English history of that era. However, I spend a lot of time reading in the Windsor library. Even when the entire castle is unbearably cold, there is always a good fire burning because my father favors that room," quipped the princess lightheartedly.

"Oh, he must be your Mr. Keynes!" The princess suddenly burst forth with delight upon this realization.

Elizabeth again had no choice but to nod.

"I long to meet him! He is my ideal husband! I wish I could marry. I had to decline a proposal five years ago because the Duke is a papist. Lord Orville—the hero in 'Evelina,' you must know him—had taken the duke's place as my imaginary husband until Mr. Keynes made his appearance." The princess placed both hands on her bosom and sighed.

Elizabeth became noticeably apprehensive when she heard longing in the princess's voice.

The princess laughed. "Do not be alarmed. I have a beau, and I love him to bits. I cannot have enough of him... ah, I should spare an innocent maiden like you the details. My sisters and I need some... outlets while being locked up in this nunnery."

Elizabeth could not hide her shock at such a frank admission from a prim and proper royal princess. Her aghast expression made the princess laugh even harder. It was then Elizabeth realized she had a genuine friend in Her Royal Highness.

"Do not worry about the Queen's reaction to our conduct. She knows full well who our lovers are, but she has chosen not to interfere. For that, we are grateful. Because I am her favorite, she does not want me to marry and leave her. It is a prickly problem for me but, no matter. As soon as we move back to Windsor, I shall have my sweet Betsy—my Guernsey cow—and my little chicks to cheer me up."

Just before Easter, Elizabeth moved with the Queen's entourage from Buckingham House to Windsor Castle. One day at teatime, she was overjoyed to see Colonel Fitzwilliam attending with the rest of the equerries. The King's equerries eating meals with the Queen's Keepers of the Robes had long been a tradition for over thirty years.

The two cousins-to be found a few moments for private conversation after dinner. Colonel Fitzwilliam said he would be on duty for the following two weeks. This made Elizabeth very glad. She felt imprisoned at Windsor. The days were long and dull since she had nothing to do. She could not even explore the castle on account of the mad King being in residence. The Queen never visited her royal husband, and so Elizabeth had no excuse to venture out.

"You must be dying to know how Darcy fares," quipped the Colonel, who could see Elizabeth wanted very much to ask that question.

"I confess, I am. His last letter said he was due for a visit to Lady Catherine at Rosings. I wonder whether he will tell her about his betrothal."

"I was at Rosings with Darcy before coming here. Lady Catherine had heard the news that Darcy had been calling on Mrs. Trumbull, and she is seriously displeased!" The Colonel expected Elizabeth to be amused, but saw a fleeting expression of worry or perhaps surprise? Disappointment? Jealousy?

"Did Darcy not tell you he had been attending Mrs. Trumbull's soirees on Thursday evenings?"

"Of course. But I never thought of those visits as 'calling on' Mrs. Trumbull. Please do not mind me, Colonel. I am not jealous of Mrs. Trumbull. It is just..."

"... difficult that Mrs. Trumbull regularly sees your beloved, and you do not?" probed the Colonel.

Elizabeth did not deny it. The Colonel felt it his duty as a future cousin to ease her anxiety by disclosing his relationship with Mrs. Trumbull.

"Miss Bennet, Mrs. Trumbull enjoys evening diversions, but not with Darcy. I visit her sometimes, but not on the evenings of her soirees."

Elizabeth's face became hot. She stuttered, "I... I... I do not know what to say, Colonel. I wish you and Mrs. Trumbull well."

The Colonel could not help smiling at the innocence of the young woman before him. "Miss Bennet, Mrs. Trumbull and I are, so to speak, experienced. You surely know such relationships exist?"

On seeing Elizabeth redder and redder in the face, he conceded, "Alright, alright, my pure-hearted future cousin, I shall cease and desist. Would you like to see Darcy before the Queen has issued her decree for you to marry?"

Elizabeth's face brightened instantly. "Oh, yes! I have an idea on which I would like to solicit your opinion. But first, what did Fitz... Mr. Darcy say to Lady Catherine's accusation?"

"Darcy said what needed to be said: being master of his own house, he could visit whomever he pleased, and he would never marry his cousin Anne."

"And Lady Catherine let it go without complaint?"

"Lady Catherine has no power over Darcy or me. We all know it, including her. Until Darcy ties the knot with you, she will continue to nag, threaten to cut him, and... oh, her favorite, 'I shall know how to act!' Darcy and I know how she will act: she will go to my father and complain, hoping he will do her bidding. In days past, my father tried to shift her attention to me, knowing full well that she would not accept me, and feeling he had performed his duty. But I doubt he will do such a thing anymore."

"Is that because of Mrs. Trumbull...? Forgive me, Colonel, I do not mean to pry," said Elizabeth apologetically.

"To be frank, neither Mrs. Trumbull nor I see matrimony in our future. No, I was rarely in England, and Lady Catherine could not get hold of me. Now, my father does not wish me the fate of having his sister as my mother-in-law unless I wish it, which will never happen."

The Colonel wanted to divert Elizabeth's attention from his relationship with Mrs. Trumbull. He asked, "I am impatient to hear your suggestion on how you and Darcy may meet while you serve the Queen."

"Oh!" exclaimed Elizabeth excitedly, assured that Lady Catherine would not be a problem. She explained she had Princess Elizabeth's support for meeting with Mr. Darcy on the palace grounds. The logistics were something the Colonel could help with.

"Since your duties are so light..."

"How do you know this, Colonel?" Elizabeth interjected.

"You are not the only one who has befriended a royal princess. Princess Sophia told me this. Being the youngest and best-looking equerry our King has had in a long time, the royal princesses had known of me since I began my duties here. All the princesses had already called on me."

Elizabeth was astonished, but she did not interrupt.

"Not contradicting me, at least about the best-looking part? Well, I am obliged," quipped the Colonel.

"Oh, Colonel, I thought you in person and address most truly the gentleman even when I first met you at Rosings."

"But not handsome?"

Elizabeth was going to object, but the Colonel stopped her.

"Where was I? Ah, since you have little to do during the day, you could name a time and meet in the park at either the Queen's House or here at Windsor. In years past, the King and his whole family used to walk out regularly in the palace gardens so their adoring subjects walking in the parks could see and even greet them. Do not be stealthy about it, as the Queen will not tolerate meetings that appear to be clandestine. And believe me, she will know if you walk on palace grounds with a gentleman.

"I do not recommend involving Princess Elizabeth in your meetings. The princesses have had a very sheltered existence and virtually no contact with gentlemen not of the Court. Can you imagine the attention my handsome cousin would attract from the man-crazy princesses? If I am not mistaken, Princess Elizabeth's lover is a fifty-eight-year-old former Lord of the Bedchamber for the King.

"Here at Windsor, if I am able, I shall be your chaperone. If I am not free, or when you are in London, Darcy may bring Georgiana. You should know that Darcy's regular appearance at Mrs. Trumbull's soirees has generated whispers, and that was how Lady Catherine heard about it. His being seen with you will throw those gossipmongers off track. They would most likely start speculating about his association with a lady at Court. Hmm... that would be interesting."

"Our meetings will look like a conventional courtship then, except royal approval may be involved. Do you think I should ask for the Queen's approval first?"

"It is perhaps prudent but not necessary, knowing Her Majesty's character. I understand the affairs of her daughters are known to her, but she has turned a blind eye. For the Keeper of the Robes, she would likely be unconcerned as long as you are not hiding from her. If she asks, inform her you are in a courtship with a gentleman, and he comes to walk with you occasionally. You still walk, do you not?"

"Yes, as much as I am able. The weather has turned spring-like. I dare not venture too far inside the castle, however, because so much is closed off on account of His Majesty."

"You do not want to run into him in a dark hallway—that is for certain. One cannot help pitying him. Before his illness, he was a most kind and solicitous man. Now, it is heart-wrenching to watch him behave like a lecher, even when lucid. He has had some lucid moments lately. I hope the trend continues and his behavior would revert to his avuncular self."

"I hope and pray our King will be well again soon. His health is a tremendous burden on his wife and daughters."

"Before I go, let me give you an urgent warning: If Prince Ernest is around, stay very far away from him. Better yet, never let him know you exist. He is rumored to have done unspeakable things to men and women alike, and those are not baseless rumors."

"Thank you, Colonel. I feel lighter already. At least, I can see through the bewildering goings-on more easily. Ah.., I am gladdened that Lillian has you in her life."

"I am delighted I can be of service to you. I have promised Darcy to watch out for you if I can. As for Mrs. Trumbull, she does not really need anyone in her life, but I am honored she has chosen me."

Elizabeth felt far more hopeful now that seeing her betrothed had become a real possibility.

Chapter 30

As predicted by her nephews, Lady Catherine went to her brother, demanding he talk sense into Darcy about marrying her daughter Anne. She had done this twice before, to no avail, but that was not reason enough to give up trying.

Has he lost his mind? Pursuing an old woman covered in filth from trade?

To her chagrin, when she arrived at her brother's house at Grosvenor Square, the Earl had left on Parliamentary business to the north, and the Countess had gone with him to see her new grandson.

She went to Darcy House next, but the master of the house was not at home; and the butler, Mr. Ford, refused Lady Catherine's entry to the house.

Lady Catherine was scandalized.

"What has the world become? Insolent servants rebelling against their superiors! I shall have Darcy dismiss you without reference!" she roared. But Mr. Ford was not concerned, as the order to bar the door to Lady Catherine in his absence came directly from his master. She went away fuming.

Lady Catherine's own townhouse had long been leased out, but she was not without friends in town. She visited her friend of long standing, Lady Mellon, and secured an invitation to stay at the Mellon's residence. Through questioning Lady Mellon, one of the more notorious gossips in town, she discovered Mrs. Trumbull's soiree was to be held that evening.

If she needed to go to the Trumbull residence to confront Darcy, so be it, even if she must pinch her nose to keep out the stench of trade.

My character has ever been celebrated for its sincerity and frankness; and in such a moment as this, I shall certainly not depart from it.

When she entered Trumbull House that evening, she was miffed no one paid her any attention, which confirmed for her that Darcy was mixing with riff-raff who did not understand the distinction of rank.

By now, Mrs. Trumbull, following Miss Mary Bennet's suggestion, had implemented a new format for her gatherings. Only invited guests were admitted to the soiree, which held a formal presentation followed by supper. The only two gentlemen who did not need an invitation to attend were Colonel Fitzwilliam and his cousin, Mr. Darcy.

Most people believed Mr. Darcy was Mrs. Trumbull's matrimonial target, and the Colonel benefitted from being a close relation of the Darcys.

Lady Catherine walked toward the grand salon, from whence voices emanated. However, since she was not on the guest list, two footmen barred her entrance.

"What is the meaning of this? Do you know who I am?" thundered Lady Catherine, nearly cracking the floor with her cane.

Mr. Darcy had been listening half-heartedly to a presentation given by a well-known historian about the recent war news from the Continent. He was usually attentive in presentations like this, but this was a special day for him.

He and Georgiana had gone to walk with Elizabeth in the Queen's House park that morning. Since then, he had been basking in the warm memories of seeing his betrothed after almost a month of separation and her sisterly interactions with Georgiana.

Georgiana had been her timid self at the beginning and listened with an astonishment bothering on alarm at her future sister's lively, sportive manner of talking to her brother. However, she had never seen her brother looking so openly pleasant. From Elizabeth herself, she had received gentle, light-hearted prodding, which made her talk without the usual fear she was saying something wrong or childish. When Elizabeth suggested she join the Bennet sisters in a private presentation to the Queen, she almost cried in gratitude. She had dreaded the court presentation ever since her aunt Lady Fitzwilliam had told her it could not be avoided. At the end of the visit, she eagerly looked forward to having Elizabeth at Pemberley soon.

The two siblings then went to Rambler Cottage for a family dinner with the Bennets. Georgiana, after having met Lizzy, was well-disposed toward the remaining Bennet sisters. She did not feel the embarrassment she invariably experienced among young ladies who were pleasant to her only to get close to her brother. The sisters were as lively as Lizzy, and they were around her own age! Even Mrs. Bennet was exceedingly welcoming and treated her as family.

On the way back to Darcy House, Georgiana was rhapsodic about becoming part of such a large, warm, and fun-loving family of ladies.

He would have stayed home to savor these precious feelings, but he had promised Bingley to attend the Trumbull soiree this evening. Bingley complained that even though his sister had been more compliant, she had not stopped nagging him about calling on Mrs. Trumbull. To maintain the peace, and to avoid visiting during daytime calling hours with his meddlesome sister, he chose to attend an evening salon with Darcy in part because he wanted to see how much truth was behind the rumor that Darcy was pursuing Mrs. Trumbull. Among his new circle of friends, there was a wager going on, and Bingley wanted to win.

When the unmistakable shrill voice of his aunt came through the closed doors of the drawing room, Mr. Darcy was rudely awakened from his pleasant ruminations. He excused himself from Bingley and the Duke of Bridgestone, who sat on either side of him, and hurriedly went out to the hall.

"Aunt Catherine, I did not expect to see you here. If you had informed me you wished to attend this gathering, I could have secured an invitation for you." Mr. Darcy offered his arm to his aunt, attempting to lead her away from the salon.

"Darcy, you should be ashamed of yourself—brazenly chasing an old widow oozing filth from her dead husband's trade money..."

"Lady Catherine, desist from your nonsensical slander. No one is chasing anyone else, as you so indelicately described."

"You cannot deny the truth of what I said. There is rampant gossip about your frequenting this foul house of a cit. Why do you, of your own accord, mix with the detritus far beneath you? Have you ever considered if your mother were alive, how broken-hearted she would be that you abandoned your betrothed and were seduced by a low woman? Are the shades of Pemberley to be thus polluted?"

Mr. Darcy cringed at the preposterous insults his aunt threw at him and the people at this gathering of eminent intellectuals and members of Parliaments. He was, for the first time, ashamed to be related to his aunt.

Once the shock of Lady Catherine's appalling language passed, he was confused. What could Lady Catherine mean by his abandonment of Elizabeth? He quickly realized the delusional woman was referring to her daughter, Anne.

Mr. Darcy thought it best to take his aunt away rather than to prolong the embarrassing scene.

Meanwhile, the presentation had ended. Guests were streaming from the salon towards the dining room for supper. Among the first to appear was George Bentinck, Duke of Bridgestone. He had come this evening because his two sons were fighting on the Peninsula, and he was hungry for news from the front lines, especially through unofficial but reliable channels.

His Grace had grown up with Lady Catherine as a neighbor, and she had set her cap at him when he was a young man. He, however, had never been interested.

The duke addressed his former neighbor, "Catherine, well met. I thought I recognized your voice." He turned to Mr. Darcy and said, "Darcy, please give me an opportunity to catch up with your aunt. Go on to supper. Lady Catherine is in good hands, I promise you."

Lady Catherine was exceedingly surprised to see the duke at a tradesman's home. She had time only to utter, "Bridgestone..."

The duke intercepted her greetings and said severely, "I heard your description of me as detritus. I am seriously displeased. If Mrs. Trumbull's home is good enough for me, it ought to be good enough for you. After all, she is descended from a line of twelve baronets, whereas you married a man who bought a title. Your indelicate and public accusation of Darcy courting Mrs. Trumbull simply fans rumors of this falsehood instead of quenching them. Darcy is like family. I need to discuss with him how to handle the vicious gossip you and your groundless accusation have caused. You might have left him no choice but to ask for Mrs. Trumbull's hand. In terms of fortune, intellect and lineage, they are well-matched. Now, let me escort you to your carriage. You have done enough harm."

Lady Catherine's face turned ashen. "Bridgestone, I... never meant this to happen. I did not know you would be in attendance. This is not to be... borne..." The last word was not audible because Lady Catherine had to swallow it.

"Catherine, on account of my friendship with your brother, allow me to offer a word of advice. You have not been to town in years. Things and people are not the same as when you were younger. Ladies such as Mrs. Trumbull— intelligent, erudite, beautiful, and with immense fortunes—have powerful influence in many spheres. If she felt insulted, she could simply hint to her bosom friend, my niece, Lady Nottingham, and you would be cut by polite society. Please do not be an embarrassment to your nephew again. I have no daughters, or else I would have gladly married one of them to him. But Darcy is his own man, and a great friend to my three boys. He will marry where he wants, even if the lady is from trade."

When the duke reentered the house, both Mr. Darcy and Mrs. Trumbull thanked him for so handily resolving a prickly problem.

275

The duke laughingly answered, "I am particularly qualified to dispatch Lady Catherine. You should have seen her attempts to catch me when we were young. I believe she will not be a problem for you anymore, Darcy. However, she did announce loudly to the people gathered here that you two were courting."

He turned to Mrs. Trumbull and said, "Madam, you have chosen your guest list well, but it is impossible to prevent talk. Even decent gentlemen could turn into a peck of squawking hens when the topic seems like a juicy worm. Unless you two are indeed courting, what will you do about this?"

Both Mr. Darcy and Mrs. Trumbull denied vehemently anything other than friendship between them. Each, of course, knew of the other's true attachment but would not divulge it.

"Your Grace, I thank you for your advice. Since Mr. Darcy and I are not courting, we cannot satisfy the gossipmongers. However, if it is a scandal they want, it is within my power to create one that will take the attention off Mr. Darcy but will not harm me at all. In fact, I look forward to such a diversion."

Both gentlemen were intrigued by Mrs. Trumbull's remark, but the lady demurred and would not disclose her plan other than to assure Mr. Darcy that all would be well.

Throughout the rest of the evening, Bingley kept hinting at Darcy he could be trusted with the truth about Lady Catherine's accusations. Mr. Darcy decided Bingley had indeed changed. It was time to distance himself from both Bingley and his sister. He was disappointed, but it could not be helped. Bingley needed to grow up, but Darcy declined to take on the responsibility.

The next day, as expected, the rumor of Mr. Darcy's and Mrs. Trumbull's impending nuptials was all over town. Miss Bingley, having eavesdropped on her brother's conversation with an acquaintance he invited back to his house after the soiree, was one of its most enthusiastic spreaders. Disappointed though she was at the loss of her chance of becoming mistress of Pemberley, she relished being the center of attention among her acquaintances.

A day after that, Mrs. Trumbull was seen boarding a ship with her Italian lover, Mr. Rocco, and none of her children. The rumor that they were traveling to Italy to be married spread like wildfire. The ton was quite sympathetic toward Mr. Darcy, but he was not available, having left town with his sister. He was sighted at Windsor, leaving people to wonder if he sought out his cousin, an equerry to the King, to lick his wounded heart.

To the Bingley siblings, the door to Darcy House was closed to them. Mr. Bingley was more chagrined than he wanted to admit. Darcy had not formally cut him but made it clear that their former fraternal closeness no longer existed. He would sorely miss his old friend's guidance, but he understood the reason: his sister had unwittingly incriminated herself and him when spreading the rumor by always beginning with, "My brother, Mr. Darcy's close friend, heard with his own ears what Lady Catherine announced..."

Immediately before leaving for a hunting party in the north, he went to his solicitor, and this time carried out the threat as promised. He never witnessed the terrible tantrum Miss Bingley threw on learning that her pin-money had been cut to half of the original size. Worse, a new condition had been added: any damage she caused to her brother's house would have to be repaired or replaced by deducting the same amounts from her dowry.

Miss Bingley, without her generous pin money, was like a snake without its fangs. She felt physically weak because she could no longer afford the fashionable dresses that gave her strength. Worse, she had been cut from polite society wherever she turned. She had no choice but to retreat to Scarborough, where her four hundred pounds a year could go a long way, and the ton's spite had not bothered to reach that far. She would bide her time there and plan her revenge on her despicable brother, who supplied her with information and then blamed her for telling others. How was it fair?

Mr. Bingley, of course, knew his actions had consequences. However, now that the last of the elder generation of the Bingley family had died, he had no pressing reason to visit his ancestral home.

He had no lack of entertainment from his ever-growing circle of friends, even without Darcy. Besides, Darcy's new form of amusements—going to lectures instead of balls—was not to his taste. In a few years, he might look Darcy up again.

He finally admitted to himself, being friends with Darcy was hard work, and he had rather not exert himself if he could help it.

Chapter 31

The religious people of Clapham had a reputation for being saintly, but when a rumor from town came their way involving two who lived among them, many could not help spreading the abhorrent news. Mrs. Trumbull aroused much anger from the usually charitable people of Clapham because she had injured the pure-hearted Miss Mary Bennet by association.

After one Sunday service, the Bennet ladies were not shunned, but their neighbors stayed a few paces away, eyeing the four handsome women. Mrs. Lytle, being hard of hearing, had not yet heard the gossip.

One of the curious matrons of the church came over to ask, "Mrs. Bennet, how could you allow Miss Mary to work for such an immoral woman?"

Mrs. Bennet had not known until that moment of any condemnation of Mrs. Trumbull.

She was disgusted by this attack against herself and Mrs. Trumbull, who had been nothing but kind and generous toward her family.

"Balderdash! My Mary told me she traveled overland with the young Miss Trumbulls and their governess and nurses to Mrs. Trumbull's estate in Wales. Mrs. Trumbull went separately by sea to meet them because she fancied a voyage. She is very rich, you know. She can do whatever she has a mind to, like any rich man. Of course, she needed a strong young man to escort her on this sea journey."

The matron asked, "Is it not indecent for a lady to have a male guard traveling with her unchaperoned?"

"How were they unchaperoned? She has footmen and maids accompanying her in addition to Mr. Rocco, who was her late husband's ward. He is a member of the Trumbull family. Busybodies in town saw Mr. Rocco in the carriage with her and started a vicious rumor that the ignorant people here spread. I am ashamed of... not you, but the rest of these hypocrites!" Mrs. Bennet shook her finger at those who, though keeping their distance, were listening to every word she uttered.

"Mr. Rocco has been traveling with the Trumbulls for years. He came from Italy as a boy to live with his cousin, who owns a pugilist club in London. Mr. Trumbull heard him play the pianoforte in the dining room of the club one day and was so impressed by the young man's musical talent that he offered young Mr. Rocco a place in his household, and brought him up like a brother. When Mr. Trumbull became ill, only Mr. Rocco's music could calm his mind.

"If he were to marry, it would most likely be to my Mary from the way she talks about him—he improved her pianoforte skills ten times over, she was the instrument God used to lead Mr. Rocco to Himself, and on and on. I have not met him, but if Mary has chosen him, he must be a young man with a good heart. Mr. Trumbull left him a handsome inheritance. He can afford to marry. He will be my son. Mark my words!"

So the good people of Clapham became the first to discard the rumor as nonsense. They were also very glad that the gentle, pious Miss Mary Bennet had found a worthy young man to marry. Within a few days, the rumor died away even in Town, for Lord Byron obligingly supplied new grist for the gossip mill.

Within the royal household, Elizabeth was gradually gaining a firm foothold. Her friendship with Princess Elizabeth was a boon to her usually monotonous existence. When she was at Windsor, Colonel Fitzwilliam was a comfort. His cheerful mien and sage advice helped bolster her confidence. Her only occupation was to wait for the next time she could meet the gentleman of her heart.

In the meantime, the Queen remained aloof, and the princesses scurried soundlessly around their mother. One day, to Elizabeth's great astonishment, the Queen halted a conversation in German with Mrs. Waldheim to say, "Miss Bennet, if you still desire a private presentation for your sisters, bring them in after the next drawing room on Thursday because I plan to remain at Windsor for the foreseeable future."

Elizabeth was flabbergasted. Just when she thought the Queen Consort was cold and indifferent to everyone around her, including her own daughters, Her Majesty exhibited such kindness and thoughtfulness. That she remembered such a small promise made months ago was unbelievable, but very well appreciated. Elizabeth took the opportunity to ask permission for Miss Darcy to be included as well.

"She is the sister of your young man, is she not?" asked the Queen offhandedly.

"Yes, madam." That was all Elizabeth could say. She had suspected the Queen knew her every move, and now she had proof.

Her Majesty abruptly returned to her conversation with the other Keeper of the Robes, and Elizabeth was dismissed soon after.

When she next saw the Darcys, it was when the siblings left London to take refuge from the scandal about Mrs. Trumbull and Mr. Rocco.

"You may want to know that Mr. Rocco and your sister, Miss Mary Bennet, are courting. So there was never any danger present between Mrs. Trumbull and him," said Mr. Darcy, a little sheepishly because his sister was present, and he did not want to appear a gossip.

"Oh, good for Mary! Mr. Rocco never said more than five words to me: 'My business is finished here.'" Elizabeth lowered her voice to imitate Mr. Rocco, who had a pleasant bass voice. Both siblings laughed at Elizabeth's antics.

"Both Miss Mary and Mr. Rocco have changed noticeably in the last few weeks. Miss Mary looks much more like you now with her hair styled like yours, and her dresses like any fashionable young lady. Mr. Rocco smiles a great deal more as well. When I first attended the gatherings, he looked almost glum."

Elizabeth wanted to say, "Just like someone I know!" But she decided against it. It was perhaps too early to tease the Darcy siblings.

They went on to speak about Elizabeth requesting leave to attend the upcoming wedding of Jane and Mr. Lytle, and the all-important permission from Her Majesty to marry.

Just then, they turned a corner and came to the farm cottage of Princess Elizabeth. Her Royal Highness was crouching down to examine the newly planted vegetable garden. In her plain dress and almost unladylike posture, one never would have guessed her identity.

Elizabeth did the introductions. Miss Darcy was completely awe-struck. She was so nervous when she performed the deep curtsy that she almost fell.

The princess was equally awe-struck, but by a different person. She stared at Mr. Darcy and said in a dreamy voice, "Mr. Keynes..."

Mr. Darcy was extremely embarrassed. With other ladies who ogled him, he put on his most haughty mien by clenching his jaws and looking forbidding. But he was in front of a royal princess, who was also Elizabeth's ally in the tangled web of the Royal household. Surprising himself, he lowered his head to hide his face from the Princess's adoration.

After a few moments, the Princess remembered her manners in public. She said kindly, "Mr. Darcy, Miss Darcy, do you enjoy gardening?"

The Princess gave a tour of her garden and small farm to the Darcy siblings, all the while stealing glances at the handsome gentleman. Elizabeth remembered Colonel Fitzwilliam's warning about not letting her betrothed be in contact with the princesses more than necessary.

At the end of the garden tour, Mr. Darcy complimented the Princess sincerely on the excellent management of her agricultural innovations, making the Princess blush fiercely with pleasure while batting her eyelashes shamelessly.

Mr. Darcy and Elizabeth could barely contain their mirth when walking away from the Princess until they heard the dreaded question from Miss Darcy: "Brother, why did Her Royal Highness call you Mr. Keynes?"

Mr. Darcy stopped short. He had forgotten half of the family did not know the truth about 'First Impressions' being partially autobiographical.

Elizabeth, quick-witted in situations like this, answered, "Georgiana, Princess Elizabeth, like all her sisters, loves 'First Impressions.' They live like hermits, and do not see many young and handsome men like your brother. You must excuse Her Royal Highness's fancy."

Mr. Darcy beamed proudly at his betrothed, pleased she considered him handsome. His smile dropped when Miss Darcy asked, timidly this time, "Lizzy must be Miss Isabella Delancey then?" Both of her companions were startled by Georgiana's perceptiveness.

When Miss Darcy realized she had inadvertently voiced her speculation aloud, the young girl lowered her head and said softly, "Forgive me, Lizzy, Brother. I did not mean to speak my fancy out loud. My only excuse is that I also lead a sheltered life and allowed my imagination to roam without restraint."

Elizabeth asked gently, "What made you think I resemble a fictional character, Georgiana? I am intrigued."

"Your... lighthearted, easy conversations during our walks have impressed me deeply. I could not name it until Princess Elizabeth's remark reminded me they are how Mr. Keynes and Miss Delancey banter in the novel. It is uncanny... to my... mind. I hope you do not mind my drawing such nonsensical conclusions from a novel."

Mr. Darcy decided he would need to speak with Georgiana once they were back in London. Continuing to disguise the truth from this point on amounted to deceit. He and Elizabeth passed each other a meaningful look, confirming that disclosure was inevitable.

Chapter 32

The rapidly approaching presentation to the Queen created feverish preparations in the Bennet household. Mr. Gardiner provided funds from Elizabeth's novel sale for a new head-to-toe ensemble for each Bennet lady except Mary, who was in Wales with Mrs. Trumbull. Mrs. Gardiner and Mrs. Bennet joined the young ladies to be presented as well. Lydia, previously determined to remain in mourning for a full year, reconsidered. She reasoned that her presentation at Court would be a valuable asset for Aiden being recognized as a gentleman, even without an estate.

The Bennet, Gardiner and Darcy ladies gathered at Buckingham House arrayed in their finery. They saw ladies in elaborate dresses leaving the palace and could not help admiring the novelty, even though none regretted not having to wear the cumbersome dresses.

"I would surely trip and fall in front of Her Majesty!" exclaimed Kitty.

Lydia thoughtfully said, "I do not see how the dress could be altered to wear on other occasions. It also does not make sense for me to save it, as my Aiden is a boy." Her practicality had become a permanent trait of her character.

Miss Darcy simply beamed at the group of ladies who would become her family. She felt she had known these ladies far longer than just their few weeks of acquaintance. Her brother had explained that Mr. Keynes and Miss

285

Isabella Delancey were indeed based on himself and Elizabeth, as Elizabeth was the authoress. The only question Miss Darcy had was whether Miss Lydia had been hurt by Mr. Wickham. Mr. Darcy wanted to preserve the secret for Lydia's sake and explained that only part of the story was taken from real life. Miss Darcy was satisfied with this answer. She fervently hoped Lizzy would write another story, especially one about her Court experience. Princess Elizabeth seemed a good story in and of herself.

The three gentlemen escorts, Mr. Gardiner, Mr. Lytle, and Mr. Darcy, looked on their loved ones with great pride. Mr. Lytle and Mr. Darcy were both from very small families, and the large crowd of ladies in their future family made them feel that life would never be lonely again.

The presentation of the Bennet clan took place after the formal receptions were over. Elizabeth came into the waiting room to escort the ladies to the Queen, who was fatigued after several hours of receiving ladies of note, but she was attentive when the Bennet ladies were introduced to her. She scrutinized the Miss Bennets closely, her eyes staying on Kitty for a long moment.

After all the curtsies had been received, Her Majesty signaled the interview was over, and they carefully backed away from the Queen to the anteroom. The ladies all breathed a sigh of relief. Being received by the Queen was a great honor, but none of them wanted to repeat the experience.

Elizabeth accompanied them to the door. She lingered with them for as long as possible. That was the first time in two months she had seen her mother, sisters, and the Gardiners.

The entire party was to dine at Darcy House that evening. Since there would be no ball to celebrate the presentations, a three-course dinner would have to suffice.

While the party was waiting for their carriages, Elizabeth hurried toward them with a joyous smile that almost split her face.

"The Queen has given me leave to be away until tomorrow. Princess Elizabeth intervened. She knew how I longed to see my family," Elizabeth said breathlessly. "Could you give me a few minutes to pack a few things?"

Mrs. Bennet answered graciously, "Of course, Lizzy! We are going directly to Darcy House and shall spend the night there. You need not hurry. I shall enjoy watching the comings and goings at the palace."

Elizabeth and Mr. Darcy exchanged another look. Elizabeth had not known the details of the celebration. She had assumed her family would stay with the Gardiners as they had done many times over the years. Somehow, the thought of sleeping under the same roof as her betrothed was enough to set her heart racing and cheeks burning.

When the celebratory party arrived at Darcy House, it did not take more than a few moments for the older retainers of the house to notice that, among the festively dressed house-guests, there was a young lady who would likely become their new mistress. Until now, they had never seen their master giving such frequent, tender looks to a young lady on his arm. They could already see little Darcys pitter-pattering around the house.

After a refreshing tea, the group dispersed to their assigned rooms to rest.

Mr. Darcy stopped the housekeeper and asked, "Mrs. Fordham, were you able to settle our guests in satisfactory accommodations?"

She smiled pleasantly and answered, "Yes, sir. The guests who are not staying overnight have returned to their own homes until dinner. I had to put our last guest, Miss Elizabeth Bennet, in the family wing. I hope that meets with your approval, Mr. Darcy."

Mr. Darcy's heart skipped a beat with this news. "Of course, Mrs. Fordham. With you in charge, I am certain our guests will need for nothing."

Mr. Darcy knew full well that Mrs. Fordham could have asked Elizabeth to share a room with one of her sisters, but he would not complain.

Instead of resting, Elizabeth and Jane met in Jane's room to talk.

"Dearest, it has been an age since I have seen you. How have things been? You have not written as often lately."

"Forgive me, Lizzy. With Mary away, I have been spending more time with Mrs. Lytle. I have also started planting the garden and preparing my trousseau."

"Oh, have you set the date for the wedding? Do you have enough funds? I asked Uncle to release some monies from the sale of my book. Could you believe it has earned over eight hundred pounds? There will be two hundred pounds for each of my sisters."

"Lizzy, you should keep some for yourself..." chided Jane gently.

Elizabeth interrupted, "You have all earned it by allowing me to cast you in the story. Without my sisters, there would have been no story. Moreover, earnings from the story continue, as we speak."

"But you are also giving us a part of your wages for serving the Queen. We have all become veritable heiresses because of you!"

"Don't jest, Jane. Both you and I will be marrying gentlemen of means. Our daughters will be heiresses, if we are to be so blessed. First, we must marry. When?"

"What do you think of marrying Mr. Darcy on the same day as Jeremy and me? That will make my joy complete."

"That would indeed be wonderful!" Elizabeth paused and became thoughtful. "I have not had the courage to broach the subject with the Queen. All my attention had been on your presentations. Now gaining the Queen's approval has become urgent. I have the advantage of having Princess Elizabeth as a friend. She is sympathetic to anyone who cannot marry because the Queen does not allow it. However, I am no princess and not bound by the Royal Marriages Act. My request should be only a formality. I promise not to wait too much longer and make you pine for your Mr. Lytle!"

"I hope all will be well with you, Lizzy. The Queen has a reputation of being kind. I can afford to wait a while longer."

Elizabeth was indeed very worried about asking the Queen. Lately, the Queen hardly spoke to her in the ubiquitous presence of Mrs. Waldheim, who conversed with the Queen only in their native German. Elizabeth understood a little German because of her fondness for Middle English, a substantial part of which was derived from German, but she tried not to eavesdrop. Madame d'Arblay had advised her that the Queen valued confidentiality above all else, and she was most keen to follow this advice.

Trying to keep her mind off such a prickly topic, Elizabeth asked about the welfare of her other sisters.

"Lydia, as you already know, has changed for the better from the brash, shameless flirt... oh, I should not be critical, since she is no longer like that," said Jane apologetically.

"Of course, Jane. I have noticed you have been far more forthright since... we left Longbourn. You yourself said that you have grown a backbone. So, criticize away! You never wrongly accuse anyone or anything in all your life."

"So long as you understand. Lydia is a devoted mother. She is lively still, but no longer frivolous. Kitty has found anchorage in her drawing. She regularly visits galleries and museums with young Miss Trumbull, who is also a budding artist. They go together under the care of Miss Trumbull's governess."

"And what of Mary? Mamma said she and Mr. Rocco were courting, which surprised me. I never got to know Mr. Rocco during the few months I was with Mrs. Trumbull, even though he was there regularly. For a brief time, I had suspected perhaps they were lovers. I am ashamed of such scandalous thoughts."

"You know Mr. Rocco was Mr. Trumbull's ward and brought up like a brother?"

"I learned recently when Fitzwilliam... Mr. Darcy told me about the daring provocation Mrs. Trumbull created to shift the focus of the emerging gossip from himself and Mrs. Trumbull."

"But Lizzy, Mary never said anything about being courted by Mr. Rocco. I think mamma is making a prediction she wishes for. Mary, however, has spoken highly of him. Apparently, Mr. Rocco grew up as a devout Catholic in his hometown in Italy but somehow became alienated from his faith. He became agnostic. Mary's piety fascinated him, and his faith in God was reignited by our gentle, honest, and faithful Mary, whose every action in life is guided by her belief. They began studying the Bible together, and he now joins the Trumbull household for church services. Mr. Rocco is also an outstanding musician—a prodigy even. Mary's performance at the pianoforte has had an astounding improvement. It is a pleasure to listen to her practice."

"I hope Mr. Rocco's heart is true toward Mary. She deserves someone special to love. What of mamma?" Elizabeth asked.

"As you know, little Aiden is the apple of mamma's eye. She sews all day long: booties, frocks, caps, blankets... everything. Even if Aiden wears one new piece of clothing every day until he turns five, he will not exhaust the pile mamma will have made! She is indeed much more patient—not at all prone to nervousness. The only thing that reminds us of Longbourn is that she keeps an eye on the Collinses through my Aunt Philips. She claims she cares only because Aiden has a chance to inherit Longbourn after Mr. Collins, especially because Charlotte's pregnancy did not come to term."

"Poor Charlotte! For Charlotte's sake, I wish the Collinses well. It seems to me the Miss Bennets of Rambler Cottage have done very well for themselves, better even than at Longbourn. However, I would give up all of this to have papa back."

"Even getting married to Mr. Darcy?"

"That is indeed a conundrum. Without his rescue of Lydia, we would not be as we are today. So, I must keep him, and you may keep your Mr. Lytle, too."

Both sisters laughed heartily at Lizzy picking and choosing her fate as she saw fit. When the laughter had died down, Elizabeth added thoughtfully, "Did you notice we did not weep when I mentioned papa?"

"Yes, Lizzy. I miss him greatly, of course. But he set us on the path toward our current happiness by collecting valuable books that led us to Rambler, and you to Mrs. Trumbull, who enabled you to publish your story, which led to Mr. Darcy's finding Lydia. I think without great trials, there cannot be great happiness. I believe with my whole heart that papa..." Jane paused and looked heavenward, "has had a hand steering us to a future of happiness."

Just then, the dinner gong sounded. The sisters separated to get dressed, each with misty eyes and hearts overflowing with gratitude and love for their dear departed papa.

Chapter 33

The celebration dinner at Darcy House was joyous. Mr. Darcy invited Mrs. Bennet to sit at the head of the table, making the Bennet matriarch beam with radiance at her future son-in-law. Everyone at the table noticed what a handsome woman Mrs. Bennet still was, despite being mother to five grown daughters.

After dinner, the men stayed behind while the ladies, led by Georgiana, retired to the drawing room. Lydia commented, "Oh, Miss Darcy, you are so fortunate to live in such a grand house, but you do not seem to have a pianoforte. Otherwise, we could have a ball for just ourselves. We were presented to the Queen today. We should have a ball!"

Kitty immediately rejoined, "Are you not in mourning still, Lydia? Dancing would be inappropriate for you."

No longer following Lydia's every move, now Kitty called things for what they were.

"You are right, of course, Kitty. But we are all family here, and I am not wearing my mourning dress. I would so love to have just one day of gay enjoyment before I go back to mourning my dear Daniel."

Miss Darcy chimed in, "There is a pianoforte in the music room. I shall play some dances if you like."

Everyone marveled at Miss Darcy's boldness for speaking up. She had only talked when spoken to. Lydia clapped her hands and exclaimed, "What a lovely idea, Miss Darcy! I shall finish my cake quickly. Please wait for me!"

Since a ball had not been held in Darcy House for the past ten years, the ballroom had become Miss Darcy's music room. Without even pushing the furniture to the wall, there was plenty of space for an impromptu dance.

Miss Darcy played a cotillion as the first dance. The ladies formed three couples. They bowed and curtsied, and the dance began!

The gentlemen heard music and ladies' laughter. They instantly abandoned their drinks and cigars and hurriedly left the dining room in search of the source of the merriment. Soon there were four couples dancing, as Mrs. Bennet insisted she did not care to dance anymore as she kept forgetting the steps.

Elizabeth took turns at the pianoforte so Miss Darcy could take a turn dancing.

The dance lasted till after midnight. None of its participants could remember a more enjoyable time. Miss Darcy felt she could face any ball during her first season after this.

As they parted for the evening, Jane asked Elizabeth, "Lizzy, would you share my room tonight? It is twice the size of our room at Longbourn. If I had not visited Trumbull House, I would have thought this a royal palace!"

"Jane, your room is better decorated and more comfortable than many of the older rooms at Windsor Castle and the Queen's House."

Elizabeth looked around, and for the first time, felt the honor and privilege of becoming mistress of such a fine house. Tonight, she wished to stay in her own room. She turned to Jane and said, "I would like to, but it is late, and I need to return to the Queen early tomorrow morning to accompany her back to Windsor. I had better get some rest. If the Queen is irritated with me, she might not allow me to marry."

"I shall see you off in the morning. Where is your room?"

"It is on the other side of the house. I believe Mrs. Fordham said it is in the family wing. Even a townhouse this large has only four guest bedrooms." Lizzy could not help blushing furiously.

Mrs. Fordham had told her she was in the mistress's chamber, but Miss Bennet should not worry as the passage between the master's chamber and the mistress's would be locked.

"I see. Good night, Lizzy. Don't do anything I would not," Jane teased.

"Jane! Good night, dear. I shall see you tomorrow morning to break our fast together."

As soon as Elizabeth returned to her assigned room, the maid knocked on the door to help her get ready for bed. She was certain she was receiving special treatment as the future mistress of the house. Had its master told the staff about their betrothal?

She examined the room, which was far more exquisitely decorated than the guest room Jane was in. In her opinion, this room suited her far better than the Queen's bedroom, which was too ornate and dark. This bedroom was decorated in sage green and cream—feminine and calming, but the gold and crimson accents added an alluring element. She could not think of anything to change. The bed was large and comfortable, and the linens luxurious and supple.

She laid under the counterpane, staring at the floral tapestry adorning the top of the canopy. The night was warm toward the end of May. Only a low fire was burning in the hearth.

Because the dance had been unplanned, no one wore gloves. Elizabeth's fingers and arms still tingled at the memory of touching her Fitzwilliam's hands. They had been betrothed for two months, and this was the first time since the walk outside Rambler Cottage that they had touched each other's bare skin. The thought of the sizzling kiss underneath Kitty's window would not let go of her mind and soul. She felt hot, and her skin tingled so much it was unbearable. She instinctively pressed her legs together to release the tension.

Just then, she heard the unmistakable click of the lock at the door that separated her room and the master's. She shot up in bed. When she saw the silhouette of her love standing at the door, she jumped out of bed and ran to him.

That night, they came perilously close to anticipating their vows, but—by exerting tremendous will power on both sides—did not. Darcy and Elizabeth now understood better why so many could not resist the temptation, and common and special licenses became necessary.

Elizabeth made up her mind that, even if she had to risk being sent to the Tower, she would approach the Queen within a week about releasing her from Her Majesty's service so she could marry.

Chapter 34

Two days after the Queen's household returned to Windsor Castle, Elizabeth asked to speak to Her Majesty.

"Madam, I wish to ask for permission to marry," Elizabeth respectfully asked.

The Queen did not look surprised. She stated matter-of-factly, "You wish to marry Mr. Fitzwilliam Darcy of Pemberley."

Elizabeth was also not surprised. The Queen had ears and eyes everywhere, some on her own daughters, who were effectively enslaved to their royal mother.

"Yes, madam. Mr. Darcy and I became betrothed immediately before I joined Your Majesty's staff. We believed it prudent to make no announcement until after obtaining Your Majesty's approval."

The Queen turned to Mrs. Waldheim, who was always with the Queen whenever Elizabeth was present.

"Wo ist der Oberst?"

"Er ist weg, madam," answered the main Keeper of the Robes.

Elizabeth could understand the exchange but did not understand the meaning of the inquiry. The Queen asked where the colonel was, and Mrs. Waldheim said he was away. There were many colonels around since equerries were usually high-ranking military personnel.

"Miss Bennet, please let me think about the matter. I shall give you an answer. You are dismissed."

The Queen, however, asked Mrs. Waldheim to stay.

It was done. The request had been made, and the Queen had not become angry. She chided herself for thinking so highly of herself that the Queen of England would be devastated about losing her to marriage.

However, two days after making her request, the Queen still had communicated no decision to her, and she was meeting the Darcys that day.

After their intimate encounter at Darcy House, Elizabeth and Mr. Darcy felt as close as man and wife. There was no embarrassment when they saw each other again so soon after having seen and touched just about every inch of each other.

"What do you think, Fitzwilliam?" asked Elizabeth, unable to disguise her worries.

"You said the Queen asked about 'the colonel' immediately after your request?" he inquired with a frown, also puzzled by this strange question.

Elizabeth nodded in answer.

"Knowing just one colonel, my cousin Richard, at the palace, I immediately associated the Queen's inquiry to reference him, but it could be any other colonel serving at Court. Have you noticed a particular colonel who is close to the Queen?"

Elizabeth thought for a moment and said, "No, but there is a General Spencer. He is one of the King's equerries. He comes regularly to report to the Queen about the condition of the King. Within the Court, he is widely believed to be 'married' to Princess Augusta. Oh, forgive me, dearest. I do not mean to gossip."

"Well, my love, as Richard would say, good gossip based on facts is intelligence. If the Queen remains uncommunicative on this matter for much longer, I shall seek help from my Uncle William—Lord Fitzwilliam. Richard should be back on duty in three days. He and I will discuss this. All will be well, dearest."

By then, Princess Elizabeth's farm was in view, and they thought it wise to turn back.

Two further days passed and, just when the Keepers of the Robes were leaving the Queen's chambers, General Spencer asked for an interview with the Queen. Mrs. Waldheim told Elizabeth to return to their quarters, but she herself re-entered the Queen's room. Elizabeth, out of curiosity, stayed where she was, and heard the Queen exclaim, "Also! Heute Abend!"

Elizabeth quickly left the Queen's anteroom before Mrs. Waldheim caught her eavesdropping. Even though she again understood the literal meaning of the simple German, which meant 'So, this evening!' she could not fathom what distressed the Queen.

The day was otherwise rather dull. She went to Princess Elizabeth's farm to help with planting summer flowers. The princess chided her for keeping Mr. Keynes to herself, but Elizabeth could tell the scolding was in jest. They worked congenially until almost dinnertime.

The King's equerries worked in shifts; only those not on duty could come to dinner. The two who were present were about to discuss the King's condition, but they were shushed by Mrs. Waldheim, who never allowed discussions about the monarch in her dining room. Despite the silence, Elizabeth could sense something important had happened.

In the evening, the Queen sent a page to ask her Keepers of the Robes to come, as she wished to retire early. As usual, Elizabeth stood a few steps away while Mrs. Waldheim busied herself helping the Queen change out of her dress.

Elizabeth was utterly shocked when the Queen suddenly addressed her, "Miss Bennet, could you go to the library to fetch me a book? It should be on the table in the center of the room. That book always helps me sleep. I shall be obliged."

Elizabeth was confused. Why did the Queen not send a page? And where was the library? She had never been shown the way to that part of the castle.

It was, however, never an option to refuse the Queen, more so when she asked politely. To make sure she carried out the errand without fault, she asked, "Madam, could you tell me the name of the book in case there is more than one book present?"

The Queen seemed surprised by this question. After a pause, she said, "It is a German Bible printed in the sixteenth century. Ask a page to show you the way. Now, go!" commanded the Queen. This was the first time the Queen had spoken to Elizabeth with agitation.

"Yes, madam." Elizabeth curtsied and left with the page, John. On the way there, John, being a gossiping type, said, "I heard the King has been lucid more and more. He loves the library when he knows what's what. I hope we do not run into him. I have seen him mad only once, and that was not a pretty sight."

Elizabeth was apprehensive hearing the King's state of health discussed openly for the first time since joining the Royal staff. She asked hesitantly, "If the King feels poorly, does he go into the library?"

John promptly answered, "No. The equerries on duty ensure His Majesty does not leave his rooms. Only his physician, Dr. Willis, may enter his chambers when the King is wild."

Elizabeth stopped and exclaimed, "Wild? I thought the King just talked nonsense when he was in his insane state."

John said thoughtfully, "It depends on what you mean by wild. He is unpredictable when he is not himself. That is what everybody says. The one time I saw him, it was at a distance. I heard the King talking, as you said, nonsense, but loudly. His two equerries had to restrain him. His Majesty is quite frail now, but he is still unpredictable. Oh, we are here."

Elizabeth looked at the imposing doors of the Royal library, famed for its immensely grand collection. She turned to the page, as if asking why he did not open the doors for her.

"Oh, I beg your pardon. I am under strict orders to remain outside, but I shall open the door for you."

Elizabeth was truly worried now. Why so much intrigue just to fetch a book?

She cautiously entered the library, which was well lit with a fire burning bright in the hearth, just as Princess Elizabeth had described. Under other circumstances, she would stand in awe and marvel at the enormous number of books in royal bindings on all four walls stretching for as far as the eyes could see. Now, she ignored the splendor surrounding her and scanned the room for the table where the requested book lay.

She gasped loudly when she saw a table standing in the center of the room at which a man sat hunched over a book. Before she could decide what to do, the man turned around. It was His Majesty, because no one else could be so casually dressed and be allowed in a public room at the palace.

Elizabeth had been trained to back away from Their Majesties at a chance encounter. She immediately backed away with her head bowed.

The King's eyesight was poor. He stood up and walked toward Elizabeth for a closer look, but she did not stop. She kept backing until she reached the doors. She turned the handles, but neither of the doors would open!

Elizabeth kept her head bowed, and hoped the King would turn away. The fact that he was in the library meant he was not mad at the moment, and he should have been the kind, solicitous monarch everybody claimed he was.

When the King was a few paces away, he suddenly rushed forward, exclaiming, "Emily, my heart! You are back from Hanover to visit your old papa? Why has no one told me about it? How are my grandbabies? You have as many babies as your mamma and papa, don't you? Oh, Emily, you have come back to save me!"

Elizabeth was trembling like a leaf. She was stunned speechless. She tried not to wince when the King embraced her tightly.

After a moment, the King released her suddenly. His eyes trailed down to her breasts.

The King said slowly, "Ah, you have been indulging in torte! You now have a womanly figure. Your husband must be pleased."

He lifted Elizabeth's head to look intently at her face. He said quizzically, "Your face has changed as well. What has happened to your eyes? Why are they so dark? My dearest girl's eyes are light, not dark, and she is thin. Your breasts are full."

Before she could react, the King took hold of her shoulders and leaned forward to get within a few inches of her face. His foul breath enshrouded her face.

Not knowing the King's intention, Elizabeth screamed and instinctively turned her head while putting up her hand between her face and the King's head.

Is he trying to kiss me?

Abruptly, the King grabbed the hand that was directly in front of his eyes and slipped the ring off her finger. She had forgotten to take off her betrothal ring when she had answered the Queen's unexpected call.

How could I be so careless!

He examined the ring with a deep frown. Elizabeth considered fighting her way out from between her captor and the door while he was distracted, but hesitated. For the first time in her life, her wits left her, and so did her courage. If the King wanted someone for any purpose, what could they do? Her father had forbidden his daughters from working as governesses, worried about lecherous employers preying on them. But if the employer was the King, could one resist? Would it be considered treason?

But he thinks I am his dead daughter!

Her mind went round and round thinking of all kinds of scenarios, one more desperate than the other.

The King muttered, "This looks like the ring my dearest girl gave me, except that mine has a white rose with diamonds, and a lock of her hair. This one has a red rose and no hair. You look like Emily, but also not. She had given me the ring to mourn her before she... *she died*!"

He stared at Elizabeth with a wild expression and asked urgently, "Are you my Emily, or are you not? Are you dead, or alive... "

And then the King started spewing nonsense non-stop while shaking Elizabeth, which shook the doors. But as soon as he began, the doors behind her opened. Two men came in to restrain the King, and John, the page, supported her from behind to prevent her from falling. Another man directed the two equerries to take the King, who continued his nonsensical babbling without taking a breath, back to his chambers.

The man who spoke with authority turned out to be the King's physician, Dr. Willis. Before rushing off to attend the King, he ordered the page to take the lady back to her lodgings, and he would examine her later. But Elizabeth refused to go. She said breathlessly, "His Majesty took my ring. I must get it back. It is my betrothal ring. I cannot lose it. Oh, someone please find the book Her Majesty asked for. It is a German Bible on the table."

John volunteered to look for the ring, but it was nowhere to be found. He also went over to the table to look for the German Bible but did not see it. The King had pulled out many volumes from the shelves, but none of them was a bible in German.

By then, Elizabeth had calmed down substantially. She thanked him profusely. "John, your timely arrival saved me. I truly did not know what to do when the King started shaking me."

John looked sheepish when he answered, "Forgive me for waiting so long to act. General Spencer locked the door once you entered the library. He said to fetch him and the doctor if I heard anything was amiss. When you screamed, I ran over to the doctor, and they came right away."

"I see," Elizabeth answered with a frown. Why did the King's equerry lock the door behind her? Even though she was not badly hurt, the trauma of encountering the mad King made her weak in the knees. Losing her precious ring, one that had been in the Darcy family for hundreds of years, saddened her. She had no doubt Fitzwilliam would forgive her, but she did not want to lose it. In the morning, she would request permission to return to the library and search for the ring.

When she arrived at her own rooms, she realized she must tell the Queen why the book could not be delivered, but Mrs. Waldheim's assistant stopped her and told her to retire for the night. The Queen had heard about what happened and was extremely distraught. Her Majesty was not to be disturbed.

Elizabeth did not need to be told twice to go to bed. The King had not violated her, but she somehow felt dirty. She knew in her heart she would have fought the King to preserve her purity if that had been his intent. Thank God that it did not go that far. She washed herself as best she could and quickly fell asleep from complete exhaustion.

The next morning, she was told again that the Queen did not need her services, and she should remain in her quarters to await Dr. Willis's visit. She was wondering when she could go search for her ring when Colonel Fitzwilliam entered her sitting room. Apart from her betrothed, not even Jane could have lifted her spirits more than the presence of the Colonel.

The Colonel hurried over and brought up Elizabeth's hand for a kiss, something he had never done before but was exactly the comforting gesture she needed right then.

"How do you fare, Miss Bennet? Or may I be presumptuous and call you Elizabeth or Lizzy?" asked the Colonel anxiously.

"Colonel, please call me Lizzy, like my family. Right now, I need family."

"Right, Lizzy, I returned from my off-time this morning and heard of the uproar caused by the King. An equerry on duty last night, Colonel Weston, told me what happened. Apparently, the King was relapsing yesterday morning, and had long periods of insanity throughout the day. Before that, and even during my last shift here two weeks ago, he had been doing well, having only brief lapses. Dr. Willis was hopeful His Majesty would have a respite from his madness. And then it happened again, but Dr. Willis was still hopeful it would pass soon. Spencer, the other equerry, allowed the King to be in the library by himself. Spencer said he was obeying the Queen's order, and the Queen herself corroborated his claim. She said she believed the books there calmed her husband. And then you came into the library, and the King mistook you for his dead daughter, Princess Amelia, whom he called 'Emily.' That appeared to trigger the madness to return fully. Dr. Willis had to put the King in a straitjacket to calm him down. As soon as I heard that the King had mistaken one of the Queen's ladies-in-waiting for Princess Amelia, I knew it had to be you. Dr. Willis also gave me this ring to return to you. He said it was in the tight grip of the King. The good doctor had to pry His Majesty's hand open to get it."

Elizabeth's face broke into such a beatific smile that there was no doubt in the Colonel's mind who had given her the ring.

Now that the big worry had resolved itself, Elizabeth could calmly and logically relate what had happened the night before.

At the end of her account, Elizabeth looked around to make sure the assistant was not present and whispered, "At the risk of being called treasonous and sent to the Tower, I believe the Queen conspired with Mrs. Waldheim and General Spencer to set me up as bait to trick the King, and they had to wait till you were away to carry out their plan. Whether her intent was to drive the King fully mad or to bring him back from madness is to be debated."

The Colonel was impressed by Elizabeth's rational elucidation after such a traumatic event. He said, "Miss... Lizzy, brava! That is precisely my thinking as well. I shall go further to assert that the Queen's intention was to shock the King back to sanity. It was the Princess's death that pushed the King over the edge to relapse into madness. She probably believed the process in reverse would give the opposite and desired result. It obviously did not, and I understand she is distraught, blaming herself for causing great harm, which may or may not be remediable."

Elizabeth was dismayed. Would the Queen give the approval she needed to marry? Did Her Majesty place on Elizabeth part of the blame for failing the mission?

When she voiced her worries, the Colonel replied, "We may have to appeal to the Prince Regent instead because the Queen is refusing all requests for an interview. My father holds some of Prinny's debts, and he owes father a favor. I shall write to Darcy and my father today. Lizzy, you were very brave. Other young ladies in your situation would have been hysterical. You seem to have recovered quickly."

"I do not know, Colonel. Having this ring back has steadied me. What happened in the library was sudden and fast. I did not have time to think or react. Perhaps in a day or two, when everything has sunk in, I shall start screaming and crying."

"You are strong. Admit it! Much like another lady I know," said the Colonel with a smile.

"You might be correct. I have had to be strong since my father's illness and death. Perhaps it has become a habit. I pity the King, but I do not hate him. What the Queen did was despicable from my point of view. I might have become a willing accomplice had she shared her plan with me; but even if I was unwilling, I would not feel so betrayed as I now do. Speaking of the other lady, have you just returned from Wales?"

"Yes, I have. I went to see Mrs. Trumbull at her estate, and escorted her and her household, including your sister, Miss Mary, back to London. It was a lot of traveling to do in two weeks, but it was worth it to me. I had never been to Wales before, and think it very fine country—untamed, and yet, not wild. I jokingly suggested to Mrs. Trumbull that, if she moved to Wales for good, perhaps I should resign my position in the army and become her personal guard. She said she would think about it!"

Elizabeth switched the topic back to herself. "All I ask is the Queen releases me before you leave the King's service."

"I am optimistic on that front. It appeared the Queen hired you strictly for this harebrained scheme. Your requesting to leave her service to marry might have made her decide to carry out the scheme sooner rather than later.

"Now that the scheme has proven both unworkable and harmful, I doubt she will want you around, or more accurately, anywhere close to where the King might run into you inadvertently."

The two friends parted. Elizabeth rinsed the ring thoroughly before putting it on her finger. She no longer cared who saw it, or whether it snared all the Queen's fine dresses.

Chapter 35

For the next week, the Queen refused to see anyone but Mrs. Waldheim and her Lady-of-the-Bedchamber. Elizabeth had nothing to do. Fortunately, Mr. Darcy conveyed Jane and Miss Darcy to visit her while he and his uncle, Lord Fitzwilliam, conferred on how to extricate Elizabeth from the Queen's grip.

The royal princesses were all close-mouthed. Against the outside world, the sisters were united, even though they deeply resented their queen mother. Princess Elizabeth visited to express her regret that her friend should have been involuntarily involved in the Queen's scheme, but that was it. Mrs. Waldheim spent all her time in the Queen's quarters and returned only late at night.

The Colonel, as usual, came by during mealtime. Cautious of his words in company, he reassured Elizabeth things were progressing well with the Prince Regent.

A few days later, a royal carriage conveyed both Elizabeth and Colonel Fitzwilliam to Carlton House, the Prince Regent's residence in London, for an audience with the Prince Regent, who again could not travel due to gout.

Elizabeth was the first to be presented.

The Prince Regent was seated in a chair in the hall when Elizabeth entered and curtsied.

"Miss Bennet, let me first compliment you on your work of fiction, 'First Impressions.' It is verily a work of art. Before you leave, I would like you to sign your name on my copies."

"You honor me, Your Royal Highness," answered Elizabeth unsteadily, wary about what the Prince Regent would say after this compliment.

She had heard the Prince Regent loved art and literature, and felt truly honored regardless of his unsavory reputation in his personal affairs. She found it unbelievable this bulky, sickly old man was the handsome philanderer he was reputed to have been.

"I would like to have a look at your red rose ring, if you allow it," the Prince Regent asked solicitously.

Elizabeth was apprehensive about handing over her precious ring again, but she could not refuse. An equerry handed the ring to the Prince Regent, who examined the ring for a long moment and said, "This is indeed the pattern favored by my sister, Amelia. She loved the white rose so much that she had a ring made with the same design and gave it to the King. No wonder the King was so affected by seeing this one."

Elizabeth started on hearing this. Would the Royals blame her after all for possessing the ring that triggered the King's recent relapse?

The Prince Regent continued in this placid manner, "Please accept the apologies of both Her Majesty and myself for endangering your person and your health at Windsor. The Queen wishes to show her appreciation for your loyal service by awarding you an annuity equal to your wages at your retirement, which is effective today. Since you will be marrying Mr. Darcy of Pemberley shortly, a monetary compensation is perhaps meaningless in view of his great wealth. I hereby grant you, in addition, the use of the courtesy title of 'The Honorable.' The Darcys of Pemberley distance themselves from the Court and the peerage unless through marriage. You will be addressed as 'The Honorable Mrs. Elizabeth Darcy' after you are married."

Elizabeth was surprised. She could only utter, "Thank you, Your Royal Highness." And then she was ushered out of the room.

She could already see her mother's delighted reaction to her courtesy title: "The Honorable Miss Elizabeth Bennet! How well it sounds!"

The Colonel was next to see the Prince Regent while Elizabeth signed no fewer than five copies of her book. The Royal librarian dictated the verbiage, and Elizabeth just wrote it on the page without understanding what she was writing.

It was only a few minutes later when the Colonel returned. He seemed thoughtful, but declined to discuss the matter until they were away.

Mr. Darcy was waiting for them when they emerged from Carlton House. He came up to Elizabeth and held out his hands to her, not caring who might have seen this intimate gesture. He had already procured a special license. If Elizabeth were to be sent to the Tower, they could still be married there, and he could rent decent lodgings for the two of them and begin married life at the Tower.

"Are you well, dearest? Did the Prince Regent say the Queen had approved our marrying?" asked Mr. Darcy anxiously.

"Oh, we do not need the Queen's approval. I am now retired from the Queen's service. You are to marry The Honorable Miss Elizabeth Bennet. Could you bear to marry a titled lady?"

It was with almost inhuman effort that Mr. Darcy restrained himself from picking his lady up to swing her around and then kiss her senseless. Her playful impertinence after such a stressful week made him giddy, a new sensation for the stoic master of Pemberley, and he smiled at his love with such overt affection that Elizabeth blushed.

A loud clearing of the throat from the Colonel broke the bubble surrounding the betrothed couple.

"Would you care to congratulate the newly minted Major General Richard Fitzwilliam?"

Mr. Darcy and Elizabeth turned to look at the General in astonishment.

"Don't look so surprised. My influential father has greased the wheels. Let us go back to your house, and I shall explain," quipped the General.

In Mr. Darcy's study, the General began:

"Technically, I am still a colonel. The promotion needs to go through the regular channels, but that is only a formality. I suspect it is a bribe to seal my lips on the happenings the night the King went mad again. I imagine my father reminded Prinny of my heroic deeds on the battlefield in Salamanca that cut short a brilliant military career, which was heading straight for a generalcy. Of course, the head injury causes my memory to be poor, guaranteeing I will not remember what I heard and saw regarding the King and the Queen. He also emphasized my friendship with you, Lizzy, and so I heard all there was to know about what the King did and said to you. He likely added his support for another increase of the Prince Regent's allowance when the bill comes up in the House of Lords. I think, out of all these negotiation points, the secrecy part was probably the most convincing for Prinny to do my father's bidding."

"The Prince Regent is not afraid I might leak the secret?" asked Elizabeth, wondering why she, the most involved in the debacle, was not feared.

"Lizzy, you are marrying one of the richest men in England. You need not blackmail for money. Darcy is also known for his impeccable sense of honor and justice. He would never stoop so low as blackmail."

"Thank you, cousin, for your generous praise," commented Mr. Darcy. "You have your wish. The promotion came from the Prince Regent instead of the King, as we discussed when returning to England. You may now retire with a rich pension to pursue any damsel you fancy and marry without regard to fortune."

"You flatter me, Darcy, by thinking I remember what I said six months ago. At the moment, I am quite fixed. I have no desire to marry any damsel, with or without a fortune."

The cousins exchanged significant looks. Mr. Darcy could never understand the sort of arrangement between his cousin and the rich heiress.

ৡৡ

The double wedding of the two eldest Bennet daughters to worthy and wealthy gentlemen was to take place two weeks after Elizabeth's retirement from the Royal household. Mr. Darcy had a special license and could marry anywhere, while Mr. Lytle obtained a common license.

Mrs. Bennet sorely wanted to have the wedding at Longbourn, but there was nobody in the Meryton environs she would invite other than her sister Philips. She was also not ready to see Longbourn as a guest and not the mistress. Having the wedding at the cottage was out of the question. Even Wayleigh, where Jane would become mistress, seemed too drab for her most deserving daughters, especially The Honorable Miss Elizabeth Bennet.

In the end, Mrs. Trumbull suggested a solution. The wedding would take place at the Trinity Church at Clapham, but the wedding breakfast would be at Brixton Park, which was stylish and richly decorated.

Mr. Samuels was to officiate at the weddings. He had been married since shortly after meeting the Bennets at their cottage. Mary never had a chance.

Mary did not need that chance. She and Mr. Antonio Rocco were head over heels in love with each other. For his own salvation, and deep down for Mary's sake, Mr. Rocco forsook his Catholic faith to be baptized into the Church of England.

The night before Mr. Rocco was to ask Mrs. Bennet for a courtship with Mary, Mary spoke with her favorite sister, Lizzy, so Lizzy would not be surprised at the announcement. She credited Lizzy for supporting her in her transformation from a rigid and self-righteous soporific to a compassionate, serious, yet witty young woman.

It was important to her that Lizzy knew how Mr. Rocco and she came to love each other.

"Antonio... Mr. Rocco had a horrific experience when he was only eight years old. He sang like an angel, and some evil men from the city heard him sing at church and wanted him to grow up singing as a castrato—you know what that is, do you not?"

311

Lizzy nodded. Many beautiful arias were composed for castratos, but she never considered how such men came to have soprano voices.

"His mother came into the room just when those men were about to perform the despicable operation that would have changed his fate forever and stop them. To save her son, she sent Antonio to live with her cousin in England to help with his pugilist club.

"Antonio was bewildered during all of this. He was devoted to the Catholic Church and had been told the operation was a necessary step toward priesthood. Since his mother refused to explain the deception, he became suspicious of all things related to his Church and refused to sing. He turned to the pianoforte, but mainly he did chores for his uncle until Mr. Trumbull by chance heard him play. The fair treatment he received from the Trumbulls made him realize decent people could enjoy his music without evil intentions. Not only did he gain access to renowned music masters for formal training, but he also received a twenty-thousand-pound legacy from Mr. Trumbull. He has always been taciturn and shy. The deaths last year of his benefactor and Master James Trumbull, who was like his own little brother, made him more so. Now, however, he has returned to singing. He still sings like an angel, but as a bass. To me and the young Miss Trumbulls, he has also become much more animated.

"As for religion, he was a skeptic until we met. Perhaps because he had never met a young woman like me, he was curious about my devotion to God, and then he could not help himself and started studying the scriptures with me as they are written, instead of being drawn in by the rituals and liturgy that appealed to him as a boy. He also gave me lessons on the pianoforte and singing because he said my performances in both were grossly misdirected, which you know to be true. Now I sing the contralto part, and he said my voice was rich and supple. So, through all this, we have discovered that we love God, and we love each other."

Lizzy nodded, simultaneously pleased and astonished. She was truly happy for Mary, but she had to ask, "I wish I had spent more time to get to know him, but I was very busy with the business of publishing the novel. But, Mary, you have had little experience with love. You were hoping to marry

Mr. Collins and then Mr. Samuels. How do you know you love Mr. Rocco for himself, and not just the poor little boy with a sad childhood?"

"How do you know you love Mr. Darcy? I remember when you deeply loathed him. Then, you announced your betrothal the day he showed up at the Cottage, and you had seen each other only once or twice in the intervening nine months," Mary inquired.

Elizabeth was taken aback by her question. To an outsider, it certainly seemed abrupt, but to them, it was anything but.

"Forgive me for doubting you could love a person in a way no one else may understand. I am heartily happy about your felicitous future with Mr. Rocco. Your children will have no need of their Aunt Lizzy to teach them to play the pianoforte very ill."

"You mean, The Honorable Aunt Lizzy?"

℘℘

On a beautiful day in June, Mrs. Bennet married off her two eldest daughters. What made this day especially splendid for her was the attendance of a Royal Princess. Princess Elizabeth, dressed rather plainly as was her preference, came with a peace offering for Elizabeth from the Queen—an exquisite set of hair combs with pearls and rubies, which matched Elizabeth's red rose ring.

The princess, with an admiring smile, said to Elizabeth, "Miss Bennet... oh... Mrs. Darcy, my congratulations and my sincere wishes to you for a felicitous marriage." She then turned to look dreamily at both Mr. Darcy and his cousin, the soon-to-be general. "I wish I could marry like this, even if my unobtainable husband were ten times less handsome than Mr. Darcy or Colonel Fitzwilliam..." She then looked at the many men in the crowd, and mumbled to herself, "So many handsome men!"

She turned back to Elizabeth and said, "The Queen's permission for me to attend your wedding means she was truly regretful of her ill-conceived scheme that put you in a frightening position. The wedding gift to you was but a token. How I wish I could also attend the wedding breakfast!"

After the Princess boarded her carriage with lingering backward glances, Elizabeth looked over to Mrs. Bennet, who was quite in her element as mother to two radiant brides, and mother-in-law to two wealthy, well-connected gentlemen. Lizzy realized her mother was far from perfect, but she would choose Mrs. Bennet rather than the Queen of England for her mother, if such a choice were hers to make.

Just then, her husband of ten minutes came over and asked, "You have a faraway look on your face. What is it, love?"

"Dearest, I have been thinking: the last eleven months have been filled with trials and tribulations, and then unexpected joys and revelations. And now, you and I are united in body and soul, and my sisters and mother have grown in wisdom and contentment. Jane and Mary have found true love just like us. I will always regret papa's passing, but I feel deeply that he, in heaven, led us to all this." Elizabeth spread her arms as if to embrace the family and friends gathered to celebrate their union. "Everything happened for a reason."

Mr. Darcy looked at his bride with a tender, smitten smile, and could not wait for the time when their union of body and soul was *complete*.

A few steps away, the Colonel surveyed the scene with Mrs. Trumbull on his arm. He whispered to his own love, "Darcy is already thinking of consummating his marriage before even consuming the wedding breakfast. So does Mr. Rocco, although he needs to get to the altar first."

"And I had thought Antonio was unaffected by such desires of the flesh! You once told me men thought about carnal pleasures constantly. I now believe you. But tell me, do you prefer this version of the Darcy-Lizzy love in real life, or the one in Lizzy's novel?"

"You are turning me into a bluestocking—asking me to analyze a novel! Let us see. In the novel, Lizzy's father lives. In real life, he died. The Bennets would probably prefer the novel version. However, Mrs. Cieran's fate would have been worse and Miss Bennet—Mrs. Lytle—would have been burdened with that immature schoolboy Bingley for life. In real life, they have far better prospects for happiness. In real-life or in fiction, Darcy and Lizzy have found each other. That is all that is important."

Epilogue

A few months after the double wedding saw many changes in the Bennets' lives.

Rambler Cottage was closed up because the Darcys offered use of the Pemberley dower house to the Bennet ladies, including Mrs. Cieran. They said a fond farewell to the Lytles and their friends and neighbors around Wayleigh and Clapham, loaded their belongings, and made the journey north.

Just when the Bennet ladies had settled into their new lodgings, they had to pack up and move again—this time back to Longbourn.

Shortly after Mrs. Cieran came out of mourning, news arrived at Pemberley that Mr. Collins had choked on a piece of meat and died. He had become quite the glutton since becoming master of Longbourn and devoured his meals with excessive zeal. Mrs. Collins, as far as anyone knew, was not with child.

Daniel Aiden Cieran, the next male in line to inherit Longbourn and end the four-generation entail, became the means of returning the Bennets to their ancestral estate, permanently.

Mrs. Bennet and Mrs. Cieran received a warm welcome from the long-time Longbourn staff, who, even though shielded by Mrs. Collins, were ordered around like serfs by their former master, who behaved as if he had been a feudal lord even more grand than his former patroness, Lady Catherine.

There was some initial conflict between the new mistress and the erstwhile mistress about the simple question of who should occupy the mistress's chambers. Mrs. Bennet was incredulous that her seventeen-year-old daughter should defy her. That was the first time she realized her days of being mistress of Longbourn had truly ended.

On another point, however, Mrs. Bennet and her youngest daughter were of one accord. They offered to let Mrs. Collins stay at Longbourn for as long as the widow felt necessary. Mrs. Bennet's initial reaction was to object, but Lydia said, "Mamma, if Mrs. Wickham had not let me stay with her when I was without a home, imagine what would have become of me."

Mrs. Bennet acquiesced because the hardship she endured in her own newly widowed state was still fresh in her mind.

Mrs. Collins, however, had other offers—one from Eliza to move to Pemberley, and a second from Jane, who invited her to stay at Rambler Cottage. She decided on Rambler Cottage because of its proximity to her family in Meryton, and, more important, to town, which would provide the chance to broaden her horizons. The practicality that urged her to accept Mr. Collins's marriage proposal had not worked out as she had hoped. Perhaps following the Miss Bennets' footsteps to Wayleigh would change her outlook and enrich her life as it had those of her friends. An added advantage was that Mary and her husband had made the gate lodge at Brixton Park their permanent home. They were active in the Clapham circle, and could ease her entry into the local community. So, she and her sister Maria, who also saw leaving the confined society of Meryton an excellent opportunity to spread her wings, removed to Rambler Cottage.

One day, two naval officers came to call at Longbourn. The older of the two was Captain Wilkes, the commander Midshipman Cieran had saved from death. With him was Midshipman Marcas Cieran, Lieutenant Cieran's younger brother. When the guests were shown into the parlor, Lydia was so astonished that she exclaimed, "Daniel!" and fainted dead away.

Marcas Cieran bore a familial resemblance to his older brother, but not so similar as to be a twin. However, to Lydia, who had spent less than two weeks with her husband, the naval gentleman in front of her was her husband coming back from heaven.

Both officers were furloughed when the wars ended in 1814. Captain Wilkes wished to visit his godson, and his midshipman, whom Captain Wilkes had handpicked with an eye to promote him for the sake of his brave brother, accompanied him to see his nephew.

Within a month, it was clear Midshipman Cieran was smitten with his sister-in-law, and the attraction was reciprocated. After consulting with Mr. Philips about the legality of marrying one's dead husband's brother and learning that the law was murky about the restriction against their marriage, Lydia and Marcas married at Longbourn Chapel, with all four-and-twenty genteel families attending. Kitty, not yet married, stood up with Lydia, and Captain Wilkes stood up with his midshipman. Mrs. Bennet was almost as radiant as the bride, and that did not go unnoticed by the Captain, a confirmed bachelor, or so he believed.

Everyone in the Bennet extended family could not help wondering if this wedding had taken place a year and a half before, whether the course of events that followed would have drastically changed.

Before the wedding, the five Bennet sisters went to visit their father's grave in the churchyard. No one said anything. Finally, Elizabeth said, "Papa, we are here, all five of us. Thank you." Then they huddled together and cried tears of gratitude.

On their way out of the churchyard, they saw their mother walking toward Mr. Bennet's grave. When they stopped, intending to turn back and accompany the matriarch, Mrs. Bennet waved them away.

Before the company dispersed to their own homes, Mrs. Bennet announced that Captain Wilkes had proposed, and she had accepted.

It was a bittersweet moment for her daughters, but they were happy for their mother, who was still young at three-and-forty; Captain Wilkes was a good man, judging from how he sought to assist the Cierans in their careers.

Lizzy, ever observant, asked. "Did any of you see mamma putting herself forward for the Captain?" The sisters looked at one another and shook their heads—their mother did not practice what she preached.

The new Mrs. Wilkes had nothing to repine. She moved to Southampton with her husband, who treated her kindly. When he was not at sea, they went to visit her daughters' families together.

Her mind was at ease, and her nervous nature disappeared entirely. After all, there was now a new Bennet mistress at Longbourn, and a new generation of Bennets growing up. When he reached his majority, Daniel Aidan Cieran became Daniel Aidan Cieran-Bennet.

1816

The heartaches and sadness caused by the death of Mr. Bennet were long past. All the Bennet ladies had followed the only way for a woman to have a secure future by marrying worthy gentlemen of means.

When the newlywed Darcys arrived at Pemberley after their wedding, Mrs. Reynolds was not surprised to meet the new Mrs. Darcy, who had made such an agreeable impression on her. Judging from how her master and mistress lingered mornings and evenings in their chambers, she went ahead and prepared the nursery for new Darcys, the first of whom, a feisty babe—the heir—was born exactly nine months after the wedding.

Mr. and Mrs. Lytle spent their wedding trip on a voyage to India and the islands beyond so that Mr. Lytle could wrap up his responsibilities with the East India Company, and to bring home his ward, who had been stranded in India.

Under the influence of the Clapham cohort, Mr. Lytle grew disgusted by some practices of the East India Company, the most egregious of which was slave trading. He decided to start his own firm with the proceeds from the sale of his father's business and focused on American trade.

In time, Jane achieved her dream of sailing the world. One of her children was even born on board ship.

Mr. Lytle's success in America not only made him immensely rich, but he also made his investors—his brothers-in-law, General Fitzwilliam, and Mr. Gardiner—even more prosperous.

One other gentleman who benefitted from his success was Mr. Charles Bingley. After having squandered half of his inheritance in less than five years, Mr. Bingley finally came to his senses and sought his friend Darcy for advice. On Darcy's recommendation, he invested half of his remaining wealth in Lytle and Sons. He could have lived comfortably on the earnings, but he decided to seek employment with the company, as he was genuinely interested in the workings of a budding enterprise. He was an able employee and was soon sent to New York as the company's agent. He had only a glimpse of his former angel when she came with Mr. Lytle to inspect the branch office there.

After two years in New York, he married an American lady with auburn hair. His preference for blondes had long faded. With his father-in-law's financial backing, he started a wagon-building business using the knowledge of carriage building gleaned from his own father. Aided by the explosive growth in commerce in America and the push to open up the West, his business thrived.

Miss Bingley, not married at age seven-and-thirty, finally received her dowry with the accumulated interest. She became quite an heiress. However, she never forgave her brother, and the two siblings remained estranged the remainder of their lives.

Among Elizabeth's sisters, the last to marry was Kitty, who married a neighbor of the Darcys in Derbyshire. She and Georgiana had become good friends. Their artistic inclinations complemented each other. Kitty's guileless bluntness helped Georgiana break through her shell, and the perfect decorum of Georgiana helped Kitty learn to be a poised young lady.

Georgiana married Lord John Bentinck when he came home after the victory in Waterloo. No one needed to help them toward felicity in matrimony. The two young people simply met as neighbors, and after three months of courtship, the couple married.

After Georgiana's marriage, many of the gentlemen who had pursued Miss Darcy switched their focus to Kitty. Even though her dowry was not significant, her connections were excellent. Both Mr. Darcy and Mr. Lytle augmented Kitty's five-thousand-pound dowry, which was made up of proceeds from the sale of Mr. Bennet's book collection and Lizzy's novel. Mr. Dewey's interest in the arts drew him to Kitty, whose talent in painting and drawing shone because of the able tutelage of masters referred by Mrs. Fitzwilliam's artistic friends. The couple could often be found side by side, painting the craggy landscape of the Derbyshire countryside.

Mrs. Fitzwilliam was the former Mrs. Trumbull. She had had no plan to marry again. However, she found herself with child. Like any sensible woman of her time, she told the man responsible, and General Fitzwilliam instantly asked for her hand in marriage. Their child, a girl, Isabella Lilian Fitzwilliam, joined her three step-sisters to become heiresses of the Trumbull fortune.

Their father, the general, never attempted to live up to his boast of being a matchmaker *par excellence, not* even for his daughter and step-daughters. Instead, he remained a working military man for years and retired with a generous pension. His disabilities had corrected themselves, but the war was over, and he had lost his taste for battles.

Because the Queen did not wish anyone at Windsor with knowledge of her regrettable scheme, he was reassigned to a sinecure position at Whitehall. With his father's influence and his wife's fortune, he encouraged advancements in issues important to him, such as improving treatment of the wounded and sick in military hospitals, and continuing the work of his mentor, General le Marchant, in training cadets at the Royal Military College.

As for his wife's immense wealth, he acted as a responsible custodian rather than its owner. Lord Fitzwilliam was perplexed his younger son turned down the opportunity to out-shine the Duke of Devonshire by joining him in driving to the Doncaster races with two magnificent coaches-and-six and sixteen outriders.

In the evenings, he donned his eye-patch and accompanied his wife at her soirees, and scowled at anyone, including Lord Wellington, who seemed too familiar with the still very handsome Mrs. Fitzwilliam.

As for the Darcys and the Royals, communication ended when Princess Elizabeth married a German prince in 1818. Her brave friend, Elizabeth Darcy, had inspired her to stand firm behind her decision to marry until her Queen mother backed down.

Eventually, everyone in the Bennet extended family knew Elizabeth had written 'First Impressions.' There were several novels published in quick succession under the name of 'A Lady,' whose style of writing resembled Lizzy's, but Lizzy adamantly denied she had anything to do with those works, which she herself ardently admired. She wrote only for her children, nieces and nephews, but not for the public.

Mrs. Fitzwilliam, connoisseur extraordinaire of talent, knew the true identity of 'A Lady.' In her opinion, if Elizabeth had continued to write novels, she could have achieved the artistry of 'A Lady.' After all, Elizabeth had written 'First Impressions' before she turned one-and-twenty. Despite the sometimes awkward changes she had made to the autobiographical first half, there were flashes of undeniable genius in many passages throughout the story. Surely 'First Impressions' was estimable enough to be compared to a late draft of one of A Lady's published novels, which, she had no doubt, would go down in history among the most beloved works in English Literature.

1817

So, what happened to the scoundrel who caused the Bennets' heartache?

Three years after Mrs. Cieran's second wedding, a ragged man came to Longbourn, looking for Mrs. Lydia Cieran. Mrs. Hill, housekeeper of Longbourn, was suspicious of the man, who had a puffy face, missing front tooth, bloodshot eyes, and threadbare, ill-fitting clothes. She left the visitor standing outside the door and sent a maid to alert Mr. Cieran.

Lydia was with her two children in the nursery, reading a story written by Lizzy and illustrated by Kitty. When Hill came to inform her about the visitor, who resembled that scoundrel, Mr. Wickham, but was in very poor shape, Lydia was curious. By now, Mrs. Cieran was a poised and competent mistress of Longburn. Her former brashness had turned into self-assuredness. She went with Hill to judge for herself whether the blackguard had had the gall to return.

When the door opened, Wickham smiled widely, which made him look even more hideous, as those teeth, however many remaining, were rotten and blackened.

"My dearest Lydia! It is I, your dear George. I have returned to be with you and my son. We shall be a happy family here at Longbourn!"

Lydia said with a sneer, "I already have a happy family here at Longbourn. You claim to be Wickham, but you look nothing like him. You are an imposter, one who has been dragged through filth. Even if you are that man, you do not have a son here. Your wife died in childbed with the babe unborn. The master of Longbourn, my husband, Mr. Cieran, will not be pleased to see you, whoever you are, but most certainly a vagabond, a cheat, and a miscreant."

Wickham interrupted, "Your sham of a husband is dead. Do not think I did not dig into your so-called marriage!"

Lydia was roused to anger and was about to rebut when, behind her, came a booming voice with an Irish lilt. "Who says I am dead?"

Wickham's face turned ashen. The giant with red hair scowling at him was approaching with a menacing gait.

After years of dissipated living, his health and strength were not what they had been. Since leaving Lydia at his wife's house, he decided working an occupation was too much exertion, and so he went back to being a lackey for wastrels, heirs who had nothing to do but wildly spend their lavish allowances while awaiting the rich fathers' demise. He rather enjoyed the expensive habits such as spirits, women and laudanum. A little flattery and the willingness to do dirty work were all that was required of him. The only downside of this life was that these habits had ruined his looks, while his debts never stopped mounting.

Then he discovered men were looking for him. They were Fitzwilliam's men. With the war over, and with his wife's great wealth, Fitzwilliam could afford to hire as many furloughed soldiers as he wanted to do his bidding. The worst among them was a man named Hughes, who was constantly at his heels. When he went back to sell his late wife's boarding house, he had heard about a pregnant Lydia marrying a dying man. He had thought if he hid in plain sight, so to speak, and became a gentleman living with his 'wife' and child at Longbourn, he might finally rest his weary bones. However, he had not expected this very much alive Irish rogue giving him trouble. It was not worth the risk. Instead, he fled, which had been how he typically dealt with difficulties, and it had worked.

After that day, no one heard anything else about the reprobate except General Fitzwilliam, but he told no one, not even his cousin Darcy.

Present day

Soon after her marriage, the Honorable Mrs. Elizabeth Darcy halted the printing of her novel because she had never reconciled herself to her guilty feeling at exposing her loved ones' private lives and conversations. No copies of 'First Impressions' have been seen for at least a hundred years. After all, a debut and only novel by an anonymous author would not make a valuable collector's item. If any copies remained, they could be at Windsor Castle had they escaped the devastating fire there in the year one thousand nine hundred and ninety-two, which destroyed a great number of valuable artefacts. The only other likely place to find copies would, of course, be the ancestral home of the Darcys, Pemberley.

Printed in Great Britain
by Amazon

25820936R00185